Twisted Crown
Alexa Michaels

Copy Right

Twisted Crown Copyright © 2025 Chowen Publishing House LLC All Rights Reserved

Kindle Edition All Rights Reserved

Print Edition: All Rights Reserved

Editor: North Pines Editing LLC

Cover design: Covers By Aura

Interior Art: Atra Luna Graphic Design

ISBN: 9798280321335

No part of this book may be reproduced or transmitted in any form or by any means, electronic or mechanical, including photocopying, recording, or by any information storage and retrieval system without the written permission of the author, except for the use of brief quotations in a review.

This book is a work of fiction. Names, characters, places, and incidents are either products of the author's imagination or are used fictitiously. Any resemblance to actual persons, living or dead, events, or locales is entirely coincidental. The author acknowledges the trademarked status and trademark owners of various products referenced in this work of fiction, which have been used without permission. The publication/use of these trademarks is not authorized, associated with, or sponsored by the trademark owners.

About Twisted Crown

She gambled with kings to save her cousin. Now, there's no way out.

Penelope
An impromptu trip to visit my relatives reveals an unexpected—and unpleasant—surprise. My baby cousin, the sweetest creature to ever walk this Earth, is getting married. It's not a love match. She's never even met the man!
I expected my visit to be chaotic. But this? This mad rush to attach two families through marriage? It's hell.
When I decide to do something about it, to push the buttons and manipulate behind the scenes, I think I finally have the upper hand.
Boy was I wrong.
Don Mancini came from Chicago expecting a Caravello bride, and he's not leaving without one. It just so happens Caravello was my mother's maiden name; their blood runs through my veins. Now I've taken my cousin's place—the substitute bride to the most feared man in the underworld. With my family's lives on the line and no escape in sight, I'm forced to say "I do" to a monster.

Alessandro
The little ball of pure energy had no business standing at that altar, no reason wear the ring meant for another. But when she made herself the sacrifice, when she looked me in the eyes and spoke those vows... something in me snapped.
She thinks she's trapped. That I forced her into this. But Penelope doesn't realize—I was never going to let her walk away.
They call me a monster, a beast who rules with blood and fear. She should have been afraid of me. But instead, she stands in my world with fire in her eyes, challenging me at every turn. Testing the control I thought was unbreakable.

I want her more than my next breath.

But in our world, affection is a liability. And if I let her in, if I give in to this heat between us... I might just become the one thing I swore I'd never be. Weak.

Twisted Crown **is the first book of the Dynasty of Queens series, set in the Midwest Underworld. It's a stand-alone darker mafia romance, with no cheating, a guaranteed HEA, and no cliffhangers. A morally grey romance, this book may not be suitable for everyone.**

Trigger Warnings

A morally grey romance, this might not be suitable for all audiences....
Violence, fighting, and other crimes of a mob
Killing
Adult language
On page romance
BDSM
Impact play

Dedication

To the bold-hearted, the rule-breakers, who believe love is worth the fire.

This one's for anyone who ever wanted the villain to get the girl...and stop at nothing to keep her.

Chapter 1 – Penelope

For this having been only the second airplane ride in my short life, it wasn't so bad. I looked down at the empty mini bottles tucked in the seatback in front of me. Those weren't even a consideration when we flew to Disney fifteen years ago. Of course, when both your parents were with, flying seemed like fun to a ten-year-old. I shoved the bottles into my large purse, even though there was no fooling the old woman on my right or the flight attendants. They knew I had a decent buzz going. But since I was calm and collected, unlike the batch of toddlers five rows ahead, I was hoping they would let me leave without trouble.

Pushing to my feet, I tested my balance. There was no shaking in my legs, which was a good start. By the time I met my relatives in the pickup area, I would have a good handle on my coordination. It was a delicate balancing act to be comfortable on the nerve-racking flight but not be toasted when the people who had all the wealth, power, and influence collected me. They had to see me as a valuable asset, and that meant making a good first impression.

People shuffled about, grabbing their overhead bags. I waited my turn, snatched my own small suitcase, and proceeded to file out of the plane.

I did it. Step one in my plan was successfully accomplished.

This whole thing was madness, but so far Lady Luck was with me. A small thrum of excitement shot through my veins. I was really doing this. I was stepping into the world my mother ran from, that she fought so hard to keep us children from. Maybe it was the drinks, but there was no twinge of guilt for undoing her hard work.

She needed me—she needed her *family*.

Stepping from the humming interior of the plane into the Detroit airport was like plunging into the roaring sea. There were so many people. I swallowed hard, clutching my bags tightly. A deep gulp of air filled my lungs. It was stale, forcefully blown through the overhead filtration system, with a slight hint of grease from the restaurants attached to it.

But it sure beat motor oil, dirt, manure, and sweat.

I pushed deeper into the airport, gaze greedily soaking up the displays in the shop windows. This was just the airport! What was the actual city of Detroit like? I couldn't wait to explore. It was so different than Carrington, although the few times I'd been to Fargo, there was this level of commerce and consumerism. Gaze darting about, taking in the different sights, I must have missed a turn. And then another.

Crap.

My small town swagger fizzled out.

I stared at the overhead signs, wandering through different halls and corridors. Speedy trains whizzed along the exterior of the far wall, but I didn't dare hop on one. Who knew where I'd wind up. So I continued to walk. The sounds faded and the crowds thinned. The fixtures overhead seemed nicer, brighter, less harsh...if that was possible.

A mostly empty wing proved to be a dead end. Turning, I spied a sliding glass door. It looked as good as any option, so I ventured inside. Soothing instrumental music with bamboo flutes and water sounds enveloped me. A large black stone fountain gurgled to the side, and opposite that was an empty desk. Although the sense that I didn't belong here tickled the back of my mind, I marched up to the desk and leaned on it, hoping to find a bell for the attendant. I would just ask where I should go, since this area was clearly above my pay grade.

"There's nothing to steal," a deep voice observed.

I jumped, nearly falling out of my skin. "I wasn't stealing!"

The first thing I noticed was his smile. It cracked across his face, making him look predatory. I'd shot to scare off wolves with that same feral look who'd come snooping around the spring calves. But no creature from the lupine family looked that good in a suit. The soft black material was a second skin, curving over his broad frame like a coat of armor. The color might be dark, but it was the lightest thing about him. Those black eyes twinkled, swallowing the light and refusing to give it back.

That voice was the texture of granite, but amusement laced his words. "If you say so."

"I do," I insisted. I had to crane my neck to meet his gaze. Damn, but he was tall.

He hummed, the sound rich and hypnotizing. I steeled my spine. That was exactly the kind of noise a beast would make to lull prey into letting their guard down.

I knew better. I was a damn good hunter, and I never backed down from a challenge.

"I'm looking for the front desk person," I stated calmly.

His brows lifted. "The receptionist?"

That was when I noticed the lilt behind his words. There was a rhythmic form to his speech that made it a safe guess he wasn't a native English speaker. Curiosity piqued in me. I swept another look over his figure but couldn't place his origins. Or his age. He wasn't young, but the years hadn't marked his features with lines or greys.

"Yes," I answered.

"You thought you'd find him hiding under the desk?" he mused.

My lips thinned. "I was looking for a bell."

"Ah." The grin broadened.

And he's mocking me. It was probably glaringly obvious that I didn't belong here. My jeans might be unripped, but they were far from new. My boots had seen a few summers, but the buckskin-brown hid their age. And the button-up shirt with the hat and belt buckle made me look like I'd come straight from the rodeo. But I was damn proud of my country girl roots, even if the big city did call my name and I'd finally had a reason to answer the summons.

The man took a container from his inner pocket, tapped it against his palm, and plucked a fat cigar from the interior. While I was still wondering who carried smokes in a shiny metal case, he put it to his lips.

"You can't smoke in here!" I gasped, stepping forward.

Didn't the idiot know that was a fire hazard? There were designated smoking areas throughout the airport. I might not be a world traveler, but even I knew that!

Quirking a brow, he held my gaze as he flicked the fancy metal lighter. There was a definite challenge in his eyes.

He isn't really going to do it.

Only, his hand wasn't stopping. He brushed the tip of the flame over the stick.

Anger bubbled inside me. Rich city people, who thought they could do whatever they wanted. There were rules for a reason! And not smoking in the airport was definitely a rule.

Right?

Yes, it was. The memory of the automatic speaker robot-lady talking about the smoking lounge as I wandered aimlessly through the corridors came to mind. *This fancy ass lounge definitely wasn't one of those places.*

"Put that out," I demanded, glaring at him.

The man blew a puff of smoke into the air. I refused to acknowledge how good whatever fancy brand of tobacco that was smelled. That wasn't a cheap smoke from the gas station full of fillers and junk. It was likely pure tobacco leaves from a really good source.

Saliva trickled on my tongue.

The man cocked his head to the side. "Now why would I do that?"

The need to make him stop swelled inside. He didn't think he had to listen. A prick who was above the rules—oh, sweet Moses! That just wasn't going to fly with me.

But I knew better than to scold. Me telling him would only fuel his need to taunt me. It was time to take action. Show this big, bad wolf who was boss.

"Because it's wrong," I enunciated every word, stalking forward as I spoke.

"Then why does it feel so right?" he drawled.

That observation sounded downright sinful. A tendril of something warm curled deep in my belly.

I faltered. The instinct to pluck the stick from his fingers, to take a drag....

But when the beastly wretch smiled, I snapped out of the trance.

"Put it out," I demanded.

"No."

"Fine." And with that, I lunged.

There was no way, given my size and stature that I should have been able to do what I did. I could only explain it by having the luck of surprise. The giant of a man swayed backward, pawing wildly for my wrist. I jerked back, escaping his grasp. He lost his balance and toppled into the serene fountain.

The suave, polished man splashed hard in the basin of water.

Holy shit on a shingle. What did I just do?

I gaped at him.

He seemed just as shocked and speechless. We stared at one another—for three heartbeats.

And then reality snapped into place.

His tanned face reddened. A dark spark lit in his eyes. That was my cue to leave. As he bellowed something incoherent, I darted to my bag, snatched the extended handle, and fled out the sliding doors, skimming against the glass panels that were opening too slowly.

My heart hammered as I ran down the airport corridor. Only after I rejoined the mass of civilization did I look back and see I wasn't being followed. I pulled my hat off, wiped my sweating brow, and blew out a long breath.

That was a close one.

But then a smile pulled up my lips. There was a spring in my step as I at last found the path to baggage claim. As far as good deeds of the day were concerned, that was epic—a good start to the new chapter in my life.

Chapter 2 – Penelope

"Ssshhwwweee, *this* is where they live?" I breathed.

The driver my uncle sent chuckled at my small town awe.

"Yeah, this is Signor Caravello's house," Enzo explained.

"This whole house? For three people?" I pressed my hand against the window, gaping at the sprawling lawn that was manicured to within an inch of its life. There was nothing natural, wild, or rugged about the landscaping. Everything was purposefully designed to fit together, and if it didn't, it would be plucked out and burned.

"Well, there are spare rooms where some people stay over regularly," the driver added.

Knowing my uncle had wealth and seeing it in front of me were two different things. I let out a long breath.

"Who stays over?" I tore my gaze away from the window and watched the expressions of the driver. He was very careful not to use a certain word around me. Part of the thirty-minute drive from the airport had been spent trying to make him admit the secret society I knew they were part of—the mob. The bugger hadn't let slip the truth.

"Business associates," Enzo said quickly.

Being the head of the mob was the big secret my uncle kept, something I wasn't supposed to know. When my mother walked away from this life, she lost the connection to that world. I grew up knowing she had a brother who had a very important job in the construction business. Curious little thing that I was, I discovered what exactly my mother was avoiding by never coming back here to her hometown.

Not that hometown meant the same thing when talking about Detroit as it did when I referenced Carrington, North Dakota. This place was a concrete jungle. And Uncle Tito ruled part of it, which was pretty darn cool.

"What kind of business associates stay over?" I pressed. "Wouldn't they have their own mansions on Park Place or Boardwalk?"

This time, the driver let out a deep belly laugh. I threw him a smirk.

"You're cute," Enzo teased.

My smile tightened. I wasn't that cute, and I didn't care for the insinuation that just because I was a country girl meant I was ignorant. I left my dead-end career in search of something *more*. Because dammit, I deserved to be seen, to be valued. I might be homegrown, but I wasn't cute.

Play the game! I took a deep breath.

"Does your boss keep them working around the clock, so it's easier if they sleep here?" I pressed, stabbing the seatbelt release. "Or is it some kind of commune. Like a cult?"

The driver only laughed harder.

Cult, mob, same thing. From my research, I knew Enzo was probably sworn to secrecy when he was *Made*. Wondering what this man would do if I admitted I knew all about my uncle's illegal organization—and it didn't matter where he got his money, so long as he shared in this hour of need—I was saved from blurting out whatever nonsense was on the tip of my tongue when a fluttering shape appeared on the front steps as the Cadillac stopped before the house.

"Poppy!" I shouted, launching from the fancy car that probably cost more than every vehicle I'd ever owned combined.

"Penny!" the girl squealed. She picked her way carefully down the steps, pretty white dress flowing around her like angel feathers.

Six years younger than me, it was hard to see my little cousin now as the high school graduate. She'd just finished kindergarten...yesterday!

I wrapped my arms around her, hauling her off the ground and twirling about. "You look like a cloud fallen straight from the sky, little mouse," I teased, pressing a noisy kiss to the top of her head. "And you definitely grew since last summer!"

"Stop it, I have not," Poppy gasped, trying to regain her breath. "I haven't had a growth spurt since I was fourteen."

"Wait!" I held up my hand dramatically, while still embracing her with the other. "You're *not* turning thirteen this summer?"

"Penny!" she protested.

I cocked my head and narrowed my eyes. "And that's not One Direction blasting from your bedroom? I swear I hear Zane!"

Poppy shoved me playfully. "You must have no access to the outside world on that farm of yours if you don't know the band broke up. Years ago!"

"Oh, we have high speed internet on the *ranch*," I clarified. "But seriously, you look good, mouse."

Whatever she was going to say dried up and shriveled in a moment as a drill sergeant in a tight pantsuit—with hair pulled back so tight it was a wonder it didn't snap off—barked her name.

"New nanny?" I whispered.

Poppy nodded. "You'd think nineteen would be old enough not to have one. But," she sighed and lifted those delicate, slight shoulders in a shrug, "it's only temporary. The nicest part about getting married is that Signora Ferraro won't be coming with me to my husband's house."

Time came to a screeching halt. I blinked at my cousin, who happened to be eye level with me due to the pretty little strappy sandals she wore.

Poppy suddenly looked young, and not because I was having a hard time seeing her as grown up. That dark chocolate hair curled delicately around her shoulders, and her big brown eyes glittered with shy excitement.

"Married?" I hissed. "You can't be getting married."

Poppy held up the ring, nearly gouging my eye out with the sheer size.

"I'm blind!" I yelped, slapping a palm on my chest and making her giggle.

The nanny squawked from the front door, but I took my time looping my arm around my cousin's waist and moving back to the house at our own pace.

"Ssooo, my baby cousin is engaged," I drawled, hiding the inability to process that behind humor. "What's he like?"

Poppy's smile faltered. "He's a very desirable catch."

The comeback I had for that didn't fit. How did one joke about a marriage being a desirable catch? That wasn't why people married. Drunk and Vegas with Elvis made more sense than that.

Clearing my throat, I tried again. "And he swept you off your feet, no doubt. I want all the details!"

"Well, there aren't many," Poppy started.

"Signorina, one does not rush out to greet guests in the driveway like a commoner," the nanny snapped.

I felt my cousin's body tense at the rebuke. Any chance of liking this particular nanny flew out the window. No one talked to my cousin that way.

Well, we'd played plenty of tricks on her nannies before. This one would be no different.

I stepped forward, putting myself between Poppy and the old battle axe. "Hiya there! I'm Penny Greenbriar, the country bumpkin—I mean, cousin! Pleasure to meet ya, ma'am."

Snatching the withered stick the woman passed off as a hand, I shook it heartily. There was the delicious feel of her bones jarring in their sockets at the force of the handshake.

My abrupt and forceful greeting had the desired effect. The nanny stuttered.

"Well, I'm parched, cuz," I droned, wrapping my arm protectively around Poppy's shoulder. "Why don't we head to the kitchen, and I'll wet my whistle while you tell me all about your boyfriend—I mean, fiancé."

Hiding her giggles, Poppy ducked beside me, and we hurried inside.

"This way," she breathed, drawing me down the halls to a gorgeous kitchen straight off the HGTV channel.

Every last detail of the space was pure luxury. The appliances had to be custom made. But the oddest part of the space was that there was no clutter. No piles of mail shoved to the side of the counter. No cardboard flats of bottled beverages that people could grab as they came and went. And no smell of anything homey.

I blew out a whistle of admiration. "This is where you live?"

Poppy continued to the fridge but paused to look back at me. "Well, yeah?"

"All this time, we meet up once or twice a year for family vacations at some remote location, and we could have been having big, old-fashioned Christmases here," I sighed dreamily. I could just see the counter lined with cookie baking stations, a pot of cider simmering on the stove, the roast lamb in the oven slow-cooking and making it smell like a dream, while my siblings ran about the place.

Except…we don't belong here.

Poppy was silent, no doubt having the same trail of thoughts.

I waved my hand. "But I loved the road trips to meet you guys at the national landmarks. There was always somewhere new to explore!"

The tension passed from my cousin's face, and we fell into an easy conversation, reminiscing about the past.

"And how's your papà and 'em?" I drawled after a long drink of the lemonade she brought me.

"Papà is doing well!" Poppy beamed. She poured an ice-cold lemonade in a dainty glass cup. "Doctor said he's never been healthier."

If that girl had one flaw, it was that she was a major daddy's girl.

I rubbed my chest, ignoring the ache there. I was the same. I adored my father, and I would do anything for him. Which was part of the reason I was here. He couldn't help my mom, and it killed him. There was no room for dreading the awful moment when he found out his little girl was signing up for mob life. But it didn't make it easier knowing he wouldn't be happy with my decision. What was he going to feel when he found out why I was really here? Betrayal? I doubted Dad would understand.

But there's no other way….

Mom's brother could help—and I would make Uncle Tito listen to reason. With time, Dad would forgive me. He always did. The plans I had for being here revolved around knowing everything possible about my uncle. Men like him needed problems fixed. I didn't have anything to bargain with other than my brawn and my determination.

Those two things had to be enough.

I gestured for my cousin to continue. "Where is zio?"

"He's out, working," Poppy rushed to say. "But he'll be back for dinner later! And he's bringing company."

The clip-clomp of the nanny's kitten heels announced her arrival. "I've had the butler take your bags to the room we've prepared for you, Signorina Greenbriar."

I nodded. "Thanks! Mighty nice of ya, ma'am."

The nanny pursed her lips, not hiding the assessing look as she gazed over my body. "Do you have something appropriate to wear, signorina?"

"What Signora Ferraro means," Poppy stammered, "is that you look very nice—"

"For a farmer," the nanny muttered in Italian.

She probably didn't know I spoke my mother's native tongue. We would keep it that way, since it was a newer development.

"—but dinner will be a more formal event." Poppy clasped her hands in front of her. "I don't think you'll be able to fit in my clothes. So, we could go shopping if need be?"

Since my bank account was effectively under three figures, that was not happening. Actually, if things didn't work out, if my uncle didn't agree to my plans, he was going to have to loan me the ticket fare back to North Dakota if he didn't want a more permanent house guest.

It will work out! I wasn't settling for anything less.

"I have a sundress." I smiled.

My cousin winced, and the nanny visibly shuddered.

"Paired with my jean jacket, it's quite nice," I added, refusing to let them make me feel bad for not being fancy. "Anyhow, tell me about this dinner? Are we expecting company?"

"Yes," Poppy said quietly, twisting her hair. "My fiancé is coming."

"Oh, goodie! I can't wait to meet him." Snatching the lemonade from the counter, I whisked Poppy away. "Show me the rest of the house!"

Chapter 3 – Penelope

"I can't find my charm bracelet." I frowned, looking once more through my leather crossbody purse. "I swore I didn't take it off."

"It'll turn up," Poppy assured me.

I hoped so. The buzz from the plane had disappeared before I climbed into Enzo's SUV, but it was hard to say where the piece of jewelry had gone. Without it hanging from my wrist, it felt as though a piece of me was missing.

And I needed every bit of my armor in this strange new world.

The sundress was barely appropriate in the nanny's estimation. It came down to the woman not wanting my cousin to leave the house so close to supper time and risk being late. Instead of a trip to the mall, we wrapped a beautiful Hermès scarf—a fancy French word that my cousin used like I should know it—around my bare shoulders. The silky soft material kept slipping down my arms. The pattern was wild and exotic. I honestly didn't care for it, but from the way Poppy kept smiling, I pretended to like the darn thing.

"Which one is he?" I whispered conspiratorially as we stood at the great window in an unused bedroom that overlooked the front drive.

Poppy chewed her lip. "The one they're all gathering around."

Since the sun was behind the house, thick shadows fell across the circular drive. Three blacked-out SUVs were parked on the flagged pavers and nearly two dozen men milled about as she'd said. The way the dark and light played tricks on the eyes, I couldn't make out the features of any of the men. But there was one undeniable source of their focus. He was one of the taller specimens and was built like a linebacker.

It was more than his size that set the fiancé apart.

It was the energy. Black and dangerous, I could almost see the invisible forcefield swirling about him. He commanded the herd. Even though all he'd done was exit the middle vehicle, it was undeniable that he was their leader.

Why him?

I scrunched my brows and peered down at the group now mingling with my uncle's friends and associates. It was hard to see my teeny tiny cousin with such a bullish brute. How the hell did she even meet someone like that? Probably some fancy party Uncle Tito threw. I peered harder at the man. Lord, he was big. And probably older, not that a few years mattered too much, but those weren't teen muscles. No, he was definitely a man-man.

Another drop of unease slithered through me. Something wasn't right about this situation. All afternoon, little tidbits kept dropping about the fiancé. I was missing some glaringly obvious piece to this puzzle. It danced right outside my understanding.

And that made me mad.

I didn't like being the one left out.

"Signorina Caravello, come downstairs this instant and welcome your guests," the nanny barked.

Poppy...trembled.

I looped my arm through the crook of her elbow and gave her a tight squeeze. "Don't let her ruin your night."

My cousin gave me a small smile.

Shouldn't she be excited to see the man she was engaged to? A kernel of anger pulsed deep in my gut at the nanny for making her feel so miserable.

Or maybe it wasn't just the drill sergeant, but rather the entourage storming through the front doors. I wouldn't want to have dinner with the goonish strangers, when a nice, quiet meal with the family would be far more preferable.

I held tight to Poppy as we descended the stairs.

Not all the men had come inside. In fact, there were only a handful with Uncle Tito and Cousin Massimo being two of the group.

"Max!" I called out and gave him a big wave. "Where have you been all afternoon? I've been waiting!"

A shit-eating grin spread across my cousin's face. Whereas I was the second oldest of seven siblings and had an extended paternal family that made up a large chunk of the population in our small corner of the world, I only had two cousins on this side of the family.

And Massimo was trouble, my favorite kind of cousin.

"I heard you snuck into town, mimma," my cousin boomed, jogging up the flight of stairs to meet us half-way.

We exchanged a quick hug. He smelled like stale body spray and...gunpowder? I took another whiff. I knew that scent anywhere.

When he pulled back, I gave him a sharp once over. He didn't look like he'd been at target practice. Had he been doing...something else? I quickly gathered my wits and didn't let him see the unease that made me want to squirm. That was the part of the mob life I couldn't yet wrap my head around. If the rumors were true, mobsters were notorious for handling disputes as judge, jury, and executioner, killing without remorse.

But I was here, ready to pledge to that life in spite of the death and destruction. It was the only opportunity for me.

"Come on, let's go introduce you to my future brother-in-law." Massimo's eyes twinkled.

Sticking close to Poppy, we scrambled down the stairs, murmuring a fast conversation that only people who were the best of friends could have after an extended period of separation. Granted, I texted these cousins every so often, but it was only when we were together that time seemed to hold no meaning, and we picked right back up where we left off.

Engrossed in the side conversation, it wasn't until we stopped right in front of the other four men that reality snapped back into place and time seemed to resume.

I shot a glance over the group—and my heart fainted.

No...no no no.

"Penny, I want you to meet Alessandro Mancini," Massimo said with a sweep of his hand.

Oh, shit on a shingle! This couldn't be happening.

The world tilted. The ground shifted under my feet. I froze in place, ludicrous smile stuck on my face. It was like a freeze frame in a movie, the bold heroine stopped mid-motion as calamity encroached around her.

I wasn't able to draw a proper breath before the man speaking to my uncle deigned to tear his gaze away and acknowledge my cousin's attempt at polite manners.

Black eyes, the color of a starless night, collided with mine. Something crackled deep in those inky pools, but there was no other visible reaction. This man might as well have been made of stone.

I, on the other hand, was suddenly too hot. Energy crackled over my skin in response to his hard stare. Damn, he looked good if it wasn't for his icy exterior.

I do not find my cousin's fiancé attractive! I struggled to shove that reaction deep in the back of my mind.

But it was difficult with his intense focus lasered on me.

"Signor Mancini, my niece and my daughter," Uncle Tito intoned, going to stand beside Poppy.

Three more heartbeats passed before the wretch from the airport lounge broke our staring contest. I sucked in a gulp of air and shook myself. The tingle of warmth in my veins ebbed slightly. At least he wasn't hideous to look at, a small blessing for my little cousin.

"Signorina," Mancini intoned, stepping toward Poppy. "A pleasure."

I didn't miss the way the wolf looked at her.

And what if he tells on me? I gulped. While I was perfectly justified in my actions, it probably wasn't the smartest idea to start off on the wrong foot with someone from Tito's world. And this businessman was undoubtedly on the down-low with the shady business dealings my uncle was part of. He had to be if he was marrying into the family.

Marriage.... I blinked at him as he lifted Poppy's hand to his lips. *Nope, I don't get it.*

What would my sweet, innocent cousin see in someone like him other than his dark good looks? And how the hell old was he? I studied that sharp jawline. While he had nice bones under that olive complexion, his mouth was set in a hard line. There were no smile lines or crow's feet, but something about his too serious air made me think he was older than he seemed.

Unlike at the airport, there was no teasing in his voice nor smirk on his lips. He was stoic, with hard edges, as if this was a business meeting, not a family dinner with his fiancée.

If I didn't already dislike him for being a rich, entitled asshole who could do whatever he pleased, I wouldn't have been impressed by this meeting.

Poppy cleared her throat and murmured something.

Oh, the poor mouse!

"I agree! Into the dining room, I'm famished," I said brightly, coming to her rescue. "Massimo, you'll sit by me?"

"You know it, mimma," he said, reaching to ruffle my hair.

I squeaked and ducked.

As the group moved toward the dining room, Uncle Tito stopped to pull me aside. Too much cologne choked me, but the hug was genuine. "It's good to see you, Penny."

"Good to see you too." A flutter of nerves broke out in my stomach. He didn't seem displeased with my sudden trip. In fact, he didn't even seem surprised. "Thank you for having me," I added.

"Always! Family is the most important thing. We're honored that your visit coincides with our celebration of this milestone." With a pinch on my cheek, he made to move along with his guests.

Determination pushed me into action. "Uncle Tito, actually, there's a reason I'm here."

Massimo moved along after a nod from his father.

I shifted on my feet, suddenly keenly aware of being alone with one of the men who my mother ran away from nearly thirty years ago. But she'd sacrificed so much for us, it was the least I could do to face the life she'd fled. Besides, the reason she remained in contact with her only sibling was because he wasn't the demonic sonofabitch their father was purported to be.

From the few things Mom had said, I didn't think I could have summoned the courage to face my grandfather, not that I'd ever met him, but his reputation was bad enough.

"What is it, nipote?" Tito slid his pudgy hand into his pocket.

"It's a business proposition," I said slowly, hesitating over the words. "I would like to talk to you at your earliest convenience."

"Ah, well, we have guests. I'll look at my schedule and find a free hour tomorrow or the day after. Can it wait that long?"

No. But right now was clearly not the time with the guests here. "Of course." I swallowed and gave him a smile I didn't feel. "Let's eat."

Tito clapped his thick palms together. "Agreed! And what do you think of my future son-in-law?"

I hid the stumble in my step as I walked beside my uncle, who was barely taller than I was. "Um, he's interesting?"

Tito hummed. "I thought you might have an opinion on the matter, since you seemed to have a moment there."

There was a question under his observation.

Did I tell him that I pushed his dinner guest into a fountain? I chewed on the inside of my cheek. I needed my uncle to agree to my terms. If I hid what I'd done, and he found out, it could go bad. But telling him that wasn't a great way to start my trip here.

I was saved from answering by my stomach growling. "No opinions! Just famished!"

He laughed. "I'm hungry too."

I scurried to the empty seat beside Massimo and some scowling man who looked like he should be a death eater come to kill Dumbledore.

"Hi, I'm Penelope, but you can call me Penny." I stuck out my hand, ready to show the sworn servant of he-who-shall-not-be-named that I wasn't scared.

Not outwardly at least.

The man slid a look over me and then flicked a glance to the suit sitting across from me. A silent exchange passed between the death eater and the lupine businessman.

I refused to look at the fiancé. It wasn't just the smoking incident, but something...else. I watched him from my peripheral, thinking about wolves in sheep's clothing. Here he was, dressed in what was probably a custom suit, a good-looking guy, but it was all pretty trappings that couldn't hide the nasty man underneath.

"I'm Dante," the scary man beside me finally menaced.

Okay, then. "Well, it's nice to meet you," I insisted, showing these men that I wasn't bothered by them.

I turned to Massimo, who was sipping his wine. "You would not believe the last rodeo. I took first in the barrel races, but Mikey stayed on a bull for the full count!"

"You never sent any pictures!" my cousin protested, nudging me with his elbow.

Purposely avoiding whatever creepy tension was pulsing in the room, I entertained my cousin with tales of the Wild Wild West. While no one back in my hometown would think the mob was alive and well, it was equally as hard for these cidiots to understand the rural day-to-day of small town life in a ranching community.

Sadly, while Massimo and I started to have a wonderful evening, I doubted very much little Poppy was enjoying her time with the businessman. Who I liked less and less.

Mother of God! Why was he so cold to her? He only spoke to my uncle, seeming to barely acknowledge Poppy's existence. If I didn't care for him before, by the time the first course was cleared, I really hated how he treated her. The unease I felt never really went away.

Chapter 4 – Alessandro

Of all the women in the world, the little fireball from the airport just so happened to be the niece of a Detroit don.

The odds were never that good.

And for some damn reason, I found myself looking across the table at her when I should be looking down at the timid wisp of a creature who was my affianced bride. Or at least paying attention to the man I brokered this deal with, who sat on my other side. There were several Italian Syndicates in Detroit, but Don Caravello ran the wealthiest famiglia. That was part of the reason we'd opened negotiations. There were many business details we still needed to sort through.

But despite my best efforts, my gaze was repeatedly drawn to the woman sitting directly across from me. The shawl kept slipping off her shoulders, and the bare expanse of sun-kissed skin tempted me to look. By the time the meat was served, she gave up trying to wear the covering and dropped it. I fisted my hand under the table.

Penny. Short for Penelope.

Dio bono! Where did she come from? She wasn't on the family tree in the dossier we created on this organization. Surprises were never a good thing. But I stopped being annoyed that she was here as my attention focused on figuring her out.

Cousin could be a loose term. Or Don Caravello could be keeping secrets. Since gambling was bread and butter to my own rise to power, I would put money on the don being up to something.

But that she was the same woman from the airport? I shook my head. She was the last thing I expected when I walked under this roof. Granted, my initial surprise was my own fault. I spared my bride only the smallest of glances as she'd come down the stairs. The threat was the father, and I hadn't taken my sight off him when he greeted me at the door.

And then I turned to see *her*.

The tiny imp who'd been up to no good in the first-class lounge. The hellcat who'd pushed me into the fucking fountain and probably ruined one of my favorite suits.

The bombshell in the pale yellow dress with a personality larger than life itself.

Her laughter flitted across the table as she regaled her cousin with a story about...calves?

Who is this girl?

I couldn't focus on their conversation, because Don Caravello gabbed my ear off. The steady stream of Italian assaulted me the moment he took a seat at my right. It only stopped when a swig of red filled his slopping maw.

"And so, we turned a hefty profit," Tito stated, food mashed between his teeth.

The man hadn't spared his daughter a second of his time. It was how things worked in our world. Marriages were another exchange of power, and Caravello wanted to cash in on his newest score—me.

I took a sip of the wine, which was decent.

"Max! You're eating your steak well-done? You monster," the lilting voice teased. "At least Dante here knows what's up. A cow this good should still be mooing!"

The exclamation from the other side of the table snapped my attention. My ruthless, fearsome enforcer was in the innermost circle of hell. To the outsiders, including our host, Dante was just another muscle, his true position in our organization hidden. When I introduced him, it was as my personal bodyguard, but Dante was much more than that.

He was here to sniff around the don and see if there was any foul play afoot. But he wouldn't be able to wander the house until our hosts were put at ease.

I didn't trust Caravello as far as I could throw him. Even once his daughter took my last name and warmed my bed, he wouldn't be a reliable ally. There was no reason for him to start now.

But when I asked Dante to join us, when I urged him to act natural, I didn't think he would be seated next to the ball of contained energy that was the niece...that was a form of torture even the famed Minstrel couldn't withstand.

"You've barely touched your veggies, Dante," Penelope insisted. A look showed her own plate was empty. "They're so fresh. You have to try them."

Dante lifted his gaze and pinned me with a black look. Just because he wouldn't speak didn't mean we didn't communicate. Like the guard dogs roaming my property, there was much to be said in those eyes if only someone knew how to read the expressions.

Right now, the killer screamed at me that he needed to escape.

I gave him the smallest shake of my head.

"May I offer you another serving of food, signore?" a soft voice murmured from my left.

Surprise jumped through me. I forced the gruff edge to soften in my voice. "No, I'm good. But thank you."

The frightened little thing was just trying to be a good hostess.

"It's delicious," I added, which didn't seem to put her at ease. Unlike her cousin, she'd pecked at her food. Very demure, very proper.

Merda. And I was going to have to fuck that on our wedding night. If she didn't die of fright, she was going to weep. I could see it play out like a horror story in my mind's eye. The girl was barely more than a child. The fact that she was mildly pretty with great big eyes made it even worse. What kind of monster did that make me by agreeing to this?

Like father, like son.

I shoved that terrible thought away. My sire might have molded me into the perfect Made Man, one that didn't show weakness, one that was always in control, but I never adopted his darker tastes for cruelty.

The dinner plates were cleared, and the dessert was brought out.

If Dante thought he was in hell, I was right there with him. My willingness to take another wife might be pure business, but it didn't make the prospect any easier.

I'll be good to her. It was the most I could do.

With access to my wealth, the timid girl would be kept in a life of luxury befitting a queen. I promised myself again that it would be enough. She would be spoiled and eventually she might be happy with me. Unlike my sire, I would never hurt her. Above all, I would keep her safe. Growing up with Caravello, she should be used to living in a gilded cage. That wasn't going to change. The limited freedom and strict rules were absolutely necessary for her protection. No enemy would see her as a weakness.

Money and protection, it was the best I could offer her.

"Oh my word, that's orgasmic!" The angelic voice laughed across the table.

I blinked in surprise.

The fool who happened to be heir to the Caravello Famiglia shushed his cousin, who was smiling around a mouthful of the dessert.

"But it is, Max! This is the best damn cake I've ever had," Penelope insisted. "And you know I can bake. But this? I need the recipe!"

She leaned to her cousin, the material of her dress shifting to reveal more of the tanned skin underneath. The sudden desire to see where the tan lines ended filled me, and a bolt of something too strong shot to my groin.

A groan stuck in my chest. I needed some air.

While not looking at my fiancée with amorous intentions wouldn't be an insult, looking at another woman under the don's protection certainly would be. I came to Detroit to forge an alliance, not start a war. I ordered myself to regain control of my thoughts.

"See! It's *orgasmic*," Penelope whispered.

I realized I'd been straining to catch every word this bubbly creature said.

The same chocolate slice sat on the plate in front of me. I plucked my fork, scooped a bite, and tasted the sweet. For someone who didn't eat many sugary things, I had to admit, it was tasty.

But orgasmic?

Don Caravello slapped his palms together, great belly rolling in laughter at whatever funny thing he'd said. I doubted he'd heard what his niece said, but the sheltered little virgin at my side was blushing bright red.

"It is, though!" Penelope insisted, teasing her cousin. The way they kept their heads pressed together, their occasional playful touching, it was all very familial, but still, something roiled inside me. I hated another man consuming her attention—even if it was her cousin!

Whoa. Where the hell did that come from? This random relative wasn't even a blimp on my radar, and here I was having such a strong reaction to her.

That was far from okay.

"Dante! You're not even touching the cake," Penelope scolded.

And then the crazed woman picked up his spoon, carved a healthy bite, and shoved it toward the killer's mouth.

Dante reared back, nostrils splayed.

"Apri!" I snapped.

The enforcer shot me a dark look but obeyed without question, opening his mouth.

Penelope pushed the spoonful of chocolate inside.

"Mangia," I warned.

Dante's dark look promised death.

Beside me, the small virgin cleared her throat. "Should we have a coffee in the salon, Papà?"

The don, who'd been talking nonstop and clearly oblivious to the scene across the table, pulled his attention to his only daughter for a moment. "Yes, yes, of course!"

I pushed the empty plate of cake away and rose, frowning down at the scrapes of decadent fudge. I didn't remember eating the whole slice. If I truly had eaten it all, it would be a first. The sweet taste lingered on my tongue, the only evidence I had shifted from my norm and eaten dessert.

We moved into the salon, where more of our men mingled. Our Mancini soldiers stayed in a close group, eyes tracking the room, while our hosts milled about, sprawled on the furniture, and drank the don's liquor.

Penelope leaned heavily on her cousin as they laughed and whispered their way to a seat. I could see how desperate my little bride was to escape my presence and join them.

Couldn't say I blamed her.

Resisting the urge to glance again at the sunny ball of laughter, I gave Dante a signal. Now that the Caravellos were good and drunk, he could slip about unnoticed.

"Signorina, I have a gift for you." I drew the attention of the room, which gave the ghost a moment more to slide away.

"The top designer in Manhattan sent this." I pulled a bracelet from my inner pocket and held it to her.

There—a sparkle in her eyes. Diamonds usually had that effect. My fiancée lifted her left hand expectantly. I clasped the piece around her slight wrist, frowning at how loosely it hung.

"We can have it resized, of course," Caravello stated, appearing at my side.

I didn't care for his immediate micromanaging.

But he was oblivious, snapping his fingers for the servants and calling for champagne.

"It's beautiful," my fiancée murmured. "Thank you, Signor Mancini."

I nodded.

Every pair of eyes stared at us, including the cousin's. They saw the gems; they approved of the lavish gift. But the success of the gesture was fleeting. My bride moved closer, turning her face up expectantly.

Oh, dio. No, just...no.

But I knew what was expected of me. I bent over her, engulfing her by the sheer size difference. I gently gripped her shoulders, only to discover she shook like a leaf. The whole scene felt wrong. I forced the burst of conscience back to the recesses of my mind. This was a business deal, there was no place for emotions here. My lips brushed chastely across hers.

When I pulled back, there were tears in her eyes.

That was the final knife to the gut.

"Let me see!" Penelope called out.

My fiancée looked between me and her father.

I gave her a small nod, letting her escape me while she could. Too soon, she'd be shackled to my side. There was no help for it.

I followed her with my gaze, but not because she commanded my attention. No, because she moved to the source of light in this haunted place.

Penelope glared at me.

Such a bold gesture. It made me wonder if she knew who the hell I was.

Somehow, I didn't think it would stop her if she did. My pulse picked up at the challenge in her flashing hazel eyes. She put an arm protectively around her cousin and held the look for a moment longer. The unspoken intent behind her words was clear. She was a protector, and I was the monster come to steal something of hers.

For the first time tonight, a real smile played on my lips. *Oh, it's on, vespina.*

Chapter 5 – Penelope

It was the wine. I could drink whiskey and hold my own with any of the boys. But whatever was in that burgundy vintage had my head spinning.

Or maybe it was the fact that you drank nearly two bottles! I pushed the inner voice aside and fought through the buzz.

An hour ticked by, and we were still sitting in the corner of the fancy room. Poppy spun the bracelet around her wrist, staring at a spot on the floor. My own wrist felt naked. At least the charms I'd spent my life collecting had meaning. That sparkle on Poppy's wrist was only meant to dazzle. If there was sentiment behind the calculated gesture, I missed it.

Massimo was off talking with some of the other guys. And that guy Dante? He kept coming and going. It was as if he made regular appearances to check in with his handler only to disappear when no one was looking.

The temptation to follow him was strong. If I hadn't felt the overwhelming need to stay close to my baby cousin, I would have.

So I sipped my red wine and stayed put. Sitting on the fancy ivory couch, it was all I could do not to spill. I was clearly out of my element, and I knew better than to drink any more. But the red in my glass never seemed to empty, thanks to the servants who appeared out of thin air to refill it. I liked the wine better than the bubbly, sweet stuff Uncle Tito brought when the beastly man gave my poor little mouse the gaudy, hideous bracelet.

I flicked a glance to the shiny thing. It was undoubtedly expensive, just like the massive rock on her finger. They looked wrong on her. As if her fiancé didn't know the first thing about the woman he'd spent so much money on.

The missing piece of the puzzle slipped into place, sobering me instantly.

Nooo....

That was just...wrong. It couldn't be the case.

"Bathroom," I hissed, snatching Poppy by the arm and tugging her from the uncomfortable couch that looked like something from *Pride and Prejudice*.

I managed to navigate us out of the room, but Poppy took over from there, guiding us to the large bathroom that only had a toilet and sink.

The door slammed like a clap of thunder.

Poppy jumped. "Jeezus, Penny, you okay?"

"No, and you aren't either." I placed a hand on either side of her shoulders. "Poppy, are you being *sold* to that asshole?"

Her eyes widened. Hushed protests fell from her lips, but I saw the truth in her eyes.

"Okay, call it whatever you want, but you're being forced into this," I insisted. "Don't bother lying, I can see it in your face."

My cousin looked away.

"Mouse! This isn't right." I pulled her close, wrapping my arms around her.

"I hadn't even met him before tonight," she croaked, voice barely audible.

Oh, mother of god! How the hell was that even possible?

I pushed the rising panic down. This was exactly what my mother fled. Why she wouldn't talk about her childhood. She too had been engaged once. While she hadn't said much, I understood now.

"You aren't marrying him," I declared.

"Sshhhuuush!" Poppy tugged at me. "Quiet, please! They can hear you."

"Poppy—"

But my teeny, tiny cousin pulled away. She straightened, chin tipping up with determination. "It's the way things work here, Penny. It's tradition, and he's a good match."

"He's a—" I couldn't even form the words.

"He's a what?" she dared.

I pursed my lips. "This is mob business, isn't it."

Surprise widened her eyes. "You know?"

"Yes, I know," I said with a touch too much bite. Pausing, I took a deep breath. "Are you in danger?"

"What?" she laughed. "No! Not that."

"Then help me understand," I insisted.

"Papà found me someone who can protect and provide for me. Signor Mancini is a don, a boss, just like papà." Poppy smoothed her hands over her pretty flowery blush dress.

Garh! She looked too young in that shade of pink with the full skirt. "You have to be joking."

"I'm dead serious."

"You can't marry a man you don't know!" I protested.

She jumped to clap a hand over my mouth. "I'm doing as is expected of me. Try to understand. And if you can't, don't ruin this for me."

Her big brown eyes begged me to understand. That wasn't possible. But somehow, I found the strength to nod. It was what she needed right now. Later, when my head was cleared, we were going to talk about this.

"Thank you," she whispered. With that, my cousin slipped from the room.

I could have fallen into the wall if a feather brushed against me. Maybe I was more buzzed than I thought.

And then an even worse realization tore at me. "Oh, shoot. No! Just...no."

What if my uncle required the same obedience from me? I'd come here to bargain, hadn't I? I was expecting to work for him—hopefully as an assistant, but I would go so far as to be a maid or something equally grueling since I didn't have a fancy business degree to offer.

But what if I was just a pound of flesh to him? Could I allow him to sell me to save my mother?

I grabbed my suddenly tight throat. I needed to go upstairs, probably take a shower, and think about this where I could have time and space to process the possibility.

Hurrying from the bathroom, I took the corner and ran into a wall.

A warm wall, one that smelled like woods and a deep, intoxicating musk.

I took a second inhale of the spicy scent before I could stop myself.

"I was wondering where you ran off to," the wall rumbled.

I knew that voice.

Our eyes clashed, and I took an involuntary step backward. While he came across as cold and unfriendly with my uncle, and icy and cruel when standing next to my cousin, there was something pulsing underneath that frozen exterior.

Something lupine and hungry.

"Goodnight, Mr. Mancini. I can't say it was nice to meet you," I blurted out, my tongue taking on a mind of its own.

The corner of his mouth twitched. "I didn't think you were one to run away."

"I'm not. But I also know that you shouldn't be alone with another woman when you are engaged to someone else," I snapped.

He had the audacity to chuckle.

My molars ground hard. The nerve! This man was nothing short of infuriating. I muttered a wish that he'd be trampled and shoved past him.

His arm shot out to capture me. He held my wrist tight. His touch burned the skin, but the look in his eyes made me shiver.

"If you have something to say to me, say it to my face," he growled.

The sound sent a shiver straight through my body, making my toes curl.

"I think you're a monster." I tipped my chin up, refusing to back down from his icy, unfeeling stare.

"You'd be right, carina. I am the worst kind of monster."

Rage spiked in my blood. There was no way in hell Poppy was marrying this man. Right there, without a plan, I vowed it to myself. I would move heaven and earth to end this engagement.

"Sleep well...Penelope."

My name was silver rolling off his tongue. He held my wrist a moment longer before releasing me.

Not bothering to offer him the same wellness, I walked away with careful, practiced steps, refusing to give him the satisfaction of seeing me flee. I felt his gaze follow me, and it took a lot of hot water and soap to banish the lingering reminder of his touch in the shower.

The sun baked the decorative stones around the glittering pool. The freshly squeezed orange juice sweated in my hand. Unfortunately, I could see myself getting too comfortable here. There were no chores to help with, no herd was demanding my attention, and no grueling shift at the local Holiday Inn & Suites was waiting for me following ranch work. Best of all, the housekeepers I managed weren't blowing up my phone with a crisis, and it truly felt as though I was on vacation—and not the annual trips with my family.

When the hell was the last time I had an escape? I sipped the cup until it was empty.

If I was being technical, this wasn't a vacation. But with the sparkling sunlight and endless availability of food that I didn't have to prepare, it sure seemed like paradise.

One blissful morning. That was all I was allowed to enjoy. There was a different kind of work demanding my attention, but since Uncle Tito was busy, I could take advantage of the moment to relax. I set the empty cup down and rose.

Poppy flipped through a bridal magazine, keeping her body carefully tucked under the shadow of the big umbrella. My cousin seemed…eager to marry. Why, I still couldn't say. But she'd woken me up with a smile and stack of magazines. She wanted my opinion on every detail and told me over and over that anything could be changed if I thought something else would be better.

I had to bite my tongue when I thought her choice in groom should be the first thing to go.

Any determination to talk her out of the situation fled with the morning sun. It was her life, and who was I to judge? Even if it felt wrong deep in my bones. I was a guest here, I had my own agenda, and there were clearly facets of this situation related to my uncle's sketchy business that I didn't quite understand. So we'd spent most of the morning chatting about the big day—which was a lot closer than I would have guessed.

"The water's calling my name," I moaned dreamily. It was clear, didn't reek of chlorine like the hotel's pool where I worked, and it was much better than the murky pond back on my brother's property where we'd let loose when too many light beers hit.

"You still haven't answered my question," Poppy pressed.

A long sigh escaped. I couldn't in good conscience be a participant in this farce. But how could I not stand by her side if she truly needed me to face her husband at the altar? Making an excuse about the timeframe or work could easily be the solution, if I really wanted to avoid being present at the wedding. It came down to whether I wanted to stand by her or not.

And the poor thing wanted me there. The eagerness shone in her eyes.

"I'll only be your maid of honor if you promise the dress won't be hideous," I said sternly, pointing a finger at her.

Poppy squealed and launched from her chair, slipping into the sunlight to wrap me in a hug. It was hard not to let the enthusiasm wash over me.

Maybe, just maybe, the surly giant was her prince charming on a valiant steed. The beast sure as hell wasn't my cup of tea.

"What's this?" Massimo cheered, coming up the path from the house.

I looked over to him, a snarky comeback on my tongue about helping him sacrifice his sister to the god of darkness, when the very monster appeared behind my cousin.

With that strange magnetism, our gazes collided. An explosion of sparks shot through my traitorous body.

Stop it!

I didn't find him handsome or worth my attention. The reaction was purely because I saw him for what he truly was. There was no other reason for these feelings pulsing through me.

I forced myself to give him a once over.

Nope, he definitely wasn't my cup of tea. I didn't find him attractive in the slightest, and who the hell wore a full suit at eleven in the morning? At the pool!

Poppy untangled herself from my side, reaching for her coverup and tugging it over her swimsuit. "Signor Mancini, I wasn't expecting you."

"I have business with your father, signorina." But he wasn't looking at her.

No, that calculating, frigid gaze was laser focused on me. Deep in those inky pools of blackness, a raw emotion flickered. If I had to name it, it resembled possession.

But that was ridiculous.

I planted my hands on my hips. "So you're the reason I can't speak with Tito this morning. Can you hurry it up so I can have my turn? I really need to talk to my uncle."

A muscle in his jaw feathered.

"Penny!" my cousin hissed. "What's gotten into you?"

That was a good question. Normally, my customer service face was easy to fake.

Ah, who am I kidding? There was a reason I was head of housekeeping and not front of house at the hotel. District management passed me over time and time again, stating that I wasn't qualified to be more than head maid.

I pushed the pain of their rejections away. I was here now, with the intent to join the mob. There would be ample opportunity for me to prove my worth here.

"Signore, may I get you a drink?" my perfect little cousin rushed to add.

Massimo, busy on his phone, looked up. "Me too?"

His sister smiled and disappeared. Whatever Massimo was going to say was cut off with the ring of his phone. He held up a finger and wandered around the pool, animatedly speaking in Italian.

That left me alone with the prick in the expensive suit.

I refused to let him know it bothered me that I was basically naked in front of him. It would take a lot more than that to make me uncomfortable.

"Did you have a headache this morning, signorina?" he said, voice deep and gravelly.

I narrowed my eyes. "I'm not a lightweight, Mr. Mancini."

Garh! How could he stand there, planning to take my sweet baby cousin and not see anything wrong with it? He was ancient! Okay, maybe not decrepit, because those sculpted features weren't touched by age. But—but—

He was all wrong for her.

In the bright light of day, I couldn't avoid the obvious. And as was my habit, I couldn't keep my damn mouth shut.

"How old are you?" I demanded.

His mouth twitched. "That's a very personal question."

He had the nerve to tease me.

I marched forward. "No, not really. Because you know what I think?"

He hummed, a deep, delicious, masculine rumble.

Which only pissed me off more.

"I think you're too old to get married."

Those lips curved up. "I don't believe there is any maximum cap on the situation."

"Too old for her," I clarified.

Amusement flicked in his eyes as he remained focused on me. There was a definite air of danger about him. Every instinct in my veins screamed not to mess with him.

And yet I was the fool stepping into his space. "You can't marry her."

"She's eighteen and has agreed to the arrangement."

"She's nineteen, you beast. Garh! You don't even know anything about her," I hissed.

The smirk playing in the corners of his mouth was all it took.

An all-consuming anger surged through me. How dare he? How freaking dare he! I lunged.

This time, he caught me. The force of my spring was enough to send us both toppling, however. The scream was cut off by the water as the pool rushed around us, and I remembered at the last second to hold my breath.

Hard hands gripped me.

I struggled and fought.

Oh, mother of god, this is it! He was going to drown me.

Only...he didn't.

The beastly wolf drug me to the surface.

"What the fuck was that?" he bellowed, the mask of careful control gone.

Good, this was the real beast, and now everyone could see him as the raging fiend I knew him to be!

"Are you trying to drown me?" he barked.

"Unfortunately, it doesn't seem to be working," I snapped and swiped at him. He dodged me easily. "Let me go, I can swim."

I looked around, ready to point a finger and show everyone just how dangerous this man was. How grouchy and how completely unsuitable.

There was no one.

Massimo was gone. No servants flitted about. And Poppy was still in the house.

I jerked, tugging on his hold. "Let. Me. Go."

A low sound rumbled through that broad chest. "Say please."

"Oh, hell no!" I protested, but my voice caught too high.

There we were, floating in the pool, entirely too close for comfort. Water dripped from his face, but otherwise he looked...handsome as ever. His touch slid up my arms, capturing me around the shoulders. My pulse beat double. Words failed me. I'd even stopped struggling, only fluttering my legs to keep buoyant.

"Penny! Signore! What happened?" Poppy called, running from the house, the tray of drinks bouncing in her hands.

Her appearance broke the damn spell—and just in time! I had no idea what the beast would do. But the painful truth was that I'd been caught in his spell, if only for a moment.

He shoved me toward the side of the pool and swiped a hand down his jaw. "I can't believe you fucking did that."

"Again," I said before I could think better of it.

His narrowed gaze promised this wasn't over.

Bring it.

I needed one or two incidents where the others could witness his meaner side, and then they would never allow Poppy to marry him. Lazily rolling into a backstroke, I glided across the pool as the businessman climbed out, accepted a towel from my cousin, and attempted to dry off his ruined suit. The smile on my lips didn't go away to see him so ruffled. I did that—and I would do it again!

Chapter 6 – Penelope

There was no proof that the delay in meeting with Uncle Tito was because Mr. Mancini was seeking vengeance. But he monopolized my uncle's time, and when afternoon rolled around, the men disappeared. Poppy didn't know where they went and said it was the nature of their business operations. She didn't admit what her father did, saying that his construction company was very demanding. She never mentioned the real business behind the legal front. Until I spoke to my uncle, I didn't want to confess more of what I knew about our family legacy, so I didn't push for details.

Lounging around her house, curiosity mixed with the impending weight of the conversation threatened to drive me crazy.

How could my cousin just sit there, working on some needle art project while the men were out doing heaven knew what? It was nothing short of insanity! Something out of a hundred-year-old novel.

But there was a wedding planner who was handling all the arrangements, which left Poppy with little to do. When my sister Jillian married, we did everything from the decorations—which were hunting themed, because burnt orange and fall were her taste—to making the food and setting up at the local rec center. While it was nice not to have to make a hundred and fifty table decorations, there was an out-of-touch feeling that made this wedding seem not quite real. I very much doubted my cousin felt that way, though.

After a quiet dinner, Poppy curled up with a book before the electric fireplace. The flickering flames made me instantly miss the log hearth back home. When Mom and Dad built their snug cabin after they first married, the fireplace was the center to Mom's vision. She even cooked over it sometimes, while us girls dressed up in prairie costumes and pretended we lived in the 1800s.

Fighting the nostalgia of home, I flicked through my phone, too fidgety to read on my Kindle but also too nervous to text my sister with an update from the Bismarck hospital. The glass of red wine on the side table wasn't helping matters.

"Whatcha readin'?" I asked, dropping my phone and scrubbing my hands over my face.

Poppy hummed and looked up from her book. "Sorry, what did you say?"

I grinned. "Must be good. What's the book about?"

"Oh, um, it's okay." She held up the hardback so I could read the cover.

And my eyes about fell from my skull. It was an inspirational treatise about happiness in marriage.

"Honey, if you need this—" I started to say but stopped abruptly. "It's not my place."

Poppy glanced to the door, double checking that the drill sergeant was well and truly gone for the night. "I was hoping it would explain things."

"Things?" I hedged, sitting up straighter and taking a sip of my wine. "What kind of things, mouse?"

She chewed her lip for a moment. "I don't know what to *do*, Penny."

I frowned, unsure what was best to say, and not wanting to tell her outright that if she had doubts, she shouldn't go through with it.

"I don't know how to...be intimate," she whispered.

She didn't.... Had no one talked....

Oh, sweet mother of god.

"You're a virgin?" I whispered back, scooting to the other end of the couch so I was next to her armchair. "That's not a bad thing!" I rushed to add. "If you haven't found the right guy, doing it can be uncomfortable."

The look on her face made me immediately want to smack myself.

Mancini was *not* the right guy.

"Do you, um, know the basic mechanics?" I fumbled for the words to make this conversation less abrupt.

Her cheeks infused with a bright blush. "Of course. The last nanny told me what happened when I became a woman."

I rubbed my hand over my face to hide the look I couldn't keep off it. "Then why are you reading that?"

Poppy dropped her face into her hands, and the book slid onto the floor with a deafening thud. "Signor Mancini is never going to see me as a woman. As a wife. This needs to work, Penny. And I don't know how to make him fall in love with me!"

That was because a beast like him wasn't capable of love! I wanted to scream the truth at the top of my lungs, but I bit my tongue.

I rushed to shut the double doors, not wanting to be surprised during this conversation. "Okay, first, do you even want him to love you?"

Poppy nodded eagerly. "He's a really good match."

Then why do you sound like you're trying to convince yourself? My hands fisted at my side.

"Can you help me?" she asked hopefully.

I fought back a groan. Could I? I would go to the ends of the world to help her, but this? How did I help her prepare to be a virgin sacrifice?

"I can try," I murmured.

"Oh, thank you! I knew you would know what to do. You've had boyfriends, and you're so worldly."

Someone save me! I cleared my throat. "What you need then is to feel...sexy?"

That earned me a vigorous nod. "A sex goddess—yes! Like you!"

I groaned again. If she knew the kinds of things I'd done to earn extra money when funds were tight.... Sex goddess? More like dancing queen in a sweaty pole building around drunk farmers and ranchers. And when they got too handsy, those couple of close calls before the bouncers stopped drinking long enough to pay attention and help—

I was not going there. Nothing bad had ever happened, and it didn't pay to dwell on things that could have been.

"Okay, first, you need to ditch most of your wardrobe. It's pretty, and I'm sure it was expensive, but you look really young."

Poppy chewed on her lip. "I can try."

Next, I pulled out my phone. "This is the Kindle Reading App. Are you familiar with Kindle?"

"Oh, yes!" She nodded, passing me her iPhone.

I clicked around the screen. "Stupid iPhone."

"What are you trying to do?" She leaned over to look. "Oh, sorry. That won't work."

The answer was obvious a moment later. "You have a parental lock."

"Yeah," she muttered, dropping back into her seat.

This poor kid! Sheltered didn't even begin to describe it.

How the hell did they expect her to marry someone like Mancini? He might be an ass, but it was clear as day that he was virile. Worldly. *Smoldering.*

That word made my stomach do a little flip.

Resisting taking another swig of wine, I drummed my fingers against my thigh.

"Okay, well, pirating is wrong, but there are good books on a place called Wattpad and other sites." I gave up and took a long pull at the glass of red. "Do you know Harry Potter?"

Poppy chuckled. "I might be green, but I'm not that out of touch with the world."

"What if Hermione and Draco ended up together?" At her wide-eyed expression, I knew I had her hooked. I proceeded to give her the blurb and hook of a certain fanfiction book as I downloaded it. "My favorite is *Manacled*, but it's dark. There are others that are spicy without the intensity—you need to work up to something as emotionally destructive as *Manacled*. Let's see."

I scrolled through the few books I knew about on the free sites.

"Here's one! Fantasy Romance with fae who are enemies but become lovers. It's very spicy," I mused. *Maybe too spicy for Poppy.* But she had to start somewhere.

"You've read it?" my cousin asked.

I shook my head. "Not this one, but it has rave reviews by people I trust. It will be good," I decided. "If you want a marriage where you drive your man crazy, reading about smoldering attraction is the way to do it."

There it was with that word again!

I blamed it on the electric fire that wasn't turning into coals.

After taking her phone back, Poppy began to read. From the small noises she made, I knew I'd just blown her mind. I mentally patted myself on the back and finally opened my own book.

It was half past midnight before the front door opened.

Loud voices broke the cozy ambiance. Poppy jumped, the haze of enjoyment swiped off her face and replaced by a guilty wobble.

"But if we go talk to Gianetti, make him see reason," Massimo reasoned, his voice carrying through the closed doors.

"Don't look like your hand was in the cookie jar, mouse, and they won't know the kind of things you read," I laughed, patting my cousin as I rose.

"This book is sssooo good!" she whispered, tagging along behind me. "Are there...more books like this?"

"Loads and loads," I promised, pulling the door open and stepping into the hall. "I've got you."

Was it smart to drop an unsuspecting virgin, who was also new to smut, into something as kinky as dark, forbidden romance? Probably not. Should have eased her into the genre. But then again, she was getting married before the end of the month. There wasn't time to introduce her slowly. If the marriage went through—which I was still determined it wouldn't—she would need all the help she could get.

"That is not an option—" Uncle Tito spat, face blotchy and anger glittering in his eyes.

I pulled up short. I misread their loud entrance. Coming from a large family, no one was quiet. So I hadn't assumed father and son were arguing.

I flashed them a smile as I called out, "Glad you're back! Did you guys want something to eat?"

Massimo scowled. "Thanks, mimma, but I'm headed to bed."

Uncle Tito growled in Italian, "Remember your place, boy. You're not a leader yet."

Poppy tugged at my arm, but I shooed her upstairs. "I'm going to make a piece of toast. Want one?" I offered my uncle.

Muttering a string of grouchy opinions, he nodded and followed me into the kitchen.

"What is it that you want to talk about?" He went straight to the point.

My fingers closed around the fresh loaf in the bread box, and I whispered a quick prayer to any saint listening.

"Spit it out, I haven't got all night," he grumped, falling onto a barstool. "And don't bother denying it, that's why you waited up all night."

"Mom needs heart surgery." I kept the shake from my voice as I slid the knife back and forth.

The dollop of butter crackling in the skillet was the only sound in the room. I placed two slices of bread in the butter, swiped the crumbs onto my palm to dispose in the sink, and proceeded to grab plates.

Only then did I turn to my uncle. "I want to give her the best chance possible. I want to send her to Mayo Clinic in Rochester, Minnesota."

"Bismarck won't do the surgery?" He tipped his head to the side, studying me.

I shook my head. "They wrote her off. They want to make her comfortable. There's a doctor in Fargo who will try. But they're not Mayo."

"She never said...." Uncle Tito's voice trailed off.

I bit my tongue. It was better he process the news, and when he was ready, we could discuss how best to take action.

The slices caramelized nicely. I put a healthy smear of butter on the toast, glad that he had grass-fed, real butter.

It would taste like home.

Because she married a rancher, Mom did everything homestead. We made our own bread, butter, and lived off the land. What we couldn't grow, we sourced locally. Those things were what kept her so healthy for so long. But heart defects didn't care about lifestyle. They cropped up when least expected.

My uncle ate his toast noisily.

I stood across the island, telling myself I was in the barn with the milk cow and not another human. No one should chew that loudly and then proceed to lick their fingers clean.

"You need money."

His question jerked me from the mental retreat I sent my mind on. "Yes, and I'm willing to work for it."

Appreciation flicked in his eyes. "When your mother left, my father warned her there wouldn't be a cent."

I knew that. "But he also said there'd be no contact. And we've spent many family vacations with you and the cousins."

Uncle Tito nodded. "I'm not my father. I know a good thing when I see it. Your appearance couldn't have come at a better time."

There was a note of something in his tone. It slithered through me, spreading a thin layer of unease. Collecting the plates, I dropped soap on them and proceeded to scrub. The very state of my world might be hanging in the balance, but cleaning—doing something that needed to be done—grounded me.

When I was done, I turned. "I'll do anything, zio. You've got to have something I can do, some job. I'll work as long as it takes."

"Don't think me so heartless that I won't help my only sister," my uncle said quietly.

Relief, sweet and beautiful, rushed through me.

"Oh, thank you, thank you!"

Uncle Tito held up his hand. "You'll remain with us while your mother receives treatment and is recovering. I have a few ideas how you can help me."

Translation: Work off the debt. That was exactly what I needed to hear.

But now that he'd said it, I braced myself for the other shoe to drop. The ultimate question played through my mind. What the hell did a morally questionable businessman like my uncle, who worked outside the legal avenues, want with a country girl like me?

"I'll do anything," I asserted. He needed to see my resolve and determination.

"I'll find a use for you," he promised, sensing my uncertainty.

"But nothing illegal, right?" I blurted out.

Ah, shit. Me and my big mouth!

Uncle Tito frowned. "Now why would I ask you to do that?"

There was no use pretending. Everything needed to come out in the open if this was going to work.

"I know what my grandfather was," I gulped. "I know the empire he left you, the legacy my mother walked away from. I want in."

There—I said it.

Tito leaned back, an impressed whistle played on his lips. "My darling niece, you want to join the mob."

"I do." I squared my shoulders. "There's opportunity in this line of work, better than I'll find in North Dakota."

"Opportunity?" he mused.

I shrugged. "It's no secret that I wasn't the best student in school. I barely graduated, and I've had no prospects to advance myself in a trade like my sister."

"Jillian became a nurse, right?" Tito rubbed his five o'clock shadow.

"Yes." And I paid in glitter and sweat to make sure she could follow her dreams. It was my turn to dream now, my turn to seize the day. "I'm a hard worker. Give me a chance to prove I can be of use to you—to our famiglia."

My uncle studied me. "But you just said you don't want to do anything illegal."

Crap. I backpedaled quickly to fix that slipup. "I mean killing," I said bluntly. "I'll beg, borrow, and steal, but I don't want to be a murderer."

"I see," he hummed.

"I'll do whatever you need me to. Let me work for you, give me this chance, and all I ask in return is to cover my mother's medical bills."

Would he do it? His poker face was unreadable.

I sent a prayer to the Blessed Mother.

The smile that curled my uncle's lips could have curdled milk. The toast somersaulted in my gut. "You're so smart, Penelope. Much smarter than your parents."

That was highly doubtful. None of my six siblings had come to strike a deal with the devil. My dad never talked about my mom's family, and Mom hadn't even told her brother about the surgery. Was I smart for coming out here? Or did I just sell my soul?

"Don't worry," he assured me. "I would never ask you to compromise yourself, carina. But the fact that you know about your heritage will make it easier to work together, yes?"

"Yes," I breathed. "You'll have me?"

"Well, of course." His grin broadened. "I'm not a fool, I know a good opportunity when I see one."

Relief flowed through me. It was done. I was in!

Holy shit. I just joined the mob. My heart began to patter with a new vigor.

"We'll talk about your conscription later. For now, I'll say goodnight." My uncle rose, kissed me on both cheeks, and disappeared.

I stood near the sink, feeling like I'd just been thrown from a horse and trying to breathe through the roiling emotions. I'd done it, but it felt more uncertain than before.

Poppy went to bed over an hour ago. It had been three nights since the midnight snack with my uncle. So far, my only duty was keeping Poppy company. But that wasn't good enough for me.

I sold myself to the mob to pay for my mother's surgery. And if I didn't find a place to fit in, my uncle could technically renege on our deal. It was doubtful he would, but I wasn't taking any chances. The second—and probably more pressing—reason for my unrest, was that I wanted to actually be useful. To do that, I should know every detail of this organization. My whole life had been spent filling in where needed. If I understood where a need was *first*, I could insert myself.

I can make something of myself.

This was my birthright after all, like a long-lost princess coming home to the kingdom. Looking at it that way helped my conscience deal with the fact that most of the business dealings weren't above board.

There was one person who might be able to show me the ropes. It was simply a matter of catching him on his way out. So I waited. Predictably, a little after ten, I heard steps on the stairs. I bolted from my room.

"Max!" I called in a stage whisper.

My cousin stopped short. "Penny, why aren't you in bed?"

I tugged the jean jacket firmly over my tee and hurried after him. "Because, silly, I'm coming with you!"

Massimo blanched. "Mimma," he warned.

I held up my hand. "I'm your newest recruit! Yes, yes, I know, I'm behind in my training. But I'm going to prove myself as an associate and work my way into being sworn as a Made Man."

Before coming to Detroit, I spent weeks watching and reading everything I could find about mob history in America. Michael Franzese, a real mobster from the Colombo crime family had a lot of fascinating information on the internet. He'd been my starting point. I dug and dug, enjoying the research process. Now

I felt confident and was familiar with the concepts of organized crime and how it differed from the drug rings and gangs.

I stopped short before my croaking cousin. With a nudge, I urged him down the stairs. "Didn't you hear? I'm going to join the family business. Your dad and I arranged it the other night."

"Penelope, women don't participate in the mob." The use of my full name, coupled with my cousin's stern expression, would have cowed a more timid soul.

Not me.

Pinning Massimo with a hard look, I began to tick off the names of bosses who were female.

But my cousin cut me off. "Rare cases. The way the mob works in America, families—women and children—are off limits. For a reason. Unlike the original organizations back in the Old World, we have a code."

Michael Franzese had said as much. But that wasn't stopping me.

"Your father said—"

"There are other ways women serve," Massimo said in a low voice.

I blinked. "Like your sister."

He paused for a moment, choosing his words carefully. "That's part of the tradition."

No, it wasn't. My cousin was being bartered. There was some arrangement between my uncle and the monstrous groom. While my blood boiled at the thought of her being essentially sold, I had to remain focused on my role in this grand scheme.

I squared my shoulders. "I'm going to be a Made Man—a Made Woman. I'm tough. I can do whatever you do, Max."

A smile cracked over his face. "Bet?"

"Bet!" I stuck out my hand.

"What I'm doing tonight is running surveillance. It's nothing compromising, so there shouldn't be a problem with you tagging along." His eyes glittered with mischief. "Let's go, recruit! Just remember, you wanted this."

I do. I wanted this.

Chapter 7 – Alessandro

Dante shifted beside me. My right hand felt the trouble brewing same as I did. The sixth sense developed at a young age, and since we were some of the lucky bastards who listened to it, we were still here, decades later, haunting the shadows of the underworld.

Of course, luck had very little to do with it.

We trained hard; we learned the art of war. We put ourselves in situations where luck could be produced. That was the thing about the elusive lady. She didn't bestow her favor on those who avoided her.

"I don't like this," Dante muttered.

"If they're dealing, I need to know," I growled.

A plague was spreading across the Midwest—across the whole of the country. While mobs sometimes dealt in the drug trade, there were a few substances I would not allow anywhere near my territory. I knew some facets of Caravello's operation were drug related, and I could in good conscience write that off. But not if he was investing in things like methamphetamine, fentanyl, or even prescription painkillers. Some of that shit was tainted and downright nasty. When we first proposed the joining of our houses through marriage, I made it a non-negotiable.

Blindly trusting my future father-in-law's word would be utterly stupid. I had to make sure his operations were above board.

It would have been so much easier to marry a Chicago girl. I could better keep an eye on her family's operations. And I'd tried! Around Christmas time, I'd offered myself to the pakhan of a rising Russian Bratva. But Dimitri Vlasov was fiercely protective of the women in his family. He wouldn't hear of a man approaching forty marrying one of his young female relatives. It was hard not to admire the pakhan for that. We'd established a friendship, however, over our shared hatred of the main source of fentanyl in Chicago—the Toro Syndicate, who were based out of the cesspool that was southern Minneapolis. They were street rabble, little better than a hood gang, but with a more organized structure like a motorcycle club. Their reach spread to neighboring states. They were a cancer, putrid and rotting, that kept coming back no matter how frequently we gunned them down.

Mine wasn't the only organization who abhorred their existence, but I was probably the only one powerful enough to do anything. The Vlasov Bratva was a newer organization, and they were focusing on growing their business. There was an old Irish faction with several prominent families in Chicago. They *could* do something—if they wanted to. But the idea of an Irish woman marrying a Prince of Rome was worse than letting a new crime faction arise in the city.

No, Vlasov was the only one willing to fight the scourge. Together, we kept that shit from our streets. But what I had with the Russians was a working relationship, and I needed something deeper to shore up my reign.

So I had to look for alliances elsewhere. That led me to another old legacy, one that we had warred with and married into before.

"Is that the Caravello heir?" Dante pointed through the broken window of the old warehouse.

I frowned. "What is he doing here?"

Massimo wasn't a capo, but he also wasn't a street soldier.

"Do you think he's going to double cross us?" Dante voiced a question that irritated me like sand behind the eyelids.

That nagging feeling in the back of my mind flared bright. Certain things about this alliance weren't adding up. Dante's sleuthing had proved effective in producing non-doctored reports. Caravello was receiving a much better bargain through this marriage than I was. The exchange of money and power didn't bother me as much as the fact that his businesses weren't as profitable as he'd claimed. If he could fib about the numbers, what else was he hiding?

The only way to back away from the contract and not start a war was if Caravello was coming to the table in bad faith. We hadn't proved that yet. And because I needed this alliance, I hoped we wouldn't.

"He looks like he's here for a regular drop." *Like a common soldier.* My tongue swiped across my teeth as I considered the scene playing out before us.

"He lacks discretion," Dante spat.

I hummed in agreement.

My second palmed his gun. "Should we teach him a lesson?"

"As fun as that sounds, I don't think we'll have to." I jerked my chin in the opposite direction. "Let's see how the kid handles himself."

Three figures emerged from the darkness. By a civilian's standard, it wasn't a fair fight. But nothing about our life was fair. We survived or fell on our own merit. It was what made a mob stronger than any legal organization. Bureaucracies and legal entities leached off those they were supposed to protect and serve. They wouldn't know the value of service if it was presented on a silver platter. Most Made Men protected their own, and that extended to anyone living in their territories. That was the sacred code I lived my life by. Even if the civilians didn't know we existed, we fought, bled, and died to keep them safe.

When the trio of newcomers shouted, the little Caravello jumped.

Dante chuckled.

But my attention was drawn to a shift of movement in the front seat of the kid's dark sedan. Massimo didn't come alone. The question of who he'd chosen to trust on this mission was quickly answered with a terrible revelation.

Nut brown hair swept into a braid fell down her back. I gaped at her. *Dio mio, no!* Penelope sprang from the car and bounded to the little prince's side.

"Shit." I pushed from the wall.

By the time Dante and I scrambled down the stairs and burst outside, gunshots rang through the night. Cool metal filled my hand a moment later, but instead of drawing a steadying breath to make the too-easy shot, blood roared in my ears.

Penelope wasn't on the ground. Neither was she taking cover near the sedan.

Fury blazed through my veins. Standing tall, and refusing to take cover, I advanced, my gun raised as an extension of my hand. I aimed and plucked off one of the newcomers. It was a clean kill, and better than the bastard deserved.

I wanted to shred the flesh from their skin.

Another dove for safety, but not before Dante managed to send a bullet straight into his center mass.

In a haze of red, I strode into the street. Two more shots, and I managed to kill the last. My second sprang after his wounded prey with a bloodthirsty snarl. He would finish him and place a final bullet in each skull for silence.

"Caravello," I shouted. "Come out here!"

The prince had taken cover behind a mailbox—not taking his cousin with him.

A thousand thoughts boiled through me. My chest rose and fell rapidly. It was hard not to strangle the boy.

"Boss?" Dante muttered, jogging to my side. "You alright?"

He was looking at me as if I'd grown another head. I might as well have. Uncontrolled outbursts weren't my style. And yet I'd just rushed into the night, inserted myself into a street fight without knowing the stakes, and was about to unleash a volley of fury on the heir to the Caravello Famiglia.

The reason for the change of conduct emerged from behind the shelter a moment later.

Calm down. Fucking now! I gulped air into my lungs.

Penelope seemed fine. But as she took a step forward, the pronounced limp in her gait had me rushing forward. She put up her hand and shook herself out.

"I'm fine, but there's a rock in my boot." Without taking my offered hand, she reached down, removed the worn cowgirl boot, and shook it out.

"What the fuck happened?" I snapped.

The Caravello kid was on his phone, stammering to his capo or another authority figure.

Calmly, Penelope's gaze washed over me. What did she see? A man on the edge of losing control and unleashing a terrible wrath on her family member? I struggled to hide that, but the flicker in her eyes told me she'd already seen me at my worst.

"Max was overseeing a drop," she explained, her voice slightly breathless. "When my uncle's guys never showed, we came to investigate and—"

Whatever else Penelope was going to say was cut off when bullets rained down on us.

I didn't even think.

I dove.

Right before I crushed her against the pavement, I managed to roll so that I took the brunt of the impact. A splitting pain shot up my arm.

Penelope squeaked but didn't resist me.

Looking up and around, I spotted a vehicle racing toward us.

Dante, the crazy motherfucker, stepped into the road. He lifted his gun and coolly took three shots.

The truck careened to the side, running into a building.

Four more shots filled the air. Dante dropped his clip, smacked another in place, and continued to fire.

The fight was done moments later.

"Clear," my second shouted.

"Did he just take out a 5.56 rifle with a freakin' handgun?" Penelope gasped, leaning over to take in the scene.

This girl knew guns.

Warmth bloomed in my chest, and I barely recognized the foreign emotion as admiration.

I didn't release her. Instead, I swept my hand over her head. When nothing wet or sticky met my touch, I continued a path down her back.

"It's not always the bigger firepower that wins the fight," I rasped, allowing my mind to focus on the philosophy of warfare to help calm myself down. I hadn't been this worked up in...ever. My pulse thundered in my veins. The organ in my chest beat double-time. I couldn't see straight.

But my assessing touch shot little bolts of reassurance through me. It had to be why I continued to pat her down.

It wasn't because I enjoyed how she felt. That made less sense than losing control.

Penelope's gaze cut to mine. "I'm fine, Mancini."

My fingers slid over her hips, brushing her back pockets and only becoming firmer as they glided over the backs of her thighs. Dante's and Massimo's conversation faded away. I murmured deep in my chest. Yes...yes, she was fine.

A shuddering breath left my lungs. "You could have been shot."

Penelope pursed her lips. "I just told you I wasn't."

"Forgive me for making sure," I said dryly.

"That's no reason to be so handsy, lupo," she snapped.

Wolf—she called me a wolf. That insult, coupled with the bite in her voice, sent a bolt of white heat through my veins.

My gaze dropped to her lips.

Such a gorgeous mouth. It tempted me, and I wasn't a man who succumbed to temptation. It was a useless emotion that could be exploited as a weakness. Until several days ago, I had been immune to its draw.

Now temptation incarnate wriggled out of my arms.

I shouldn't want to taste that luscious mouth. Penelope wasn't for me. I had an accord with her uncle; I was promised to her cousin.

But damn me, I wanted her.

I shifted my weight, pushing to sit, and drawing her leg over my thighs. From the glow of a distant streetlamp, I could make out the torn denim and dark splotch staining her skin. Her knee was skinned and bleeding under the ripped denim.

My voice came out rough and harsher than I meant. "It doesn't hurt?"

"No," she breathed, the fire suddenly absent from her tone. "I've had worse on the ranch."

"Hmm." I drew my hand down her calf, applying the slightest pressure. "Nothing hurts deeper? Muscles? Tendons?"

"No," she insisted, the bite in her voice lessening.

I lifted my gaze back to hers. So damn beautiful, in a raw, real way. Other women didn't carry themselves like this. I held out my other hand for her to rise. She avoided the offer and sprang nimbly to her feet.

The sudden urge to *do* something to this woman struck me. I wanted to drag her back down, pin her with my weight, and—

What?

Penelope *wasn't* for me.

With a growl, I fought back the sudden rush of possession in my chest. Planting both hands, I went to push off the pavement.

And nearly bellowed.

My arm, the one with the pain. I hadn't noticed it before, but now—

"Che cazzo!" I hissed.

Penelope squatted beside me. "What happened?"

Breathing through the burst of pain, I looked at her.

Those bewitching hazel eyes were filled with concern. It did something to me. Dark feelings twisted in my chest. I would give up half my kingdom to keep her staring at me with that searching, beautiful look.

"My arm. It's fine," I lied.

And she knew it.

A snort flared her nostrils. "Men. You're all the same. So tough."

She straightened, staring down as I struggled to my feet.

The truth was, something was very wrong with the limb. Since it caught both our weight, I would be lucky if it wasn't damaged to the point of needing a sling. Something I wouldn't be caught dead wearing. Dante would simply have to pop the joint back into its socket, and I would hide the weakness.

We wandered over to where other Caravellos were showing up.

I kept Penelope in my line of sight, continuing to sweep the area for danger. While it was probable that the excitement was over, I wasn't taking chances where she was concerned.

The truth was, I couldn't stop thinking about this country cousin. After tonight, it was going to be impossible to content myself with the timid bride the Caravellos were presenting me.

And then, a darker thought sprouted. Was there any way, even a snowball's chance in hell, that I could have this woman instead of the one promised me?

No, not without breaking the deal. Taking this woman for my own would be a declaration of war. It would be cataclysmic, bringing disaster on those I was sworn to protect. I had to push my own desire away, bury it deep within me.

But a little voice whispered in protest that anything was possible. If the opportunity presented itself.... If there were a way to make Penelope mine.... I had to admit, if the chance came, I would take it. Immediately and without hesitation.

"And what, pray tell, were you doing out in the streets of Detroit?" Don Tito glared at me across the desk. The piece of furniture was littered with papers, stubs of pencils, and a laptop sat helter-skelter to the side. The rest of his home office wasn't much better. How he was productive in this chaos was beyond me.

I took another sip of my whiskey, numbing the throb in my arm. "Sightseeing."

The older man growled.

He might have a few more years than me, but I never had my legacy handed to me in a gift-wrapped package. No, I'd bled to become don.

"What I want to know is why the fuck you let your niece go out for mob business?" I demanded, voice holding steady.

"That's a family matter," Caravello snapped.

I bristled. "I'll admit, I didn't know you had a sister, let alone a gaggle of nieces and nephews. Penelope's sudden appearance in Detroit has been quite the surprise."

Caravello's tone was defensive. "My sister left the Famiglia, and we haven't had much contact with her."

"What's to say one of her sons doesn't come sniffing around for a piece of your empire?" I pushed.

"They're ranchers! They care about their trucks and cows, not the underworld."

The postcard image of a ranch played in my mind's eye. I could see the spirited woman there, riding horses, free and wild. Why would she choose to come to a city like Detroit if that was her life? I shifted, wondering at the pieces of the puzzle. Something was missing. I told myself the reason for my fixation on the subject was business related.

I almost believed it.

"And yet Penelope is here. Supervising with your son and heir," I countered.

The don didn't like being pushed. That much was obvious. His plump face reddened, and the jowls on his cheeks shivered.

"Like I said, she's not your concern," Caravello repeated, tone sharp and decisive.

In the corner, Massimo fidgeted on the grey metal chair. He'd been so quiet, it was easy to forget he was present for this interview. Well, if his father wanted him to witness me being taken down a peg, that wasn't happening.

"She's just here for the wedding," the don lied.

"But not the rest of the family?" I countered.

"No—they weren't invited. Penelope and Poppy are close."

"So she'll be a guest in my wife's house?" I pushed.

The don's face became a dangerous shade of red. "That is unlikely, signore. And if she does, her visits won't be unsupervised."

I leveled my stare at the don. He dared tell me how to conduct my affairs? This conversation was treading on dangerous territory, and it would be wise to drop it. But in order to do that, I had to clench my jaw tight and force air into my lungs.

"It still doesn't explain your spying." The accusation flew across the desk.

I finished my whiskey. "I am first and foremost a businessman, signore. And that is why I don't like surprises, especially unknown relatives popping up right before my wedding."

"Penelope won't be a problem." The automatic answer came too quickly.

The warning bells chimed in my head. What the hell did he mean by that?

"We're dealing with the niece situation, and it won't affect my daughter's acceptance of your hand in marriage."

"See that it doesn't," I ground out.

Caravello shot me a disdainful look. "I'm a man of my word."

A twisted, warped word.

"It's late. I'm going back to my hotel," I said. This conversation was going nowhere.

"I'll walk you out," Massimo offered.

"You'll stay," Caravello barked. "I'm not done with you and that stunt you pulled tonight."

Ah, so the don was waiting for me to leave before he ripped into the boy. There wasn't a drop of pity in my veins for the kid. He messed up bringing the girl into a street fight, and now he would have to answer for that.

"Goodnight, signore," Caravello said tightly.

I gave him the same icy reply and left. As I met Dante by the SUV, I paused to look up at the night sky. Like Chicago, there were too many lights to see the stars well.

I bet that's different on the ranch.

Without a conscious thought, my fingers reached to the tiny piece of metal dangling against my sternum.

The moment I felt the small object under my shirt, I snatched them back and shook them as if they'd been burned. I told myself when I took the trophy that it was madness. But then I started wearing the damn thing.

Never touching it, only wearing—because I just couldn't help myself.

My gaze skated over the front of the house. Somewhere in there was the woman who was messing with my head. I clenched my jaw tight and refused to wonder if she'd cleaned her knee. That was none of my business.

If I was smart, I would walk away and let her fate play out.

That wasn't happening.

Whatever the Caravello Famiglia did going forward was my business. That included the girl. They were planning something with Penelope. Every single move her uncle made would affect me in the future. The lie flitted through my mind that I needed to know for my own wellbeing.

"Find out what they're doing with Penelope," I instructed my second the moment I was safely behind the wheel and the doors were shut.

Dante shot me a side look. "What happened?"

I shifted my arm. The joints were in the sockets, but the damn thing needed ice to stop the inflammation. It was going to be an uncomfortable night.

"Caravello plays dirty, and I don't think she knows it." The engine started with a purr.

"And you care why?" my second countered.

I slammed my foot on the gas, sending the wheels spinning. "Because I don't like men who use women as pawns."

Dante only grunted.

I knew what he was thinking. I was marrying a girl for an alliance. But Poppy grew up in this world. She might be scared of me, but there was no fear of becoming a don's wife in her eyes. The way she accepted my opulent gifts, the eagerness with which she talked about the grand wedding...she wanted her moment as a mafia princess. Even if it meant the groom was seventeen years older than her.

"Just do it," I snapped.

Wisely, Dante nodded. "Sure thing, boss."

Chapter 8 – Penelope

Just as Massimo promised, there was no blowback for me going with him on the nocturnal run. In fact, it felt like Uncle Tito was proud of me on some level. He made sure to smile more at the two breakfasts where we sat together as a family. He asked my opinion on several trivial matters. While I didn't think the answers I gave were profound, he listened. That had to be worth something. It made me want to work harder to show him my worth. I would serve this organization, I would pull my weight—I would save my mom.

So when he called me into his office, I was ready to be put to work.

"A date," I repeated.

Uncle Tito nodded before leaning forward to rest his double chin on the steepled fingers. "Jax is very eager to meet you."

I opened my mouth, thought better of the snarky response, and closed it.

"He'll pick you up around seven," my uncle added.

Be brave! I could do it. I could stand up for myself. I knew my own worth, even if he didn't. "Respectfully, is there some *other* reason you want me to spend an evening with the capo?"

The pause was unreadable. My uncle studied me for a few beats before finally agreeing. "Such a smart girl."

The muscles in my shoulders relaxed. Tito did have a legitimate reason for wanting me to interact with his soldier. I wasn't being shown off like a prized heifer. There was more to this, and I passed whatever test my uncle just put before me.

I gave him a bright smile. "Thank you."

Tito chuckled. "I need to make sure my men are loyal. They're more likely to lower their guard around someone...like you."

Excitement teemed in my veins. Uncle Tito was making me his own personal spy! "Anything in particular you suspect him of?"

Tito shrugged, lips pressing like a duck. "Nah, just feel him out."

"And he'll probably boast to impress me," I surmised. "Alright, easy. Done!"

"I knew you were the right person for the job." Tito smiled.

Fueled by his praise, I left his office with a pep in my step. The first stop was to collect Poppy, who was reading an ARC book by the pool, and then she could help me find something to wear.

"I think I would like to have a bookish account," she confided as we hustled upstairs. "Help authors promote these new releases. Like the social media ones you showed me!"

I squeezed her arm. "That'd be great!"

"We can't actually *be* on social media. Too much of a risk." She slipped a lock of hair behind her ear. "But I could do a faceless one, right?"

"Right! I find some of my favorite reads from other readers. It can be a great community." *And it's official. I've corrupted my little cousin.*

"The only drawback is how much Signor Mancini will monitor my phone," she said reluctantly.

I frowned. "He would do that?"

But I knew the answer before she nodded. "Probably. I expect the same kind of rules Papà has."

Insufferable! How could she be willing to do this? I chewed on the situation as we looked through my small suitcase. We changed the conversation from the unfairness of her restrictive world to my evening plans. I didn't tell her I was spying on her dad's capo, but only that one of his men asked to spend time with me. That made her perk up.

After laying my clothes over the bed, I swept my hand over them. "What do you think?"

"You only brought the one dress?" my cousin gently nudged.

"Well, yeah." I fumbled. "So you think the dress?"

"If you want the date to go well. Do you think you would ever fall for someone like Jax? Someone on the...inside?" She gave me a funny look.

But it wasn't me who I was thinking about.

"Do you love him? Mancini?" I blurted out.

Poppy turned, but not before I caught the wave of sadness that consumed her delicate features. "Marriage is a partnership, Penny. Love is a bonus. Come on, let's see if you can wear something of mine. I found some clothes that were too big in the very back of my closet that never were altered."

I stalked after her but didn't continue the conversation until we were in her walk-in closet. There were more clothes hanging on one wall than my two sisters' and my dressers combined. It should have been a wonderful distraction, the thought of wearing something this luxurious.

But even the prospect of being a femme fatale wasn't enough to pull my thoughts from the conversation.

"And you think what you and Mancini have is what a partnership should look like?" I grabbed her arm gently and forced her to look at me.

Her gaze shifted to the rows of clothes in her closet. "I'm not sure what will fit. You're muscley and curvy compared to me."

"Poppy!" I hissed.

She threw up her hands. "You keep harping on this issue but Penny! It's out of my control. It's done. Names are signed, contracts bind me. I'm making the best of it."

If that were true, then why was there a tremor in her voice?

This isn't my battle.

Yet as much as I wished I could walk away, forget about the situation and worry about my own mess of problems, that wasn't an option.

"This was a little big, and I was going to have it taken in, but it should work," she said with forced brightness, taking down a very fancy dress.

It took every drop of strength, but I gave her a short nod and let the conversation drop. Already we were making progress. She'd finally admitted she wasn't keen on the situation. Maybe there was enough time to talk her out of marrying the wolfish businessman.

As I unbuttoned my blue jeans and reached for the flowy chiffon maxi dress, a horrid thought settled in my mind. What if she agreed that this marriage was a terrible idea?

She won't be able to escape.

"You really have no body image issues," my cousin breathed, awe filling her voice.

I chuckled. If only she knew how comfortable I was in my own, thick skin. Desperation was the mother of invention, and there had been a season where I was desperate enough to stop caring that people looked at my body. They paid well for the privilege, and I exploited the hell out of them.

"I'm so comfortable stripping that I've changed at a truck pull when some jackass spilled his beer all over me. Took my top off and everything. It's just a body. No big deal," I said just to see her eyes widen.

"I wish I could be that brave," she murmured.

"You can, and it's not bravery." I winked at her before shimmying the dress over my head. "It's called not giving a fuck."

She chuckled. "I wish I had that then."

And that was the answer. Poppy had a voice; she just needed a little help finding it. I wouldn't stop until she learned to use it, which I silently promised her that she would.

But there wasn't much time to find it. Her wedding day was coming soon.

If there was a contract—and I wasn't sure if that was literal or just a verbal agreement—it didn't matter if only she could gain the strength to decide for herself. Because then, if she wanted Mancini, it would be her choice. And if she didn't.... The first step was convincing her that marrying the brutish monster wasn't her only option. This was the Twenty-First Century, she wasn't trapped! Fuck the mob and its traditions. Once she believed it, we could find another course for her to follow.

Jax rubbed his nose.

Again.

I curled my fingers into a fist. I was seconds away from grabbing his linen napkin, putting it to his nose, and commanding him to blow. Just like a damn toddler.

"That's the wrong fork," he murmured, and because of the nasal drip, the words held a slight sneer.

I purposefully stabbed another piece of cooked vegetable with the implement. As I popped it between my teeth, a little voice in the back of my head reminded me that I was supposed to be getting along with this capo for my uncle. It was hard to be sweet and charming to someone I wanted to stab in the eye.

Sighing, I set the fork down. "Which is the right one?"

"The correct fork is the three tine." He pointed.

No...he touched. Those fingers that had just been rubbing his nose brushed against the spikes of the fork.

Looking away quickly, I tried not to gag.

A shadow moved on the other side of the restaurant.

The jabbering date faded away as my focus narrowed on the advancing pair. Surprise flashed through my veins. Was he stalking me now? What else could he possibly be doing here? The wolfish monster must have felt my stare, because his glance swept in the direction of our table.

My gaze was ensnared by one that was black and endless. Something shifted deep in those dark depths. It was a predatorial look, making the businessman look absolutely animalistic.

I arched a brow, silently demanding the reason for his presence.

Mancini gripped the back of a chair and gave it a tug, not breaking eye contact with me. A wisp in pink slipped into view beside him. Damn, but she was a pretty little thing. My heart clenched tight at the sight. Poppy slid into the seat he held a second later, answering half of the question running through my head.

A date.

She'd never said.

Of course, it was highly possible she hadn't known.

I gave my cousin a big smile. She returned it with a wave before placing her napkin on her lap.

"Excuse me, beautiful, while I use the little boy's room," the voice across the table stammered.

Jax rose and stumbled away. Twitching. He was twitching as if there were ants in his pants.

Sighing, I dropped my elbows to the table and scrubbed my hands through my hair. Not only was the capo impossible to talk to, but now I felt like my efforts were on display. Luckily, Poppy didn't know this was a setup, and it was unlikely

Mancini did. For the sake of appearances, I was safe. But I wanted to do a good job! I had to find it in me to be enchanting with such a companion.

Just pretend you are up on the stage again. I snorted. What would the fancy patrons of the restaurant think if I pulled out an erotic dance routine and used the chair as a prop?

"Miss, the Château Cheval Blanc."

Looking up, a waiter presented me with a jug with a swirly neck filled with red wine and an empty glass.

"I didn't order that," I hedged. A sudden rush of dread slithered through me. How in the hell was I going to pay for this meal? If the date fell through, would the capo still pay? The don set it up. Maybe I was supposed to foot the bill?

Shit.

"It's from the gentleman behind me," the waiter said implacably. "He ordered it to be served decanted."

"Oh," I breathed, reaching for the glass and container.

"Allow me." The polished server set the cup down, pouring a little more than a splash into it, before presenting it to me.

Uncertainty ringing through me, I picked it up, saluted my cousin's table, and shot it back. A burst of rich, decadent flavors too broad to narrow down flooded my mouth.

"Dang, that's good," I whistled.

The waiter couldn't hide his wince fast enough.

Yeah, I'm out of my element here, bud. "Thank you," I breathed, sitting up straight and reaching for the decanter to fill my glass.

"Please, miss." The waiter gently brushed my hand aside.

Jax fell into his chair, nearly missing the seat.

The waiter had to think we were barn animals. At least I was trying. Jax was…a mess.

His pupils were blown. He had fuzzy snot under his nose. And his whole body vibrated.

"What's that?" he demanded.

The waiter repeated the vintage.

"Thank you so much for it, and please thank Signor Mancini and his date," I told the waiter.

Smiling professionally, the waiter disappeared.

"The Blood King is sending you wine," Jax bristled.

The Blood King? "Poppy sent it," I lied.

My attempt to diffuse the sudden tension failed.

Spectacularly.

"He's staring at you," Jax spat.

With that, he dropped his hand on my leg. The stubby paw was moist.

I wiggled away, but his touch lingered. "They're my relatives. It's a nice wine. Do you want to try?"

Jax glared at me. "No, I don't want to try the fucker's wine."

"You have a little something under your nose," I said, tired of staring at it. "Next time you blow your nose, make sure you wipe it well."

Jax sniffed hard, then rubbed the protruding part of his face hard on his sleeve. "Crap, that's a lot to waste."

I frowned. "What is?"

"Ah," he grinned, and that was more freaky than the hold he still had on my thigh. "I knew you wanted to party, beautiful."

Episodes from TV clicked into place. This date was high. The skeletal appearance, the tweaking, it all made sense. If he was drunk, I would have been able to interrogate him. But high? *Crap*.... What was I going to do? My uncle wanted to know if he was loyal. If there was some big secret to pry from him, I doubted we would be able to get to the truth of the matter with him in this state.

It would probably be best to end this dinner before matters grew worse. Maybe a second date—a morning coffee or brunch—wouldn't end in drugs? That setting might encourage a real conversation.

Jax slid his hand farther up my leg. Panic lurched through me. It was too familiar, dredging up the nightmarish aspects of my past. But thanks to the bouncers, nothing horrible had ever happened, although there'd been too many close calls for comfort.

There were no bouncers guarding me tonight.

"I'm going to use the bathroom," I said with forced calm, trying to overcome the spike of sickening anxiety.

As I rose, I slid the steak knife out from the place setting. Jax nearly fell out of his chair as he tried to keep his hold on my leg. I had to shake him off as I stepped back, but I managed to flip the knife and keep it pressed on the inside of my wrist as I moved away from the table.

I caught Poppy's eye and gave my head a small shake. As I hurried away, I shot her a text explaining that I wasn't feeling well and was going to grab a cab back home.

Not that I had cash for that either.

There was nothing left to do but take off my cousin's too-tight shoes and hike it back on foot. While asking her for a ride was possible, I didn't want to ruin her date. If she stood a chance to find common ground with her fiancé, they needed every opportunity to become better acquainted.

Or for her to be so fed up with him that she was willing to say no to the marriage. And I knew which option I was rooting for!

The spiked heels clipped across the floor of the back hall. At the end was an employee-only exit. I flagged the waiter going into the dish pit.

"I'm going to head out for a smoke, is there an alarm?" I pointed to the door.

He shook his head and disappeared.

Leaning against the frame, I tugged off the first shoe.

Pain exploded across my scalp as I was yanked back. I didn't even hear Jax following me!

"You little bitch," the date from hell sneered. "Running away? That's bad manners!"

My heart stuck in my throat, but I struck out without hesitation.

The knife sank into the flesh of his leg. A satisfying yowl filled the hall. But I didn't stay long enough to revel in the damage. Defending myself was one thing. Hurting a member of the mob was another. I needed to get to my uncle first, make sure he heard the story from me. I was already risking my uncle's kindness by failing the mission. Dinner was a bust. Hopefully, he'd understand there wasn't a chance to learn anything useful about his capo.

I ripped open the door and fled, wearing only one shoe. As I ran, I hopped and pulled at the buckle.

The door banged open. Jax's roar filled the shadowed alley.

Once the second heel was off, I ran. A quick glance showed a healthy distance between me and the drug-addled pursuer. But then I pulled up short. The alley was blocked by a chain link fence. I shook the gate, noticing the padlock too late.

The panic turned my veins to ice. No, *no!* This was what I always feared. I'd never been caught by the slimy men, but it felt like it was going to happen now.

Jax sensed the advantage and bounded forward.

Shakey, breaths filled my lungs. At least the fear wasn't freezing me in place. I turned, ready to intercept his spring. If I could shake him off, there might be enough time to scramble over the gate.

I braced for impact.

But Jax never collided.

Darkness shifted, and a shadow lunged. Jax flew through the air like a sack of vegetables.

Mancini—Mancini was here.

Oh, good grief. This had gone from bad to worse.

My cousin's fiancé stalked after my date. Mancini reminded me of a bull. That great body shook. His nostrils flared as his lungs worked double time. A rough sound, part grunt, part growl, bellowed from his chest.

I rubbed my scalp, picked myself away from the wall, and stumbled forward. My body trembled, but the instinct to flee gave way to the urge to fight. It would be stupid to step between the men. There was nothing I could do, and I was physically smaller. But even if I had an advantage—a weapon or maddening strength—I doubted I would use it. These were prominent players in the criminal organizations.

"Lay a hand on me, and you declare war," the capo wheezed.

Mancini took a step forward.

I faltered. My heart shot to my throat and began beating violently. No! *No, I can't let him.* Not for me. I forced air into my lungs, the plea for Mancini to retreat formulated on my tongue.

"It would be worth it to end you," the wolf said, voice cold and completely at odds with the lethal energy vibrating off him.

"I'm a capo! You can't do this," Jax whined.

I bounded the last few feet, ready to reach out and tug Mancini away. Not that I was able to move him. But I had to try something!

Mancini smiled down at my date as if he were about to gobble him whole. "Try to stop me."

"Why?" Jax wailed. "Why would you do this?"

The wolf's words came out as a pure growl. "Perché, é donna mia."

My technical brain picked apart the grammar. The thing about native speakers, they didn't always use the rules when they spoke Italian, which made understanding them take two mental steps. When the meaning behind the sentence clicked, I gasped.

Holy shit on a shingle. This cold, cruel monster just called me his woman.

What in the hell did that mean? Was there some weird familial relationship lost in translation?

No...there was no mistaking the possessiveness of his tone. That transcended language.

Oh, mother of god, what have I done! I had to undo this—now!

Chapter 9 – Alessandro

"Because...she's my woman," I snarled, the words coming from a place deep inside.

There wasn't time to process their origin, neither could I fathom their significance. They felt right.

Besides, it wasn't as though anyone heard the moment of madness—insanity, that was what this was. I felt sure that later, when my head was clear and I was back in control, that was exactly what I would call this. Who was going to talk? This putrid specimen of flesh wasn't long for this world. My outburst would be something this dead man took to his grave.

And the farmer's daughter? Her cousin said she spoke no Italian, other than a few phrases or cuss words her mother dropped.

I dragged the date back, through the alley. Pushing his twitching body behind a dumpster, I stepped on his hand to pin him in place. His howls filled the space.

"What are you doing?" There wasn't even a tremor in her voice. It was a matter-of-fact question, piqued with curiosity.

But no fear.

I cut her a look. "Go inside. Sit with your cousin. Order some dessert."

Penelope drew herself up straight. "You're going to get in trouble if you do this."

My lips twitched of their own accord. "Worried about me?"

"You're Poppy's fiancé and from a rival mob," she huffed. "And this is a *capo*."

Those weren't the answers to what I'd asked.

I tugged the leather driving gloves over my hands. "Go, Penelope."

Bending down, I put my back to her. I would have preferred if I ended this scum after she vacated the area, but time was of the essence.

Reaching into the sleezy fucker's limp suit jacket, I found the baggy of powder. The moment I laid eyes on him tonight, I knew he'd been using. This amount, however, was unexpected. There was enough here to tranquilize a horse. It would be far more efficient to shoot him up with the stuff, but I didn't have a needle or any supplies to liquify it.

A calm settled over me as I prepared to make the kill. This was how I usually operated. The heat of the moment, when I found his filthy hands on Penelope, was foreign. I never lost control like that.

"Go, Penelope," I barked.

She stepped closer. "Not a chance, lupo."

Fine. I knelt on the capo's chest. Before prying his mouth open, I checked his pulse. It raced.

"Time for your last hit," I said in a low, sing-song voice.

There was probably already enough coke in his system that he might OD from the amount he'd taken coupled with the frenzy of the chase. But I wasn't taking any chances. He'd touched Penelope. His hand, slithering up her leg—

A snap cracked through the air as my heel broke the wrist.

His howl made it easier for me to force his jaw open, and I poured the powdery contents of the baggy down his miserable throat.

As I worked, I contemplated my reaction. The only way it made sense was realizing that Penelope was family. If anything happened to her, it was my wife who would be very upset. Therefore, it was in my best interest to protect her.

That has to be it.

"You're going to pass off his death as a drug overdose, but what about the stab wound?" the object of my thoughts asked.

"What stab wound?" I shot her a look over my shoulder.

Penelope crouched and jabbed at his thigh. "The one from the steak knife."

Something close to admiration filled me.

What is happening? I didn't feel emotions. Certainly not such things as admiration.

And yet what else was it called when a pretty little hellion stabbed a man?

"I was going to tell my uncle about the date groping me under the table after he took a hit of coke," Penelope explained.

"I'll do it." The words slipped free of their own accord. "I have to explain why his wrist was broken. Might as well say I stabbed him too."

Penelope put her hand on my shoulder. "You're sweet, but I don't need a man saving me. Never have, never will."

With that, she straightened and moved away.

The urge to fight, the desire to yell, they mixed and fizzed inside. *Oh, it's on, vespina. It's on.*

Penelope left her uncle's office just as Poppy and I walked through the front door. She'd slipped away at the restaurant, and it'd taken some convincing to make my little fiancée leave. Poppy insisted repeatedly that her cousin was just fine and had instructed us to finish our meal. So that was exactly what my fiancée said we were doing.

I hadn't taken the timid thing as having a backbone. I was happily impressed with the development.

"Mancini," Don Caravello barked. "Care to explain?"

Penelope shot me a look as she scurried past. My fingers twitched to reach out and grab her. Was she okay? She didn't look hurt—other than she had dirty feet. I remembered her being barefoot in the alley, but why was she still?

Poppy murmured something about having had a lovely evening, and then she too was hurrying away.

"What's there to explain?" I folded myself into the stiff-backed modern monstrosity some interior decorator tried to pass off as a chair.

"My niece just told me that one of my capos assaulted her."

"In public." The rush of red was still there, even now. But sitting here, facing a force like Caravello, I was able to keep it at bay.

"And she stabbed him." The don stood at his swanky gold bar-cart and poured a brandy.

I shook my head when he held one out for me. "That would be why she left in a hurry."

"One of my boys found Jax out by the dumpster."

The moment of truth. I waited calmly, waiting to see where the cards fell.

"He was high, Penny said. And then, it seems he took another hit to cope with the pain of being stabbed."

"Sounds like a winner," I drawled. "Tell me, don, are all your capos made of such stuff?"

The air between us crackled.

"No." Caravello slammed his empty tumbler on the side table. "He had the problem from the beginning, but after a stint in rehab, I thought the situation was fixed."

Then why did I smell a lie? "I see. And Penelope, what is her role in all of this?"

"Are you asking if we can trust her?" Caravello sank into a chair. The cushions whooshed from the sudden impact. "That was what I was ensuring by setting her up with Jax. He is the only one who she might have found appealing."

The bastard was going to marry her off to one of his men. Like a damn prize for their loyalty. The truth sent a deep, resounding thud through me. I guessed as much at the restaurant, but hearing it from the don's lips created a powerful surge of disgust—and something else I wasn't able to name.

In the pause, the don watched me.

So I threw the situation back at him.

"Does she need to be controlled?" I leaned forward. "I can't have this coming back on my new wife."

The don shook his head rapidly, waving away the warning in my voice. "I'll handle her."

That was exactly what I'd feared. "Very good. Now, if there's nothing else—"

"You tell me, did you see anything else I should know about?" The don stared intently at me.

"Only a coke addict sitting across from your niece, signore." I rose and left, not wanting to give him anything more. "Other than that, it was a lovely meal with your daughter."

Caravello grunted.

Turning quickly to hide my look of disgust, I left. It should come as no surprise that the women of the famiglia were chattel. I planned to make up for my part in the charade by spoiling my wife as the princess she was. But the whole arranged marriage tradition was far from ideal.

I wonder what Penelope thinks of being married off.... Somehow, I didn't think she was a willing participant. There had to be something Caravello had on her to force her to agree. Running my tongue over my teeth, I paused at the sweeping staircase and looked towards the upper floors. She was up there. Doing something.

Maybe she was washing her feet.

I chuckled. I couldn't believe she let them get so dirty. But...she was also the woman who didn't flinch at the murder of the man who'd attacked her. From Dante's research, she was a civilian. Her family hadn't even visited Detroit, always meeting Don Caravello and his children at far away locations. That made her appearance here all the more sudden.

Stopping at the banister, I looked upstairs. The stolen item throbbed in the pocket of my suit jacket. The past few evenings, when I'd come to visit my fiancée, I meant to slip away and return it. Just like the other times, there wasn't a chance to do it now.

I needed to rid myself of the connection, cut the ties. That meant ridding myself of the fascinating piece of jewelry.

A small weight against my sternum seemed to burn.

Rid myself of *most* of the connection. A black soul like me always kept some memento of our sins.

"I'll do it next time," I promised myself and stepped toward the front door.

About to push into the night, a noise from down the hall caught my attention. I spared a glance.

And stopped in my tracks.

"What is she doing out there?" I muttered.

A smart man would leave. Normally, I was that smart man.

But not tonight, apparently.

Drawn by instinct, I followed the wisp outside, heat pulsing violently in my veins. Long, tan legs sprinted into the dark. The frayed edge of jeans appeared just in time to cover the slope of skin and muscle of her curves. But at the waistband, more skin was bare. The expanse spread until the triangles of cloth covered the upper swell of curves.

At the side of the pool, Penelope dropped the shorts to reveal the teeny little bikini, and my dick thickened in response.

Right before she leapt into the pool, I spoke. "What are you doing?"

Penelope squeaked but didn't move her hands to cover herself. "What the hell, lupo?!"

Luckily, she was on the side of the pool that was close to the pergola, where the shadows were deepest. It wouldn't bode well for me to be caught out here.

"I needed to blow off some steam," Penelope snapped.

"And why is that?" I stalked forward.

She didn't budge, holding her ground with more strength than many brutal men. I closed in on her, and she tipped her head back to hold my stare in the dark.

"It was a hellish dinner, and I wasn't able to help Uncle Tito."

I cocked my head.

"I don't like failing," she added with a sharp bite to her tone.

Hearing the self-deprecation in her tone made my fists clench. The cold hard truth tumbled from my lips. "Whatever you think you failed at, you didn't. Your uncle is using you as a reward."

Why did I tell her that?

Because...she deserved to know.

And there was part of me that wanted to know if she already knew. That was answered a second later when she wrapped her arms around herself.

The fierce need to do something for her—maybe comfort her—reared inside me.

I stepped forward, fingers itching to snatch her, to pull her close. *To protect her.* "Penelope—"

"Don't." She held up a hand and took a tentative step back only to collide with the pergola post. "You belong to Poppy."

Forbidden—yes, it was. This woman was off limits. But why could she see that, and I was the fool taking a step toward her. Words spoken earlier tonight in the heat of the moment came surging back through my mind.

É donna mia. *She's my woman.*

Another step forward on my part made her breath catch in her throat. A shaft of moonlight fell across her face. The enchantment reached full power, and I couldn't take another second of it. I reached out and cupped her cheek.

Her sharp inhale was the sweetest music.

An ache pulsed in my groin. I needed to hear her make it again. Needed it more than I needed to breathe. My thumb brushed across the soft skin of her cheek. This close, I couldn't see the faint freckles in the dark, but I knew they were there.

But I had to do the right thing. Holding tight to my iron control, I forced my mind to stay focused on what mattered. "Penelope, listen very carefully. I don't know why you are here, but your uncle is not a good man, neither are his men. You need to leave. Now. While you still can."

Her voice came out breathless. "Then why are you here? Doing business with him? Doesn't that make you bad as well?"

A dry laugh escaped my lips. She had no idea. "He will use you. Tonight proved that."

"Like he's using his own daughter." It wasn't a question, neither was it an accusation.

"You can leave. Poppy was born into this world," I insisted. My chest tightened, heart beating hard with the need for her to hear me out.

But she only shook her head. "I can't."

"Why?" I demanded.

She jerked her head away, but I slid my hand into her hair.

"Why, Penelope?"

"Drop it."

Such a sharp tongue on this little wasp. "No."

"I'm not your concern, Mancini."

"It's Alessandro."

But she shook her head. "Not to me, it's not."

With that, she slipped from my grasp.

I let her go. My hand fisted at my side. She wasn't mine to protect. I turned sharply, marching back into the house. That was it, I was cutting off the last vestige of interest in the woman before she tempted me into an unwinnable situation. And that meant slipping into her room to rid myself of the trophy that tied me to her.

Chapter 10 – Penelope

The timer on the oven buzzed. I set the last tray of cupcakes on the counter beside it, grabbed the hot pads, and pulled the tray out from the heat and replaced it with the last batch.

"That smells so good," Poppy moaned, sailing into the kitchen.

I flashed her a smile. "They will be!"

I didn't add that it was my form of stress relief. This was the eve of *her* wedding. The rehearsal dinner was in less than twelve hours. The last thing she needed to worry about was how I felt.

"I wish I knew how to bake." She reached out, thought better of it, and retracted her hand.

"Have one," I insisted, pushing the chocolate pile of goodness to her.

"Thanks!" She snatched it, tore down the wrapping, and pulled off a huge piece. Steam shot from the cupcake.

"They can't have frosting until they're cooled, but I have it made if you want a spoonful to smear on it," I offered.

She nodded, cheeks puffed like an adorable chipmunk. *An innocent woodland creature.* Who would march willingly into the lair of the beast in one more sunrise.

I turned away.

"Oh, you found your bracelet," Poppy observed. "Where was it?"

I shook my wrist, the charms tinkling with their metallic lyrics. "In the bottom of my purse. I swear I looked there, but it was in a tear in the lining."

I didn't add that the purse hadn't been broken when I left. I would sound like a crazy lady. Because who would have broken my purse? It didn't make sense.

"I see. Well, I'm glad you found it. You've been collecting those charms since you were a kid."

"Mhmm, since Dad gave me the chain and the cross charm when I was seven," I agreed.

There was a moment of silence before my cousin whispered in a changed tone, "Penny?"

Looking through the kitchen window at the perfectly manicured yard that I hated I murmured, "Yeah?"

"I don't think I can do this."

Those words! I latched onto them, my heart bursting with joy.

"Never mind, I shouldn't have said anything," she added quickly.

Oh, no you don't! Glancing around the aperture to make sure there were no household staff loitering about, I hurried to her. Grabbing her elbow, I drug her into the butler's pantry and shut the door.

"What does that mean?" I asked eagerly.

Poppy shook her head, dark curls swaying over her shoulders. "We have nothing in common. I've spent the last three evenings with my fiancé and there's nothing. No spark. No connection. How can I marry someone like that? Make a promise for life when I know we'll both be miserable."

"It's not right," I agreed.

"He kissed me, you know. On our last date." Poppy brushed the tips of her fingers over her lips.

I balked.

"There was nothing, Penny! No kernel of heat or explosion of passion. It was like kissing the Mother Superior on the cheeks." Poppy dropped against the door. "He's a good match, but only on paper. There's nothing between us."

Guilt dropped in my stomach. I wasn't able to say the same. A raging fire zipped through my veins at the memory of how that beast looked at me. I knew he felt it too. The raw hunger, the desperate need. We'd avoided each other since the night at the pool, but that didn't make the electricity any less real. There was no lack of spark, no end of chemistry...with my cousin's fiancé.

Liquid heat pulsed between my legs. Mother of god, I was turned on just thinking of his hands on me!

Stop it!

Mancini used those hands to kill without hesitation. But the reminder of what he was capable of didn't shut down the rush of arousal in my veins.

"What should I do?" Poppy whispered.

The thickness in my throat wouldn't let me respond quickly enough. I coughed and tried again. "What does your gut say?"

"Read more books." Her laugh was halfhearted. "Maybe I can find a way to spice up our marriage," she added hopefully.

That wasn't the right trail of thought.

"So that's the *only* reason you don't want to marry him?" I pushed.

Poppy lifted a shoulder. "There's not another option for a girl like me. You're lucky, coming into the famiglia with worldly experience. You can bargain your way into a position of power."

Could I? What did a girl like me really know about climbing the ranks? Just because I wanted to, didn't mean I was able.

That seed of self-doubt, the one that was always front and center to tell me I wasn't born capable of achievements like my sister whispered through my mind. Jillian was smart. Studious enough to become a nurse once I found the money to pay for her degree.

The tumble of thoughts in my mind nearly consumed me. As I struggled to put the negativity back in the box where I tried to keep it contained, another thought flitted through my mind. This one from the moonlit conversation with Mancini.

Uncle Tito told me yesterday that I would have a date with another capo for the rehearsal dinner, and a third for the wedding. After that, I would start meeting top-ranked soldiers, since his other capos were married.

When I'd pressed, my uncle had readily agreed that these dates were for me to feel out his capos. But I wondered: Why would a don suspect his captains? All of them? And his soldiers? That wasn't good business, and the mob was more complex than a corporate structure. Disloyalty would be severely punished. There was no way these men needed their loyalty questioned.

Which meant Mancini might very well be right. I was little more than a prize to reward the loyalty of one of my uncle's men.

The oven buzzed in the next room. The stress baking was my way of coping with the situation.

I squeezed Poppy's hand, and we reentered the kitchen.

"I don't know how, but it will be okay," I promised.

"I wish I could trade places with you," Poppy said wistfully. "You know about animals. You know how to work a kitchen. You have a job! In your world, you could marry for love."

Trade places.... I set the last batch of cupcakes on the island. Because I needed my uncle, I signed up for a fate exactly like hers. There was no going back to Carrington and our ranch. Not anytime soon.

But my mother had done it.

"What would it take to dissolve your engagement contract?" I whispered.

Poppy looked around nervously. "A series of master chess moves."

Every eBook I'd consumed about organized crime in America, every video interview of the mobsters who walked away, what I knew from fiction TV—it played through my head in a rapid succession.

I hurried to her and grabbed her hands. "What if we did trade places?"

An eager spark flashed in her eyes. But then fear—the kind that had been nurtured in her no doubt since a young age—sprang up.

"The one thing the mob fears is the law. They've been enemies as old as time. It's how a lucky few have walked away," I whispered quickly.

"They'd kill me," Poppy murmured.

I shook my head. "Not if we have the right leverage. We can place you in my old life."

"What about you?" Poppy hissed. "No, I can't sacrifice you to do that."

But I smiled, shaking my head harder. "You wouldn't be! I *have* to be here."

And then the whole story about my mother's condition came tumbling out. "So you see, I'm already prepared to stay, to do whatever it takes. If I can free you at the same time, then two birds with one stone!"

"I don't know. There would be some consequences for Papà—"

"Nothing he can't handle! It's now or never." I wasn't losing this momentum. This was the opportunity I'd been praying for, the little spark in her heart that I could blow into a great conflagration! Admitting she wasn't invested in the marriage was the first step, and I would take it from there. "Your hair and makeup artist comes at four. We have until then to make the arrangements."

With that, I abandoned the cupcakes and dragged my cousin upstairs.

"Just a few more hours, hun," I murmured, sending a burst of good energy in Poppy's direction.

Not that my cousin could hear me across the crowded room. The glamorous space pulsed with wealth and privilege. I felt like something the cat drug in. Once again, I was poured into one of her slimmer dresses that was too short on me. The capo I was supposed to spend the evening with was at least twenty-five years older than me, double my age. He'd mentioned how he had a son going to graduate school. That made me young enough to be his child.

I wasn't sure what my uncle expected me to do with this one. It was apparent after just a few minutes of conversation that he lived, breathed, and bled Caravello Famiglia.

This isn't a question of their loyalty. I took a long sip of my champagne. It slid easily down my throat, and I reluctantly resolved it had to be my first and last glass.

Did my uncle think so little of me that he assumed I wouldn't figure his game out? And how would I play this development? I set the empty flute down and declined a second from my date.

Poppy needed me to have a clear head tonight. She would leave with cash and documents. Sherriff Forge would meet her at the Fargo-Moorhead border, and the whole Foster County Force was prepared to protect her. The documents would be kept safe and unused so long as her father didn't come after her. If anything happened to Poppy, the local boys would raise Cain.

I smiled. Small towns had a way of protecting their own.

And it was up to me to distract the players here until the last possible moment. It was a thirteen-hour drive. If she left around midnight, she could make it to North Dakota before the wedding was supposed to take place. The biggest mercy was that my cousin knew how to drive, even though she'd never traveled far and never by herself.

But she was going to do it! She was going to escape.

Running through the plan once more kept me calm. Distracting the hairstylist would be easy. Tell them to be somewhere and tell other people they were supposed to be somewhere else. It would be a grand cluster mess.

Losing the nanny would be the trickiest part.

Another shiver rattled through me at that part. I would slip something into the drill sergeant's coffee that would send her to the bathroom for the entire morning.

That idea was all Poppy. She'd given me the pills, and I was ready to drop the powder first thing in the morning.

Ruthless. With the potential of freedom dangling in front of her, that ruthless side came out of my little cousin. And I was so damn proud of her.

I watched her smile and nod to people she knew. It didn't matter if she was running from this life because she had some notion of true love. Whatever it took! Maybe with age and scope, she could learn how messed up it was to be sold into marriage.

And yet here I stood, pretending to be amused by a wiry old capo of my uncle's crime family.

"Don Tito is looking for you, Bruno," a deep voice said smoothly.

My date straightened, almost as tall as I was, prattled his farewell to me, and ambled off in search of his boss.

I turned toward the man of the hour, ignoring the small jump of excitement in my chest. "Having a nice time, Mr. Mancini?"

That dark gaze studied me from behind the cold, unfeeling mask he wore in public. Try as I might, I couldn't read him. What did he think when he saw me? Probably like every other person in the room: I didn't belong? The poor relation who was no better than the help.

"I wanted to thank you, for standing with Miss Caravello tomorrow."

It was impossible to tell if he was sincere.

I snorted and took a step away. The motives behind that sentiment didn't matter.

A hard touch slipped around my wrist. "I mean it."

"Shouldn't you be by her side, lupo?" I hissed. "Not talking to *me!*"

Those fingers slid up the inside of my wrist, producing a crackle of heat and the corresponding burst of gooseflesh. "I know you don't approve of this marriage."

"You're right, I don't!" I snapped, wrenching my arm away.

He didn't hold me. "In time, you'll come to understand our ways."

"This isn't some grand tradition! These people are here to celebrate a lamb who's being led to the slaughter," I growled, glaring up at him. I wouldn't show the monster a drop of fear.

He nodded once. "I wish there was another way."

Of all the twisted, messed up—wait. *What did he say?*

"You might find this hard to believe, but I'm not the villain you make me out to be."

"Like hell you're not," I spat.

"I'm not," he insisted. Something that could only be described as hunger slid through his eyes. "I'm coming into this with no choice."

I sucked in a short breath, before gathering my senses around me once more. "You need to leave me alone. You're supposed to be with her."

The tip of his forefinger brushed down the length of mine. "Trust me, I know."

That made my heart shudder. But I set my shoulders, jerking backward. "Good. I'm glad we're on the same page."

His voice roughened as he fell into Italian. "I've never allowed myself to want anything and yet I can't seem to get you out of my head. It will screw everything up. But maybe in a different life, vespina."

As my brain scrambled to process that long declaration, my tongue took on a mind of its own. "What the hell did you just say to me?"

His gaze narrowed. "Nothing."

"That's what I thought. Go charm someone else," I snapped and turned away. Mother of god, that man was trouble! He might be kind to my cousin, but only because it was what a good husband was supposed to do. He was downright dangerous in every other aspect. And I counted the minutes until I could save Poppy from that fate.

Rejoining my date, who was flustered that he hadn't actually been summoned by the boss, I accepted the glass of bubbly from him, not having any intention of drinking. I held the flute like a lifeline, fast breaths filling my lungs. Funny how the chilled liquid felt frozen against my still-burning fingers.

Chapter 11 – Alessandro

Something possessed me. I didn't have the first idea why I told Penelope any of that. There was no way to end the engagement, and yet a compulsion I wasn't able to resist consumed me to speak.

My fiancée shifted beside me.

"Are you cold?" I asked, forcing my voice as gentle as I knew how to make it—which wasn't much.

"No, I'm fine." She smiled up at me.

I studied her. This was the perfect mob wife, raised to shine in the position. And yet her cousin's words rang in my ears. I was the villain. The unbreakable bargain that bound us was something I agreed to in good faith.

Signorina Caravello might be a mafia princess, but she wasn't ready to be a queen.

Despite her age and disposition, Poppy would submit to the rules of my house. She would have access to unlimited wealth. With the proper precautions, she would even be allowed out of the house to mingle with civilians. And there were the endless functions that required my presence as a businessman. Otherwise, Poppy would stay at home. She knew it; I knew it.

That was the challenge her cousin presented. Already, Penelope had been in more dangerous situations in the short time we'd known one another than most mob wives were in their entire lives.

She can't be caged.

I sighed and threw back my whiskey. Even if I could break the engagement, if I could take the woman who fascinated me, it would end in disaster.

And I would not have my wife put in that situation—not again.

Moving away from my fiancée, I wandered to the bar. "Could I show her how important the safety measures are?"

Penelope was a reasonable woman. Perhaps she wouldn't see life married to a don as a cage.

The tiny metal object dangling against my chest pulsed.

No...not that one.

Penelope was used to a life of freedom. She existed in a world wild and free, and captivity would break her. I drummed my fingers furiously against the bar top. That indomitable will was part of the attraction. No woman had mesmerized me in decades, and the one instance in the past was nothing compared to this inferno.

I wanted Penelope.

But there was no logical way to take her, no sane way to keep her.

"Another drink, sir?" The bartender appeared in front of me, white catering uniform spotless.

I nodded. "Flat water."

Only after I ordered, did my gaze shift across the room. It was what the object of my obsession was drinking. I found myself suddenly parched.

What would my father say if he saw me? I beat that thought back. I wasn't losing control, I wasn't giving into my emotions. If there was a logical way to take what I wanted, he would be damn proud of me.

My tongue ran viciously over my teeth. My fingers curled tight into a fist. And the air barely seemed to be able to fill my lungs.

There just wasn't a way.

And yet as I watched Penelope throw back her head in laughter, a swirling darkness slid through my veins like a black poison. What did that laughter taste like? As good as her soft screams? Damn, it was torture.

I won't touch her. The vow reverberated through my mind. But it was absolutely necessary. To sample the forbidden would be disastrous. I was a don, the leader of my organization. My actions affected more than just me. Bringing the consequences of dissolving the contract down on my people would be irresponsible.

If it was only my life at stake, I might just try.

But it wasn't.

Yes, it might kill me to spend my life resisting her. I would exist with the knowledge that Penelope would end up with another, that she would be forever out of my reach.

I need to forget about her.

It was absolutely necessary.

Taking my water, I wandered back to my station on the other side of the room. As I passed close, I heard Penelope's rich laughter, the teasing lilt in her voice as she gossiped with the Caravello princeling. It shook my resolve.

"Yeah, that's not going to happen," I muttered. There was no conceivable way to wipe her from my memory. There had to be a way, even if it took divine intervention, to make her mine.

This was why men started wars over women. It was a story old as time. The only question left to ask myself was: *Am I the kind of man who could do that?*

Penelope's gaze drifted to mine. She raised her glass of water in a small salute, before turning back to the cousin.

I am.

Chapter 12 – Penelope

"You call me with updates," I commanded, squeezing her shoulders tighter.

Poppy nodded vigorously. "Are you sure about this? There will be blowback and—"

"Enough of that, mouse!" I pulled back and gave her a huge smile. "You go and live your life out in the wide-open spaces. I'll join you as soon as I can."

If she knew that wasn't likely to happen, my cousin kept her mouth closed. The evening wind whipped through the parking ramp. Under the glare of the industrial lights, our escape plan didn't feel as foreboding. There was a reassurance buzzing through the space that lent an air of confidence. I reached for it with every fiber of my being, praying that my cousin made it through the night. It was up to her now to seal her destiny.

"I'm really doing this," she whispered, excitement edging her voice. "I'm leaving the mob."

"You're leaving the mob." *You're free.*

I pushed her into the car, the keys for which we'd stolen from the valet stand. It belonged to a wedding guest spending the night at the hotel, so the theft wouldn't be noticed until morning when they tried to leave for the ceremony.

By then, Poppy would be safe.

"I can't thank you enough," she said, eyes glowing with hope.

I wished I could latch onto that particular feeling and let it brighten my days. But as she traveled into the light, I was voluntarily remaining in the shadows.

"I love you," I murmured and shut the door on her smile.

The engine started, Poppy put the car in drive, and the taillights soon faded around the turn. Whatever happened next, whatever storm of fury descended here, Poppy wouldn't have to face it. I would survive. We knew Uncle Tito would be furious, but that would probably be the extent of the broken engagement. If there was a problem between the two dons, they could work it out. There wasn't going to be a consequence so terrible that it would make me regret my actions tonight.

I did the right thing. Relief, sweet and wholesome, gently washed over me.

Cloying smoke drowned it a moment later. A firm step sounded on the concrete as the door to the hotel's walkway banged closed. I threw on my game face, only to drop it a moment later when I realized who was here, stalking through the shadows.

"Where's my fiancée? You two came out here twenty minutes ago," he drawled, cherry blazing between his fingers.

I stilled. "I didn't realize you were paying any attention to her."

"I pay attention to everything, Penelope."

The way the beast's tongue slid over the words sent a shiver through me.

"Poppy went home for her beauty rest," I lied smoothly. My fingers crossed tightly at my side, hoping he wouldn't question that.

He didn't. It was there in his eyes. "And you?"

"No rest for the wicked; I have a date to charm." Smiling broadly, I began to sashay toward the ritzy downtown hotel and its stifling ballroom.

"I am going to rip the fucker's lump head off if he puts his hand on your waist again," Mancini growled in Italian.

I stopped short, glared pointedly at the smoldering stub on the ground, and back at the man who'd thrown it. "What did you just say to me?"

Those midnight eyes studied me. "I said, I don't like your date."

Close, but not quite, mister. "Well, that makes two of us." When he didn't move to stomp out his cigar, I did. "You should really pick that up. Littering is gross."

The smirk on his lip told me he'd done it only to see my reaction. And his words confirmed it. "Make me."

My hands fisted. I'd been known to throw a punch before, and a few times I'd knocked out men twice my size.

"You're an awful person," I said and turned away in disgust. I needed to keep my distance with this beast. Too close, and he might take a bite.

A shiver raced through me at the thought—traitorous body.

"Trust me, I hate it too," he drawled. But he stooped, snatched the butt off the ground and walked it to the trashcan with a sand trap at the top.

Chin held high, I marched to the door. He beat me to it, opening it and stepping aside. I narrowed my eyes at him. "See, that's the thing. I don't trust you, Mancini."

"And that shows your good sense."

I rolled my eyes at the ceiling. "Argh! You're horrid."

His dark suit whispered as he sprang. The next second, my back slammed into the glass wall of the walkway. My gaze locked with his, and my chest rose and fell with a deadly mixture of excitement and arousal. This close, the warmth of his body was tangible.

"I am horrid," he rasped. "But not for the reasons you think."

Air whispered through my dry lips. His gaze dropped to my mouth, making me turn to stone. My heart barely dared to beat. Would he do it? What would it take to make him close the distance? We weren't touching. His hand braced the wall over my head and his body hovered over mine. There was part of me that screamed to reach for him and pull him closer, but the next move in this twisted game was his and his alone.

"Aren't you going to ask me why, vespina?" he said, voice deep and rough.

I shrugged. "It doesn't matter, does it?"

A harsh laugh barked in his chest. "I didn't take you for a coward."

"Fine," I challenged. "Why are you so *horrid*?"

He lifted his other hand, and with the back of a knuckle, he traced my lips. "Because the only thing I've been able to think all night is how much I want to taste you."

Not kiss me.

Taste me.

My insides clenched in response. The need to experience that was a desperate pulse roaring through my veins. I wanted it more than I wanted my next breath.

"But you're the forbidden fruit," he continued. "I never let myself be tempted, but there's something about you that is breaking down every defense in my arsenal."

It was the gravel in his voice that did it. I reached up and brushed the tip of my finger over his lips. Would it really be so bad? This thing clamored at us to give in.

Poppy....

It wasn't because this man was her fiancé. No, that might be what stopped him from giving in. He thought the wedding was still happening in the morning. His honor was admirable. But for me, I needed to keep up the ruse.

"Go back into that ballroom and forget about me, lupo," I demanded, voice as strong a whisper as I could manage.

His jaw tightened. I dropped my hands to my sides, fisting the dress so as not to make contact again. Even pushing him away was dangerous enough to start a conflagration.

With a low bark of frustration, he shoved off the wall and took a step back. I used the distance to flee as my pussy wept in protest.

Chapter 13 – Alessandro

Something slithered through the church. The intangible buzz was laced with an uneasy energy. It wasn't the majority of the guests, but the members of the Caravello Famiglia. Dante and I shared a look. He felt it too. From where we waited at the side entrance to the sanctuary, there was a direct view of the mobsters, who'd begun to shift and look about. Their whispers flitted as a hushed buzz of undertones to the soft jabber of conversation from the other guests.

"Find out what's happened," I said under my breath.

Dante slid a piece of apple off his paring knife, popped it in his mouth, and gave me a short nod. "You think Tito crossed us?"

"That would make him look bad," I surmised.

For that same reason, I was certain this wasn't the beginning of an attack. Not with the number of witnesses. To the world, Tito was a prominent member of the community. His wealth and lavish ways made him popular.

No, something else had happened.

I didn't wait for my second to move away before I strode off in the opposite direction. Toward the end of the corridor, where it opened into church offices to the left and curved to the right to the main entrance, Caravellos scurried about. I took in their nervous expressions and the way no one seemed to be in charge. The moment I stepped from the shadows, they suddenly had somewhere else to focus their attention.

"Where's Tito?" I demanded.

The soldiers looked between themselves.

I counted to ten in my head. An itch made my fingers curl. Shooting one of them would be a declaration of aggression, but damn it would feel good to spill blood this early in the day.

Fuck, I need to leave this city.

The days of inaction were wearing on me. I wasn't made for retirement, a life of ease. A vacation? Ha! More like hell.

A memory flashed through my mind of bronze skin, sparkling with water. Maybe I could be the sort to lounge about the pool, but only with the proper incentive—

Dio bono! What the hell is wrong with you?! My conscience, the morally twisted little fucker, screamed at me. It was my wedding day, and this wasn't the first thought of the country cousin that I'd had to chase away. And last night? When I'd been seconds away from giving in to temptation?

Fuck me.

I swiped a hand down my face. This madness was bad for business. It would have been easy to blame my tangled thoughts on the whiskey, but I'd only had two drinks at the rehearsal dinner. No, it was an insanity that I wrestled with during the night and conquered right before dawn.

This wedding with Signorina Caravello was happening. There was no alternative.

"Tito's in there," Dante said, sliding to my side.

Together, we cut a path through the atrium of the church. The guards at the opposite door shuffled in place as we approached.

My second smiled and popped a piece of gum in his mouth. "Move."

"Signor Caravello is occupied," the bolder of the two stated.

Dante stepped right in front of him. He snapped a bubble with his gum. "That so?"

There was probably piss in the guard's pants. It wasn't that Dante was a large man. Hell, I had three inches on him and about twenty-five pounds of muscle. It was the dissociated look in his eye. The politically incorrect term was bat-shit crazy.

Which was exactly why we were friends.

But right now, I didn't have time to enjoy the show where my right hand scared grown men into tears. We had a wedding, a party, and then a plane to catch. What Tito didn't know was that we weren't sticking around for his wedding breakfast. It wasn't as much a middle finger to tradition so much as pressing matters in my own kingdom that needed my immediate attention.

I'd been away from the Windy City too long.

Gripping the handle, I pushed into the room, leaving Dante to deal with the guards.

A splotchy-faced Tito took another step forward, reached out, and grabbed the bare shoulders of a woman. And then the bastard made the biggest mistake of his life.

He shook her.

There was a split second where I recognized the lady's face. Not because of its otherworldly beauty, but because it wore a look of pure defiance.

Wrath surged through me, violent and consuming. I pounced. Gripping the don by the suit jacket, I lifted his squat body into the air—and shook.

"Alessandro! Don't!" Penelope gasped.

Through the haze of anger, it barely registered she'd used my name. But right now I was more beast than man. My breaths came in great bellows. Every muscle in my body shook with barely contained fury. Blood roared in my ears.

I tossed Tito across the room. He didn't fall, but he stumbled, pitching forward for a few steps before he righted himself and turned.

"I can explain, Mr. Mancini."

I paused, but only to throw a quick and thorough glance over Penelope. She was breathing hard, her pretty cheeks were flushed, but she seemed otherwise unharmed.

Rounding on Tito, I got right in his face and menaced, "What the fuck do you think you're doing?"

Those muddy eyes nearly fell from his purple face. "She—she messed this up! It's all her fault."

A throat cleared, and a gentle touch brushed against my forearm.

I dropped my gaze. Penelope was holding *me* back. She must have sensed I was about to strangle her uncle.

"It's me you want, Mr. Mancini," she said, voice clear and without a tremble.

Yes, and I shouldn't.

Vaguely aware of the soldiers filing into the room, guns drawn and pointed in my direction, I took a healthy step into the cleared middle. Dante popped a bubble against the roof of his mouth as he pointed twin handguns at the Caravellos. Whatever was happening over there, he had it under control.

Penelope slipped between her uncle, his men, and me. This woman, this beautiful, vibrant woman, was placing herself as *my* shield.

A deep breath filled my lungs. No one did that. Ever. Not even my second in command. She was something else.

Awe filled my chest as I stared at her.

"Start talking," I demanded. There was a split second of clarity where I realized I'd lost my iron control yet again—over this woman who wasn't my bride.

Tito barked at the guards, who reluctantly lowered their weapons. I didn't need to do the same to make Dante lower his twin handguns. There was no reason for the bullets to fly...yet.

"There's been a change of plans," Penelope said evenly. "Poppy won't be getting married today."

Fear pulsed in the room, all eyes on me. This wasn't a simple wedding day disaster. The ominous drone of war drums beat in the distance.

"Is that so?" I mused, managing to keep my voice steady, bored even.

Penelope tipped her chin up, inviting me to be judge, jury, and executioner. "Yes, she's left the mob."

Dante let out a long whistle. The same surprised noise whispered through my mind, but I kept the reaction to myself.

"People don't leave the mob, Miss Greenbriar." I pulled the sleeves of my tux over my wrists, straightening the cuffs. "Once you're in, you're here for life."

"That's not always the case," she countered.

Tito rumbled, and I shot him a warning look.

"She'll keep quiet, live a life without bringing attention to herself. But if any of you interfere, you'll find the long arm of the law will meet out swift and decisive retaliation."

She has no idea what she's done. A rough laugh threatened to bark up my throat, but I squashed it. Here was this quaint country girl, the object of some of my darker fantasies, standing before her uncle and me, telling us she had no problem with breaking a binding contract.

"Are you—" I held up my hand, disbelief surging through me. "Are you *threatening* a king of the underworld?"

Something glittered in her eyes. "Two of them. But there's no threat, not if you leave her alone. We can continue with business as usual, simply forgoing the wedding."

How simple it must seem to someone from the outside world. What this vibrant fireball didn't seem to understand was that bargains like the one that we'd struck were what made empires rise or fall. Her actions might have come from a place of good intentions and ignorance, but the result would still be devastation. I would be perfectly justified in burning her uncle's organization to the ground, exacting whatever penalty I saw fit, and no one would condemn me.

No wonder Tito physically assaulted her. This could be pinned on him. A clear failure of his ability to control his kingdom and his daughter. And the weaker man proved his cowardice by lashing out at the sheer determination and defiance it took to bring him down. He'd lost control to his fear. The red evidence of his outburst marked the bare skin of his niece's shoulders.

Which prompted my own tangled reaction.

I am not subject to my feelings. It took every drop of strength to draw in calming breaths. But the bright handprints taunted me mercilessly.

"And you helped her? Arranged all this?" I demanded, addressing the heart of the situation.

"She didn't want to marry you," Penelope explained simply. "I made sure it didn't happen."

I rubbed a hand along the line of my jaw. *You little wasp.* Such a sharp sting in her words, mirrored in her eyes. Admiration spread through me.

"If she doesn't return, if she doesn't marry Don Mancini, you two idiots started a war!" Tito raged.

He stank of desperation.

Penelope shifted. It was a subtle tell. A small crack in her façade.

And here I thought I was the one coming to the table at a disadvantage. I sought Caravello out, since he had a daughter of marriageable age. It was my proposition that we join forces to stop the pests invading the Midwest with their drug poison.

But this sudden change from him had me wondering what I didn't know. There had to be something. His raw reaction proved it was as beneficial to be joined to me as me to him, which we hadn't found hard evidence of when snooping through his organization. Yes, we suspected it to be the case, but here was the undeniable proof.

Interesting—very interesting.

It was a pity we weren't being joined. I wanted very much to see how he would try to play me. Plus, his resources were a valuable asset to my plans. Unlike him, there was always another tree to shake down. My determination to accomplish the impossible would drive me to discover an alternative.

But I might be this don's only hope.

The surge of power felt too good to resist. And then I swept a look over the other temptation—the one I was tired of resisting.

"I was promised a Caravello bride," I mused, the idea forming as I spoke. "Miss Greenbriar *is* your blood, correct?"

Those hazel eyes widened with horror. Penelope's chest rose and fell, each inhale more rapid as horror dawned on her.

"No!" she gasped. "You can't do this!"

A dark possession twisted the corner of my mouth up. "Oh, but I can."

Fight fueled her body, not flight. She took a step forward, glaring daggers at me.

Yes, little one, you just stepped into the trap of your own making. She might have been trying to free the cousin from my clutches, but that only positioned herself to be taken.

And damn me, I wanted to take her.

Tito sucked in a sharp breath, finally catching on to what we already knew. "Yes, she is. She is my blood!"

I shrugged. "Then I see no reason the contract can't be amended so that I still take a Caravello bride today."

"We could arrange that," Tito rushed to say. He snapped his stubby fingers, and a lackey hurried over. They exchanged a rapid series of commands in Italian.

So eager to sell to me.... I continued to smile victoriously at my new bride.

"I won't do it," Penelope warned.

"You've left very few choices," I drawled. "Marry me or start a war."

"I'm not part of that bargain. It's not my problem," she said, but there wasn't that unwavering bite of resistance in her tone.

Moving forward, I brushed the tip of my finger over the red spots still on her shoulder. She flicked a glance, snorting when she saw the marks.

"The moment you set out to visit your uncle, you declared your involvement with the mob." I lowered my voice. "I still don't know why you came to him, but you're in this, Penelope. Which means this deal affects you too."

Her whole body shook with the violent shudder. My dick stiffened greedily.

"You can't do this, lupo," she whispered, violence dancing in her voice.

There! That beautiful fight, flaming beautifully inside her. I was going to taste it after all. A dark possession shot through me. "The moment you crossed me, you staked your position on the board. And you played well, but you lost. Checkmate."

Instead of stepping away, of doing anything that would come naturally to a cornered creature, Penelope pressed into me.

The contact sent a jolt of raw heat straight through me.

"I'm warning you, don't do this," she hissed.

Fucking hell, the things I wanted to do to this woman. Things that I now *could* do to her. *Santa Madonna*...this change of plans was too good to be true. The endless possibilities of how I would exhaust that warm body, explore its secrets, and make it unravel—time after time—until Penelope was a spent, sated mess.

The custom-tailored pants on my legs did nothing to hide the hard length that was equally delighted at the prospect of a different bride.

"Oh, trust me, vespina, this is happening," I whispered darkly.

"I'll fight you."

Oh dio. My dick pulsed painfully. "Are you sure that is how you want this to happen?" I drawled.

Penelope pursed her lips. There was something she wasn't telling me. Some reason that kept her from screaming and spilling our secrets to the civilians gathered in the sanctuary. She wasn't summoning help from the high-powered players. But...why?

I wanted to know that leverage.

"I thought so," I said with a smirk.

"I didn't agree," she said through clenched teeth.

"One way or another, I'm meeting you at the end of the aisle. The choice of walking there on your own two feet or being dragged kicking and screaming is up to you," I offered, just to see the flames in her eyes.

"Won't kicking and screaming send the wrong message?" she spat.

I shrugged. "Stranger things have happened."

"It's settled." Tito mopped his forehead as he invaded the space between us.

"Uncle Tito, you can't—"

"Do not tell me what I can and can't do, girl," he barked.

I narrowed my eyes in warning.

The fool was oblivious.

So I pointed my hand right in his face. "Have the papers delivered to my dressing room."

"They'll be there in a quarter of an hour," Tito said, shaking my hand.

I brought my opposite hand on top of his, pinching the tendons viciously. "And if you ever raise a hand against my wife again, signore, no accord between us will save you. Capisce?"

"Ho capito. Ho capito!" Tito gasped.

I straightened. "I'll see you at the end of the aisle, Miss Greenbriar."

The last image of my bride was a pure vision of a terrible beauty. Her bridesmaid dress was black and evoked the idea of sin and wrath.

But the feeling had very little to do with what she wore.

No, it was the way this woman carried herself. The way she defied me with every fiber of her being. The perfect queen to bring back to my underworld kingdom.

Chapter 14 – Penelope

"This has to be illegal," I shouted as the door shut behind the beast and most of the guards. But my voice was suddenly hoarse, and the words didn't come out with conviction.

My uncle rounded on me. "Are you really that stupid, girl?"

I pressed my lips into a thin line.

"You wanted to play mobster? Welcome to the life of crime," he sneered. "We don't need your permission to do this."

"There are witnesses. If you drag me down the aisle kicking and screaming, they'll put a quick stop to it." The threat bubbled up of its own accord.

Tito walked to the ice bucket with champagne. He poured a healthy flute and chugged. A burp exploded from his chest. Those fat lips smacked as he wiped drips from his chin.

"You cause a scene like that...." He pointed a sausage finger at me, while pouring another glass. "And your mother won't see another doctor for the rest of her very short life."

My body jolted, every function stopped, and ice formed over my heart. He wouldn't. That was his sister. I tried to breathe, but air didn't fill my lungs.

"Did you forget about that?" he sneered. "Was that never a consideration in your little scheme?"

He chugged again, a series of smaller hiccups exploding through his barreled chest.

"Or are you stupid enough to think that what we'd agreed to was still going to hold despite your actions today?" He slammed the empty bottle down. "That's it, isn't it? You thought I wouldn't come after your mother because of what you'd done."

"She's your sister, and she's sick," I croaked.

My lungs moved a fraction, fighting desperately against the rising panic.

"Family is everything, but only if it never becomes a nuisance. And you, dear niece, are a fucking pest." Tito ripped open the door. "Meet me at the sanctuary doors, ready to walk down that aisle with a smile on your damn face in ten minutes, or I pull the plug on your mother's care."

The door slammed with a terrible finality.

A petrifying chill leached into me. Numb, I looked around helplessly. There was...there was no way out of this.

I staggered to the ice bucket. The bastard hadn't left me any alcohol. I was going to need that to get through the next hour.

Because now that the moves were played, there was nowhere else for me to maneuver on the board.

"This is not checkmate." I fisted my hands.

I let my thoughts fly away and focused only on my breathing. I had to do this, so I would. Air in—hold. Air out—hold. The next moments were reduced to those simple steps. Walk out the door. Breath in—hold. Smile down the aisle—breath out. Don't faint, just marry the monster—

I choked.

Brutal coughs wracked my frame. I was the sacrifice. There was no one to save me. This was the price for Poppy's freedom and for Mom's medical care. The option to choose myself no longer existed, and if I was being honest, it never had. Something terrible was always the price I was willing to pay to save my mom. Adding Poppy's life to the list was a small price to add to it.

Too soon, there was a knock on the door.

I smoothed my hands through my hair. *Take a step.* I did. *Good, now another.* And that was how I made it to my uncle's side.

"Where's your dress?" he demanded.

The black lace of the bridesmaid gown shifted around my legs. "I'm wearing it. What? Did you think *I* would fit in your daughter's custom frothy white cupcake?"

He began to snarl something.

Done with his threats, I took several fast steps forward, pushing through the double doors. Confusion filled the crowd, because it was the bride's procession, but I was clearly not the bride they anticipated.

"Yeah, it's a surprise to me too," I muttered.

Halfway down the aisle and panting hard, Uncle Tito caught up to me. His clammy hands bit down on my wrist. He tugged me beside him.

"Slow down, now," he snapped under his breath.

Murmurs swirled through the room. We waded through them like a thickening fog.

At the end of the aisle, I jerked away from my uncle and stepped before Mancini. Horror welled from the pit of my stomach. This was happening. Me, tied to this cold and vicious wolf.

Mother of god preserve me! Standing here, facing the situation with no escape, the fight instinct quickly fizzled out and gave way to flight. I looked wildly about. Where was the exit? Would they shoot if I ran? My pulse roared in my ears. I faltered, spying a door just to the side of the chancel. If I was fast enough, I could make it!

Something hard and warm slid against the skin of my inner arm. The monster—it was the monster, and he was offering me some form of comfort. The touch cut through the chaos, drawing my immediate attention.

He pushed me into this mess. It was all his fault! Why didn't I bring something to stab him with? I ground my molars and glared at his fingers moving against my skin.

I should have told him to fuck off.

Instead, I let him continue to brush his fingers up and down my arm.

"Treasured friends and beloved family," Tito boomed, his natural charisma pushing through the sweating, nervous exterior as he grappled with the situation. "There has been a change of plans. You came to witness the union of my daughter to Mr. Mancini. It turns out, love cannot be staunched. An attachment has formed between my niece and the groom. My sweet, darling daughter has stepped aside, wishing them all the happiness in the world. While I should shoot this man for trifling with my Poppy's affections—"

Giggles flitted to the vaulted ceiling, the civilians taking his statement as hyperbole.

"—I cannot be the one to stand in the way of true love. So!" Tito clapped his hands. "It is with my family's blessing that Penelope Greenbriar and Alessandro Mancini are joined in the union of Holy Matrimony."

"Proceed, padre," Mancini commanded the priest.

From the look on my uncle's face, he clearly had more to say on the issue. But the order from the groom was enough for the prelate to scurry into action.

Before Tito could reach and place my hand on the mobster's, I clutched both of Mancini's hands.

This is of my own accord.

They might have trapped me in the impossible situation, but I would be damned if they bartered me like flesh.

Those hard fingers wrapped firmly around mine. They engulfed mine, but I didn't feel uncomfortable. In the midst of this nightmare, the connection had the odd effect of grounding me.

But the moment I looked into his face, that cruel and calculating enigma, the trickle of fear came back in force. He was a stranger, and I was surrendering myself to him.

For Poppy. For Mom.

I can do this.

Conjuring images of their smiling faces was the only thing that bolstered me through the beginning of the service. The address on marriage, the psalm, the introit—the tedious pieces should have been soothing because they were similar to the liturgy of Sunday Mass, but I found little comfort in them.

Probably because it was all fake.

We were making a mockery of the Holy Rite.

I swore I could feel a black mark forming on my soul for standing before these people in the sight of the altar and lying about something as sacred as matrimony. What a fitting punishment for my sin—to be shackled to this lupine beast.

The priest droned on and on. Right before he moved to the pulpit to deliver the sermon, Mancini leaned in. "Make it short, padre."

The priest's eyes flashed wide. For changing brides on him, he was handling the situation well. But the ice dripping from the mobster's command would make even the most pious saint falter.

As the priest scuttled into the pulpit, Mancini and I sat to the side of the chancel. The white satin ribbon on the high back chair tickled my shoulder. I had to admit, the church looked breathtaking. The fresh flowers, the ribbons and lanterns, even the greenery draping along the pillars, created a lush and soft side to the otherwise stuffy interior. Poppy's thoughtful touches surrounded us.

My heart clenched tight. It would be wrong to let such a sweet-natured creature, such a beautiful little innocent, be handed over to the brute next to me.

I was made of sterner stuff. I would survive whatever was thrown at me.

But I was still human. I needed a distraction to keep from screaming.

So I studied the icons and paintings decorating the walls. I tapped my toe against the smooth floor. This was happening. It felt like a dream. I never daydreamed about a lavish wedding. While it would have been big—with most of the town in attendance—it wasn't this. It would have been in the country parish church, the one I'd gone to since I was born, baptized, and had my First Communion—home. An ache weighed on my sternum. But try as I might, I wasn't able to push the thoughts away. After the service, there would have been a big dinner. We would have had a tent in the field. The boys would have been stinking drunk, probably tip a cow.

Hell, who was I kidding, I would be right there with 'em.

A long sigh blew through my lips. There were probably no cows to be tipped tonight. Neither fireworks nor bonfires that would roar until dawn. Tonight, there would be a fancy, stuffy dinner at the most prestigious country club in Detroit. Followed by dancing, with everyone looking and whispering. And then, the groom would whisk me away—

Oh, mother of god, don't think about that.

Too late! I would be spending the night with him. The mob boss. I gulped. The shiver that rattled down my spine was unstoppable.

Something rough brushed against my wrist. The charms jingled. I glared down at those fingers, hating their proximity. Who did he think he was? Touching me whenever! Wherever!

My husband.

That was who.

Whenever the exegesis on Corinthians and the attributes of love was over, this man would be bound to me. He probably assumed I was his to embrace as he saw fit.

I am no man's possession.

Mancini gently lifted the silver horse. "Do you like to ride?"

The simplicity of the question made me blink. "Only weirdos don't like riding."

He snorted. "I've been called a lot of things, but weirdo is a first."

"You don't like to ride?" Of course he didn't ride.

Holy Virgin, preserve me! A life without horses. No more galloping over the fields as the wind snapped and crackled in my face. The sun blazing down on the open landscape as the hooves thundered across the unobstructed expanse. Cows lowing in the distance, and the warm lights of home always on, ready for me to return.

It was gone.

The door to that world closed. Probably forever, unless I found a way to escape this nightmare.

I yanked my wrist away, clutching the charms protectively to my side.

Mancini exhaled softly. "You don't have to fear me, Penelope."

My name, on his lips...I steeled my spine against the confusing feelings mixing with the rest. "I don't fear you, lupo. I hate you."

He stiffened.

The priest wrapped up his speech and summoned us back to the front. That hard touch captured me again, gripping my fingers in a bruising hold. I might have admitted to this man that I hated him, but what I disliked more was the crackle of sensation at his touch. How could my body respond like this? It betrayed me at every turn! Of all the things I was enduring today, this had to be the worst.

It's not real. I didn't actually feel excited at the contact. I couldn't possibly feel anything. Anger kindled in my chest and it was directed at his horribly beautiful face.

Distracted and annoyed, I didn't realize it was time for the vows until the monster began to speak. Meaningless words that were meant to bind us.

"Penelope June, you stand there before me, the vision of my future. Everything I dreamt of surmised in your alluring presence. As your husband, I promise to stand by your side, to protect you and keep you safe through every storm life brings our way. I vow to support you endlessly, to be your shield, your strength, and your unwavering shelter. Today, I give you all of me—my heart, my devotion, and my promise to always be the home where you feel safe and secure."

That didn't sound like a man about to acquire a possession.

Don't let him fool you! He jumped on the opportunity to own me. I was the perfect substitute, the next best possession for this power-hungry player.

The ring was clearly too small. Mancini slipped it on my pinky, the blood flow immediately clamped.

"Penelope?" the priest urged.

My turn. "I vow to be the perfect little wife. I'll be whatever you need me to be."

A shuffle in the crowd drew my attention in that direction.

I should probably pretend to like him—just a little.

"I promise to be faithful, taking you as my lawfully wedded husband," I added, drawing on the memories of past weddings, but altering the traditional vows to suit my enraged feelings at the situation. "To have and to hold, from this day forward, until we part."

Because we would be parting. One way or another, this wasn't my future. It couldn't be the end to my story. I wouldn't allow it.

Fueled by that determination, I kept speaking. "For better or worse, I'll be there, a thorn in your side that you can't dig out. For richer or poorer, wealth and status will never sway me. Come sickness or health, I will be the cherished wife you need me to be."

For some reason, I left off the *till death us do part* line. Perhaps it was the spark deep in his black gaze. Perhaps it was the fact that no matter what, I didn't see a situation where I became a murderer.

No, I would leave that to whatever other enemies this man had.

This little enemy wasn't going to kill him. Drive him to madness? Sure, I would happily do that. Create an unlivable hell in his home? Sign me up!

Take his life? No.... It wouldn't need to come to that.

"By the power vested in me by God and the Church, I pronounce you husband and wife. Let these guests take witness to the vows spoken, and let what has joined never be torn asunder," the priest proclaimed.

Those words held a terrible finality. They were a thunderclap to my senses. The air left my lungs, and I staggered.

But two arms snatched me, tugging me into a hard embrace.

Before I could scream at being caught by the monster, his mouth crushed against mine. That contact brought precious air to my lungs. But his hard, demanding kiss cut off the blast of panic.

This close, the ice monster was anything but cold. No, his touch burned, and his body was warm.

Warm enough to make my own body forget we were enemies.

It had to be the reason I melted into his hold.

I gasped at the overload to my senses. Mancini struck, taking advantage of the sharp intake of air. His tongue plunged into my mouth, sweeping and tasting me.

Mother of god, he kissed like a sinner.

And I didn't hate the way it felt.

As if drawn by invisible strings, my hands roved over his body, pushing up his hard torso that had to be cut from living stone. I fisted the lapels of his jacket—and so help me, I tugged him closer!

The kiss deepened, our tongues clashing. The spot between my legs ached with relief, and at the same time demanded more. I pushed against his body, desperate for more. We were making out, devouring one another in front of the entire church! But neither of us seemed to care. The tingling chemistry that we'd been avoiding since the airport was finally released.

It consumed us.

Mancini groaned. At this point, he was fucking my mouth with his tongue. And me? The good girl from the country, who never broke any law worse than speeding? I was about to climb him.

A rough cough somewhere far away eventually reached us.

We broke apart, staring hard at one another and panting for breath.

"If you touch me again, padre, you'll lose that hand," Mancini rasped, quiet enough for only us to hear.

"Please, sir, don't continue that public display of affection here," the priest muttered.

Vaguely aware of the suddenly roaring, cheering crowd, that I'd somehow been oblivious to in the heat of the moment, I was now acutely aware of the steamy, rated-R smooch I just had with the man I swore not five minutes ago that I loathed.

Get a damn grip! I struggled the entire way out of the church to regain control of myself. It barely worked. There was one thing that service proved. Lust was a powerful force, and I was addicted after that one hit.

Chapter 15 – Penelope

Everything after that kiss was a blur. The story I told myself was that it was the lack of breakfast, the extra cup of that dangerous coffee my cousin's housekeeper made, and the stifling press of strangers in the church. My senses were overwhelmed, and that was why I couldn't think straight.

It wasn't the kiss.

The tingle in my lips was from dehydration.

When the back door of the town car closed, I dropped my head back against the seat. Silence caressed my tortured ears. I pushed every unnecessary thought from my mind and focused on drawing deep breaths.

The opposite door opened, and Mancini slid into the back beside me. The moment a delicious woodsy scent tickled my nostrils, I changed to inhale through my mouth.

His presence was stifling! There was no escape.

If the driver felt the tension, he didn't comment. He did his job as a professional, not jabbering to fill the void as I would have done. But I was keenly aware of Mancini's proximity. I refused to open my eyes. To engage with him. But I couldn't stop being aware of him.

That was the very reason I lost track of time and when the car finally slowed, I prepared to bolt. The lock popped as I opened the door, not waiting for the driver or my husband to escort me. Tires squealed as a car rushed by, and then a horrible metal screeching tore through the air.

Mancini grabbed my waist with a growl. "Are you trying to get run over?"

Horns blared. Drivers shouted, and the door hung askew from its hinges.

I gaped at the chaos. "Why was he going so fast?"

"While that is a very good question, it's not what concerns me right now." Mancini gently gripped my chin and turned my face to look at him. "I'm going to ask you this, Penelope, and I'm going to need you to be honest with me."

I felt myself fall into those inky depths. His tone was deadly serious, but there wasn't any anger or threat behind the words.

I gave him a small nod. "Okay."

"Are you considering harming yourself to escape this situation?" he pressed.

The way his thumb slid over my jaw delayed my brain processing his question. When I finally did, I jerked back.

"No! Why would I—no!" I shook my head.

But he held his grip, continued to brush that rough pad back and forth. "You just tried to jump in front of a moving vehicle."

I blew out a long breath. "I can't say that I'll never have depression so bad that I consider harming myself. But know this, mobster, I'm a fighter. I love being alive. So I would rather battle you to the end of time than give up."

He continued to look at me for a moment before he was convinced of the truth of my words. "That's good to hear."

"Do you plan to be so horrible that I'd choose death rather than life with you?" I bit back in turn, following him out his door.

"No, in fact, I plan to make your life comfortable. You'll have whatever your little heart desires…my little wife." Whatever else he was going to say was cut off when his phone rang.

A jet roared overhead.

I snapped my gaze upward and stumbled.

Mancini caught me, and this time, he didn't let me go. That firm touch slid around my back and guided me over the walkway. The driver passed a piece of luggage to an attendant, who we followed through private security.

"Why are we at the airport?" I hissed.

Mancini continued to chat on his phone, but the amused look he threw me showed that he'd heard my query. He didn't even put the device down for the TSA. I glared at him the whole way to the private lounge.

The scene was all too familiar.

"Mrs. Mancini, may I offer you a beverage?" the receptionist, who hadn't been there just a few days ago, asked.

Mrs. Mancini.

Tearing my eyes away from the fountain and the haunting memory of our first meeting, I croaked, "Water, please."

She left without asking the monster in a tux about a refreshment.

I stared at my husband, who was doing more listening than speaking into the phone.

Enough was enough.

I marched over, jumped because of the height difference, and plucked the phone from his hands. "He'll call you back!" I shouted into the receiver, before holding the device over the pool of water and sliding my thumb over the red button to end the call. "Start talking, lupo."

The surprise on his features was worth everything. I doubted very many individuals were bold enough to stand up to him. Well...that was something he was going to have to get very used to if he planned to keep me around.

"Isn't it obvious?" he ground out. "We're at the airport."

"There was a wedding reception, or did you forget about this?" I held up my hand to show the teeny, tiny pinky ring.

A muscle in his jaw flexed. "I didn't realize you were so eager to be trotted in front of Tito's friends."

I wasn't.

"Does my uncle even know we're skipping town?"

"Does it matter?" he countered.

Touche. "And...where are we flying to?"

He grinned. Those pearly, lupine teeth flashed sharp. "Home."

Which was...I scrambled to remember. *He's the don of where?* I narrowed my eyes.

"Chicago," he drawled and held out his hand. "Any more questions or may I continue my conversation?"

There was no reason to drop his phone in the fountain. No *good* reason. I slammed the device against his palm. As I turned on my heel the world suddenly tilted from a violent push. I swayed. The dress tangled about my legs, and my heels lost their grip.

Mancini held me, dangling me over the pool of water. "Watch yourself, vespina. I'm not the kind of man who can be easily coerced."

He dropped me an inch.

It was just a little water. I'd fallen into the cows' water trough before. But the thought of sitting in the lounge soaked—and who knew how long the plane ride was—didn't sound fun.

"Are you looking for an apology?" I snapped.

He chuckled. "You won't give that to me. But I'll settle for a kiss."

Outrage burst from my lips. "As if!" I scoffed.

He dropped me again.

I squeaked. "Fine. Fine!"

He pulled me up and wrapped an arm around me. This time, he didn't bother closing the distance. He patiently waited, looming above me. I stared up at him, too aware of how tall he was. He expected me to bridge the distance. Well, good thing I was resourceful.

I'm only doing this so I don't get wet.

The muscles in my stomach tightened as I stepped onto the edge of the fountain, bracing myself on his broad shoulders for a moment, and then clapped both hands on his cheeks. This wasn't romantic, and he needed to know that. I wasn't here to pleasure him whenever he demanded it. This whole situation was messed up. The sooner he understood that, the better.

I gave him a loud, sloppy smooch.

When I pulled back, he was smirking. "You are going to make life a hell of a lot more interesting than your cousin would have."

How dare he!

I was tempted to slap him. I even raised my hand. But he caught it.

"Don't insult her," I hissed. "She would have made you a good wife."

Mancini shook his head. "Maybe divine intervention knew I didn't need a good wife."

With that he moved away. And I had to jump off the edge to avoid tipping into the fountain.

The receptionist came at that moment with my water. Snatching it violently off the tray, I saluted her. If only I'd eaten something this morning, then I could be drinking something stronger. But I wasn't about to get sloppy and lose my edge around the mobster.

By the time we loaded onto the private jet, I was fidgeting. Badly. Mancini disappeared through a door at the end of the cabin. The chairs in this main area were sprawled out, some with tables between them and others set by themselves for maximum leg room. The space reeked of comfort and wealth.

The plush seats were cozy. I slipped my strappy shoes off, tucked my feet under my dress, and stared out the window, my fingers drumming against my thigh. Soon, the runway began to speed by, and the metal can we were trapped in gained speed. I slapped the blind shut.

But just because the world rushing by was invisible, didn't mean I stopped feeling it.

The moment of weightlessness when the metal bird proved it could fly had me digging my fingers into the armrests.

Booze would've helped, but I would never like this feeling.

Keenly aware that we were climbing higher and higher into the sky, I pushed long gusts of air from my lungs one after the other.

"Miss, can I get you anything?" the flight attendant asked, a slight sneer marking her voice.

Screw it. Empty stomach be damned. I squinted at her. "Bourbon. Neat."

She shook her head. "Mr. Mancini said you needed to eat something first."

Anger spiked deep inside. *Oh, he did not just do that.*

Of all the controlling, rotten things to do! It didn't matter that in principle I agreed with him. My fingers curled tight, creating little half-moons in my palm. If he thought I shouldn't have any, that was between us. He shouldn't be telling this—this—

Smirking wench with big tits!

"What's your name, honey?" I smiled tightly.

"Chelsey, miss."

Of course it was. A typical 90's it-girl name, right up there with Ashley and Britney.

I drummed my fingers into the armrest. "Okay, *Chelsey,* here's what's going to happen. You are going to bring me three of those little bottles of booze. I would prefer bourbon, but I'll take what you've got. If you don't, or if you tattle to my husband, I will hog-tie and brand you in three minutes flat."

The threat held no weight with her. Condescension dripped from her eyes. "Mr. Mancini gave his orders, and—"

"I don't give a rat's ass about Mr. Mancini or his orders." I launched out of my seat, brushing past her.

"Miss, miss! Where are you going?" she called.

But I was already marching down the aisle of the small cabin. The gallery had a second attendant, who was preparing a pot of coffee.

I gave the man a clipped nod and began to rummage through the boxed compartments. There were better treats in here than peanuts and pretzels. I grabbed a few that looked appetizing. The writing on the chocolates weren't in English, so they had to be good.

"Stop. What are you doing?" the blonde bimbo hissed from behind me.

"Chelsey, don't," the man warned. "She has every right to be back here."

I hid my laughter. The anger wafting off the woman was tangible. It made me dig even harder through the stores. Cracker-like breadsticks from Italy, dried organic fruits, and a little tin of nuts that I would pick through added to my pile.

Her reaching out to touch me was a mistake.

I gripped her wrist, spun her around, and wrenched her arm up her back. The treats in my other hand tumbled to the floor. Like any barnyard animal, she squawked helplessly.

"Where's the mini bottles?" I asked the male attendant.

He gulped, stooping to pick up my snacks, and placed them on a tray. "What would you like, Mrs. Mancini?"

That name crawled down my spine. "Something strong—and a bottle of water."

He plucked a cut glass from a shelf, dropped ice in it, and pulled out something clear with weird letters. "Vodka, ma'am?"

"Sounds great!" It really did.

"Anything to cut the taste?" the attendant asked.

"Cranberry juice." I smiled. "Thank you."

"Of course, ma'am. I'm sorry for Chelsey's behavior. She's new."

"Well, let this be a lesson to her." I shoved the attendant, plucked the glass with swirling red tendrils, and returned to the main part of the cabin. The man followed with my treats.

"What's your name?" I asked, dropping back into my seat.

"Alec, ma'am." He set the tray on the table before me.

"Thank you, Alec, I appreciate it."

Now that the victory had been won, there wasn't as strong a need to lose myself to the pull of forgetfulness. I slowly nursed the cranberry vodka and made sure to finish the entire bottle of water. Chelsey didn't make a reappearance.

To occupy the time and avoid going to find the mobster through the partition, I scrolled through the book on my phone. Even the dragon-riding warriors weren't able to hold my attention. So I logged into the WIFI and began to binge short videos about recipes. Thirty minutes into the flight, Alec brought a fancy board of crackers, meat, and cheese.

"Do you have any Sunny D?" I asked, flicking a glance at him.

He cleared his throat. "I have fresh-squeezed orange juice."

"You know why my generation is obsessed with these charcuterie boards?" I took the last sip of my cranberry drink and handed him the empty cup.

"Not sure, ma'am."

"Because we grew up on Lunchables and Sunny D." I plucked a piece of cheese and popped it in my mouth. "I'll have the orange juice, but just plain please. And some more water."

"Still or sparkling?"

I blinked. "Regular?"

He smiled. "Coming right up."

The far door unlatched and Mancini ducked through it. His presence suddenly filled the interior of the cabin. One look at me, and a frown tugged at his lips.

I refused to squirm under his gaze.

"Hungry?" he asked, folding into the seat across from me. "They do have more than snacks on here."

I shook my head. "I'm fine."

This time it was Chelsey who brought the beverages. There was a teeny, tiny coffee for the force of nature sitting across from me. If the attendant leaned over a little too far and bent a little too low, I refused to notice.

Only, I did see it.

And it made me want to take her to the floor.

Damn, what is wrong with me? I might not have wanted anything to do with this marriage, but that was my husband this flight attendant was flashing her cleavage in front of.

Mancini didn't look up from his phone at her.

It shouldn't impress me. But dammit, it did. I needed to hate this man, and something as simple as looking at another woman, on this our wedding day, would have helped!

I hate him plenty. Nothing was going to change that.

The orange juice sloshed as Chelsey dropped it in front of me. A splash bounced out and landed in my lap.

"Oops! I'm so sorry, miss," she gasped, her cheeks reddening.

I curled my fingers tightly in my lap. She was trying to provoke a reaction from me. "It's fine, honey. Why don't you bring me a wet towel, and I'll dab at it."

Not playing into her hand made her fume.

Mancini clicked off his phone, lifted his tiny cup, and pinned me with a look. "We'll be in Chicago soon."

He didn't look back at big boobs.

I cocked my head, studying every minute detail of this man. "What happens then?"

One broad shoulder lifted in a small shrug. "They'll have a meal prepared for us at the house."

"And then?" I pressed. "What happens tomorrow, or the morning after?"

Chelsey appeared and held out the tea towel with the edge wet like it was a dirty diaper. But I was done with her and the petty display of dominance. There were bigger problems to deal with. My life as I knew it was changed.

When we didn't ask her for anything else, the attendant disappeared.

Stabbing a finger into the table, I leaned forward. "What am I supposed to do with my life?"

Mancini popped an olive in his mouth. "Whatever you want."

That simple? I frowned. "Alright, I'm leaving."

His chuckle was dark and rich. I hated that it felt better than the fancy chocolate. "You don't want to do that." He rose and tugged on the cuffs of his dress shirt. "Besides, I just caught you, Penelope. I don't intend to let you slip away anytime soon."

I picked up the cut glass and hurled it at his retreating figure. The orange juice splattered on the wall, but the crash didn't make him pause as he slipped back into the far cabin.

Mother of god, what do I want more than leaving him? But maybe, through the twisted tangle of my thoughts, I already knew the truth. There were other things I wanted way more than not being this man's wife.

"And maybe he's my ticket to having them," I mused, pushing around the bottle of water. I lifted it and chugged. I really needed a clearer head to think through this new turn of events.

Chapter 16 – Penelope

"Well, I'll be," I breathed, staring up at the grand house. It was double the size of my uncle's home.

A man with a scrunched face stood at the front door. The poor thing looked as though he needed a good fiber supplement. Possibly an enema.

"This is Shepherd, the butler. If you need anything, he'll know how to supply you with it," Mancini intoned as we climbed. "There are a handful of maids and understaff, but we currently do not have a housekeeper. Shepherd manages everything beautifully, however."

"We're not in a rush to find one, sir." The man said with a bow. "We prize discretion above all other forms of character."

I felt like I was walking into Downton Abbey. The double entrance spilled into a grand opening. Stairs swept up the left side, cutting to a second-level walkway that disappeared into the bowels of the mansion.

While there were blisters forming on my toes, I was glad for once that I wasn't in blue jeans and boots. I resisted the urge to rub my opposite arms. A girl like me did not belong in a place like this. The portraits on the wall seemed to agree.

"Mr. Baldwin is waiting for you in your office, and Miss Serena is in the east sitting room," Shepherd informed his boss.

Mancini stopped short. "When did she arrive?"

"An hour ago, sir. Shall I bring cocktails?"

Mancini shook his head. "I think we'll head straight in for dinner tonight, Shepherd."

I narrowed my eyes. Maybe I wanted a drink before I faced whoever made the mafia don look like that.

"Tell Baldwin that I'll be with him in a moment." Stepping close to me, the beast slid his arm behind my back, forcing me to move.

Lifting my skirt, I scampered out of his reach. "I don't need herding."

He let out a harsh laugh, and his touch hardened. "Please, Penelope, I'm begging you, no games right now."

"Who's Serena?" I said sweetly. "Your mistress?"

A shudder rolled through his frame before his iron mask fell back into place. "Hardly. And besides—" his fingers curled possessively around my waist "—now that I'm married, there's no need for girlfriends."

My stomach did a small flip. I wished he wasn't touching me. The contact muddled my senses. The harder I tried to pull away, the tighter he held me.

I gave up with a huff and let him guide me into a creamy, fresh room. A woman sat before a piano, her fingers lifting the moment we stepped through the door.

"Sandro!" She rose and moved gracefully towards us. The chic dress floated around her like a cloud. "I'm so sorry I didn't come with gifts. Your marriage was so sudden! I came straight back home once I heard."

Mancini stilled. "It's good to see you, Serena. But you didn't have to leave Tuscany."

She stopped in front of us, turned her gaze to me, and swept a quick look over my body. It was fast, barely a blink! And yet, it had the resulting effect that I was lacking in her estimation.

I pulled myself straight. My initial response to wanting the regular clothes vanished, and I wished I was in jeans and boots. Spurs too! I wouldn't let a wispy, willowy model like her make me feel like anything less standing here.

"Well, aren't you going to introduce us?" she purred.

"I'm Penelope—his wife." I stuck out my hand.

One perfectly manicured brow flicked. "Spicy. Wherever did you find her, Sandro?"

Alessandro shifted behind me. "She's the niece of Don Caravello."

Serena let out a high-pitched laugh of disbelief. "What happened to the pretty little poppy seed?"

"My cousin was unavailable. I stepped in. And you, Serena, are...?" I jerked my hand in front of her.

Her slender fingers slid into mine. They were stronger than they seemed. For such slim digits, they had a good, solid grip. But my calloused, rough paw wrapped around them like a vise.

Those blood red lips parted in a small gasp as my grip tightened. "I'm Serena *Mancini*. The sister."

I released my hold. A sister...that deflated the horror story forming in my mind.

"Play nice," Mancini growled in Italian. "Or you won't like the consequences, Serena."

To me, he added, "I'll see you for dinner in ten minutes. Make yourself at home."

His hand brushed against my lower back, and then he was gone.

Serena walked to the wall and pressed a button before returning to the piano and closing the lid over the keys. "So, Penelope, how did you ensnare the don?"

The challenging look she threw me sent my defenses rising high. Maybe correcting her wasn't the path I wanted to play.

I shrugged. "I have more to offer than my cousin."

Her short laugh grated on my nerves. "Doubtful," she muttered.

Before I could call her out on the insult, a maid came through the door.

"Miss Notaro, please bring a bottle of champagne. The '89 Armand de Brignac would be fine," Serena instructed the woman. To me, she smiled. "After all, we have some celebrating to do."

I wasn't about to tell her that cocktail hour had been canceled. Let her brother be upset about ordering what I could only assume was a fancy bottle. Their relationship was...strange. She might not be a rival in the traditional sense, but if I assumed she wasn't going to protect the don, I was sorely mistaken. Their lack of affection, however, was confusing.

"You were in Tuscany." I moved around the room, not wanting to sit in front of her despite my aching feet. "Do you not live here?"

Her hand waved delicately in the air. "I come and go."

She sank into the armchair, filling it and commanding the space around her like a damn queen. If this was an old English abbey, was she the dowager countess? I snorted, hiding the reaction by drumming my fingers against the top of the piano.

The maid came with the bubbly, popped the cork, and poured. She took one to the sister, but I went to collect my own. It might be nice not to have to scrub my own toilet—or the other hundred in this brick-and-mortar behemoth—but I didn't need anyone serving me.

"Thank you, I appreciate it." I gave the maid a huge, genuine smile.

Her lips flickered, and then she left.

Serena took a long sip of her drink. "Well, you aren't much to look at, but at least you won't be easy to find in a crowd."

What a bitch. I sucked in a sharp breath and bit my tongue. *And you're proof that God makes all kinds.*

Unlike the easy flight attendant, it wouldn't be a good idea to take her to the floor and mop it with her thick, long hair.

"Why, thank you!" I smacked a hand over my chest. "That is probably a good thing considering we're living, breathing criminals."

Something flashed in her eyes. "So you're aware of our world? Of Alessandro's position in it?"

I only smiled and took a sip of my drink.

"I see." Serena toyed with her glass, dangling it from the tips of her fingers. "Know this, my brother doesn't change his mind easily. So if you're trying to trap him, he's one step ahead of you."

I'm the one who's trapped. Me! I clenched my jaw tight, refusing to let those words find a way past my lips. At that moment, a bell rang.

"Ah, that's dinner." Serena pushed to her feet.

Chapter 17 – Alessandro

"Show Signora Mancini to our room," I spoke low to Shepherd.

"Does she have luggage, sir?" the butler responded in perfect Italian. One would never know he'd been born and raised in Surrey. He spoke six languages, each without a discernable accent.

"No, but I expect Caravello to send it eventually." I dabbed my mouth. "I'll be in my office if you need me."

"Very good, sir."

I rose and left the table. My baby sister had spent the entire meal sipping her wine and staring between my bride and me. I didn't like the way she expressed her clear disapproval. It was my decision to marry, to bind myself to Detroit.

Serena liked drama and the spotlight. She was just mad she hadn't been involved in the selection of the bride, the bargain with the in-laws, and the party. I kept her away from events like that for the very reason that she was too unpredictable. If I couldn't control her outbursts, I was unable to protect our image, but more importantly, I wasn't able to protect Serena. For her safety, I kept her away from business, society, and any other situation where I couldn't predict the outcome.

But if there was anyone who was a match for my spoilt little sister, it was my wife. I flicked one last glance at Penelope. Dio bono! The way she'd put that flight attendant in a surrender hold. My wife didn't know I could see the whole thing, and that I'd commanded the other flight attendant to stand down and give Penelope whatever she wanted.

Because that was my wife's new life. Within reason, so long as it didn't compromise her safety, she would have whatever her little heart desired.

And if my sister tried anything.... I chuckled to myself as I pushed into my office. I almost wished Serena would try something.

But Penelope eating dinner in her bedraggled bridesmaid dress brought an issue to light. She needed clothes and other feminine necessities. It made no difference what she wore, whether it was the flirty dresses or the blue-collared working girl look, it all appealed to me. The bikini, however...fuck. That starred in several R-rated dreams. I woke every morning since meeting her drenched in sweat with a painful, rock-hard erection.

Shifting in my seat, I played with the small crown around the leather strap at my throat.

Penelope wasn't vapid like the other mob wives. It was going to be fun watching her spend my money.

"She's going to be a breath of fresh air," I mused to myself.

Sitting at my desk, I started up my laptop. The banking information blinked onto the screen moments later. But I wasn't able to easily navigate the dashboard to do what I wished. Frowning, I dialed my phone.

"Liliana, I need a new charge card," I clipped the moment the line connected.

The financial officer answered promptly. "Yes, signore, at once. What is the limit?"

The corner of my lip twitched. "No limit. But I want the spending reports sent to my phone so I can monitor the purchases."

"No limit, signore?" The talented accountant clucked her tongue. "That will require connecting it to several accounts, and looping the trusts through a holding LLC, which would create a stream—"

"I don't need a business lesson, Lilliana. Make it happen. No limit, no restrictions on purchases. Do you understand? You'll put it in my wife's name—Luca will give you her details."

"Very good." Liliana was a treasure with a talent for numbers. She could calculate the numbers at an illegal gambling event just in her head, and that was only one of her many skills. When she came to the city, seeking refuge, I made a deal with her in exchange for her services. She was invaluable, and we weren't letting her leave—which was preferred by her. "The physical card will be delivered first thing in the morning, signore. The accounts will be tied by ten a.m. at the latest."

"How are your kids?" I asked after a moment. With the trip, I hadn't been able to do a regular check-in with her.

"Oh, they're great, Signor Mancini! Thanks for asking." That note of motherly pride always made me smile. "But, signore?"

"Yes?"

There was a low crackle on the other end of the line as she hesitated. "Did Dante not come back from Detroit with you?"

My smile widened. "He rode his bike back. Should be home today."

Her relief was tangible. "It's just, the kids missed having him around," she explained quickly.

When I gave the assignment to have my newest accountant watched, it surprised me that Dante demanded the job. He was my enforcer, my right hand. House sitting a mom and her kids was regular soldiers' work. But he told me in no uncertain terms that if I gave the job to anyone else, he would kill them.

Liliana was his to watch over.

Why he continued to keep a professional relationship with her confused the hell out of me. But interfering with the enforcer's personal feelings wasn't something I had the time or energy for. So long as Liliana and my accounts were safe, I let them sort it out for themselves.

"Have the card delivered as soon as you can," I repeated.

"Will do, signore."

The moment she gave me verbal confirmation, I cut the call. Step one of wooing my wife was in play. Penelope said she hated me? Well, I was the one in control of her life now. She could have whatever her little heart desired, but it came from me.

She would depend on me for *everything*. Every crumb, every scrap of clothes. And every drop of pleasure.

My dick stirred, pressing against the seam of my pants.

It was time to show her that there was something between us. That chemistry, that *fire*—we'd danced around it the last few days at her uncle's. Now that every obstacle had been eliminated, we were able to explore this heat.

All other business could wait until after I sated my wife. Leaving the office, I made my way to our bedroom, anticipation for the exciting evening ahead pulsing in my veins.

The door opened with a crack, and Penelope screamed.

I barely managed to duck as the thick bedside clock sailed across the room. Damn, that woman had an arm on her. I would have to remember that.

"Was that really necessary?" I muttered, shutting the door behind me and throwing the lock.

Penelope's body shook. Venom leached from her pores, and her gaze promised death from a thousand cuts.

Dio, had there ever been a more beautiful sight? I crossed my arms and leaned back against the door, enjoying the view.

The seething wasp stood there in nothing but a black strapless band around her breasts and a whisp of lace hugging her hips. I had to keep my jaw clenched tight to keep from falling to my knees and licking every delectable inch of her.

Somehow, call me crazy, I didn't think she was as excited over the prospect of our marital extracurricular activities as I was.

"What are you doing in here?" She spoke slowly, each word dripping with pure, unadulterated wrath.

I tugged at my tie, giving her an amused look. "What does it look like I'm doing?"

She lifted a finger. Whether it shook from anger or fear, perhaps a mixture of both, it was hard to say. "Out. *Out!*"

Dropping my tie on the settee at the foot of the bed, I frowned. "Why would I leave?"

"I'm not having sex with you," she said through clenched teeth.

I blew out a short breath. I half expected those words. Had I hoped for a different answer? Naturally. But given the rollercoaster of events, I was prepared to just fall asleep beside her, hard as that was going to be.

But it still was disappointing.

My wife looked like a goddess sent to bring mortal men to their deaths. And I would happily fall on the swords of my enemies just for a taste of that.

I had to recognize and admit my attraction to this woman. If I didn't want it to rule me or dominate my existence, it couldn't be ignored.

"I'm tired as well. Tonight, we'll just sleep," I said softly.

The last thing I want is to force you, beautiful.

"Great! Goodnight," she barked, flicking her fingers in a dismissive gesture.

I cocked my head, studying her. It took a moment, but the objection dawned on me. Penelope thought this was her room.

Forcing down the dark laughter, I asked casually, "You thought this was *your* room, wife?"

Penelope flung her arms wide. "It's where Carson brought me!"

I frowned. "Carson?"

Penelope waved her hands in annoyance. "A British drama show reference—wouldn't expect an ape like you to have enough culture to know it."

I might not, but Shepherd likely would understand the reference.

"Oh, please call Shepherd that to his face," I muttered. He would eat her alive for that comparison. Louder, I added, "This is *my* bedroom."

A beat passed. If she had a gun, I had no doubt she would have pulled the trigger to fill the silence. "Fine!" she snapped. "I'll leave."

Shaking my head, I stepped into her path. "I'm afraid I can't allow that."

Penelope didn't stop. She advanced. Shoved me. I narrowed my gaze, but she didn't budge. "Move, lupo."

"Since you seem so confused by the situation, let me explain it, but listen closely because I'm not in the habit of repeating myself." I took a deep breath, fingers itching to grab her and close the remaining distance. From this proximity, her intoxicating scent swirled to my nose, it was floral with a hint of dark musk. "You're my wife. You'll sleep in my room. You'll wear my ring. And you won't talk to any other men."

"Oh, is that all?" she snapped, tugging the wedding band from her pinky. Arm flung wide, she tossed the ring across the room. It bounced and rolled away.

Not that it mattered. I planned to buy her a beautiful set sometime this week.

"For now," I smirked. "Follow these rules, and we'll have an amicable relationship."

Her chest rose and fell with hard breaths. If she was prone to crying, this would be the moment where the waterworks started. Those blank orbs might sparkle a little brighter, but she didn't shed a single tear.

"That's all I am to you, a possession." She threw her arms wide. "Fine, do your marital duty."

I jerked forward before I could stop myself. But I didn't touch. I was *not* that man. Unlike the demon who raised me, I didn't hit, didn't force myself on anyone, man or woman.

But how would Penelope know that? To her, I was the man my father tried to mold, and mostly succeeded.

"I said, we don't have to do anything tonight," I ground out.

"Why wait? You clearly want it." She pointed to the hard length in my pants.

I blew out a hard breath. "I'm not the villain you make me out to be, Penelope."

"You forced me into this match—"

I began to protest, but she continued to talk over me.

"You drug me to this city. You are forcing me to sleep in your room, so why the hell not take my body too? Huh? It's your husbandly right, isn't it?" When I didn't answer, she raised her voice. "Isn't it?!"

"Is sharing a room with me really that bad?" I demanded.

Penelope shrugged. "It's another layer of control ripped away from me."

Fucking hell, didn't this woman see that she had it a thousand times better than most females in the mob?

She didn't grow up one of us. She truly didn't know.

"So do your worst." Penelope backed up until her thighs hit the bed. She sat hard, but never broke eye contact. Pulled like a damn marionette, I moved until I stood over her. "I don't consent to this. You can force me, and I can't stop you, but I won't give it to you."

I let out a burst of pure anger. "I'm not that kind of devil!"

Penelope shrugged. "But you're not a saint."

Leaning over her made her wince. "I am not touching you, wife, until you fall to your knees and beg me for it. This I vow on my mother's grave."

Spinning on my heel, I stormed to the bathroom.

"I'm not the kind of girl who begs," she called after me, but the door to the en suite cut off her response.

The shower blasted cold water onto my crawling skin. Her words cut deeper than I would ever admit. There were real demons in the underworld. Hell, I'd known them. Suffered at their hands. Killed them.

Become one? No...I somehow escaped that horror.

But how was she to know that? I wrenched the soap over my body, viciously scouring the skin in a failed attempt to cleanse the feeling.

Cursing, I dropped my head against the shower wall. "What do I do now?"

I had a wife who had kissed me like she needed it to breathe. Yet the next moment, when I cleared the obstacles, she turned away.

There was an undeniable chemistry here! Was I a bastard if I wanted to pursue it? Was that so wrong? When I knew on some level she wanted it too?

Through the chaos, the answer dawned on me. I was the monster who tried to marry her baby cousin, only to substitute at the last second when an alternative became the only option. And she no doubt saw her own actions as saintly, salvific. *Righteous.* I groaned.

"She needs to get to know me." I banged my head into the tile.

Patience....

"I can do that." After all, it was how I built this empire. Penelope had no idea the force she was messing with. She could wait years, and eventually, she would have to admit there was something physical with us.

When I emerged, ready to apologize and explain that I would sleep in the guest room for tonight, I found my bride curled up—on the floor. That angered me. I would never ask a woman to sleep on that hard surface, and yet from the way she held herself rigid, I knew it would be more of a fight to demand she return to the bed.

Fine, play it your way. I took the thin sheet, flopped into the bed, and eventually lost myself to sleep. But only after I vowed to every saint listening that I would show her I was not the vile being she claimed me to be.

Chapter 18 – Alessandro

A knock on my door interrupted the tangle of thoughts. The emails were endless. Just when I thought I was seeing the bottom of the pile there were dozens more flying into my inbox.

"Come in," I barked.

When no one announced themselves after the door swung open, I looked up sharply and sucked in a tight breath. My wife stood in front of my desk, having ghosted on featherlight steps across the room. She was barefoot, toes painted a pretty purple shade. There were bandages on her heels and across a few toes. I frowned at that. Those were the only unsettling details about her. Those and the fact that she'd made no noise entering.

No one surprised me; no one snuck up on me either.

I leaned back and studied her. There was a nervous air swirling about her, but she was working very hard to keep it hidden.

Cute. So very cute.

"They said you wanted to see me first thing," she said by way of explanation.

Wet hair hung down her back instead of braided tight. It was a darker shade of brown that could have been black in the right light. Her face was freshly washed and bare. The clothes she wore were simple but completed the picture perfectly. *Mio Dio,* she was stunning.

"Thank you for these," she gestured to the plain black tee and jean shorts.

My gaze immediately swept down her toned, tanned legs. An ache pulsed in my groin, and I shifted in my seat. "You're welcome. Everything fit?"

She nodded. "The care package the maid dropped off was a good surprise. These clothes are perfect. I was half expecting to wear the bridesmaid dress until my luggage came."

They were perfect. Not the typical clothing of a Made Man's wife, but they suited this country girl, which was what I'd instructed the maid when I sent her shopping. I wanted Penelope to be comfortable.

"Yes, well, I don't expect your uncle to be sending that anytime soon."

Her eyes flashed. "Not even my backpack? I had my laptop and journals and...things in there!"

I held up a hand. "I've put in a request that it be packed up and sent immediately, but knowing him, he'll delay to spite us."

"I don't even have a charger." She lifted her phone and sighed. "I don't suppose you have one I could borrow?"

I peered at the device. "I'm not sure, but we can figure it out."

"Okay. Good." She shifted, letting out the smallest bit of nervous energy.

I glanced at my watch and let out a sharp whistle. "You're up early."

Penelope shrugged. "My internal clock is up with the sun."

Mine too. Hmm...something in common.

I cleared my throat. "This came for you."

I held out the black card. She took it and her brows nearly shot to her forehead. "It has my name on it."

"It's yours, why wouldn't it?" I hummed, keeping my amusement under wraps. Now was the moment of truth, to see how she reacted to the untold wealth at her fingertips. "It's already been activated, and there's no spending cap. If you'd like, you can take a driver and a guard to go shopping for whatever else you need."

Penelope nodded slowly, eyes still glued to the card. "I didn't realize credit cards could be so heavy."

My lip twitched despite the rigid control. So very cute. "One thing you will need to pick up, there will be several important dinners in the upcoming weeks. I need you to have some outfits prepared for those events. My assistant Luca can send you an itinerary if you need help preparing for them."

As I spoke, her eyes closed. Clenching her jaw tight enough for her molars to crack, she took a deep breath. Her nostrils flared and her chest heaved. When she opened them, the full weight of that hazel gaze fell on me, all traces of annoyance were wiped away.

The effect was unsettling.

"Of course, dear, whatever you need." She beamed at me, a completely different woman.

I would have preferred the wildcat with claws to this forced ball of bubbles and rainbows.

"And the charger," I added. "Don't forget your charger."

The flicker deep in her eyes told me she was mad. Good. She would spend a ton of money to get back at me. The fun was just beginning. Watching her burn my money was going to be the highlight of my day. It would be a game to distract me from the mountains of work that piled up while I was gone.

And it would give her something to do to distract her from this new life. Penelope was used to a life where she came and went as she pleased. Today she would learn that was no longer the case. Bodyguards were absolutely necessary, and they had orders only to take her to certain places.

She didn't comment on the restriction as she turned to go.

"Hold up." I rose from my chair and followed her to the door.

"Is this the part where you tell me what else I'm supposed to do with my day?" she sniped oh, so sweetly.

I shook my head. "This is the part where I kiss my wife good morning."

Penelope's shocked expression was priceless. I caught her in my arms before she could flee. My lips cut off her protest.

Her fists clenched against my chest, as I pulled that decadent body tightly against me and slowly tasted her. Dio, she was intoxicating. A man could get used to this every morning—every day. Every *night*. I pushed my tongue into her mouth, only to rear back in a burst of pain.

She bit me.

That beautiful smile shone up at me. "What? Something the matter?"

I gripped her jaw, fingers digging into the hollows of her cheeks to force her head backward at an unnatural angle. She breathed through the pressure, continuing with that insulting smile.

"Do that again, and I'll put you over my knee and spank that pretty little ass until it's too sore to sit," I warned, moving back for another taste.

"You wouldn't!"

"Try me," I dared.

My mouth crashed into her, stifling her outburst. She tasted of sin and triumph. I was hooked. My tongue slid between her lips, testing for a moment before plunging deep.

Her tongue swiped at mine—the only assault she dared.

Good, so good, vespina.

Penelope didn't melt into me as I'd hoped. She remained firm and defiant. So I kissed her—hard. Fucking her mouth. Showing her the lengths I was capable of going.

When I finally pulled away, there was a moment where she shivered. Her unfocused gaze fluttered.

I bit back a groan. Penelope pulled herself together, gave me a tight look, and left without saying anything.

A hiss escaped my mouth as I sank back into my chair. That woman—that feisty little woman.

"Shepherd," I clipped into the phone at my desk.

"Signore."

"Tomorrow, hold my breakfast until Signora Mancini awakens for hers," I instructed the butler.

"Very good, signore." The intercom disconnected.

I didn't want us missing meals together, and if my wife was an early riser, there was no reason to dine separately. I was going to wear my fiery hellcat of a bride down until she caved.

Early afternoon meant the neighborhood park was cleared of the crowds. I strolled down the path, taking random turns until I was sure that there was no tail. I ducked into an alley and rapped on the door. It swung open, the gamer dude giving me a clipped nod as I entered.

Stepping into the VR lounge, I sat on the stylized lime green ball that was supposed to be a seat. Minutes later, a suit walked through the doors.

"You look tired," I drawled.

Mier gave me a dry look. "And you aren't dead yet."

I pulled my ankle over the opposite knee and leaned back. The ergonomics of this chair were wanting, but the material formed in an oddly satisfying way to my backside. "Now what would be the fun in dying on you? There'd be no one else to help you keep the streets clean."

"You mobsters are a dime a dozen. I could negotiate with any number of the crime lords." Mier sat down hard, scrubbing his hands over his face.

"Seriously, let me send you some of my nonna's pastina. You could use an immune boost."

"Fuck off, Mancini."

Grumpier than usual today...something must have happened. "What's wrong?"

The suit pinned me with a dry look, which I knew from past experiences meant he was about to drop a bomb. "There's a new special agent in town. He's been assigned to my division, and he's on the warpath."

I hummed. "Nothing new. We've seen eager Feds come and go over the years, haven't we?"

"Not like this kid. He's just shy of thirty and highly decorated. Served in the Marines for a short tour of *active* duty. Graduated top of his class and has made waves over in the Big Apple."

"Then what the hell is he doing out here? Don't his sort go to be groomed for top brass in D.C.?" I stretched my neck.

"He *wanted* to be assigned here."

I sat up straighter. "Then there's a reason."

Mier clapped slowly. "You're a smart one, cookie."

"Ya know, if you're going to be the harbinger of doom, you could at least set these meetings for places that serve alcohol," I muttered.

"I don't drink."

Surprise flickered through me. After all this time working with him, I thought Mier was like every other suit, deep in the bottle and depressed as fuck. "You don't say."

"What do you have for me?" Mier coughed into the lapel of his suit. It was rough and barking. The Fed was sick as hell.

I swept my hand through the air. "None of the organizations will pull together to stop the influx of drugs into the city. The good news is that it's coming from one main source."

"The Toro Syndicate, damn roaches," Mier rasped, and then began to cough violently into his elbow.

I winced and moved back. "Seriously, let me send soup to your office—anonymously, of course!"

The suit's red-rimmed eyes pinned me with a dark look. "It's just a cold."

"And if you're feeling unwell, criminals can slip past your guard and take advantage of you." I slapped my thighs and stood. "Forgive me for not shaking your hand, officer."

Mier gave me the bird. "You haven't managed to pull one over on me yet, Mancini. Don't get cocky. I can still knock you over with a flick of my wrist."

I grinned. "Nah, you know we're good for each other's business."

"Wait up, do you have anything more?" Mier raised his hand but doubled over in another coughing fit.

I shook my head. "No. It's the same as it was at Christmastime. The Vlasovs will help us if there's a direct mission on the streets against the drug runners. Flannigan won't speak to us, but he's managed so far to keep the rabble out of his turf. The other Chicago Famiglias would rather I die, and the smaller players are shaking in their boots."

"So while they care about keeping drugs off the streets, they won't unite to do so," Mier said, voicing the disgust I felt.

"Exactly."

"And your trip to Detroit? How was Caravello?"

Merda.... "Should have known you'd figure that out."

The suit smirked, but it was pained. He opened his mouth to speak but ended up coughing instead.

"Seriously, man. Go. Rest."

"I'm fine," the Fed croaked.

I shook my head. "Caravello's daughter skipped town. She's holed up out west somewhere."

"Will her father send resources to collect her?"

My phone buzzed. I pulled it from my pocket. A possessive flicker of satisfaction slithered through me. It was a notification for the bank attached to my charge card. But as I opened the app, the dark glee turned into confusion.

My wife spent a grand sum of forty-five dollars—at a Walmart.

"What's got you seeing thunderstorms, mobster?" Mier broke through the perplexing situation.

I clicked off the phone, putting it away for later. "I don't know what Caravello is doing. The girl supposedly has blackmail on him, and she's united with the local sheriff."

Mier wheezed. "A sheriff? Are you shitting me?"

I nodded, amused by his incredulity. "Yep. Big gold star and everything."

"What the fuck did she think a sheriff could do against an organization like the Caravello Famiglia?" His outburst triggered another coughing fit.

Madonna! I was going to need to bathe in sanitizer after being confined in close quarters with this oozing mess. "Don't know. Don't care. I wish the girl well, and hope her father isn't too hard on her when he does bring her back home."

"You think he will?"

"She's leverage." I shrugged. "He won't let that go easily."

"And you're extremely calm for having been jilted. You must have gotten something out of this to be willing to let the girl go?" The thing I admired most about this suit was the way he struck when he had a good hand to play.

"I might have," I answered carefully.

"According to a Detroit informant, felicitations are in order."

"They are."

"I'll send you a card. Shall I put Mrs. Mancini or use her first name?" Mier smirked.

I stepped close, nose to nose with the Fed. "My wife is off limits, Mier. Understood?"

He only smirked harder. "You like her."

"Remember how I told you my sister was off limits? That same threat applies to Penelope. Or do you need a reminder of what I'm capable of?" I hissed. Fun and games with the law were over.

A couple of moments ticked by where we just stood there, a couple of enraged beasts staring off.

Until Mier broke out in a coughing fit.

I stumbled back in disgust, wiping spittle off my face.

"I'll leave her alone," Mier wheezed. "But the new guy? Agent Frankie Tribiano. That's the guy you need to watch out for. Keep your business tight and above board, Mancini. This kid isn't fucking around."

"Soup. Rest. Go!" I ordered with a stern finger.

Mier batted me away, staggering through the door and coughing the entire time.

Gross.... Just fucking gross.

I stopped in the bathroom to scrub my hands in scalding water. I would have a dossier about Tribiano on my desk by nightfall, and I would probably want to call my business partner. If Baldwin thought my marrying the niece was the worst thing that could have happened, he was going to have a field day about the new Special Agent in the Organized Crime Division.

Once more, I checked my phone, but there were no new credit card charges. I left the bathroom, shaking my head. I resisted the urge to text the driver for five whole minutes. When I couldn't stand it any longer, I tapped out a short message. The guard driving my wife responded instantly. No, they'd only gone to Walmart and then straight home.

"What the hell is your game, little wasp?" I muttered, cutting back through the streets and disappearing into the suburbs of West Chicago.

Chapter 19 – Penelope

His low voice broke the stillness of the breakfast room. "You made me look bad, Penelope."

I jumped in my seat, the cappuccino splashing out of the quaint cup that was more teacup than coffee mug. Moving too fast, I winced and grabbed for my neck. Most of my muscles were sore, and my back was stiff as an iron bar. My neck wouldn't survive many more nights on the floor, but I would be damned if I crawled into the bed with the don.

"What are you doing here?" I snapped, turning slower this time to glare at the looming figure leaning against the doorframe.

Alessandro studied me behind the cold mask of indifference. His walls were tight this morning; there was no seeing the beast that lurked behind the curtain. "Isn't it obvious? Having breakfast with my beautiful wife."

He advanced, pausing beside my chair to bend down over me. Too busy glaring at him, I didn't move away. And the bastard stole a kiss.

I fisted my hands, refusing to reach for him.

The hunger behind the caress was contained, but it was there. He lingered for a moment, unfazed by my lack of participation.

When he broke the kiss, he smiled serenely down at me, looking every bit the feral wolf playing with its prey. "I'm not in the habit of sitting down for the morning meal, but having you here makes it worth it, Penelope."

"It's Penny—or Pen. No one calls me Penelope." *Why?!* Why was that the hill I chose to die on?

A rich hum vibrated in his chest. "No, I prefer your full name. It's regal, befitting a queen." He sat smoothly in his chair beside me, and a maid appeared with another tray. "Which brings me back to my original statement: You made me look bad yesterday."

I flagged down the maid and kindly repeated my original order. "I would like a cup of coffee. Not espresso, not...this. Good old-fashioned Folgers, or whatever you have. In a Mr. Coffee maker. A big mug, please."

The woman's eyes widened, and she looked rapidly between Alessandro and me. "Ma'am, I'm so sorry. We don't have that kind here. If the cappuccino isn't to your liking, we can make a macchiato or an Americano?"

English. *English!* We drank cowboy brew back home. So black it would put hair on your back, and my dad swore he could stick a pencil in it. Remembering him joking about it with my mom sent a wave of emotion through me. I wanted to sob in frustration. It had been the same in Detroit. No one in my uncle's house knew how to make a good old cup of joe.

I'm homesick.

"It's fine," I breathed, reaching out to pat her hand. "I'll be fine with this. If you don't have normal coffee, I'll learn to love this."

"Ma'am—"

"I said it's fine." I shooed her away. Later, I would explore the kitchen. It was hard to believe that in a house this grand, with this many employees, there wasn't a coffee pot or maybe a percolator like we used on the campfire. One way or another, I was going to have my fix.

"You don't enjoy the European style of morning beverages?" Alessandro drawled.

I took a deep breath. This man was overbearing and insufferable. If only I could have my cup of coffee, I could deal with his nonsense.

"And how, pray tell, did I fail to uphold your image?" I snapped. "I did exactly as you requested. I took the driver—which was unnecessary. And I was followed through the store by a second guard. Again, he was completely unnecessary! But because my husband required it, I did it. So please, explain to me exactly how I messed up? Or is this how our marriage is going to work? I'm criticized for every little thing? Hmm? Are you a nitpicker, Mr. Mancini?"

A second passed.

And then the great, stony ice beast bent over. Riotous laughter boomed from his chest. It rolled through the room, filling it like the staccato of thunder. He laughed and laughed until he gasped for breath.

I threw my napkin on the table, shot to my feet, and moved toward the door—only to have him catch my wrist and tug me back. I fell onto his lap.

"Turn me loose," I snarled, writhing and bucking.

"Calm down," he gasped before another burst of laughter cut off his words.

I tried to pummel him with my fists, but he only succeeded in capturing those as well.

"Penelope, calm the hell down," he rasped. "I'm sorry, you just looked so cute sitting there and biting my head off."

"Glad I could be your court jester, my liege." I jerked hard to the left. "Now, let me go!"

Still breathing hard, he cupped my cheek while still holding me captive. "Penelope." His touch brushed back, pushing the wisps of hair back into the long braid. "How did I end up so lucky?" he murmured in Italian. "Such a beautiful wasp to be my queen? No one stands up to me. But my brave little wife does. Oh, how I enjoy having you around." The soothing tones rumbled through me as his fingers drew down over my shoulder and along the length of my arm.

"What the hell are you saying to me?" I demanded, but the words lacked the punch I would have loved to give them. "I don't like when you speak *at me,* and I can't understand."

Later, I would have to have a long think about if and when I ever wanted to reveal I spoke his native tongue. It would be all too easy to be caught, but feigning ignorance would also give me a chance to eavesdrop. So I wouldn't make the decision either way just yet.

"I said, I need you to spend more money, wife," the don lied. Reaching up, he traced my cheek with the back of his knuckles.

I blanched. That was not the thing I expected him to be controlling about.

He must have guessed the thoughts behind my surprise. His mouth quirked up. "I am a very wealthy man, Penelope. It makes me look bad if you don't spend the money. Like I'm not providing for you."

"But I bought everything I need," I protested before thinking the response through.

He shrugged. "What did you buy yesterday from the...superstore?"

Holding up my fingers to tick off the items, I rattled the list off. "The mascara brand I like. Deodorant and flipflops. A cell charger, a notebook, and a dress for whatever godforsaken event you're dragging me to."

The mob boss gave me a pained look. "A dress? From Walmart?"

I shrugged. "It's pretty and it will go with the shoes from the bridesmaid dress."

The big, bad don scrubbed a hand over his face. "Beautiful, fiery, and frugal," he muttered in Italian, voice full of disbelief. In English, he added, "That's not going to work, darling."

I bristled and tugged away. He held me tight.

"The kinds of places I'm taking you, they can scent a designer label, and they won't look kindly on you for being economical. Plus—" he grabbed my heel and crooked my knee "—you aren't wearing those shoes again."

His touch as he stroked the bandages was impossibly gentle.

This side of him, the caring, concerned husband, I didn't like it. I needed to hate him, to remember how much I wanted out of this nightmarish situation. Promising me untold wealth was something I could feel insulted about and resist. But the gentler side, the side that was bothered by the blisters cutting my feet open, it would get to me.

Hell, I had to look away! My chest was pattering too rapidly. The way he stared at me battled through my defenses.

I'm his trophy. He's only doing this to bolster his image.

Those truths grounded me.

"Fine," I said through clenched teeth. "You need me to buy something expensive? Just to prove you have money to spend? I can do that."

"I know you can, vespina." He chucked my chin and set me down.

Careful not to seem like I was running from his touch, I walked slowly to my seat, folded back into the chair, and picked at the omelet. "Do you have a preference where I go? Which store says your ego and cheque book are bigger than any other mobster?"

"Not really." He stabbed at his own plate of scrambled eggs. It was hard to tell if that was a twitch of humor playing on his lips or not.

"Oh, come now, you look down your nose at the places I shop at." I gave him the sweetest, saccharine smile. "You must have specific instructions where a wife befitting *your* status should shop?"

He cut a side look toward me. "You don't know where to go, do you?"

I shoved a forkful of food in my mouth to keep from answering.

Which only made the bastard chuckle. "The driver will take you to the stores."

"I can go by myself," I grumbled.

"Not an option."

I rolled my eyes. "Don't your soldiers have better things to do than babysit me?"

His tone warned me to drop the issue. "No, they don't."

I made short work of my food, done with the rapid back and forth. My husband was insufferable. I was done with his nonsense. After shoveling the breakfast into my mouth, I took my plate and sprinted to the kitchen…where the poor maid nearly had a heart attack because I cleared my own dishes. When I started washing them in the sink, she nearly fainted. But I was too damn mad to stop.

What she didn't know was that we were cut from a similar cloth. One that I needed the familiarity of right this second. The hot water and soap grounded me. Calmed me down. Let me *breathe*.

Alessandro thought he could order me around? That he could sleep in the same bed as me? Invade my breakfast? Fine! Two could play at that game.

It was time to get even.

Nico pulled the car in front of an expensive-looking store. The whole street glittered. The shop windows were large, the displays decadent. Some of the names were recognizable. Others I'd never heard of, but if they were neighboring buildings, I assumed they were just as swanky.

My guard, Giulio, opened the door, and I swallowed hard before stepping out of the vehicle.

He repeated the bargain we'd made yesterday. "I'll stay back, as you requested, signora."

It wasn't that I minded having the muscle shadow my footsteps, but before we had a little chat, he'd practically been breathing down my neck. That wasn't going to work. Ever. My dad didn't raise a girl who needed to be protected, but rather one that others needed protection from as I'd proved on several occasions.

However, I wasn't naïve enough to compare the criminal underworld of Chicago with the late nights at the bar. And if I was being honest, there were times I hadn't been able to take care of myself. Like when the drunk farmers tried to touch me in a pole barn as my body was covered in cheap glitter that won me their hard-earned cash. If it hadn't been for the bouncers....

No, I wasn't thinking about those times.

"Thanks, I appreciate it," I smiled and pushed into the first store, patting my pocket to assure myself the card was there.

"Miss, can I help you?" A salesperson hurried over. She wasn't smiling, and my own friendly grin faltered. Her gaze swept over me, and when she stopped in front of me, a grimace scrunched her manicured face. "Are you lost, miss?"

"No, I'm here to shop." I spread my arms.

She gave me a pained look. "Honey, this is ARKLI. I can safely assure you, even our travel size toiletries are out of your budget."

A disbelieving laugh exhaled from my chest. "Of all the presuming things...." I shook my head. "Do you turn all your customers away like this?"

"Miss, please, let's not make a scene," she said quietly. "You can't come in here without an appointment. And our clientele doesn't wear Daisy Dukes."

I planted my hands on my hips. "I have an obscene amount of money to spend. And you're telling me you don't want it?"

"If you don't have an appointment, you're out of luck," she said, her voice holding a slight sneer. "I don't care how much your John gave you."

I fisted my hands at my side. Giulio lingered by the door, and I was tempted to call him over.

"Imogen! Do you have the clutch in the dusky rose or not?" a familiar voice called from farther in the shop.

Looking around the nasty salesperson, I watched Serena appear, looking at an ugly little bag in mint.

"Oh! Look what crawled in here," my sister-in-law minced.

"Do you know her?" The salesperson's voice faltered.

Serena nodded. "Unfortunately. She's my brother's new wife."

"Oh, well, maybe we can make an exception." A second salesperson, who'd heard the whole exchange came over and nudged the first's arm. "She's a Mancini."

"Nooo." Serena laughed. "She's *not* a Mancini."

"Is there a problem?" Giulio called out.

But I moved into the first salesperson's space. I was perfectly capable of fighting my own battles. "I have a credit card that says otherwise. It doesn't have a spending limit either. But you know what? I don't care to spend my husband's money in a place with such rude staff."

"We really do have a policy about appointments, but let me see if I can fit you in my schedule," the second clerk insisted.

While I wanted to take pity on the man, and was sure he'd be much nicer, I was done here.

"Thanks, but I'm taking my business elsewhere." I cut a look to Serena. "Have a great day, *sis*."

With that, I spun around and marched out of the shop. My flipflops slapped against the floor.

"Penelope! Wait," Serena called out.

An equally burly looking man stepped beside Giulio, no doubt her beefy shadow.

"Your card doesn't have a limit?" she sniped.

I shrugged. "That's what your brother said."

"Unbelievable!" Serena threw up her hands.

"Yeah, well, I don't get it either." I waved my fingers for Giulio. "Again, have a great day."

Hurrying away, I could feel her daggers being hurled at my back. Which was sad because I wanted to like my sister-in-law. One friendly face in that huge house would be nice. The maids wouldn't talk to me, not like a person. I understood. Hell, no one talked to me like a human when I was in their orthotic shoes just a few weeks ago. But unlike the guests at the local Holiday Inn, I was trying to be friendly. With time, I might wear them down.

I sighed.

"Where now, Giulio?" I asked, once we were a few shops away from the horrid place.

"I hear that Dior is a popular place amongst the wives of Made Men," he said with a grin.

I followed where his finger pointed, bracing myself for another scene. But I was distracted from the strangely dressed window mannequin by a yellow cab. The streets were busy, but something prickled my neck. I focused on the cab...and gasped softly.

The driver was looking fixedly at me.

I held his gaze, and when he didn't look away, my skin began to crawl.

Temptation to point him out to the bodyguard was strong. But I didn't know what this mobster was capable of. He no doubt had orders, and I wasn't in the mood to see a fight on the ritzy street.

"Alright, well, here goes nothing," I said, tearing my gaze away from the cab-driver.

"Right behind you, signora." Giulio held open the door.

Bolstered by his confidence, I marched into the luxury store.

Chapter 20 – Penelope

Shouting filled the foyer, ascending to perfume the vaulted ceiling. I faltered in the middle of kicking off my flipflops by the front door.

Giulio chuckled, tossing a quiet observation to Nico, who was also carrying armfuls of bags, in Italian. While it was funny, it was also concerning that he called the boss's sister a holy terror.

Curious, I padded barefoot to the door of the sitting room. Serena was in a rage. She screamed at her brother, who stood by the window with a whiskey.

The mighty don looked...tired.

I frowned and rubbed my chest. I did not feel bad for him. If he was exhausted, it was his own damn fault. He hadn't come to bed at a reasonable hour, only to wake at the crack of dawn and interrupt my breakfast.

"She comes from nowhere and you let her have free reign of your wealth!" Serena spewed.

Mancini set his glass down. He loomed over his sister. "Stop it. This isn't you, sorellina!"

"Maybe it is!" she seethed.

"You've been a damn shrew since you came back from Europe. I'm about to lock you in this house." He swiped a hand over his face. "I need you to leave Penelope alone. You don't insult her."

"She didn't." The outburst came out before I could stop it. I closed my eyes and took a breath.

"See! She's eavesdropping!" Serena shouted.

Walking into the room with my chin held high, I said slowly, "Hard to eavesdrop when you've got the volume loud enough the neighbors can hear."

I braced my hands on the back of the fancy, uncomfortable couch. The carved wood was smooth under my fingers.

"How was shopping, Penelope?" the don asked pleasantly.

Sharing a look with my sister-in-law, I said simply, "Lots of fun. I did exactly as you asked and spent your money. What the hell I'm going to do with all those fancy clothes, I don't know. Seems to me there's more there than I can wear in a lifetime. *Bbuuttt....*" I paused to pin him with a look. "No one will question your status based on my clothing, Your Highness."

The don smirked and went to refill his drink. "How many bags?"

"Too many," I countered.

Serena scoffed. "Hardly. Nico said you barely bought anything."

"Spying on me?" I demanded.

She smiled. "Didn't want to run into you again. You still managed to ruin my morning."

What the hell was this woman's problem? She was determined to hate me. We didn't even know each other!

"How much did you spend, wife?" Mancini approached from the bar cart with a filled glass, stopping in front of me.

I gulped. Here was the moment of truth. What would he do when he found out the outrageous sum I burned? It was ridiculous. Hundreds of dollars for underwear. A thousand for a purse and one pair of pants. And the fancy dress? More than a yearling at auction.

"The total was just over five grand," I murmured, suddenly feeling very guilty about the shopping trip.

As he passed, the don reached out and tugged gently on my braid. The gesture was hidden by his body, and the action so unexpected, I froze. His words came out soft, for my ears only. "So, you do know how to listen. Good girl."

I felt those words warm through me. Tightness, delicious and sensual, formed deep in my core.

And I hated the traitorous reaction.

Something flashed in those inky black depths. It was as if the monster *knew* what his words did to me.

"Now do it again," he murmured.

"You're freaking joking!" I exploded and took a step back. "I don't need all these things, Alessandro. Expensive shit that I have no plans to use. Five grand—*five* thousand dollars! It's insanity."

"Little wife, I have more where it comes from. And I need you not only to be comfortable, looked after, and have everything else you require, but I need every other man who sees you to know I can take care of you." He brushed a knuckle across my jaw, setting off the butterflies in my belly.

I loathed my reaction to his proximity.

As he left the room, he turned and looked at his sister. "You could learn something from each other."

Serena let out a mocking laugh. "Yeah right."

"If you thought about money like she did, I wouldn't put a cap on your cards." To me, he added, "Learn to shop like she does."

"Well, that makes no sense," I stated, but the door was already closed behind the don.

"On that, I can agree with you," Serena scoffed.

For a moment, only the briefest of seconds, there was a comradery with my sister-in-law.

But her sour expression returned, and she sailed through the far doors muttering about pigs and lipstick.

I sighed. My plan to piss off my husband failed spectacularly. Granted, there were a few pretty things I found, and I was going to enjoy the Mr. Coffee Maker. Knowing that there was coffee just waiting for me to brew, I hurried to find the pot, filters, and grounds.

From an expensive boutique, I had an assortment of beauty products. These were brands I'd never heard of but instantly loved. There were no cheap filler ingredients, which made all the difference. I poured the salts and oils into the steaming tub, eager to experience what had to be the most costly bath I'd ever taken.

One foot in, and I sighed.

This was luxury—and I was in danger.

Serena could have the pretty clothes and funky, impractical purses. I was going to spend the don's money on this stuff.

Leaning back in the tub, I let my mind clear. The sweet floral scents melded with the bright citrus notes. The heat made my skin tingle. Bliss and contentment filled my soul.

A heavy knuckle rapped on the door.

Ripped from the haze, I groaned. "Go away."

The door jiggled.

"It's locked...stronzo." I added the insult under my breath.

Silence pulsed.

The sound of nothing buzzed in my ears. Relaxation effectively ruined, I debated leaving the tub. Most of the bubbles were popped and the water was tepid. This was the point where I would have refilled the water, added more soap, but right now, I wanted to rinse off and find my book to read.

The soft clicking at the door sent my heart jumping to my throat.

He wouldn't dare.

He did.

"Shit on a shingle!" I yelped. "You can pick a lock!"

The door swung open. "That I can."

I fumed silently, pulling my arms over my chest as the don filled the doorway.

Amusement glinted in his eyes. "I was raised in the mob and educated in the streets, vespina. Opening locked doors was a lesson I mastered as a child."

I rolled my eyes. "Your mother must be so proud."

Something passed through his face, but it was gone before I was able to read it.

The don stepped forward, owning the large bathroom with his presence and making it feel suddenly small. "I came to tell you I'll be gone for the night." Any amusement at having bested me was gone from his face.

I sighed. "Thanks for the news update, but you could have just said so."

Mancini kept walking. I fought the urge to squirm in the water. At the side of the tub, he bent and braced his hands on the side.

"But then I couldn't kiss you," he growled.

My protest was cut off by the hard press of his mouth.

His lips were demanding, insistent, stealing my breath and scattering my thoughts. I shouldn't have responded, shouldn't have arched up from the water to press closer, but my body betrayed me like it always did with him. For a dangerous moment, I melted into the kiss, my wet hand rising to clutch at his expensive shirt collar before I caught myself and pushed against his chest.

"You're getting your suit wet," I managed, pulling back just enough to see his eyes darken.

"I don't care," Mancini murmured, his voice a low rumble that sent an involuntary shiver down my spine despite the warm water. His thumb traced my jawline, leaving droplets of bathwater on my skin.

The man of iron control didn't care that he lost it. Again. I would have smiled if I wasn't furious.

"That wasn't fair," I whispered. "You trapped me."

The corner of his mouth lifted in a half-smile that didn't reach his eyes. "Nothing in this life is fair, vespina."

Touché. I shifted in the water.

This man was dangerous—not just because of who he was or what he did, but because of how he made me feel. Confused. Reckless. Alive.

"Where are you going tonight?" I asked instead, deflated by how easily his touch manipulated me.

I watched him straighten, adjusting his cuffs with meticulous precision. Something was off. The tension in his shoulders, the tightness around his eyes—this wasn't just business as usual.

"Work."

"One word answer. Fine, don't tell me." I glowered at him.

His lack of trust made sense, but it was still frustrating. I was an outsider. We had no common ground on which to form any kind of real relationship. But at least I was trying.

"There are thugs pushing drugs in my streets," the don explained, surprising me with his openness. "This is the kind of problem I like to deal with personally."

"Oh," I breathed. "Oh, well, good luck."

He let out a short laugh through his nose. "Thanks. I'll need it."

As he retreated, I pulled myself to the edge of the tub. "Is it...dangerous?"

The suddenness of the feelings inside confused and bothered me. But I didn't want him hurt. Not only because it left me in a tricky situation, but because...I didn't want him hurt.

"Concerned for me?" He shot a look over his shoulder.

I shrugged. "I just don't care for widow's black."

"Well, for your sake I'll be extra careful," he said and left.

I rested my chin on the edge of the tub, closed my eyes, and whispered a prayer. No, I didn't want him hurt. The reality of his work was too real. He might have learned obnoxious tricks on the streets, and my sacred bath time was clearly no longer my own if he wished to invade it. But the other facet of the job was that he was in constant danger.

"Please be safe," I whispered into the stillness of the room. "Or I'll kill you myself, lupo."

Shaking the eerie feeling away, I roused myself and left the uninviting water. It was going to be a long night.

Chapter 21 – Penelope

As a rule of thumb, I hated running. It didn't matter that I was good at it, that I'd been top of the cross-country team in high school. The jolting rhythm of a jog, the way my lungs heaved for air, the strain on the small joints and tendons, were bad enough when I was in shape and used to the physical strain. But it had been well over a year since I last put on my athletic shoes and ran up and down County Road 40.

I didn't need to worry. Mancini came home this morning and joined me for breakfast as if he hadn't been out all night cleaning up his territory. Annoyed at the turbulent feelings, I knew I needed something more than a bath to calm down. I waited as long as possible, but exercise was the only solution to temper the feelings in my chest.

Tying the blue laces, I began to bounce up and down, warming the muscles. I would stretch at the end of the driveway and pound my emotions into the asphalt. The dopamine rush of a workout was just the thing to clear my head. That was why I'd purchased the fancy shoes and stretchy clothes the other day. I knew I would need an excuse to leave the mansion, if only for a little while.

The afternoon sunlight trickled through the high windows of the vaulted ceiling to paint the stairs in a kaleidoscope of shadows and bright hues. I pushed outside without meeting a soul. Shaking off the haunted feeling of the silent, stoic mansion, I let out a burst of speed as I sprinted to the front gate.

The iron bars didn't budge.

Breathing hard, I frowned at the behemoth. There wasn't a latch or knob. It was as though the stately display was to keep us in, more than keep anyone out.

"Screw that," I panted.

Grabbing the vertical bars, I shimmied up the gate, carefully avoided the ornate spikes, and vaulted to the pavement. A broad grin spread across my face as I selected a high beat playlist, stretched my legs, and then began to jog.

The running app would create a map, so there was no fear of being lost. The afternoon sun hung lazily in the sky, bathing the quiet street in golden light. There were no shadows on this side of the street. The eerie vibes from sitting around alone wore off the farther I ran. The warmth pressed against my skin, coaxing out a light sheen of sweat as my feet pounded against the pavement. My breath came deep and even at first, filling my lungs with air tinged with the scent of fresh-cut grass and the faint sweetness of blooming flowers.

The neighborhood was still, save for the occasional rustling of trees in the soft breeze and the distant hum of a lawnmower. These houses were set back on the properties just like the don's, but I doubted they were mausoleums. Most rich people were normal, with noisy families and bustling homes—or so I imagined. At least out here, I wasn't alone. Birds chattered in the branches overhead, their songs blending with the rhythmic slap of my sneakers against the ground. I was tempted to turn the earbud off so I could enjoy their company, but the music helped keep my pace even.

As I pushed forward, the burn in my legs deepened, but I welcomed it. Each step, each breath, each bead of sweat rolling down my temple felt like proof of something—strength, endurance, determination. The air was thick with the feeling of life. My pulse thrummed in my ears, my heartbeat matching the pounding of my feet.

Out here, I didn't feel like a prisoner.

Not that Mancini mistreated me. Other than breakfast, I rarely saw him. But I felt like a captive nonetheless.

I need something to do with my time.

That became obvious the day after my shopping trip. Reading books and drinking coffee always seemed like a dream scenario. And it was...at first. What I soon came to realize was that I was used to activity. While being a maid was a job, I missed the demands of work.

If I could find a balance, find something that gave me purpose, something I loved....

Being married to a wealthy, powerful man opened a door a girl like me never thought was possible.

Granted, my uncle strung my fantasy along, telling me there was a way to make something of myself. But I didn't want to lose that.

The more I ran, the more I felt it—the rush, the clarity, the sheer aliveness of movement. I felt like I was running toward some great revelation. My worries slipped away, lost in the rhythm of my body propelling forward. The endorphins coursed through me, lighting up my veins with a quiet euphoria. This was why I ran—not just for the exercise, not just for the sweat, but for this feeling. The feeling of being unshackled, of freedom, of pushing forward and knowing, for this moment, nothing else mattered.

The roar of an engine broke the serene neighborhood.

The matte black bike tore down the street, but instead of passing me, it hopped over the grass and onto the sidewalk. My heart shot to my throat, and I stumbled to move aside.

The crotch rocket stopped short, not intending to hit me.

I darted around it, ready to flee for my life.

"Signora! Stop," a muffled voice shouted.

Yeah, fuck that! I tore away, ready to climb another gate and pray the neighbors were home and would shelter me from the danger.

"Penelope! I said stop," the voice menaced. The man slapped his visor up, and the death eater pinned me with a glare as I stopped hard.

Slapping my hand on my chest, I let out short, staggered gasps. "Dante! What the hell? You scared the shit out of me."

"You can't be out here," he growled.

I gave him a skeptical look. "What? What are you talking about?"

"Get on my bike and let me take you back to the house."

Who the hell did he think he was, ordering me around like that? I tipped my chin up. "That's not happening."

I dug my heels in, ready to take off and sprint away. I was under no illusion that I could outrun a motorbike, but I wasn't going to comply with his demands.

Dante cursed violently in Italian, increasing my vocabulary with the colorful expletives.

Pulling up my phone, I tapped on the running app. "You're slowing down my average," I grumbled.

"You can't be out here," the mobster snapped.

"I'm in a cozy neighborhood and going for a run," I explained carefully as though he were dense. "I'm not doing anything wrong."

"Did you ask your husband?" he sneered.

My lips pressed tight. We both knew the answer to that.

"Didn't think so." Dante shifted. "Hop on or I'll drag you over my lap."

One brow shot to my forehead. "I doubt your boss will like that."

"Listen, lady, I was the closest soldier to the manor. So it was my job to collect you. Boss won't care so long as you're brought back safely."

I was done with this. With a burst of speed, I took off. A fire ignited in my veins, and my legs ate up the distance. When the bike roared to life, I began to use evasive maneuvers to avoid easily being caught.

It worked for the next few feet.

Dante dashed by, plucking me off the ground. I struggled, but his grip was firm. He tugged me against his chest, leaned to the side, and took off in the direction of the mansion.

I debated launching from his arms.

At the gate of Mancini's house, I jerked hard. The roll and tuck came naturally, just as if it were a horse. Standing up, I brushed the dirt and grass from my body. The wide-eyed expression on Dante's face was priceless.

"Touch me again, and I'll castrate you," I hissed.

The soldier opened his mouth, but a dark voice thundered from the road. Mancini stepped from the town car, face a dangerous mask of wrath.

I shivered, unable to hide the natural reaction.

"Sir, I was collecting her, just as you ordered." Dante's voice held a respectful tone, despite the anger in his words.

Mancini glared daggers at his second. "She could have been hurt."

"She launched from the bike!" Dante protested. "I wasn't holding her tight, because I know how damn possessive you are. You told us not to touch her, and I didn't want to be shot."

"You're lucky you're my favorite," Mancini growled.

Dante narrowed his eyes but kept silent.

Since their conversation had been in Italian, I chose my next words carefully. "Care to explain why you sent your dog after me?"

That black gaze turned on me. "You ran."

I gestured to my attire. "It's called exercise, Mancini."

His voice hardened. "You're not allowed out of the house without a guard."

That was the last straw. "So I am your prisoner!"

A muscle in his jaw ticked. "It's for your protection."

I held up a hand. "No, don't play with words, lupo. I'm your prized little wife, and you can't stand the thought of me running away. Glad we finally have that straightened the fuck out."

Turning on my heel, I marched through the open gate.

Heavy footfall marched behind me. I knew the don was right there, following, but I still tensed when his fingers gripped my wrist. All the struggling in the world didn't stop him as he drug me behind a copse of oak trees.

Mancini pushed me against a trunk and caged me with his body. "You don't get it!"

"Oh, I get it!" I yelled back in his face.

His chest rose and fell as he tried and failed to reign in his emotions. "I have enemies, Penelope. People who will hurt you—badly, very badly—just to strike me."

"So the solution is to keep me behind iron gates, got it." I pushed against his hold, spewing venom back in his face.

"Cristo, woman!" Mancini swiped a hand over his face before pummeling his fist in the trunk above my head. Flecks of bark sprinkled down on me. "Why are you fighting me? I'm doing this for you!"

"No, you're doing it for you." I tugged away.

It was useless.

"Let. Me. Go." It was his only warning. When he didn't comply, I struck. My knee landed with a satisfying thunk into his groin.

The mob boss doubled over with a grunt of pain.

Instead of fleeing in the burst of victory, I gripped his shoulders and tried once more to make my position crystal clear. "I will never stop fighting you on this. I need my freedoms. No bars, no shackles. I won't fight the marriage, but I will fight you on this, Mancini. It was just exercise. I'm not running away."

The beast snarled through clenched teeth, "Take the guards, and we won't have an issue."

Was that really such a terrible request? I paused. What if Dante had been a threat? I wouldn't have been able to outrun him. Maybe having Nico and Giulio wouldn't be the worst thing in the world.

But I wasn't caving to this man easily.

"We need ground rules," I demanded.

Those black eyes glared at me. After a moment filled with his heavy, pained breathing, the don nodded.

"I won't be cooped up here," I began.

"You're not."

I snorted. "I was just abducted by your henchman while I was destressing."

"And he'll be punished for touching you," Mancini snapped.

I reared back. "Don't you dare!"

But a deadly mask of cruelty was there in the boss's face. "He broke my rules and touched what's mine."

"On your orders!" This was unbelievable.

It shouldn't have been. The don was a psycho. A twisted, warped monster.

Mancini straightened, crossed his arms over his chest, and glared down at me. "Not only did he break the rules, but he didn't protect you."

"When I jumped from his bike?" I let out a bark of disbelief. "You know what, fine. He's your man, do what you want with him. But Mancini?"

A black brow quirked. "Yes?"

"That just proves you're incapable of basic humanity," I spewed. "So next time I fight your tyrannical authority, remember that is why."

I slipped away, taking off for the house at a run. Tears blurred the mansion, but I didn't let them fall. Swiping my hands against my eyes, I tore into the house. When I realized I hadn't been followed, I grabbed a change of clothes and took off for one of the guest bathrooms. It was the only other unoccupied room that had a huge soaking tub.

I hid there, trying to drown my emotions until my skin was raw and red from the hot water. But I didn't need to hide. The don never came looking for me.

Chapter 22 – Penelope

The three maids scurried from the kitchen as I entered. Their quiet movements made this mausoleum feel haunted. I knew they were there, that they cooked and cleaned, but the fact that they didn't speak to me or even stay in the same space long enough to wave was truly disheartening.

I rubbed my opposite arm, shaking off the eerie feelings left in their wake. What would they say if I started cleaning toilets next to them? Would they respect me for my former employment?

Setting my new, leatherbound journal on the counter, I reached for the filters and grounds. I needed to figure out my next moves, and fast! As the pot coughed and spluttered, I opened my journal. Thoughts from last night stared back at me.

What do I want?

My fingers drummed against the countertop. This pampered life had its perks. My skin hadn't felt dish soap or cleaner in weeks. The backs of my hands were no longer red and chapped. But if I went any longer without working, the callouses would fade.

"I won't turn into a spoilt princess," I reaffirmed.

That declaration was underlined, but I scribbled an arrow next to it once again.

The truth was, I could fill my days however I wanted. I was Mrs. Mancini. The name had started to hold potential instead of dread. There was opportunity to do something good, something worthwhile, with my time.

One idea continued to draw my attention. When my kid sister wanted to be a nurse, she crammed classes and worked long hours at the hospital. I helped her pay for school so she could focus on gaining experience. Now she was an RN in Bismarck and made a reliable income. I was delighted she had the chance to pursue her dreams, and I would do it again! Work those long hours and help her achieve her goal.

What if this was my turn?

Mancini had money. There were no responsibilities clouding my day.

But....

"What do I want to be when I grow up?" I laughed as I wrote those same words at the top of a new page.

It might seem silly, but now that I was faced with endless possibilities, none jumped up and down for my consideration. The present was all about me, and while the future was unknown, I could seize the day. Pouring the beautiful medium brown liquid into a clear drinking glass, because it was the only thing big enough to sate my caffeine addiction, I stopped by the fridge for a splash of milk.

A tut of disgust sounded behind me.

"Good morning, Shepherd," I sang out, putting the milk back and scooping up the loaf of bread.

"Ma'am, may I assist you?" the petrified piece of wood asked.

"No, I'm just going to make a quick peanut butter toast. Don't go to any trouble over me," I assured him with a smile.

The old geezer was looking down his nose.

"What is it?" I asked, refusing to tiptoe around the elephant in the room.

The butler sighed dramatically. "Perhaps no one told you, but a lady never makes her own coffee."

Oh, good grief. "Well, good thing I'm not a lady then."

I took the weird nut spread that wasn't peanut butter from the fridge door, found a knife, and waited for the bread to toast.

"On that, we can agree," the butler muttered as he left the room.

That jab hurt. I didn't know why, normally my skin was thick. Squeezing my eyes closed, I tried—and failed—to let the old man's words roll off.

It didn't work.

The toaster tinged in warning, then popped my toast out. I smeared it, took a bite, and then cleaned up after myself. There was no way in hell I was giving these people cause to complain. They might not like how a self-sufficient girl like me did things, but I wasn't going to create messes and extra work for them.

Gathering my things, I ventured into the breakfast room. "Oh, crap."

The butler could have said something.

I lifted my eyes to the ceiling in supplication for patience with the old man before sitting down in my seat where a covered breakfast tray sat warming. He was probably insulted I wasn't in here, eating the food prepared for me. Normally, the maids brought the food to me. I figured my appearance in the kitchen would make them avoid the stuffy formality of waiting on me.

"I'll check tomorrow before I make toast," I muttered, sinking into my chair.

Bringing the drinking glass of coffee to my lips, I glanced to the head of the table. At least Mancini didn't seem to mind that I wasn't the perfectly behaved mob wife. In fact, my oddities seemed to intrigue him. Not that I was sure that was a good thing. Drumming my fingers into the table, I flicked a glance at my notebook.

I was going to do it.

I would use this time, chained to this monster, to invest in myself at his expense. When I came out of this marriage, I would be a butterfly.

Lifting my mug at Mancini's empty seat, I saluted him. The mobster was opening doors a poor girl like me would never think possible. The least I could do was be nice to him.

"Come in!" I called in response to the knock on the door.

When a dark head of hair ducked through, I started. Looking between the time on my phone and the head of the Chicago Famiglia, confusion flickered through me.

"I brought you something." Mancini held out a square box. "I apologize for my behavior yesterday."

Words failed me.

While my first reaction upon entering the house in tears had been to smother the bastard in his sleep, by the time I soaked in the tub, I calmed down enough to see the foolishness behind that action. I might hate him for forcing me into this marriage, but the smart thing to do was use his position to my advantage.

Which was exactly what I'd spent the day plotting.

This gesture, however, was unexpected. I took the box from him, running my fingers over the soft velvet.

"You can wear them to the benefit this weekend," he intoned.

A sinking feeling pulled my gut down as I unclasped the box. The lid sprang up, and thousands of dollars glittered back at me.

My chest rose and fell rapidly as I battled down dark emotions. This wasn't a thoughtful gesture. The necklace and matching earrings were his way of adorning his prisoner. I snapped the lid closed and tossed the box onto the coffee table, bumping my glass of Joe.

"If that's what you want, sounds good," I said coolly as I plucked my glass and drained the coffee. Not only was I fueled by two and a half pots of caffeine, but hot spite filled my veins. "What are you doing home from work? It's the middle of the day."

Mancini frowned down at me. I tried and failed not to notice how good he smelled this close. "I'm afraid I'll have to work late tonight and won't be home for dinner."

I nodded. "Okay then."

"So—" Mancini swept his hand through the air "—I cleared my afternoon to take you shopping."

I gaped at him. Unbelievable. Un-freaking-believable. "You what?"

"I cleared my afternoon—"

"No, no, I heard you." I held up my hand, shaking my head. That was a whole separate issue, one I didn't want to think about. He cleared time for me? Who did that? I shook my head again. "Let me rephrase: Why the hell do I need to go shopping again?"

Mancini shrugged. "It's what women do."

"Hold up, mister." I shot to my feet, not liking the height difference. While I wasn't anywhere close to as tall as he was, sitting on the sofa in front of him made it all the worse. "I'm not some pampered Real Housewife. I don't need hordes of consumer goods to fill my days."

The don nodded slowly, as if he were really taking that information into account, and it was reforming the opinion he had of me.

"I bought enough crap two days ago to last a lifetime," I insisted.

"While you did find some nice clothes, I'm afraid you're still missing some key things." The corner of his mouth smirked. He was enjoying how much I didn't like this.

Which was a very odd thing to find entertaining.

I bristled, but he cut my protest off. "I looked over your choices, and you don't have any dresses appropriate for some upcoming events we'll be attending."

Play his game. There was more at stake here than simply shopping. If I gave in to this simple request, it could forge the groundwork when I made my own demand.

I groaned. He wasn't going to stop pushing, and I might as well have the things he needed me to have. "I don't know, I'm not the fancy type."

"Have you ever tried?" he countered matter-of-factly.

No, I guess I hadn't. If this was the price for a lifestyle where I could pursue a degree, which my morning of research and goal setting was pointing toward, paying the piper might not be so bad.

He needs someone classy and elegant. I was no My Fair Lady.

But if Audrey could do it, if Julia could do it, and granted those were films, there wasn't anything stopping me from trying.

"Let me put my cup in the kitchen, and then I'll be ready," I agreed reluctantly.

The don gave me a strange look but nodded. I hurried into the cold, sterile room and shivered. This spot was in desperate need of a makeover. Housewives decorated, right? Maybe I would add that as a minor project. If I was going to spend a significant amount of time in this house, I would need to be in the kitchen.

Squirting a dollop of soap into the glass, I scrubbed it with my fingers, since there wasn't a brush or sponge readily available. It felt good to have the suds on my skin again.

The nerves along my spine prickled a moment before two arms caged me against the sink. Heat radiated off his large frame, and while we weren't touching, I *felt* Alessandro from the back down to my toes.

"You didn't say anything about the jewels," he murmured, hot breath brushing the side of my neck. "Don't you like them?"

My pulse picked up a notch. "I'm sure they're nice."

"Hmm." The sound rumbled deep in his chest. "You hate them."

"I do," I bit out before I could stop myself. "But if you require it, I'll wear them."

"Fucking hell, woman," he laughed, but there was no humor in the sound. "I don't know what to do with you."

"Mhmm," I muttered, but only because I didn't trust myself to speak.

He leaned forward, making my heart hammer against my ribs. His lips connected with my skin. Sparks shot through my veins as he pressed a kiss against my throat—as if tasting my heartbeat. "What would you prefer, Penelope? Pearls? Gemstones? It doesn't have to be diamonds."

Spinning around, I held my damp, dripping hands upright, and pinned him with a look. He was so close. His presence dominated my senses, overwhelmed my decisions. I needed air. I needed space!

"What the hell made you think they were a good apology?" I challenged, trying to force my voice to sound normal.

Those black eyes stared hard at me. He seemed confused, and there was a genuine desperation to understand me. This close, I stared into the abyss. His eyes weren't as cruel and cold as I initially thought.

No, they had sparkles deep in the inky darkness.

But I doubted few were brave enough to be in this proximity to him. He was overwhelming. My lips parted slightly as I tried to catch my breath.

His gaze dropped to my mouth. "I am sorry for the way things happened. When I was informed you jumped the gate, I panicked."

"You panicked?" I repeated, not able to fathom this wolfish beast as anything but in control.

He nodded. "I did."

"I like to exercise, Mancini."

"Say my name," he whispered, a small plea attaching itself to the request.

"Okay. I hate running, but I enjoy being outside...Alessandro." I gave him the truth.

"Take the guards next time," he insisted.

I narrowed my eyes.

"They could use the exercise." He smirked. "You have a fast mile. It will be good for them."

That sounded like a compliment, and my traitorous body warmed. It had to be why my chin dipped in a small nod.

The wolf grinned.

I struggled not to squirm under his gaze.

"To hell with it," he rasped in Italian.

His lips crashed on mine before my brain fully computed the meaning.

The kiss was hungry and desperate. And my body lost no time responding with as much desperation.

I closed the distance, pulling him to me. It felt good.

Really damn good.

I moaned a little, enjoying the way his hand snaked up my body to cup my cheek. I was at his mercy, bent over the sink, pinned in place.

And yet, what I wanted was to be closer to him.

The kiss was nothing but fire and wanting. His body was hard and hot against me.

Need pulsed between my legs.

He was *really* hot. As if his skin radiated like a damn furnace. I slid my hands over his dress shirt, feeling the heat and wanting it against my body.

Heaven help me! I wanted this man.

The carnal drive wasn't something I would be able to fight for much longer.

Mancini pulled back with a groan. He cleared his throat.

And then cleared it again.

"We should get going," he finally choked out.

I pursed my lips. "Fine, I'll go put on some jeans."

Chapter 23 – Alessandro

If anyone were to ask, I was here to make sure Penelope looked like the goddess I knew she could be. While my assistant should have been able to instruct the stores exactly what my wife would need, I used my reputation for control as my reason for overseeing the shopping excursion. It had nothing to do with missing her wholesome, smiling face at the breakfast table, and the fact that I wouldn't see it again tonight.

My schedule was not conducive to family life, and yet I didn't want my wife to feel neglected.

That would never happen again.

This time around, this marriage, would be different. I swore it on a solitary tombstone of a girl who died too young—if I had to stretch myself thin to keep that vow, so be it.

But coming with Penelope, making time for her, wasn't the burden I predicted married life to be. I had no idea how intoxicating it was to watch her try on gowns. Torturous was the better word. Each dress brought a new fantasy to play out in my mind. Sheer torment wracked my body, making my bones ache, and all because I wouldn't allow myself to reach out and touch.

Not a burden. Not by a long shot.

Penelope stepped from the changing room in a shimmering forest-green dress. I shifted on the sofa. The semi-hard arousal, which was tucked up in the waist of my pants, was growing increasingly uncomfortable with each dress. The way this one brought out the jade in her hazel eyes...fuck me.

"Not that one," I said gruffly.

Penelope put her hands on her hips, and I had to suppress a groan. "This is the fifth dress! What's wrong with it?"

Her ponytail snapped as she jerked her chin. My fingers involuntarily clenched. Dio! How I wanted to wrap that length around my palm, use the shimmering hair to pull her neck back as I drove into her—

"Mancini," she barked. "Seriously? What is wrong with this? It's not red, my tits aren't going to fall out, and it isn't too tight, which means I can breathe."

Nothing's wrong, gorgeous. Except that if I had this strong a reaction to her, every other male who set eyes on her would as well.

It was the color. The green transformed her from beautiful to divine.

"Not that one," I repeated.

With an outraged groan, she stomped back into the dressing room.

I leaned forward, elbows on my knees and pushed my hands through my hair. This was the trouble with a beautiful wife. Everyone was going to see her and want her.

"They can't have her, she's mine," I rasped. The tickle at the back of my throat had me clearing it yet again.

I reached for my bottle of water and chugged. It did nothing to relieve the scratch.

"Alright, we have a problem," Penelope called out.

I shot to my feet, gaze darting about for a threat. With the two guards stationed at each entrance, and the store to ourselves, there shouldn't be danger, but I hadn't been paying attention. Not with her to distract me.

"Alessandro! Get in here," Penelope instructed.

Eyes narrowed, I stalked forward.

"Help me with the zipper...please." It was the way she looked up at me. Gaze hooded, eyes flashing with emotions, but trying to be polite.

Wait...she used my name.

A deep breath filled my lungs. "Since you said please."

She rolled her eyes. "But seriously, what is wrong with this one?"

I smoothed my hand down her side. "It's a beautiful dress, but it's not the right one."

Penelope shivered at my touch. "The zipper's stuck, and I don't want you to buy it if it breaks and it's not right for the events."

I drew the tips of my fingers back up her spine, a low, rough hum rumbling in my throat. "You look stunning," I confessed.

"What! Why? Wwhhat—?" she stammered, shaking her head. "Then why can't we just get this one and be done?"

I tugged her back against me. Our gazes clashed in the mirror.

"Not this one."

"Is it me?" she murmured. "Do these dresses not work for someone like me?"

"On the contrary."

"Then why not?" she insisted.

My fingers splayed over her belly, pressing her tightly against my erection digging into her lower back. Those hazel eyes popped when she realized what that was.

"Do you see what you do to me?" I rasped against her ear.

Another shiver raced through her. "So...it's not me."

I shook my head. "It most certainly is—just not in the way you're insinuating."

As she watched, I continued to touch her, tracing the lines of the dress, and freely exploring her body.

"I am a very jealous man, vespina," I warned. "And because I know what dogs men are, I won't have them salivating over you like a damn bone."

Penelope snorted. "Wouldn't be the first time."

She spoke so low, I wasn't sure I heard correctly. Was she talking about the incident at her uncle's restaurant? Because if there was more....

"I'll pummel any man I catch looking at you. Destroy any who dares touch you," I promised, rage making my voice gruff.

"Well, we can't have that, now can we?" she drawled. "Can't start trouble over your pretty little charity case when you're trying so hard to convince the world that I'm a catch."

She doesn't believe me. It was probably a good thing. She'd seen me kill already, but granted, forcing an addict to overdose was probably far more tame than what I should have done.

"You are mine. I won you, fair and square." I pressed my lips against her fluttering pulse. "And I will kill anyone who tries to take you from me."

Penelope gasped.

I chuckled darkly. "It's a promise."

She cleared her throat. "Fine, sure, whatever. Just get me out of this, okay?"

"If that's what you want."

She moved her arm. "It is."

The zipper ran up the side. I tugged, but it didn't budge. There was likely fabric caught in the teeth.

"Hold still," I instructed.

I slipped my knife from an inner pocket. At the click, she jerked away, stammering protests. I caught her shoulder and slid the blade down her spine, with just the right amount of pressure not to graze the skin.

Penelope clutched the fabric to her breasts, breathing hard and staring at me in disbelief. "These dresses are one of a kind!"

I shrugged. "It was in my way."

"Your way? You destroyed a luxury garment because it was in your way?"

I tugged it down. "Don't keep me from seeing what is mine, vespina."

"Unbelievable!" She tried to cover her bare breasts.

My heated gaze drew down her. She shivered again.

"Cold?"

"Yes, aren't you?" she stuttered.

"I'm burning." I was. My body was hot and clammy. Even my bones ached with the heat. All because she was right there, temptation incarnate.

"You are flushed." She stepped forward, a sudden concern written on her face. She placed the back of her palm against my cheek. "Mancini, you're—"

"Alessandro," I rasped, catching her arm and placing my kiss against the sensitive skin of her inner wrist. "To you, it's Alessandro."

She swallowed hard. "Okay."

"You taste so good," I murmured. My lips drew a path up the inside of her arm. "I want to devour you, vespina."

She groaned.

That was all I needed to hear. I reached out and traced along the expanse of her cotton panties, pink with red cherries on them. "These are hiding what I want to feast on."

"You're an animal," she said, voice hoarse with desire.

I pressed my fingers against her sex, feeling her heat through the material. "Mio dio, you're soaked for me."

"I am." She gulped. "And I hate it."

A dark chuckle rippled from me. "I know."

I continued to move my fingers against her sex. Penelope moaned. Her hips tipped into my touch, body more than interested in my attention.

"This pussy belongs to me, vespina," I growled, cupping it in my palm.

"Why didn't you cut those off too?" she muttered, clearly annoyed with her own interest in the matter.

I chuckled, pinching the elastic band, pulling it off her body, and then let it fall back with a snap.

Penelope gasped softly.

"If these were gone, I couldn't touch you." I knelt and pressed a kiss against her center. "Spread your legs wider."

There was a beat of hesitation.

But she did it. She inched her feet out once, and then again.

"Better, much better," I murmured, leaning forward to lick her panties. "This is what I want, but I'm not going to take it."

Her fingers ran through my hair, tugging and pushing. I mouthed against the cotton material, enjoying the forbidden nature of the chase.

"What if I never give it to you?" she rasped.

"You will." I continued to kiss her pussy. I could almost taste her through the material.

Her legs shook. Those fingers dug against my skull.

Penelope needed time. She needed to trust me enough to give into this fire between us. If I showed her how much I wanted her, how much she craved me, but without giving into it until she was ready, I hoped she would learn to trust me.

"Fuck it. Please, Mancini, just move them aside," she pleaded.

I grinned. That note of desperation was a victory. A small one, but still the same. "No, maybe you need to wait for your relief a little longer."

Even if it killed us both.

It nearly did as I rose and brushed a final caress over her panties.

"You bastard! You're edging me," she panted.

I cupped her cheeks in both hands and pressed a hard kiss against her lips. That hot tongue slid out to taste herself on me. The provocative action made my dick throb. My fingers slid into her braid, pulling the strands loose. I would burn my empire down to see this woman come undone.

The fact I contemplated that price showed how thin my control was when it came to her. But as I burned with desire, I couldn't bring myself to care.

Soon, I promised myself.

Tearing away, I stared down at her. Our hard breathing filled the space. Her hazel eyes flashed with predominant shades of amber. My wife was beautiful. It took every ounce of strength for me to step away and leave the dressing room before I gave in to her siren's call.

Her curses at being denied relief followed me like stinging darts. The little wasp was incensed, but the evidence of her desire lingered on my tongue. It wouldn't be long before we collided. And when that happened, the fireworks would be triumphant—or they would create an explosion that we wouldn't recover from.

Chapter 24 – Penelope

We managed to find several dresses the man I married deemed suitable. None of them were green—he insisted no more green. It was hard to say what his problem with that particular color was. I looked really good in most shades. I couldn't bring myself to look at the ruined dress, which the don insisted we bring home, let alone think about what happened in that dressing room. Burying the vivid images wasn't possible either. Not when one look at the mobster and his wicked mouth sent a flush of heat through me.

I tried to focus on the patterns of the floor tiles, and then the buildings we passed as we walked down the sidewalk, and finally, I searched the passersby for familiar faces. Of course, I didn't expect to see anyone I knew, so when I locked eyes with someone whose laser-focused attention was on me, my heart shot to my throat.

The man standing across the street was a stranger, but the way he stared was all too familiar.

"One more stop." Mancini's words broke my concentration.

I turned into him, stammering a question. The glint in his eye immediately put my guard on edge. But the sign above the shop only brought confusion. What the hell were we doing at a leather goods store?

The don pulled the door open. "Corwin Blau has the best stones in the city, and probably the whole world."

I looked over my shoulder. The walkway across the street was empty. The stranger was gone, and I couldn't for the life of me place where I knew their face.

Unable to shake the creepy feeling, I entered the shop. It was replaced with an equally uneasy feeling. This was a jewelry store, and nothing like the chain ones in the malls. This place reeked of pure luxury. The warm lights offset the cool hues of blue and gold. Glass cases stretched as far as the eye could see. Their contents dazzling under brighter lights mounted inside the walls. Prim associates stood at the ready, even though we were the only customers in the space—probably by design. Just like at the designer boutique. Mancini didn't seem to enjoy shopping with onlookers.

"These cases out here are all for show," Mancini explained, running his fingers over the polished surface of the nearest case. "Corwin has a more selective stock in his vaults. And he can create whatever pieces we commission."

The sour feeling that had begun to spread through my gut the moment I realized where we were now threatened to creep up my throat.

"It's an impressive display," I commented, because it felt like I had to say something.

The don took a step forward, forcing me back against a case. "You'll be honest with me? Tell me what you like?"

There was something under his request. The way he studied me was unguarded. As if he was really, truly interested in my opinion. That red flush to his skin, however, was hard to place.

"Sure," I agreed. "But you know more about this stuff than me."

The don nodded once. "Just trust your gut, vespina. You're good at this stuff if you just give yourself the chance."

A wiry man appeared from a backroom, saving me the trouble of answering that loaded statement. "Signor Mancini! You honor me, my friend, coming to visit on this fine day."

"Grazie, signore," the don murmured, inclining his head. "This was something too important to trust to my men."

"Ah, I see." The jeweler's beady eyes twinkled as he appraised me.

I stood up straight, meeting his gaze. The man didn't look as if I were out of place, but rather some puzzle he wanted to solve. "It's nice to meet you, Mr. Blau."

"Corwin, this is my wife." There was no missing the possessive way the don's tongue curled over the title. It shouldn't be a sound I liked.

"Beautiful, beautiful," the jeweler murmured.

"As Luca informed you, we need items for several events, but also, I have a more personal need," Mancini said but stopped to clear his throat.

I shot him a quick glance. His cheeks were infused with bright color. It was unnatural, and my fingers itched to reach up and feel if his forehead was warm.

"And how did you like what was sent last night?" The jeweler pulled out a pair of spectacles and began rubbing them with a cloth. "I might have lost at five-card stud at your tournament, but you, my host, were gracious enough to purchase one of my most prized pieces. Thank you, don, for that, by the way."

"You're welcome. Next time, don't bet against the river with such a bad hand. Well, Penelope? How did you like the diamonds?" Mancini asked with a shit-eating smirk.

No, I didn't want to feel his forehead. I wanted to smack that grin off his face.

I chose my words carefully. "They were very nice, but I'm afraid they weren't my style."

"You have a long neck, elegant lines throughout your frame." Blau popped the glasses on his nose, blinking like an owl at me. "But yes, simplicity over weight will be better for you. Come, let me show you my treasures."

Mancini coughed into his elbow as he followed us into one of the vaults. That noise sounded more than a tickle in the throat.

Cold air swept through the pipes, making the space feel as though it should be underground. More of the bright lights shown on us, but there was no mistaking the claustrophobic feeling of being buried alive—in a cave of wealth. If that heavy door shut, there would be no escape.

"Your bracelet is unique," Blau commented. His back was to us as he began to set velvet lined displays along the length of counter. "You prefer jewelry on your arms, signora?"

I lifted the dangling mass of charms. Whatever I was going to say died on my tongue as I noticed an empty spot between the sun and the moon.

No! Not the crown.

That was the first one I bought with my babysitting money. I promised myself I would live like royalty someday, not change poopy diapers on the neighbor's five babies. I treasured that charm, a reminder of my dreams.

But it was gone. Sadness swept through me. I lost another charm. It'd only happened twice before, when I bought cheap clasps. I was religious about checking for loose connections, and it had been years since one fell off the bracelet.

"Signora?" the wizened man blinked up at me.

"Um, yeah, I like bracelets," I croaked, cradling mine in my opposite hand.

Blau held up a braided gold chain. The yellow hue crackled in the light. There was a simplicity that immediately piqued my interest.

"You like this," he surmised, a smile playing on his lips.

"I do." *Unfortunately.* My resolve not to become a spoilt princess was being tested by something this perfect.

"Allow me." Blau reached for my wrist.

Before he made contact, I was forcefully pulled back.

"I'll do it," Mancini growled.

Growled! Like the beast that he was.

"Of course, Don Mancini." Blau didn't seem fazed.

Hard fingers wrapped around mine, and the monster quickly undid the fastening of the charm bracelet. I scowled at him, desperately wanting to tell him I could do it myself. If we were alone, I would have.

But causing a scene in this enclosed space seemed wrong.

Mancini plucked the braid of gold and deftly draped it over me. Once it was secure, he lifted my fingers to let the piece dangle from my skin. His brow rose as he met my gaze.

Angling my body so the jeweler couldn't see, I narrowed my eyes at him.

That predatorial smile curved on his lips.

Oh, what I would give to tell this wolf exactly what I thought of him buying me off.

"We're going to need more pieces like this," Mancini instructed.

Greed lit the jeweler's eyes. "I have just the thing."

"Whatever you say, dear," I mused and flashed the don a sickly-sweet smile.

Between the jeweler and the don, they found things I actually liked. It made the prospect of wearing them a little less horrid. But the thing that kept me quiet was that I didn't want to fight Mancini. Not over something like this. I wouldn't win.

In fact, the way I saw it, if I wore his stupid fancy stuff, he would be more likely to agree to my ideas. When the perfect opportunity came, I would have my counter offer ready to push on him. The don wanted a glittery trophy wife to show off? Fine, I could play that role. But in exchange, he was going to pay for my degree or help me find a job where I would gain valuable experience.

"We'll take them all, but there's one more piece I need you to show me," Mancini said before clearing his throat again.

A knock on the door made the jeweler frown. "One moment, signore. I do beg your pardon."

As Blau scampered away, Mancini took my hand and carefully slid the charm bracelet back over my skin. "There, back to normal."

It felt strange, this small connection. There was more heat blazing between us now than any of the kisses we'd shared.

The look in his eye was equally perplexing. It was almost as if he were looking past my defenses to study the real me.

I had to give myself a hard mental shake.

I'm just his prize.

It didn't mean anything more.

"Thank you," I said, pulling away from him.

"That wasn't so bad," he teased. "You don't have to admit it, but I know you enjoyed that, Penelope." I bristled, but he held up his hand. "Spare me your wrath, vespina, I can see how much you hated this errand."

A long exhale huffed from my lungs.

The don caught my fingers again. I didn't fight. He lifted my hand and twisted it, searching the charms. His phone rang, but he ignored the insistent chime.

"Talk to me," he coaxed. His voice was hoarse, but likely from the congestion and not emotions. He didn't have those. "What do you want? Say anything but freedom and it's yours."

"I want to become someone." The unformed plan blurted out in a whisper. *Shit.* That was not how I wanted to make the proposal. My mind backpedaled, trying to reform the vague request. "I need a purpose, Alessandro. I can't sit around at the house all day; I'm going crazy!"

His eyes fluttered closed at the sound of his name. When they opened, the black irises blazed with heat. "We can work with that."

That sounded too good to be true.

After what happened with my uncle, I was going to be very careful with these underworld kingpins. They might say one thing, but the devil was in the details. Once I had a better formed plan, I would make him sign his name—in ink or blood, it made little difference to me.

"Good, so long as we can work something out," I said with finality. My fingers plucked the empty place on the charm bracelet.

"Don't worry, vespina, you can keep the jewels and your pride."

I jerked out of his hold. "I don't want your blood money or gems. I want your promise that you won't screw me over like my uncle tried to do. When I come to you with a proposal, you'll listen to me."

Whatever he was going to say was cut off when his phone rang again. Lips pursed in annoyance, he plucked the device from his breast pocket.

"What?" he snapped.

Needing space, I wandered into the front of the shop. I wasn't sure I liked this change to my life. Sure, girls dreamed of the fairytale where there were servants and clothes, wealth and an endless supply of consumer goods. But now that I had everything I could ever want, I didn't feel comfortable with the change in circumstance.

Pausing by the small mirror next to the display of pearls, I looked at my reflection. I was still the same old me. I didn't have to change just because there were faucets flowing with dollar signs.

The front door banged open.

That sixth sense that all animals have if they only listen rose in warning before my senses were fully able to decipher the scene in front of me. I spun around, body immediately going on the defensive. On the surface, it was only a handful of men entering the shop.

But something about them didn't look right.

"Penelope, come here," the don said calmly, although his tone was cold enough to freeze boiling water.

I moved toward where he stood at the vault door without taking my eyes off the newcomers.

"Blood King, you crawled out of your cave to visit the likes of us common folk." This one was the largest, great beer belly draping over his belt.

"We didn't believe the report," another chuckled. "You never leave your fortress."

"Or headquarters," the beer belly agreed.

"Not without a heavy guard," the other added.

I looked toward the front. Where were the guards? They'd stayed outside in the vehicles. But surely they'd noticed these men drift into the shop? And then my heart pattered double. What if something happened to them?

That left Alessandro to face this threat alone.

I looked around for a weapon. There was a pair of ornate swords, crossed and mounted to the wall. Not only were they out of reach, but it wasn't likely they would do any good. So I stepped beside the monster and crossed my fingers that the situation deescalated quickly.

The don's fingers curled into my back, pushing me slightly behind him. "You're on the wrong side of the tracks, boys."

"It's a free market."

"Last we checked."

"Blau is under *my* protection," Mancini snarled. "You need to leave."

I leaned against the corner of the display case, wishing there was something—anything!—I could do. But I didn't have a clear idea of what was happening. The store associates had disappeared, and the wiry jeweler was nowhere to be seen.

"You killed my brother," the beer belly antagonist growled.

"That was never proven, Marco," Mancini said too calmly.

"Bullshit! We know it was you." Marco's chubby cheeks puffed with wrath. "Why else would you make his widow a proposition of marriage?!"

I arched a brow, but Mancini didn't look my direction. "Vincent had what was coming to him, Divine Providence knew that."

"Murderer," Marco seethed.

"You have one chance to leave before you start a war between the Mancini and Moretti families that you cannot possibly win—not without a true leader, which you will never be, Marco." Alessandro's words dripped with disdain.

One of the men spat on the ground. "You're a dead man, Blood King—"

The don pushed me down and pulled out his weapon. I yelped, stumbled forward, and dove behind the counter, but a mixture of adrenaline and gravity resulted in me crashing hard into the rigid corner. Pain exploded on my side.

Shots fired overhead.

Glass shattered and alarms blared.

I turned, biting back a scream of pain, but I had to look!

The don stared coolly in front of him. He wasn't bleeding, not where I could see.

Rapid Italian filled the space, but that black gaze dropped to me. Volatile emotions swirled deep in those inky depths. I sensed fear trickling from his pores.

Struggling to my feet, I winced and clutched my side. The don's soldiers stood at the door, barking orders and holstering their weapons. The alarms cut off a moment later as Blau reappeared.

They'd just shot the intruders. Shot them! In broad daylight.

This was the mob. This was what I signed up for. I drew a deep breath—or tried to. Mother of god, my rib was bruised. Living on the ranch, I was no stranger to these kinds of things. But shoot-outs? Between rivals? Oh, dear lord, I was not mentally prepared for that.

"Penelope?" the don growled, stepping close.

"I'm okay." Dropping my hand, I gave him a shaky smile.

His brows drew together.

"Really," I insisted. And then...I placed a hand on his arm. "Really, Alessandro. I'm okay."

His look said he didn't believe me.

"So...any more rivals for Mrs. Don that I should know about?" I asked to change the subject. "What other skeletons are in your closet?"

Mancini barked a rough laugh. "I have plenty of skeletons. Pray that you never meet them. And Isabella Moretti? That was purely a business deal, vespina. One that I would have regretted."

I swept my hand through the air. "And this? How is this not a business deal?"

His lupine smile flashed feral. "It's one I'm enjoying—the first one that doesn't feel like work."

There were dead bodies not ten feet away, and yet my insides shivered with a dark heat. Good lord, what was wrong with me?

Chapter 25 – Penelope

"I want the doctor to look at you," Mancini barked as we moved through the front door.

Ignoring him, I marched to the kitchen. I'd tried to hide the injury. I hadn't wanted to have the don fuss over me in the aftermath that ensued.

There was no fooling him.

"I'm fine, Mancini," I snapped as he stomped into the mansion's kitchen behind me. "I've been kicked by our hinny and thrown from more horses than I care to remember."

The mobster paused beside the island, bracing his hands against the side and breathing hard.

Too hard.

I narrowed my eyes at him.

Space, I needed space. Today had been too much. The kisses, both on the mouth and the ones between my legs, were threatening to mess with my head. Part of me wanted to give in. My brain was tricked into believing he wasn't a complete monster. Hell, I felt my resolve disappearing as we spoke! There was no way I found this violent beast attractive.

My pussy clenched in protest.

Okay, yes, he would be a fantastic lover. But at what cost! The deeper I entrenched myself with this life, the harder it would be to escape. Besides, one look at Mancini and it was obvious he wasn't the kind of man who was capable of love and devotion.

He's a protector. A provider too.

I took the frozen veggies out and lifted my tee and placed them against the skin.

"What's a hinny?" he croaked.

I snorted. Because right now, this stubborn man wore the same look as that cranky little snowball I bottle-raised.

"The dad was a stallion and the mom a donkey," I explained.

"A mule."

I smiled, shifting the veggies higher. "No, that's a dad donkey and a mom horse. Both are technically sterile, though. They don't make their own breed of babies. I did a science project on them in high school. Won top prize at the county fair."

Jeeze, could I sound anymore small town than talking about sperm quality on farm animals?

Mancini cleared his throat—twice. "What if the rib is broken?"

I shrugged. "Wouldn't be the first time."

"Penelope—"

"Fine, bring the doctor, but I want him to give you an exam too." I planted my other hand on my hip and stared the mobster down.

His metaphorical hackles raised. "What for? I didn't get hurt."

"But you're getting a cold," I countered, enjoying the shock that flashed through his unguarded gaze.

His protest would have been more convincing if he didn't have to wrestle the frog from his throat to speak. "I most certainly am not. Made Men don't get sick."

"Mmhm, pretty sure humans do. So unless you're confirming that you're an ice planet barbarian in disguise, Mr. Polar Vortex, I think you're coming down with something." As I spoke, I stalked him around the island. He looked warily at my hand, which I slapped on his forehead.

Hot—very hot.

I knew he felt unusually warm. Earlier, I'd chalked it up to the passion of the kiss.

The don jerked away. "I haven't been sick since I was a child."

"Good for you. But your body begs to differ." I took the veggies from my side and slapped them on his neck. "You should go lie down."

"Not happening."

"Then so be it," I sighed. "I'm going to hunt up some Epsom salts and soak in the tub before I spend the afternoon on the couch with a heating pad and ice alternatively. If you send a doctor in here, I'll raise Cain until he sees you too."

The impressed look on the mobster's face did things to me. He clearly wasn't used to this level of defiance, and I secretly was enjoying pushing his buttons.

"I'm not seeing a doctor," Mancini insisted.

"Act tough, just like every other man on the planet! When the sickness takes you down, don't cry to me," I called over my shoulder, leaving the kitchen.

"Stubborn woman!" he shouted after me.

"Impossible man!" Smirking, I went to take care of myself.

Lost in a book, cozy on the couch, it was well after eleven at night when a noise deeper in the house drew my attention.

I crept down the hall and poked my head into the dark kitchen. The don was back and sat at the island looking like death. His fingers played with a tumbler of whiskey, but it looked untouched. Dante spoke rapidly in Italian. Something about image and strength.

Tiptoeing forward, neither man noticed I was there until I popped to my husband's side. Dante jumped—actually jumped—and garbled a string of curses. It was sweet payback for the death eater interrupting my run.

Only then I remembered Mancini's threat because Dante touched me. I frowned, hoping the don hadn't actually hurt one of his men for following an order. That would be insane, even for the beast I'd married.

"You don't sneak up on Made Men, sweetheart," Dante barked.

"Dante!" Mancini scowled at him, but the effect was lost because of the hoarse quality of his voice and the putrid color of his face. "That's my wife. Watch how you speak to her."

I pressed the back of my hand against Mancini's cheek. "You're burning up, Mr. Don."

His gaze swung to me, and lost was the powerful frigid quality. "I'm fine."

"He fainted," Dante snapped.

"Dante." That one word packed a violent weight.

The number two didn't take the warning. "He did. Passed out in the middle of a negotiation."

"I'm fine!" Mancini shot to his feet but leaned heavily against the counter a second later.

Turning to Dante, I clasped my hands in front of me. "I wonder if you would be so kind as to run to the store for me? Since I'm new to town, I'm not sure where to go."

The scary man arched a brow. "I'm not a personal shopper, sweetheart."

"And I'm not your anything. No...wait." I gave him a sardonic smile. "I'm your don's wife. And I need you to run an errand for me. So you're going to give me your phone number. I'll text you a list. You'll go to the store to get me what I need, and you're going to do it with a fucking smile on your face. Capisc?"

"*Capisce*," he corrected.

"I know that, dumbass. But that's how we say it in America." I tugged the don's arm, wondering how the hell I was going to carry him up the stairs with my incredibly sore side. But like every other male across the species, he was too damn stubborn to admit his condition in front of another.

I began to rattle off my cell, but the death eater cut me off.

"I have your number," Dante said tightly.

Of course he did. I pushed down the feeling of annoyance. It could always be worse. Poppy had said that she expected her phone to be monitored. At least there'd been no mention of my apps turned off or my accounts banned. The breech of privacy wasn't the point right now, but I would bring up the fact that someone had my number without my permission at another time.

"Good. Now hurry," I snapped, tugging the swaying mob leader toward our bedroom.

It took ten minutes to reach the space. I ordered the don to strip and climb straight into bed as I began to tap out a list. We needed vitamin D3 with K, a zinc and vitamin C pack, and organic kombucha amongst other things. I also told the number two to pick me up an Ace bandage.

"If you wanted to get me into bed, all you had to do was say so, vespina."

I looked up from my phone. "Did you just...make a joke?"

"I'm capable of more than you think, including the occasional joke," he muttered before coughing again.

Going to the bathroom for the bottle of over-the-counter pain pills and a wet cloth, I returned. "You should have stayed home this evening."

With an angry huff, he rolled over. "I'm fine now. Just let me sleep this off."

Staring at the ceiling, I let out a strangled breath. "A cold is not a weakness! Shit happens, Mancini."

He didn't respond.

What a big, fussy baby. "Are you going to take these?"

"No."

"Alright then." I sent a second message to Dante, telling him to leave the purchases in the kitchen. Being nice to the don was a quid-pro-quo. We had to coexist in this close proximity, so it wouldn't kill me to take care of him.

What surprised me was how easy it was.

That was not something I was prepared to deal with. So instead, I shut off the overhead light and moved to the far side of the bed to slip under the covers.

Mancini's voice broke through the dark. "You're joining me?"

I sighed. "The floor isn't an option with my ribs. Looks like we're stuck together."

He hummed roughly. "What an interesting turn of events."

"Indeed." It took a half-hour of shallow box breathing before I was able to quiet my mind enough to fall asleep—where I began to dream about being kissed by a monster.

Chapter 26 – Penelope

Sugar and spice filled the air. My side ached, but if I moved slowly enough, it didn't impede the baking process. Which was good. I needed this homely activity to quiet my mind after the chaos of the last few days.

I pulled a tray of perfectly golden cookies from the oven as a fancy gust of wind blew into the kitchen. Sliding the parchment paper onto the rack, I turned and smiled at my sister-in-law. "I baked. Want a cookie?"

The look of shock on her face was priceless.

"I have three varieties," I continued, gesturing to the platters. "I wasn't sure what everyone around here liked."

"You—" Serena gaped.

"Yes?" I cocked my head, bracing for her snide comment.

Serena cleared her throat. "You can bake?"

"Mhmm," I confirmed the obvious. "I can cook too, but it's just not the same as crafting sweet treats."

"Gold diggers don't cook," she muttered in Italian. "Where in the seven hells did my brother find you?"

I grabbed a small plate from the cabinet. It'd taken all morning, but I was familiar with the space and could find whatever I needed.

"Here, grab whatever looks good to you." I held out the plate. She thought I was here for her brother's money? Well, I was just going to have to prove that was not the case. "Or if you prefer something special, I can whip up a batch if we have the ingredients."

Serena stared at me as if I'd grown two extra heads. She didn't move to take the plate. "Why are you being nice to me?"

I sighed and set the plate on the island between us. Today started with good intentions. Between her feverish brother, who still swore he wasn't sick, and this cold, hostile greeting, it was hard to keep that resolve.

"There's no terrible ulterior motive," I promised. "I'm being nice because that's who I am. It doesn't make sense not to try and get along. We have to coexist."

"Coexist...the perfect way to live." The bitterness in her tone made me pause and look over my shoulder as I prepared to load the oven with another tray of cookies.

Was that my future? Poppy was frightened and docile. Serena was jaded and spiteful. They were both so young! What kind of life was this, wealthy but lonely, growing up with the big secret of the mob hanging ever-present in the background?

"I'm going to fix your brother some lunch," I chatted, going to the fridge to find ingredients. "Do you know what he likes?"

Before the flabbergasted mafia princess could respond, the crusty old butler sailed into the room. "The maids will do that, signora."

I waved my hand dismissively at him. "It's really no trouble. I need to eat, and so does Mancini. I'll just make him a plate and—"

"Madam," the butler clipped out. "That is not how this household runs."

Turning sharply—and quickly hiding the wince from the sudden movement—I pinned him with a hard look. "Is that so?"

"Yes," he insisted. "I found Miss Notaro hovering in the corridor, and your presence in the kitchen is not only irregular, but it is interfering with her and the other maids' work."

"She's welcome to come work in here with me," I insisted. "In fact, I wouldn't mind the company." It would make this place feel less like a haunted mansion.

"If you're going to live in this household, there are certain things the lady of the house must and must not do." Shepherd glared down his aquiline nose at me.

"Uh-huh, and you don't think I'm lady material. So what's the problem?" I countered, glancing at the oven and realizing I didn't set the timer for the cookies.

"The problem, signora, is that you'll never live up to the expectations—"

"Shepherd!" The don's voice thundered through the kitchen.

The old man paled.

Serena's eyes widened. She'd been unusually quiet, watching the drama unfold. It was probably the most entertainment the poor woman had around here.

Dante burst into the kitchen, Mancini a step behind him.

I sent a quick prayer to the heavens for strength.

The don prowled toward his butler, anger momentarily chasing away the fatigue of illness. "What the fuck did you just say about my wife?"

Oh, good grief. "He was explaining how I could be a better mafia wife," I said quickly. "I'm taking notes so I can be the perfect little bride for you—in public."

Mancini shot me a cold glare. "That wasn't what it sounded like."

I planted a hand on my hip. "And what did it sound like then?"

"An insult." Mancini's voice hardened. "No one insults my wife, I don't care if he's been here a long time."

"He might not have had the most tactful delivery, but that's not a problem. I happen to like prickly old cactuses! He makes life interesting, and your house wouldn't run like a well-oiled tractor if it wasn't for him," I insisted.

The don paused, looking between us. "He wasn't insulting you?"

"No!" My brain scrambled to twist the truth. There was no reason for the don to come down hard on the old man. I could take the criticism. In fact, I didn't mind sparring with the butler. The look in Mancini's eye told me he didn't believe me, so I added, "Okay, yes, Shepherd might need to warm up to me, but I like the challenge. So don't you dare lay a finger on him or you'll have *me* to answer to!"

A thick silence filled the kitchen.

I either crossed a line by defying the boss in front of everyone, or I just saved the old man's hide. To make sure it went my way, I forced a sweet smile and pointed to the cookies. "Would anyone like one while they're still hot?"

"I would," Serena piped up.

It was my turn to feel shocked. Her readiness to diffuse the situation surprised me when I would have expected her to escalate it. But I recovered quickly, pushing the plate to her.

"Watch how you speak to my wife," Mancini warned in Italian before he and Dante left.

I caught the second snatching several cookies on his way out the door. The butler left a moment later.

Sighing, I leaned against the counter. "That was close."

"You stood up for Shepherd," Serena murmured, fidgeting with the cookie on her plate.

"Well, yeah." I shrugged. "He didn't need to be chastised for his opinions. He only thinks that way of me because he really cares about this place and the family."

Serena nodded before taking the cookie plate and standing. At the door, she turned. "By the way, it's cacti, not cactuses."

The teasing lilt to her voice, coupled with the smile on her face, was promising. Hope fluttered through me. Was this an olive branch? Or just a demented game to her? Either way, I went with it.

"Really? I didn't know that," I said and checked the batch of cookies, which were perfect.

"I can find the dictionary," my sister-in-law said dryly.

"You have one of those?" I smirked.

The woman rolled her eyes and left. Maybe, just maybe, I was getting through to her after all.

Sitting down in the spacious dining room with a plate of warm cookies and a large glass of coffee, I pulled out my phone. It took every drop of my remaining strength to dial the number I'd memorized as a little girl. The old rotary dial in the kitchen and the matching one in the living room didn't have caller ID. In my head, I could hear the sharp peal of the bell chiming at the incoming call.

I hope you're home....

"Greenbriar residence," the baritone said through the void.

Relief swept through me, followed by a surge of emotions. He wasn't in the field with the boys. "Hi Daddy, it's Penny."

"Well, I'll be! It's good to hear your voice, baby girl."

I closed my eyes. "How's Mom doing?"

"Oh, we're fine, everyone's fine," he assured me. It wasn't like he would say anything different. "How's your trip? The kids have been giving me updates, but you've been gone a long time."

"Yeah, about that—" I sucked in a deep breath. The truth was long overdue, and yet I couldn't bring myself to say the words. So instead, I asked, "Jillian said mom's heart surgery is scheduled at Mayo?"

"Oh, yeah." Something fumbled in the background. "Don't know how your sister pulled strings, but supposedly she wrangled some fancy surgeon and team to do the surgery."

"I know." *I helped.* "When do you guys drive down there?"

"We'll go down a day or two before. Your sister has all the details worked out, don't you worry your pretty little head about it. Now! I want to hear about this great big road trip you took."

How did I lie to my father? I'd told them as much of the truth as I dared. If they found out where I'd gone, what kind of bargain I'd struck to make this possible....

No, I couldn't risk it.

"I've actually got to catch a bus, but I promise I'll call soon and tell you all about it!" I croaked.

"Penelope June, are you okay?"

Crap. Tears prickled in my eyes. It would be so much easier to deceive him if he wasn't a good parent.

"Fit as a fiddle," I assured him. "And I plan to be there, for the surgery."

"Now, don't be cutting your trip short for us, sweetie. You enjoy your adventure; you've earned it. Promise?"

I needed a hug. A great big bear hug.

"Promise," I said with forced brightness.

"Good, now get along and don't miss your bus," my dad insisted. "Call when you can."

"I will."

The line cut off. I dropped my head onto my arms. The tears I refused to shed stayed locked up tight. I would do anything for my family. They were the only ones who loved me unconditionally.

Chapter 27 – Penelope

I woke up sweating. No...that wasn't right. I wasn't the one producing the heat. A furnace shivered next to me.

Mancini groaned in his sleep. That large body tensed, hands curling into fists. And then he muttered about blood and his father. It was another nightmare. Something from his past plagued his feverish sleep. This wasn't the first bad dream he'd had. A few were about a woman named Elena, but most were about his father. Mancini muttered incoherently in Italian, making the details nearly impossible to piece together.

The only solid conclusion I'd come to was that, unlike me, the don hadn't had a happy childhood.

Which made perfect sense. Only a terrible past would forge a man of cold, unyielding iron like the don.

I sighed. There was no asking him for details when he was conscious. We weren't close enough for me to pry, but the names and details had me imagining the worst. Carefully untangling myself from the inferno, I padded to the bathroom. My own side ached from the meds wearing off. After popping a few more ibuprofen, I brought some to the very sick don.

Sitting gingerly beside him, I offered the pills. "Please take these. Not because you're sick," I lied—because the man's logic was like a damn toddler. "But you need them, okay?"

"Okay," he rasped.

It was painful to watch him try to gulp the pills down. The dim light from the bathroom fell across his features, showing the haggard figure.

"You want to take a shower?" I offered. "Might make you feel better."

"You joining me?" he whispered hoarsely.

"I might," I laughed softly. "But neither of us is in any condition to do more than let the water make us feel better."

He tried and failed to climb out of bed. "I...can't."

I smoothed back his hair. "It's okay, we can in the morning."

"That offer will still be there?" he pushed.

What the hell was I saying? It was the lack of oxygen to my brain that stifled coherent thought. But...maybe he wouldn't remember this.

"It will," I murmured.

He flopped back onto the pillow. After I shut the light off and climbed in beside him, he rolled into me. My body's natural reaction was to tense, which sent a shot of agony through my torso.

"Careful," I gasped.

Mancini stilled. "Shit, I'm sorry."

"It's okay." The breathless quality of my voice was far from convincing.

"No, it's my fault. I should have ordered my men to take care of the Morettis outside, instead of setting the trap for them in the jewelry store."

I curled my arm under my head and studied the don through the thick shadows. "So you knew they were coming inside?"

Mancini nodded. "That was the phone call in the vault. You were supposed to go in there while we dealt with them. Instead...."

"Hey, don't feel bad. I'm a mafia wife now. This wouldn't be fun if I wasn't dodging some kind of danger."

He growled—dangerous and threatening.

That was the wrong thing to say. I reached out and pressed a finger on his lips to stifle his rebuttal.

"I'm fine, lupo. A bit worried they tried to assassinate you in broad daylight, but I'm fine." With a groan, I rolled back over. "Look at us. Just a pair of gimps."

Burrowing beside me, the don stayed quiet for a few heartbeats. "Life doesn't faze you, does it?"

"Not much."

After another long pause, this time, long enough that I thought he was asleep, he murmured, "This is why I wanted to marry you, Penelope. You can handle the underworld. It would have broken your cousin."

His praise made my heart thump hard.

"Go to sleep, Mr. Don," I murmured against his still-warm scalp.

He shook his head. "It's Alessandro. Why won't you use my name?"

I squeezed my eyes tight. *Because then I'll see you as a person.*

When I didn't respond, he didn't push. We remained quietly lying there as the intricacies of our forced situation swirled around us. This, whatever it was, was easy. In the dark, I could pretend he was someone I wanted to know better, to spend my days with—someone to build a life with.

This wasn't the enemy I married. And that thought scared me more than if he did something horrid to me. There was no way he was trustworthy. If I softened, if I saw him as a man instead of a monster, I might end up permanently in this life.

I need to learn more about the mob. See if it was something I would ever be willing to endure. Just because he thought I was capable didn't mean I was up to the role.

With the big, bad don in bed, it was easy being nice to the mobster. He was really sick, but the doctor was a reasonable man. He didn't want to throw narcotics at the situation, and antibiotics wouldn't fix this since it was likely viral.

"You're doing everything right. If you want, there are services that do vitamins as injectables. Might be easier than trying to make him swallow the pills," the doctor commented as he left the afternoon of the second day.

"We'll think about it," I agreed.

The truth was, the chain of command was blurry. Did I make the call to inject the boss? Should that be Dante or Serena? There had to be a protocol for this kind of thing.

Before I could go seek out my sister-in-law, the click-clack of stilettoes announced her arrival.

Bracing myself, I turned with a smile. "He's out of the woods, but not back to normal."

Serena stopped short. "Really? That's good to hear."

Odd. She was taken aback by my statement.

"Why's that so surprising?" I pushed, wanting to get to the bottom of her strange reaction.

"Oh, no, not that." She waved her hand dismissively. "The fact that you would tell me. I didn't even have to twist your arm."

Her smile told me it was a joke, but the glint in her eyes made me wonder.

"Of course I would tell you," I protested. "He's your brother. You have every right to know how he's feeling."

"It's just...you and I didn't start off the greatest."

And you've been avoiding me. I shrugged. "I'm not catty, and I hate women who are."

"A straight shooter. I see why my brother likes you so much."

I opened my mouth to protest, but she continued.

"I made soup. Do you think Alessandro would eat some?" She shifted.

I bit my tongue, fighting back the urge to ask what the prim and proper butler thought of her cooking, since he took such issue with me doing the same.

"We can try! And if he doesn't, I'll take some. Soup actually sounds great." Padding after her on my bare feet, I followed Serena into the kitchen where a pot of rich, nutritious noodle soup simmered.

Pastina—I sighed, instantly transported to my childhood. "My mama said this could cure anything."

Serena laughed. "Mine too."

But she wasn't smiling.

Whatever this truce was between us, I didn't want to break it, but there was something there.

"What's that?" a gruff voice asked from behind.

"What are you doing here, Minstrel?" Serena's voice softened, and she smoothed back some of her perfectly styled hair.

Dante smirked. "Checking in that you aren't poisoning my best friend."

"Do you want some soup, Dante?" I asked, scooping a bowl for Mancini.

"You look the picture of health." The number two gave me a skeptical once over.

I shrugged. "I'm taking high doses of the vitamins that you so kindly picked up for us."

"And here I thought you two concocted some scheme to make the don sick, so you could take over," he mused, but there was a menace behind his words.

Serena sashayed to the number two and leaned into him. "If we wanted to kill the don, we wouldn't waste time trying to heal him."

There was something there—at least on her part. It pulsed in the air. That girl had it bad for the don's fixer.

Unfortunately for her, Dante didn't look at her.

Wondering what they would do if left alone, I lifted the tray but set it back down. "Since you're both here, I have a question. Who takes the chain of command in the don's absence?"

"That would be his underboss, Antonio," Dante responded cautiously.

I faltered. "So not you."

Dante gave me a crooked grin. "Not me. I don't want that power."

"But you know Alessandro well," I insisted. "I want to give him vitamins through shots and IV treatments. It will speed his recovery. But I don't feel that I can make that call. What do you two think about it?"

"Me?" Serena's brows shot to her forehead. "I'm the least qualified person to offer an opinion about my brother's well-being."

I sighed. Her answer was unsurprising. "Dante?"

"Sweetheart, you're his wife." Dante shoveled a spoonful of soup in his mouth. "He wouldn't have married you if he didn't want you in that position of authority."

"But you joked about the soup being poisoned. Is he going to be mad if I let an outside company come in and inject him?" I insisted.

"You read too many novels," the fixer muttered.

I jerked back in surprise. "How do you know what I read?"

Dante only grinned.

"You're monitoring my phone," I surmised. I suspected it after he told me he had my number, but to hear him admit it sparked that anger I was trying so desperately to keep in control. "Unbelievable."

"*Mated to the Alpha*. Really?" he countered.

I wasn't defending my reading choices to him. They were mine, and mine alone. Tipping my chin in the air, I left.

But the mobster's laughter followed me from the kitchen.

Oh, if we were back home, what I wouldn't give to whip him into shape! Vengeful thoughts played through my head as I slowly climbed the stairs, breathing through the discomfort.

Chapter 28 – Penelope

"He's definitely feeling better." Serena set the tray down on the island. "He nearly bit my head off for not telling him where we hid his phone. Don't be surprised if he hobbles down here and yells at us."

Snorting, I put the lid on the fresh batch of soup. It was the fourth in as many days. Everyone, including the patient, was eating it like it was the only thing that would keep us well.

I gingerly sat down on the barstool and scooted the cheesy bread ring to her. "It's still hot."

"Dio, this is so good," she moaned around the bite. "You're bad for my waistline, Penelope."

It seemed the truce between us was growing stronger. If I played my cards right, it might even be permanent. One less thing to worry about. I didn't want Serena as an enemy for the remainder of my sojourn here.

"It's Penny or Pen," I offered.

Serena arched a brow. "Is my brother going to like that I call you that?"

I shrugged. "I don't care. It's my name, not his. He doesn't have to control everything."

It was her turn to laugh. "Then you don't know him well yet."

Stretching, I tested the muscles. I hadn't overdone it by being on my feet all day, which was a good sign. None of the staff bothered me about spending so much time in here. The last few days had felt more like a fairytale than all the glitter and shopping from the first few days of my captivity. The huge kitchen was feeling more homey. It was where I spent my time when not reading or looking up possible career paths. While it was in need of some color and cheer, I loved the extra room to bake and cook. And there was no shortage of ingredients or gizmos, gadgets, and tools. I was in my element. If only I could add some more personal décor to the space, make it less sterile....

I hadn't been alone in here either. Serena made excuses to pop in from time to time. It wasn't clear what reason made her like me. Perhaps because I wasn't a gold digger who expected the staff to wait on me or at least clean up after me. And me standing up for the butler probably won me brownie points too.

Serena popped another bite in her mouth. "To tell you the truth, it's nice to have another woman in the house again."

"Again?" I snapped my head up. A double thump beat in my chest.

The other woman paled. "Merda! You didn't hear that from me!"

"Fine, I didn't." I waved my hand. "But what do you mean?"

She cleared her throat. "*That* is not my story, and I'm not going to risk the ire of my brother to tell it."

One of the skeletons in the don's closet. My heart skipped again, this time with a note of pain, and maybe something greener.

"And so you'll let me imagine the worst," I grumbled.

"It's not that bad. Plus! It was over a decade ago." Serena dismissed the conversation. "Ancient history."

"How old is your brother?" I asked.

"You don't know that either?" She cocked her head. I gave her a withering look. "Mid-thirties, twelve years older than me."

A banging and bumping ended our conversation and announced the arrival of company. Three burly figures pushed into the kitchen. I immediately felt my guard go up. These weren't good men. Not that Made Men were good-good. But these ones seemed like they would slide a knife between my ribs because the humor struck.

My instinct was to reach for a weapon.

Serena hopped off her seat to stand beside me. The quick look she shot me blazed with fury, and the energy of a fight crackled around her, confirming my own instinct.

"Joe Adonis, long time no see," she said coolly. "I can't believe Shepherd let you in."

I casually scanned our surroundings. The knife block was out of reach, plus these men probably had guns.

"Told that old fart that we needed to see the boss. He's been M.I.A. too long." The man in the center of the group tapped his fingers against the island. He was the shortest and had the smallest build. But the glint in his eye sent a shiver down my spine. "Where's Alessandro, girl?"

Serena tipped her chin up. "Signor Mancini is indisposed."

The man with greasy hair plucked the whole loaf of cheese braid, tore off a huge chunk, and began eating. I suppressed a groan of dismay. There was no way those thick fingers were clean, touching and ruining our dinner.

"Shouldn't you be offering us a bowl?" the greasy one garbled around the bite of food and jerked his chin to our soup bowls.

Serena's impending explosion radiated off her. Perhaps it was what the men wanted. Hating that I didn't know the dynamics of this organization, I didn't know if I should back her outburst or pacify the intruders.

"There isn't much left, but you're welcome to a bowl of soup," I hurried to say, deciding that peace was the better course of action. I plucked clean bowls from the cupboard, wishing that they would contract whatever illness the don had just by breathing the air in here.

When I was sure they weren't looking, I used the patient's dirty spoon in one of the bowls—just for good measure.

"Penny," my sister-in-law hissed. "They know they're not supposed to be here without the don's permission. You can't feed them."

"Ah, so you're the boss's new piece of ass," the leader sneered. "Where's your husband, donna?"

"I'm Mrs. Mancini and this is my home. I'm happy to offer friends of the family whatever they require." I scooped the soup into the dishes, hating my good upbringing. It would be so much more fun to yell at them. But I knew from past experiences that men like these were dangerous to lone females. It didn't matter if they were backwoods hicks, trailer trash, or greaseballs dressed like actors from a bad mob movie.

If they were here when they knew they weren't supposed to be and risked the wrath of the don, then I wasn't taking any chances. Our status might not save us, and I wasn't going to risk anything happening to Serena. So I served soup and said a little prayer to any saint listening that they left it at that.

"Where's the boss?" the leader insisted.

"I told you, Joe, he's not available." Serena scowled.

The two men slurped down the soup, but the leader watched us. That shrewd gaze seemed to strip us bare, while the slimy mind no doubt planned all the heinous acts his sort would do.

"You can't keep him locked away," Joe hissed. The sound of his voice made my skin crawl. "If something's happened—"

"Nothing has happened," I countered. "Unless you count the fact that he married me just a week ago. Do I need to draw you a picture of what newlyweds spend their days doing?"

I stood firm against their glares. Those licentious looks were nothing new.

At least my clothing's on. And they weren't sticking bills in my G-string.

Joe pointed a finger at me, moving toward the door. "I'm going to find the boss. And if I find out you've been lying—if you two little donnacce are keeping his body somewhere—you'll be sorry."

He was bold calling us a pair of whores.

"How dare you!" Serena stormed after him.

"S! Don't," I gasped, moving too fast and making my slowly healing side ache.

But the goons stepped to block her.

The moment one reached those grubby sausage fingers at her, I saw red. We girls stood up for each other, period. I grabbed the first thing I could reach and hurled it at the goon.

He cackled. "Little missus has an arm."

I continued to blindly snatch objects and launch them at the man as he came around the island, only taking my eyes off him to watch where Serena struggled in the other's hold.

My fingers latched around the long, thick wooden length. Triumph surged in my veins as I swung the mattarello at his head. The rolling pin cracked against his skull with a satisfying thunk.

Unfortunately, there weren't enough brains there. The blow didn't faze him. The goon bellowed, leaping to snatch the weapon. We struggled. While I held tight, it was obvious he would win this.

A deafening pop reverberated through the room.

My heart jumped to my throat, beating wildly and making it nearly impossible to draw a proper breath. The second gunshot following rapidly made the damn organ stop beating altogether.

The goon staggered and fell. A tight red hole began to leak on the side of his head. The exit wound, however, was a garbled mess of bone and grey matter.

Gagging, I turned away.

This was worse than the jewelry store. That day, I'd been ushered away from the bloodbath, not wearing the corpses. I didn't dare touch the sticky substance spritzed over my face, neck, and shirt. But it wasn't the blood and gore that bothered me half as much as the deeper, emotional wounds this attack clawed open. That goon...nearly overpowered me.

If he had, he could have done whatever he wanted, and I wouldn't have been able to stop him.

A raw, sickening shudder made me convulse.

He didn't touch me. I'm okay.

Serena kicked the body off herself, looking nothing but beautiful and disgusted with the filth at her feet. I could *feel* the green taking over my skin palette. They'd been too close!

I staggered to the sink, slammed on the cold water, and shoved my head under it.

"Signore, that was my cousin and his brother-in-law," Joe growled. "Two of my best men!"

Silence pulsed in the kitchen.

No...not silence. My pulse roared in my ears. Water rushed from the sink. And a deadly presence prowled through the space. That quiet whisper of sound was the loudest noise.

It stopped beside me.

"I'm okay," I rasped, not trusting myself to open my eyes and meet Mancini's gaze.

"Signore, this is uncalled for," Joe protested. "All my years of loyalty and this is how you treat me?"

The lightest touch ran down my arm. I shuddered but managed to reach for the faucet to turn it off. A soft towel was placed in my hand. I fisted it, dabbing my face.

"Thanks," I croaked.

"Get out, Adonis." The don's order sliced through the air.

"But, signore—"

"Consider you walking out the front door with your life the reward for your loyalty," the don said coldly. "But if you ever allow a soldier under your command to touch my wife, your death will last weeks. Loyalty be damned."

Joe spat on the floor. "I came to make sure you were alive, Alessandro! No one has heard from you in days."

"You forget yourself." The eerily calm way the don spoke was far more frightening than if he'd shouted.

Since he stood between me and the ghastly mess on the floor, I gazed at his face instead of the carnage.

A beautiful mask of wrath covered his features. My body instinctively stepped toward it, feeling the unspoken shelter coming off him. For today, and today only, he could be a rock I leaned on.

Chapter 29 – Alessandro

Shepherd appeared at the opposite door to the kitchen. Dante stopped talking, looking between the aged butler and me.

"Mr. Baldwin is here, signore," Shepherd intoned.

The old man looked prim and proper despite the two body bags on the floor and the overwhelming stench of bleach.

Dante let out a low whistle. "Better go see what the shark wants."

My shoulder blades shifted as I worked the muscles of my upper back. First Joe's unscheduled appearance, and now the businessman's? Did none of the men who worked for me have a self-preservation instinct?

"Fix Baldwin his drink and show him into the office," I ground out.

Thankfully, the clean team was making a trip back to the vans and hadn't heard the announcement that one of the elite members of society and top dog in the business world was there. Baldwin and I kept a great deal of public distance to our interactions. I ran the darker side of our business, and he was our organization's biggest front. Our symbiotic relationship was so secretive that even my men didn't know it existed. And while I trusted my men not to betray us, I didn't need to give loose tongues fodder.

"Did you know he was coming over?" Dante questioned, rubbing his chin.

"No, Baldwin generally schedules our meetings weeks in advance."

"How healthy of you two," Dante chuckled.

I clenched my jaw tight. My number two knew more than most, but he didn't have any true insight into the careful scenario Baldwin and I took years to concoct, fine-tune, and maintain.

"You got this?" I snapped.

Dante saluted. "Course, boss."

Needing to find a release—a punching bag would do, but a warm body across the ring would be better—I stalked into the office. If my muscles were still weary from the sudden and intense illness, I ignored them. It might be the punching bag for the time being.

"Tonight's not a good night," I snapped, slapping the door closed behind me.

"I heard," the leather-clad figure at the window with his back to me said. "Don't you have a rule where your capos need your permission to come here, and your presence is generally a requirement?"

I worked my jaw back and forth. "You know damn well that I do."

"And yet Joe sniffed an opportunity and came uninvited?" The businessman turned but stayed in the shadows. His arms crossed over his muscled chest.

"An action for which I taught him a valuable lesson." I crossed my own arms over my chest. "Do I need to teach you the same one?"

"As if."

"What are you doing here, Leo?"

His black gaze looked me up and down. "Serena messaged the other day."

Now that was surprising. I went to the tray where my neat whiskey sat next to Leo's gin martini. I passed the business shark his drink. "I didn't know she had your number."

"In case of emergencies." Leo gave me a pointed look. "She considered your illness an emergency."

I threw back my drink. "I'm fine."

"You should have messaged, Sandro," the businessman said tightly.

His tone made me do a double take. Like me, he didn't show emotions. Having it hammered out of us was one of the bonding experiences we shared.

"I would have sent you an update, especially if it was serious—which it wasn't." I raised my voice at his skeptical look. "But it seems I've misplaced my phone."

A beat passed.

And then Leo threw back his head and laughed.

The explosion of mirth had me staring wide-eyed at the man in front of me. Disbelief rocketed through me. In the thirty-four years I'd known this man, I could count the times he'd laughed on one hand. The most recent was a decade ago, at the late don's funeral.

"You're whipped," Leo wheezed, wiping his eyes.

My fingers curled into fists. Maybe my body wasn't that tired from the illness to kick his ass. "What do you want, Leo? If this was about Serena's text, you would have been here several nights ago."

Gasping for air, Leo waved a hand. "I've been keeping touch on your condition with Shepherd. He's fiercely devoted to your wife. Serena too. And now...this? You stayed in bed and let her play nursemaid? I'm going to have to meet her."

Leo wasn't ever breathing the same air as Penelope if I could help it.

He must have read the resolve in my face, because he cracked up again.

"Leonardo," I snapped. "Tell me why you're really here."

"That fed—the one with a chip on his shoulder—infiltrated your ranks," Leo gasped as the hilarity died. "You have a leak."

The seat of my rolling chair rose up to meet me as I collapsed into the thing. *Oh, dio bono.*

Leo perched on one of the leather seats before my desk. "I came over as soon as I found out."

"How did you hear?" I managed to ask the semi-intelligent question.

"Poker match. Has Mier said anything?"

I shook my head. "He hasn't—"

I stopped short. Scowling, I stared at the door.

"Because you don't have your phone, you don't know," Leo surmised. "Incredible. She has you by the balls."

"Fuck off."

"Make me."

I should. If I hadn't spent the last five days in bed....

"Look, with the special agent in town, we need to take care of this mole. And possibly the agent. Do you want me to see if any of my connections can have this pest removed?" Leo threw back his drink.

"No, I told you the other night, we don't want to owe any politicians favors right now," I said, shaking my head. "Plus, we don't know if this special agent would go after them."

Leo flicked a brow. "True."

"We find the leak in the organization. We take the mole out in a demonstration that will leave the men questioning ever crossing us." I leaned forward, mimicking the businessman's stance. It was an unconscious habit, one that we worked hard to hide. Right now, the unity felt right. Leo was one of the few who could be relied upon without question.

"Work fast, fratello."

I nodded. "Always do."

Leo plucked his helmet and moved to the door but paused to look back at me. "You don't look so good. You sure you're okay?"

The note of concern in his voice was as foreign as his laughter. "Fine."

"I would have come if Shepherd said it was dire. I only stayed away because, well—" he shrugged "—it's the way things are between us."

The rare display of vulnerability tugged at the dead place in my chest where most people had a working organ. I had the famiglia, and for what it was worth, Serena preferred me. Leo was alone, living as a banished king up in that ivory tower our enterprises had built.

So I threw him a bone. "Should have seen me a few days ago. I was pretty out of it. But my wife wouldn't take any protest from me. Kept me in bed, rested, shoved heaven only knows what witchcraft down my throat."

I stopped talking, realizing that I'd been waxing on about the merits of my bride.

A sad smile played at the corner of Leo's mouth. "Sounds like you enjoy married life."

"It's not bad." And it wasn't.

The fact that I still hadn't done more than tease my wife was a tragedy. We hadn't even taken that shower together, a fact I lamented greatly. But I wanted Penelope to be intimate willingly. I needed that. After everything I'd seen as a kid, I needed that knowledge that she was here and with me of her own free will.

Until then, the ache in my groin was nothing.

"Talk soon, Sandro."

"Soon. Don't let anyone see you on the way out."

Leo lifted his matte black helmet, pushed it over his head, and flipped me the bird. "I know the drill, fratello."

I grumped, not that he could hear it through the muffled layer of the helmet. When he was gone, I left my office, putting the problem of the leak behind me. A good shower, a small nap, and I would be able to tackle the problem. Just because I would never admit a weakness to anyone else didn't mean the exhaustion in my bones should be ignored. I'd been sick—actually sick—for the first time in decades. And overdoing it would only give the mole leverage to wiggle.

Chapter 30 – Penelope

The hot water turned my skin red long ago. It was not yet pruned and wrinkled, but the feelings of dread still lingered.

This was what I signed up for.

First with Tito, offering him my life and service for the money to help Mom. Being shot at on the streets with Cousin Massimo was thrilling—almost fun. It probably didn't say anything good about my psyche that I enjoyed the rush of nocturnal street fighting. But I hadn't been scared.

Because I didn't have to look the bad men in the face, knowing they could overpower me.

That was the difference with tonight. It was too close to past nightmares. I never imagined I would be faced with demons like Joe and his goons. It might have been naïve, but when I married Mancini to save Poppy, I thought he was the only monster I would have to deal with. And as much as I told myself I hated the don for that stunt, I had to admit that he wouldn't actually hurt me. He wasn't the sort to violate women.

"Alessandro shot him…just in time," I whispered to the swirling pool over the drain.

What if Alessandro hadn't been there? I shivered despite the heat raining down from above.

"Penelope?" the monster's voice broke through the tangled web of dark.

"Yeah," I said, voice hoarse. I cleared it. "I'm here."

"You've been in there for an hour." The glass door vibrated, but he stopped before sliding the door open.

He was waiting for permission to open the door.

That small, minuscule gesture sent a visceral throb through my chest. When I set boundaries, it was because I was pissed that he manipulated me. I didn't actually hate this man. His illness made him more human.

And damn my traitorous body. My inner goddess buzzed with longing. I wanted Alessandro to touch me. To make me feel the fire his gaze promised.

With only one arm crossed over my chest, I tugged the door open. "What's up?" I chirped.

Steam belched from the enclosure, perfuming around the dark and terrible form standing there. As the mist cleared, his black gaze studied my face. "Are you alright?"

I shrugged. "I will be."

"Such a strong woman," he whispered in Italian.

I swallowed hard, suddenly feeling overwhelmed. He hadn't dropped his gaze, not once, to look over my wet, naked body.

Me, on the other hand, I couldn't stop myself from taking a peep. He was naked except for the boxers on his hips. And oh, good lord was he gorgeous. My core clenched tight. This close, the lines of his body were tangible. The horny little fiend on my shoulder wanted me to run my tongue over them.

My gaze dipped lower, taking in his thick legs like twin trunks and that present hiding between them.

Virgin have mercy—the outline of his cock was something to behold!

That was a monster piece of equipment. There was no hiding it in the restrictive shorts. What would it be like unleashed?

Anticipation buzzed through my body.

"I was just getting out," I rushed to say, sliding past him.

Alessandro caught my wrist. "It gets easier."

Electricity tingled where our skin connected, scrambling his words. When my lust-drenched brain finally computed the meaning, I sucked in a sharp breath. He meant seeing humans shot.

"That's what I'm afraid of," I confessed. Because it was, even though it was only part of the truth. "I believe in the sanctity of life."

His voice hardened. "The luxury that modernity and this first world country gives is that we're safe. It's a delusion, Penelope. Humans used to understand that it was kill or be killed. Not out of malice, but for survival. I wish more than anyone that it was different, but the best way to deal with that harsh truth is to protect those in our lives. I'm sorry those soldiers invaded my home. I should have been there. I'm supposed to be their leader and in charge of their actions. I apologize for my lapse. It won't happen again."

As he spoke, he rubbed his thumb over the pulse on the inside of my wrist.

"You can't control everything all the time, Alessio," I whispered, the diminutive form of his name slipping easily off my tongue.

It felt...right.

Something dark flashed in his eyes. "If I don't, who will? No...you, my sister, this house, they're mine to protect. I won't fail you again."

His determination was heartbreakingly beautiful. More little pieces chipped away at the barriers I erected to keep him away. More sentiment like this, and it was entirely possible that I might end up falling for this man.

And that would be a dangerous thing indeed.

"How's your side?" His question interrupted the mental discussion.

"Oh, it's stiff, but I barely notice. It wasn't the worst bruise my ribs have had."

The corner of his mouth twitched. "You should probably sleep on the bed a few more nights. Just to be safe."

I pulled from his hold, eyes narrowing at him. "I see what you're doing, lupo. And no, I think I'll change that and take the floor again. Can't have myself growing too comfortable in this captivity."

That made his smile tug even wider. "Most prisoners would kill for the cell you've been given."

Roling my eyes, I pushed past him. Standing there, with endless supplies of hot water, joking about prison cells, it was too much.

Too twisted.

I needed air, because—mother of god help me—I didn't want to escape.

He didn't say anything, didn't try to stop me. As I scurried away, I caught the slight motion of him shucking his boxers.

That was the last straw. I had to look back. It would be a sin not to.

The sight was mouthwatering. Delectable. *Tempting*. That chiseled backside—oh, mamma mia! My pussy wept at the sculped mafia god disappearing into the cloud of steam.

Hurrying from the room before I did something foolish like join him, I gulped down breaths of the cooler bedroom air.

The truth was, there was no way I would be able to resist him for much longer. If he'd come to the shower, stepped into it like he owned it—which he did—and reached for me, I would have pushed him away. But he hadn't. It made the idea of being with him desirable.

We both clearly wanted the thing we were dancing around.

And here I was, refusing to give in.

Only...I didn't want to anymore. Alessandro was just as much man as monster. He might pretend not to be caring and sensitive, but he asked about me. *Me.* The concern about how I was handling the situation from tonight was evident. And he wasn't just asking about my side to keep me sleeping next to him. He actually cared. He might have been sick, but this whole time he'd remembered to ask me about it. He'd been gentle when he'd been near me.

"It's not real," I insisted.

But if it was just the physical I gave in to.... I didn't have to believe he would fall for me. That this relationship would ever be anything more than a strange partnership with sex attached.

Ah, screw it.

I turned around, left the closet, dropped my towel somewhere in the bedroom, and ventured back into the sauna that was the bathroom.

Where the sound of strokes was evident despite the rush of the shower.

I tugged open the glass door. Steam rushed out to caress me, but as it cleared, the sight that greeted me was my husband viciously tugging at his length.

His hand paused.

His gaze snapped to mine.

My heart tripled in speed, and I stepped into the shower. Arousal so intense swept through my veins. "My turn, lupo."

The don was perfectly still as I closed the distance. My pulse jumped as I grasped him. The length was rigid and stiff, but the texture was impossibly soft and smooth. I palmed his cock.

A guttural hiss escaped his lips. "Don't tease me, vespina."

"Never." I shook my head.

His large hands slid over my sides, my waist, my hips. "Are you finally giving in?"

"I am."

A low, rich growl rumbled in his chest. The sound was nothing short of possessive. His pitch-black gaze ran down my body. Under the intense focus of his dark stare my nipples hardened to the point of being painful.

"Finally," he breathed, and then his mouth was on mine.

The kiss was crushing and dominant. It was the staking of a claim—mine or his, it was hard to say.

I swept my tongue against his lips, only to have his invade my mouth a second later.

Those large hands settled on my hips. The don lifted me, pinning my back against the shower wall.

"Is this okay?" he rasped against my kiss.

I nodded vigorously.

Leaning his weight into me, he reached up with one hand and captured my chin, keeping my head in place. He pulled back, hard gaze boring into mine. "You tell me the moment it doesn't feel good. I'm not risking your ribs being irritated."

Trying and failing to shake my head, I snapped, "But I need you to fuck me, Alessio. Fuck me *hard*."

He groaned. "If I go too hard, and you get hurt, we can't do it again until you're healed. I'm not risking that, Penelope."

"What if this is a one-time deal?" I murmured, already retreating into myself at the intensity of his dominating presence. This man was going to overwhelm me, my senses, my body, and if I wasn't careful, my soul.

"No, vespina, this is us. You give yourself to me now, there's no turning back." His gaze was pure hunger.

It mirrored my own.

Leaning forward, he pressed his lips against my racing pulse. "Decide, Penelope."

"I don't want to."

Teeth scored across my throat, right over the heartbeat pounding under the skin. "If you give yourself to me, there's no going back."

He was right. I had to ask myself, did I want that? To go back to a stiff formality where we lived as a strange pair of roommates?

I don't want to go back. "Alright, I'll tell you if it bothers my ribs."

The don's body shuddered at my assent. He sucked hard on the delicate skin of my throat. It came out of his mouth with a deep pop. "That goes for everything we do. You don't like something, you tell me. If I'm too rough with you, you speak up. I'll stop. Understand?"

A sob that was part gratitude, part relief threatened to burst from a place deep inside. This man was an enigma—the best kind. With one breath he told me his claim was permanent but then followed that by giving me control over our interactions.

I wrapped my legs tight around his body, threaded my hands up into his hair. "Understood."

"Good. So very good."

Those words sent a thrill of pleasure through my body. It settled between my legs at the same time his hand dropped from my face to stroke the sensitive flesh.

My pussy wept with relief.

And he noticed the embarrassing amount of wetness.

"Mio dio, vespina, you're soaked for me."

The shyness disappeared the moment he pushed one finger deep inside, swirling and curling in me. I moaned, head dropping back against the tiles. The relief was instantaneous, and yet the need increased tenfold. This was going to be unlike anything I'd ever experienced.

The don continued to explore my body. His hand pushed gently over the planes of my stomach and palmed my breast. The sensitive flesh was kneaded under his touch. Below, the one finger became two, stretching my pussy.

I gasped, my hips bucking against his hand, seeking more friction, more pressure. The don chuckled, a low, throaty sound that sent shivers down my spine.

"Patience, little one," he murmured, his accent thicker with arousal. "We have all night."

His thumb found my clit, circling it with maddening slowness as his fingers continued their relentless assault. I whimpered, my nails scraping against his slick shoulders as I fought to keep from coming quickly.

Never had I been this affected in a romantic entanglement.

This was another level. Some raw connection drove my need for this man—this nightmarish fiend who held his dark power over me.

No...he's a monster, but I'm not caught in a nightmare. Not that.

More of my resolve to hate him chipped away.

The don's lips found my neck, sucking and nipping at the sensitive skin. His beard scratched deliciously against my flesh, leaving a tingling trail in its wake. I turned my head, seeking his mouth, desperate to taste him.

He obliged, capturing my lips in a searing kiss that stole what little breath I had left. His tongue mimicked the movements. Pulling back, that dark gaze studied me.

"Do you have any idea how sexy you are?" he rasped, voice tight and strained.

It made me smile to know he was just as affected by this as me.

His fingers moved inside. Pleasure shot through me, and my eyes fluttered closed.

"Dio, I've waited so long!" he breathed.

I snorted. "It only seems that way."

"No, vespina."

I cocked my head. "How long?"

His motions paused, touch remaining as a taunting presence, but he drew back to watch me. Something akin to pain crossed through those onyx depths before he shut his deeper thoughts away from the world. "Before we married. You pushed me into the fountain, and even though I was traveling to my fiancée, I couldn't get the girl in the hat and boots out of my head. Imagine my surprise when she was waiting for me in the home of my would-be father-in-law?"

Why did it seem like there was more to it than that? To lighten the suddenly heavy mood, I teased, "You were thinking about me naked?"

Alessandro nodded. "But not just thinking, Penelope. I was *scheming*. It was a long shot, but I started reasoning ways to make you mine. Do you know how close I was to ending the engagement?"

Whoa. That was heavy.

I knew he'd wanted me. Hell, I'd been guilty of the same hunger. But I never once considered an alternative to be with him.

"Wouldn't that have been war if you did?" I murmured, overcome with the severity of it.

A dark sound rumbled through his chest. "It would have been worth it to have these legs wrapped around me."

"Was that the little fantasy I interrupted in here?" I smirked, driving my nails along the ridges of his skull.

He nodded. "But the real thing is far better than what I imagined."

Whatever smartass comment I was going to say was cut off when he pinched my nipple hard enough to sting. He withdrew his fingers suddenly, leaving me aching and empty. I whimpered at the loss. Lifting me higher, he adjusted me against the tiles as he lined himself with my entrance.

"Your ribs?" he demanded.

"Fine." I rocked against him.

My protest at the delay quickly turned into a gasp as I felt the thick head of his cock pressing against me. Alessandro entered me slowly, inch by agonizing inch, stretching me deliciously. The sensation was intense, bordering on pain, but the pleasure far outweighed any discomfort. I clung to his broad shoulders, panting against his neck as he filled me completely.

"Perfetta," the don growled, his hands gripping my hips tightly. "You feel divine, vespina."

He began to move in long, deep strokes that had me seeing stars. I wrapped my legs tighter around his waist, pulling him closer, desperate for more. The don's pace quickened, his hips snapping against mine with increasing urgency. His lips found my throat, and this time there was nothing gentle about the caress.

"So responsive," Alessandro murmured against my skin.

The praise sent a convulsion of pleasure through my core. Water cascaded over us, steam rising around our entwined bodies. The heat, the slick slide of skin on skin, the intoxicating scent of his bodywash mingling with our arousal—it was overwhelming.

I urged him deeper with a flex of my pelvis.

His responding growl was a reward.

The don's control began to slip as our passion mounted. His movements grew more urgent, more primal. I felt the tension building, coiling tighter and tighter in my core. Alessandro sensed my impending release, his fingers finding my clit once more. He rubbed tight circles as he pounded into me, the dual stimulation pushing me closer to the precipice.

"Come for me," he commanded, his voice rough with need. "Let me feel you."

His words pushed me over the edge. I cried out, my body clenching around him as waves of pleasure crashed over me. The don's thrusts became more erratic, his breathing ragged against my ear. He groaned, burying himself deep inside me as he followed, his release hot and pulsing. With a final, powerful thrust, he joined me in ecstasy, spilling himself deep inside me.

We stayed like that for a long moment, panting and trembling in the aftermath. The water had cooled, but I barely noticed, lost in the warmth of his embrace.

Slowly, he lowered me to my feet, steadying me as my legs threatened to give way. His hands cupped my face, thumbs stroking my cheeks as he gazed at me with a strange emotion I couldn't name.

"Talk to me," he urged, voice breathless from the combustion. "How do you feel?"

My thoughts scrambled as the pleasure continued to surge through me. "You need to quit worrying I'm some fragile little doll, Alessio. I can take more. I'm not going to break."

"I'm going to put that to the test." That promise held a note of darkness, which in turn sent a wild thrill shooting through me. "But," he clarified, "I need to know if you hate me."

I had seconds to sort through my feelings. It was too loaded a question. One I wasn't fully capable of answering.

So I lied.

"Yes." The flash of pain in his eyes made me add a truth. "I hate that you forced me into this marriage."

Carefully, he pulled back and set me down. But before he let me go, he cupped my chin. "I'm not the horrible fiend you make me out to be."

With that, he stepped out of the shower.

I tipped my head back against the wall. It was true. He wasn't. But I would never be able to see him as anything but a monster.

"Monsters aren't always bad," I whispered to the empty room.

Chapter 31 – Penelope

I groaned as Serena set yet another outfit on the cushioned bench in the center of the changing area.

She cocked her head and looked at me. "You really don't like this shopping business, do you?"

"Not one bit." I laughed. "We bought clothes that lasted until they wore out. New pieces were kept nice for special occasions."

"Huh, another thing I was wrong about when it comes to you." Serena scooped her waist-length, bronze hair off the back of her neck and fanned the area.

"I'm not some gold digger," I insisted.

The other woman snorted. "You could have thrown a party to show off his fortune to all your cheap friends. At least there would have been some excitement."

"I'm not exciting enough for you?" I drawled.

"Eh, a little." She shrugged.

I plucked at the ridiculously short dress and considered everything she'd said. The conclusion was right there, staring me in the face.

Serena was lonely.

She didn't leave the mansion unless it was to shop or have a spa day—which she did alone. She didn't even have a pet to keep her company.

"You do have good taste in shoes," I said, snatching the strappy pair and dangling them in the air.

She gave me a withering look. "You don't have to force the girlfriend stuff. I'm perfectly happy shopping without the commentary."

"But I'm serious, S," I protested. "I don't know how to pair things like this. Hell, the stores we go to back home don't *have* these things."

"Sorry," Serena muttered. "I'm not trying to be so prickly."

"S'okay," I drawled.

"Not really. If you didn't already figure it out, I don't have friends, Penny. I don't know how to not be a raging bitch. Having thick skin is the only way to keep from getting hurt in our world."

No sisters, no mom...no friends. "Not one?" I pressed gently.

"Not one." Serena tossed me the dress. "Even in preparatory school, my actions were very limited. I was the rich recluse who didn't speak to anyone."

"Well, I'm here." I lifted my hands.

Serena rolled her eyes. "You were forced into prison. If you could, you have a life to return to. There's nothing for me here."

I snatched the dress, mentally wondering how she could exist in such an aimless vortex. "Quit the pity party, S. You have the world at your fingertips, and all I've heard from you is whining about how awful it is to be born rich and pretty."

Her flashing brown eyes widened.

"I don't mean that your life hasn't been hell—heavens, I can't imagine being so sheltered!" I gave her a sympathetic look. "But don't you want to *do* something with your life?"

Flicking a glance around us, Serena leaned in. "We're mafia women, Penny. That is our life."

I shook my head. "I refuse to let that define me."

"You're delusional."

"Probably, but I'm going to treat it as a tool and mold it to my will." I dangled the dress. "A bold statement. I'll use it when the opportunity strikes."

Serena held up her hand. "Eww, gross. That's my brother you're talking about."

Laughing with her, I went into a room to try on the dress. But it felt hollow. Alessandro hadn't touched me since the shower. He hadn't really been around either. We'd had one glorious round of unprotected sex, and now nothing. I remedied the situation with birth control, hoping my deeply religious mother never found out. But it seemed that move was all for nothing.

"Does this thing come in a size meant for girls with boobs and thighs?" I gasped as the material threatened to suffocate me.

"I'll see what I can find," Serena called out. Her heels clipped away as she retreated from the space.

The don's cold, aloof behavior wasn't going to keep me down. I had plans and ideas littering the pages of my bullet journal. This experience was going to open doors for me. I would settle for nothing less.

The woman who stared back in the mirror's reflection was a stranger. While she looked like me, the short dress reminded me too much of the creature I created as another tool once upon a time.

Are you really any better than the old you?

I was scheming to use a man's interest in me to accomplish a goal.

"A maid by day, an entertainer by night," I said through clenched teeth.

The thing about having a past, it was either going to hold me back or propel me forward. And I knew which one I chose every morning, again and again.

Still, my past had its uses. I shimmied in the dress, dropping into a provocative squat. The material stretched and the seams groaned. Yeah, I couldn't work the pole in this. And there was no strategic way to remove it.

"If I use this time to grow, to make something of myself, I'll never dance for the drunk local boys again." I smiled to myself.

I knew better than anyone how to fight for the future I wanted. Serena thought thick skin meant being cold and heartless? I needed to show her that thick skin was a defense, but that the true self didn't need to fear the world.

I tugged on the zipper, wincing when it stuck.

You've got to be kidding me.

"Serena? You back yet?" I called out.

The curtain slid back, and she slipped into the room.

Only...it wasn't my sister-in-law.

"You!" I snapped, rounding on the man who'd been stalking me. "What the hell do you think you're doing?"

The man flipped open a leather wallet. An I.D. was on top and a shiny badge on the bottom.

Anger made my heart thump hard. "This isn't the place to talk to me, cop."

"I'm not a cop, and I'll talk to you wherever I damn well please." His gaze was full of disgust.

I pulled my inner armor over myself. His intent to intimidate was a stench stronger than the bad cologne filling the space.

"Get out," I menaced.

"I need you to come into the station and give a statement about your husband," he sneered, stressing the last word.

"Am I under arrest?" I countered.

His eyes narrowed to slits. "No."

"Then I don't have to go anywhere." I planted my hands on my hips. "And I'm not telling you shit."

The man stepped forward. If his body stank, his breath was worse. "You're going to give me the information I need to make a case against your husband, or my friends are going to pay a visit to your brother."

I faltered.

It was the smallest slip. A moment of panic.

But the bastard latched onto it like a bass on a hook. "Yeah, his friend's meth lab is going to lock him up for good."

Theodor wasn't friends with that trailer rat anymore, but it was no secret they'd rolled together as teens. A properly motivated bastard like the one in front of me could make the case that Theodor was still in cahoots with the trash.

Taking a step forward, I refused to back down. "I plead the fifth."

"That's only for criminal trials," he scoffed.

"Yeah, and you can't make me testify against my spouse. So fuck off and get the hell out of my changing room."

"Penny? Who are you talking to?" Serena called out.

Shit! I glared at the man, arching a brow in question.

"Better go out there and distract her, so I can leave," he hissed. "Don't think your husband will like knowing you were in here with another man."

An idea dawned on me at those words. I didn't know how to tell if that badge was real. But it was entirely possible this whole thing was one big test.

After all, snitches got stitches—or so the movies would have me believe.

I hurried from the changing room, deciding to keep the whole interaction quiet.

"Help me with this," I breathed. "I was cursing every holy saint in there, and I'm going to have to go to penance. Don't tell anyone, but I rant when I'm frustrated."

None of those statements were lies.

"Hot damn, you look good, slut," Serena whistled.

I gave her a dry look. "No, just no."

"Yeah, I said I'm not good at the girlfriend chit-chat." She chuckled.

I angled my body so that Serena's back was to the changing room. "Just get me out of this, will you?"

The cop who'd been watching slunk out of the room and scuttled from the area. I didn't draw a proper breath until he disappeared.

Holy crap on a cracker.... If that wasn't a test, this situation was bad. But it would have been far worse if he was a test and I failed.

Serena sniffed. "What reeks?"

My stomach dropped. "Bad perfume?"

"Yeah, that." Serena peered around the changing area. "Whoever the hell that is, she should know that's more a man's scent, if the man was cheap."

There was no reason for her to suspect anything. And if she was in on the test, she was a damn good actress.

"Yeah, it does stink," I agreed.

"I saw this buried in the back. I can't believe the saleswoman didn't pull it. I'll be speaking to her manager," Serena huffed.

Shaking my head, and trying to focus on the normalcy of shopping, I glanced at the gown. The vibrant purple creation was the most beautiful thing I'd ever seen.

"That's...elegant," I breathed.

"Yeah, you can wear it to the gala next weekend." Serena pointed at the skimpy gown. "Sorry I chose that. I didn't think you'd actually wear it."

I gave her a smirk that I didn't feel. "I told you, your brother would like it."

She grimaced. "Well, this gown will be just the thing for a *public* appearance. What you two do in private is not something I ever need to know."

I took it into the changing room, once the curtain closed it was just me and the stench. I took deep breaths through my mouth. "What are you wearing to the gala?"

"Oh, Alessandro won't let me go," Serena said flippantly.

I poked my head out to glare at her. "Did you ask?"

"Yes," she insisted. "Nicely too, so don't give me that look. But it's useless, Penny. I don't go places."

Rolling my eyes I zipped the gown up and emerged. "I'll talk to him."

Something flickered in her eyes. Hope, it was hope.

"No promises," I insisted, but already I was scheming exactly how I would make the mob boss bend. And when he did, he was going to tell me if that cop stunt was a test of loyalty. Along with some other things—like who was the woman he muttered about when the nightmares came. Because if he was dreaming about someone else....

No, no it wasn't that. The maids whispered in Italian because they thought I couldn't understand. From what I gathered, she was long dead. It was her role in this world that still perplexed me. I was pretty close to finding the truth about the mysterious Elena without having to go full nuclear on my husband.

Proud of how I handled the twists and turns of my situation, I ran my hands over the royal material. Whatever happened, I was in this world now.

Chapter 32 – Alessandro

The documents were spread over the desk. My eyes felt glazed. Pinching them between my thumb and pointer, I rubbed the lids. If I was smart, I would call it quits and go to the family room.

Where my bride was reading on that device she'd purchased.

Being the head of my security, Dante showed me the titles she read. I still found it hard to believe that those kinds of books were written, let alone read! Fairy smut? Men with bat wings? And that was just the twisted beginning of the rabbit trail.

Stalkers and hitchhikers, blue aliens and actual sea monsters, secret societies and hockey players, the list was endless.

What they all had in common was dominant men and strong women. It relieved some of the tension at knowing how hard I took Penelope against the shower.

My dick stirred at the memory—and at the resolve to take her even harder as soon as I could be assured that her side was healed.

"Alessio, you busy?" the siren called out from the other side of my door.

A dark grin spread across my face. "Come in."

The curvy sight framed in the doorway sent my dick fully erect.

Fucking hell.

She took in the pile of papers and the stack of folders. "You sure I'm not disturbing you? I can come back later when you're less busy."

"Did you wear that in public?" The question came out harsher than I meant it to.

"So what if I did?" She arched a brow in challenge. "It's my dress."

"Just tell me who I am going to kill, because I am going to destroy anyone who looks at you in that," I drawled.

Penelope didn't flinch. Oh, no. My pretty little wife marched into the home office, slammed the door, and planted her hands on her hips.

"Save your death threats. I'm here to make a deal with you, Don Mancini."

Oh, damn. This I couldn't wait to hear. I swept my hand graciously in front of me. "What do you need, vespina?"

She hesitated only a moment before speaking up. "Something you need to know about me is that I'm resourceful; I'm not afraid to do whatever is necessary to get what I need."

I hummed. Where was she going with this?

"When we needed a laptop, I found the extra money by doing chores at the neighbor's ranch—" Penelope took a deep breath "—and when my sister decided to be a nurse, I moved heaven and earth to make it happen."

"I know." *And I've been wondering how you did that with your salary.*

"I bought this dress with the intention of putting on a little show for you."

Leaning forward, I steepled my hands and pressed my lips against the tips of my fingers. "What's that going to cost me?"

Her smile was stunning. Dazzling with the strength that could easily knock a man down. "I want Serena to come with me to the Jefferson Children Society benefit."

So that's what you've been plotting, little one. "Out of the question."

"Come on." She sashayed toward me, and I stifled a groan to see her hips shiver in that flashy, shimmering dress. "Isn't there anything I can do to convince you?"

Pushing back, I rose. "I must say, wife, I'm surprised. This is an entirely new side of you, one I didn't anticipate."

That observation had Penelope's gaze dropping to the ground, but just as quickly, she lifted it. There, shining back, was the defiant streak I was coming to adore.

"How much do you know about my past?" There was a breathless quality to her voice.

I shrugged. "You worked since high school at the Holiday Inn. Two years ago, you were promoted to head housekeeper."

"Maids don't make a lot of money."

Dread coiled in my gut. "Yet you helped put your sister through nursing school."

Penelope nodded. "Without debt."

"I remember. And I haven't discovered how exactly you did that."

A triumphant smile shone on her face. "I danced."

"You danced—" The incredulity died on my tongue as I realized exactly what kind of dancing she was talking about.

Oh, dio, no.

"I'm sharing this secret to explain how I know how to do this, but don't you dare judge me, lupo. Your past isn't squeaky clean either!"

I cleared my throat, suddenly finding it hard to breathe with the weight on my chest from the news. "I'm not judging. But how did you keep it off the records?"

"The owner paid cash, plus the tips were cash." Penelope held up her phone, finger hovering over the play button of the music app. "It's been a few years, but I still remember a few routines. I'm hoping I can use them to barter your sister's company."

My voice came out sounding like I ate gravel. "And here I was planning to fuck that pretty mouth for daring to buy such a dress."

Instead of being turned on by my words, Penelope's nose wrinkled. "We never serviced clients. Anyone who asked was thrown out."

There was something else she wasn't telling me. It was there, buried in the tangled web of her past.

"You can stop being worried about me being scandalized by the lengths you went to earn money, Penelope," I promised, hoping she was convinced by the tone of my voice. "As you say, we're not saints in the mob. In fact, the famiglia owns several gentlemen's clubs."

Daggers flashed in her eyes. "You spend your time there?"

"Rarely. That's not part of the business I manage." This jealous side of her was intoxicating.

Her chest heaved as she struggled to control her emotions. "Is that so?"

"It is." I made a point of looking up and down her body in a long, lingering look. My cock strained against the slacks at the thought of her shimmying and twirling. "Penelope, tell me, am I going to have to kill every man in North Dakota?"

She snorted, not taking me seriously. "No, just in Carrington and the surrounding county."

That was still a large list and would require a vast amount of bloodshed.

"Show me." I leaned against the desk.

"You'll pay?" she asked eagerly.

I both liked and hated her enthusiasm. Would I? It was a hard rule that Serena stay out of the spotlight. Assassins were everywhere and staying alert while conducting business was difficult without having to worry about my sister's safety.

But I was bringing Penelope into that arena. There was no doubt in my mind that she could handle herself. Serena was cut from the same strong cloth. Why not bring her along? Especially if she kept my wife company.

Leaning back, I pulled a wad of cash from the drawer. "Will this buy me a dance?"

Penelope scowled. "I want Serena to come to the gala."

Stabbing the screen on her phone, Penelope tossed the device on the seat of a chair and began to shift her body.

"You said your country boys paid cash," I countered. "Let's call that the opening rate."

With a dramatic eye roll, Penelope began to move.

The music pulsed through the dimly lit room, its seductive beat throbbing in time with her body. She moved with a fluidity that was both sensual and commanding, her every motion a tantalizing invitation to take—to claim.

"Did my sister put you up to this?" I asked, hoping she hadn't.

"No, but she wants to go." Penelope wasn't even winded. Her silhouette, outlined by the light, was pure temptation. Each sway of her hips, each arch of her back, radiated an intoxicating power that drew me in like a moth to a flame.

"Why do you want her with?" I tapped a finger against the armrest, gaze locked on her twirling figure. I struggled to resist the urge to touch her, to feel the heat emanating from her skin. Her movements were deliberate but effortless, as if she had been created by the music itself.

I shifted in my seat, stifling a groan as my wife bent then snapped straight. Her legs, strong and graceful, moved with a feline precision that left me mesmerized. And when she dipped low and caught my gaze with smoldering eyes, I knew I couldn't resist her any longer.

But Penelope still hated me. What had I been expecting? A moment of passion to solve all our problems?

She won't hate me forever.

The resolve behind that statement felt stale. Already one soul was lost because I failed as a husband. It didn't seem I was doing any better this time around. My money didn't appeal to her. Neither did the clothes or jewels.

It has to be enough. I would make a more expensive gesture. Just because I hadn't figured out what to buy for her, didn't mean there wasn't something. Part of the fun was in the challenge. There was something out there that would make her happy, make her stop hating her life here, and I would find it!

The world seemed to fade away as she danced for me alone. With every step, she whispered promises of mystery and pleasure. And when the music finally came to an end, she stood before me, beaming and glistening with sweat, a vision of beauty and desire.

In that moment, it was just her and I. And as she smiled at me with a knowing look, we both acknowledged the fact that I would give her whatever she asked—because she was a goddess brought to life by the rhythm of the music.

It took every fiber of my being not to reach for her. "Again."

"Oh, so you liked that?" Her smile was coy and knowing.

Fucking hell, I couldn't tell her how much. This was going to be how she controlled me.

"How much for another dance?" I ground out.

"I don't want your money, lupo," she said tightly.

I pushed the cash toward her. "You earned this. You'll take it."

She glared at the pile. "Fine, but don't be pissed when I give it to a needy family at church on Sunday."

This woman. "I said it was yours, and it is. Now...how much for another dance?"

"Serena comes to the gala," was her immediate demand.

Rising, I went around my desk to stand in front of her. I reached out and plucked the thread-thin straps on her shoulders, snapping the silky material.

"Fine," I agreed, unable to believe I was giving in. "Serena can come, but this time...take. It. off."

Penelope smiled happily and leaned over to select another song from her phone. Her body grazed against mine. My jaw clenched tight at the contact. To distract myself, I moved some of the papers, no longer caring about the precise organization, and perched on the edge of the desk.

The sultry notes of a new melody filled the air, slower and more sensual than before. Penelope's eyes locked onto mine as she swayed her hips, her fingers trailing along the hem of her dress. With agonizing slowness, she inched the fabric upwards, revealing smooth thighs inch by tantalizing inch.

"I'm going to North Dakota first thing in the morning," I growled.

She cocked her head, but her body didn't break from the lithe movements.

"I'm going to blind every man who's seen you dance," I vowed, gripping the edge of the desk until my knuckles turned white. "I'm going to cut the ears from anyone who's heard about your performance."

"Did I mention I wore a mask?" she stated lightly. "They don't know it was me."

Interesting. "Why's that?"

"Couldn't have my family finding out." She laughed. "Or the parish priest."

"Ah, that's very kind of you not to tempt him out of celibacy," I mused.

This time, her laughter made the rhythm of her body falter. "I'm not *that* good, lupo."

I reached out, snatching her arm. Those beautiful hazel eyes watched me.

"You could tempt a priest to sin, vespina," I promised. "Don't ever underestimate yourself like that again."

Her chin bobbed.

For a second, I considered ending the dance and taking her. But instead, I released her and resumed my death grip on the desk. I paid for the dance, and I wanted her to finish it, even if it killed me to wait.

Penelope stepped closer.

My breath caught in my throat as she turned, presenting her back to me. Looking over her shoulder with a smoldering gaze, she unzipped her dress, letting it fall to the floor in a whisper of silk. The sight of her bare skin, illuminated by the soft glow of the room, sent a jolt of electricity through my body.

She moved with feline grace, her body undulating to the rhythm. Every curve, every dip and swell of her form was a work of art, and I couldn't tear my eyes away. Her hands roamed her body. The skimpy swaths of lace that covered her intimate areas teased me, forbidding me from seeing everything.

"Take those off," I growled.

She spun around, wrapped her hands loosely around my neck, and curled her body over me.

"No." The word popped next to my ear.

An animalistic sound clawed from my throat. "Penelope," I warned.

She smirked. "I'm in charge."

I pinned her in place, my hands digging into her waist. "I said, take them the fuck off."

Penelope's eyes flashed with defiance, a wicked smile playing at her lips. She rolled her body despite my hold.

"And I said no," she purred, her voice low and husky. "You wanted another dance, and that's what you're getting."

She sauntered closer, her hips swaying hypnotically. The lace material barely concealed her most intimate areas, and I could feel my control slipping with each step she took. She placed a finger on my chest, pushing me back.

"Patience," she whispered, her breath hot against my ear. "Good things come to those who wait."

With that, she spun away, her body moving in perfect sync with the music. Her hands glided over her curves, teasing and tantalizing. She arched her back, letting her head fall, exposing the long line of her throat. I longed to taste her skin.

Fuck, what was I waiting for? She was right there.

I surged forward, grabbing her wrist and tugging her body against mine. My hands slid over her body, slowly, carefully feeling every inch of her.

"This is my dance, and I'm paying for it." I pulled the clasp of the strapless bra. The hooks came undone with a pop and filled the room with a dark promise.

"Touching's extra," she panted. Her eyes blazed with excitement. It was hard to believe she used to do this professionally. The only way I was going to survive this show was to push that from my mind.

But the wicked voice that sought to torment my every waking hour pushed me to know the truth.

I hummed under my breath. "You're very good at this."

"Thank you."

"I swear to you, I don't judge your past, but if another man touched you—"

"No one," she murmured, voice as delicate as the lace. "Not while I danced."

Now while she danced....

"But they did?" I insisted, stopping her and holding her still.

Penelope pursed her lips. "They tried. They never succeeded."

Blood—there would be so much blood spilt when I was done.

"I've gotten over it, Don Mancini, so wipe that murderous look off your face and don't ruin this moment," Penelope said fiercely.

For her sake, I wrestled control of my features. There would be names on my desk by morning, and soldiers sent to collect the culprits by tomorrow night.

But right now, I focused on my wife.

With deliberate slowness, I tugged the bra from her body.

It fell to the floor, revealing her perfect breasts. The lower regions were covered with a slip of black cloth—which I would tear from her later. I cupped those full beauties in my hands, savoring their softness, their weight. Penelope's breath hitched as I brushed my thumbs over her nipples, feeling them harden under my touch.

"Alessio," she moaned, her body arching into mine.

I fucking loved that name on her lips. No one called me that, and now, it would only be her name for me.

"You're doing so good, vespina. Don't stop now," I growled.

"It's kind of hard to move with you holding me," she panted, her chest rising and falling under my touch.

"Hmm," I growled. "Then kiss me."

Her brow arched. "Kissing's extra."

Leaning over my desk, I was about to pull a wad of cash from the drawer when a stack of yellow squares caught my eye instead. I handed the post-it note to her and a pen.

"Whatever the price, write it down and I'll pay it," I said, running my hand over her body. She didn't like cash, she didn't like jewels—this way, I would learn what it was that drove my beauty.

Penelope let out a long whistle. "Whatever I want? That's a dangerous proposition, Don Mancini."

"Whatever the fuck you want," I enunciated each word.

"For a kiss?"

I nodded. "For a kiss."

Penelope set the post-it note down and stepped between my legs. "Come here then."

Her fingers slid against my neck and gave a gentle tug. I dipped my head, and she captured my lips in a searing kiss a moment later. Her mouth opened beneath mine, our tongues dancing together in a passionate collision. My hands roamed her body, tracing every curve, every dip and valley. She was a masterpiece, and I intended to worship every inch of her.

When her teeth sank into my tongue, holding it in place for a moment, before smiling against my mouth, I groaned roughly.

Pulling back, I gazed down at her. Part of me still couldn't believe she was real—that she was here.

"You feisty girl," I growled.

"You like it." Penelope closed the distance. Her fingers tangled in my hair, pulling me closer. I could feel the heat of her body against mine, the rapid beat of her heart echoing my own. The music faded into the background, replaced by the sound of our shared breaths as I pulled her onto my lap.

She didn't resist. She didn't pull away.

Encouraged, I reached between her to the slip of black cloth. It was wet.

Fuck me. I loved how turned on she got for me.

As I stroked her through the pitiful excuse for panties, her fingers fumbled with the buckle of my belt.

I let her unsnap it before I caught her wrists. "Not yet," I murmured against her lips. "I'm not finished with you."

Penelope whimpered in protest, her body trembling with need. I trailed kisses down her neck, savoring the taste of her skin, the scent of her perfume. My hands cupped her breasts, thumbs circling her nipples as she arched into my touch.

"I want this," she gasped, rocking her hips against mine.

I smirked, nipping at her collarbone. "Patience, vespina. You teased me; now it's my turn."

I lifted her so her knees braced the desk and her body was within reach. My lips traveled lower, kissing a path between her breasts and down her stomach. Penelope's fingers tightened in my hair. I paused, looking up at her flushed face. I drove my fingers into her slick center.

Her moan sent a bolt of pure need shooting painfully through my dick.

Standing and turning, I laid her out on my desk. Her back scattered the papers, but my inner control was long gone, my mind focused on something far more important than organization.

My voice came out hard. "Spread those legs for me."

A moment of hesitation flickered through her eyes.

"Come on, Penelope, show me that pretty little pussy." I wasn't asking, and she realized it.

When she opened her thighs, I groaned. She was beyond beautiful. There were no words to describe how perfect this fiery woman was.

It was time to devour her.

Bending, I licked her pussy.

Penelope gasped and arched her back. I savored her, relishing every moan and whimper that escaped her lips. My hands gripped her thighs, holding her open as I feasted with a passionate hunger.

"Let me hear you. Don't hold it in," I growled.

Penelope's legs trembled as my tongue explored her most intimate folds. Her fingers clutched at my hair, urging me closer as breathy moans escaped her lips. I savored her taste, intoxicating and uniquely hers, as I teased and pleasured her with my mouth.

"Oh, mother of god, Alessio," she cried out, her hips bucking against my mouth.

I slipped two fingers inside her, curling them to stroke that sensitive spot within. Her walls clenched around me as I sucked her clit, bringing her closer and closer to the edge. Penelope's fingers tangled in my hair, urging me on as she chased her release.

"That's it," I murmured against her slick flesh. "Let go for me."

With a passionate cry, she shattered, her body quaking with waves of pleasure. I sucked until she shivered.

"That's too much," she protested.

I flicked my tongue over her clit. "Is it?"

She hesitated. "No...but you told me to talk."

"I did, what a good girl." I pressed a kiss to the inside of her thigh, making her hiss. That delicious sound in my ears sealed her fate. I pushed to my feet and held out my hand. "Come upstairs."

Chapter 33 – Penelope

I watched the don, unable to tell if that was a question—or a command.

We were so far down the rabbit hole now, there was really no reason to turn back. This physical attraction wouldn't be ignored. I knew it when I bought the dress, when I plotted to dance for the head of the ruthless mob.

Jumping to my feet, I walked past him as if I wasn't naked in heels. I wanted more. While I was still high on the pleasure, while there was limited blood in my brain and a strong pulse between my legs, I was going to give into the primal call.

Hand on the doorknob, the door closed with force as I tried to open it. The wolf held the door tight, hot gaze staring down at me.

"Wait." There was a hard bite to Alessandro's command.

He crossed the room to a rack where his suit jacket hung. He brought it to me and draped it over my shoulders.

"No one else gets to see this," he said roughly, wrapping the material around my front and placing my palm on the closure. "It's mine, and mine alone."

The possessive tone sent a thrill through me.

Being the object of his obsession shouldn't feel this good. But it did.

The precaution was a good idea, since I had been planning to make a run for it instead of slipping back into the skimpy, too-tight dress. We moved from his downstairs office to the second floor without meeting anyone. My pulse beat wildly with anticipation the whole way.

No sooner were we through the door than his dominant command cracked through the room. "Take it off."

The suit jacket fell from my shoulders. Hands fidgety, I fluffed my hair and glanced at the bed. With the high from the orgasm waning, a note of shyness crept through my veins.

But I didn't need to feel strange about being exposed. The hunger radiating off the wolf was volatile.

"On your knees." The next order slid across my skin with a velvety darkness.

The mob boss was really hot when he gave instructions.

But I wasn't the kind of girl who easily listened. Every instinct told me it would be more fun to defy him.

I crossed the room and folded onto the bed. The don watched me darkly from where he stood at the door. The lock was thrown closed with a deafening click. He didn't say anything as he began to undo his clothing. Tie and shirt fell to the floor. Shoes and socks joined them. My mouth watered as he undid his unbuckled belt, the slacks slowly sliding down his thighs. He paused by a side table and pulled a leather cord from his neck.

Huh, I didn't realize he wore a necklace under his shirts.

The curiosity fizzled out the moment he began to stalk across the room. The monstrous beast stopped in front of me. Slowly, I spread my legs, embracing his infatuation with me, and ran my hands along the inside of my thighs. He leaned forward. My pulse beat wildly. The hunger raging in his eyes was tangible. When he loomed right in front of me, I laid back, arms above my head. The vulnerable position felt good.

"I said, on your knees," Alessandro growled.

Moving with lightning speed, he flipped me onto my stomach. One hand pressed against the middle of my back.

The other slapped with stinging force over my ass.

I gasped, the sharp sting blooming across my skin. How dare he? How freaking dare he?!

"Where's your stinging response now, vespina?"

My body tensed. But beneath the shock, a thrill of excitement coursed through me. I'd never encountered such brutal dominance before. It didn't scare me.

Heaven help me, I wanted more. "Make me."

Alessandro's hand remained firmly on my back, holding me in place.

His voice was low and dangerous. "Do you know what happens to those who defy me?"

Another slap landed, harder this time.

Liquid heat pooled between my legs.

"No, what happens when I defy you?" I snarled through clenched teeth.

The dark chuckle was the only warning. He spanked me again—and again.

I bit my lip to stifle a moan, my fingers curling into the bedsheets. The heat of his palm lingered on my skin, a stark contrast to the cool air of the room. It was hard to be enraged when the mixture of pleasure and pain sent an intoxicating shot of energy through me.

"You asked for it rough. Is this what you had in mind?" he demanded.

"I don't know, you're not even fucking me yet," I panted, my voice muffled by the mattress.

"All in good time, little wife," Alessandro purred. His hand trailed down my spine, leaving goosebumps in its wake. "It seems there's a lesson you need to learn, vespina."

"Do your worst," I dared.

The wolf's grip on my back loosened, and I seized the opportunity. In one fluid motion, I rolled to the side, evading his grasp. My heart raced as I scrambled off the bed, putting distance between us.

"You think you can escape me?" His body radiated pure danger.

The thing was...I trusted him.

In this space, in this time, I was completely at his mercy, and yet I was safe. So I played along.

I backed away, my eyes never leaving his. The room suddenly felt smaller, the air thick with tension. "I'm not your puppet, Alessandro. I won't just roll over and submit."

I meant that.

But it didn't mean I wouldn't let him dominate me here.

His eyes flashed with a mixture of anger and admiration. "Oh, vespina. You have fire. I like that. But make no mistake—I will tame that flame."

My body shivered with anticipation.

He advanced slowly, like a predator stalking its prey. I retreated, my back hitting the cool surface of the wall. There was nowhere to go.

In one fluid motion, he caught me, pulled me to the ground, and trapped my legs under one of his. Before I could react, he pinned my wrists. I glared at him over my shoulder. His eyes blazed with desire and dominance as he loomed over me.

"You think you can challenge me?" he growled. But there was no malice in his voice.

"Yes."

It was so simple, so perfect.

His fingers raked over my throat.

Leaning into his heavy touch, I stared back, never dropping my gaze. "I'm not one of your obedient lackeys, lupo. You can't just order me around."

He grasped my chin, hard enough to make me squeak. His thumb brushed my lower lip. "No, you're far more intriguing than that. But make no mistake—I will have your submission."

I turned my head, breaking free of his touch. "You'll have to earn it."

Quick as a snake, his hand came down on my ass. Over and over it connected. The pain melded into pleasure. I arched my back into his touch. My pussy on his thigh and my bare breasts on the floor, I writhed, letting the moment of friction heighten the pleasure.

The monster growled, a primal sound that sent shivers down my spine.

"You dirty little girl, you're enjoying this," the don snapped, annoyance sharp in his voice.

In one swift motion, he pushed me onto the floor and his powerful body covered mine. I felt the cool carpet against my flushed skin. My nipples ached from the rough contact as he positioned himself behind me. His hand tangled in my hair, pulling my head back.

But he didn't give me what we both craved.

Instead, his fingers slid against my drenched sex. "On our wedding night you said you weren't the kind of girl who begs. I want to hear you now, vespina. Beg for it. Fucking *beg*."

I shook my head. "No!"

His finger pinched my clit. "I can wait—all night if I have to."

I whimpered. The exquisite touch was too much.

"It's right here, Penelope," he rasped. "I'm waiting for you."

His fingers slid into me, curling in a delicious way, teasing and taunting. I half gasped, half cried out.

"Let me hear you, beautiful." His touch slid away, returning to that agonizing pressure on my clit.

Something was definitely wrong with me because the next words out of my mouth were ones I swore I would never utter. "Please, monster. Fuck me—hard."

"You want this? Then take it all," he hissed in my ear.

Without warning, he drove into me, filling me completely. I cried out, the sensation overwhelming. He drew my hips up while my forearms and chest braced on the floor. The pace he set was punishing, each thrust pushing me harder against the floor. The friction against my sensitive breasts only added to the building pleasure.

As he pounded into me, his hand came down on my ass again and again. The sharp sting created a heady cocktail of sensations that left me gasping and moaning.

I pushed back against him, meeting him thrust for thrust. Each powerful connection sent waves coursing through my body.

"Alessio," I whimpered, my fingers scrambling for purchase.

"You're mine," Alessandro snarled, gripping my hips, bruising tight.

I came hard, unable to help it.

The don fucked me through the orgasm and then pulled out only to roll me onto my back. Capturing my hands and dragging them over my head, he leaned down. "Rib. How is it?"

"Fine—completely healed. Exactly what I told you this morning, what I told you yesterday morning, the day before that," I said through deep breaths.

"Good," he said harshly. "Because I think it would kill me to stop."

And then he pushed one leg up, bending my knee, and drove into me with a punishing force.

His powerful body covered mine as he pounded into me relentlessly. His dark eyes blazed with intensity, never leaving my face as he watched every flicker of pleasure cross my features. I arched beneath him, my breasts pressing against his chiseled chest with each thrust.

With my leg captured at my side, the angle made it deeper.

Built the pleasure higher.

Bent and reshaped the universe.

The carpet beneath me offered little cushioning, the friction against my back adding another layer of sensation to the overwhelming experience. The wolf's hands roamed my body, leaving trails of fire in their wake. He cupped my breast, thumb circling my nipple before pinching it hard enough to make me scream.

"You're so beautiful like this," he growled, his voice husky with desire. "Spread out beneath me, taking everything I give you."

I moaned in response, unable to form coherent words as he hit that perfect spot inside me over and over. My other leg wrapped around his waist, pulling him deeper, urging him on. His muscular form loomed over me, sweat glistening on his chest in the dim light. I was desperate to feel him come undone.

In a million years, I never would have guessed it could be this good.

It was him—it was *us*.

I knew he felt it too. The thing between us had been raging from the beginning, and it had taken this long to truly give into it.

The knowledge that we were crossing a line, one we could never come back from, didn't scare me half as much as the idea of never feeling this explosive chemistry again.

He released my hands, trailing his fingers down my arms and sides before gripping my hips. I quickly wrapped my freed leg around to hook with the other behind his back. The change in angle sent sparks of pleasure shooting through me.

I cried out, my fingers clawing at his shoulders.

"That's it," he growled. "Let me hear you."

His pace quickened, each thrust hitting deeper. The room filled with the sounds of our passion—skin against skin, breathless moans, and our mutual surrender to moment right within reach.

I tightened my legs, pinning him closer. Limiting his movements. The restrictive position allowed him to hit that perfect spot.

His muscles tensed, jaw clenched as he fought for control.

There was no holding back.

Alessandro's rhythm faltered as he felt my walls clenching around him. His eyes locked onto mine, burning with primal intensity.

"That's it, vespina," he growled. "You're doing so well."

His thrusts became more forceful, more erratic. I could feel him swelling inside me, pulsing with need. My oversensitive body trembled, every nerve ending singing with pleasure.

"Alessandro," I moaned, clinging to him.

"Come for me," he urged, voice breathy. "I want to feel you."

I shattered, the orgasm making me scream as stars exploded in my field of vision.

With a guttural groan, the wolf buried himself in me. I felt the hot rush of his release flooding me, filling me completely. His powerful body shuddered above me as waves of pleasure wracked through him.

The sensation of his pulsing cock and warm seed was a beautiful epilogue, sending a rush of pleasure through me. I clung to him, relishing the feeling of being so completely filled and claimed. My back arched off the floor, leaving me panting in the aftermath.

Mother of god, what have we done?

Chapter 34 – Alessandro

I studied my wife as she lay under me. Penelope was breathing hard. She swore her ribs were fine, but I knew how badly she'd fallen into the counter when the gunfight started. It sometimes took weeks and months for bruises like that to heal.

I was too rough with her.

But dio! It felt good.

It felt *right*.

And the look on her face said she agreed.

Still, she was breathing harder than I liked.

Gently untangling her, I reached for my dress shirt and dabbed between her legs. That lush hazel gaze focused on me the entire time. When I was done, Penelope lifted her arms above her head and stretched.

"Come." I held out my hand for her.

The smirk on her lips told me she wasn't going to take the proffered help. So I bent and scooped her into my arms.

"Put me down," she squeaked.

That wasn't happening. I enjoyed touching her too much. Once we were in the bathroom, I perched on the tub ledge, balancing her carefully as I reached for the tap. Water spluttered and rushed out. Next came the salts, bubbles, and other items.

Penelope didn't speak, for which I was glad. I didn't want her to reassure me how much she hated our marriage. Not after the raw and brutal claiming.

My inner beast couldn't take that rejection.

So I held her tight and drew her a bath.

"You know where everything is," she mused as I dropped the essential oils into the water.

A lush, floral scent perfumed the space. I drew deep gulps of it into my lungs. The smell was nothing short of intoxicating.

"I've been watching you, little wife," I murmured.

Her light, amused laugh was musical. "Well, that's not creepy, lupo."

Wolf—a beast without mercy. That was all she saw me as.

Gently, I lowered her into the hot water. The bubbles enveloped her decadent body, and she leaned back with a sigh.

"Call out if you need anything," I instructed, pushing to my feet.

"Okay," she whispered.

The fact that she'd agreed and hadn't given me some snarky comeback sent my heart pattering. I slipped into a pair of sweats before sprinting back to my office. I didn't want to be out of earshot in case she did call for me.

Collecting my phone and turning off my computer, I paused. The yellow square of paper stared back at me. I plucked it carefully off the desk.

What the hell had I been thinking?! It was madness to offer her whatever her heart desired. My business was at risk, the lives of my men! I was first and foremost a leader in the mob. The famiglia always came first. And yet, in a burst of madness, I raised the stakes and gambled.

So why did it feel like I'd won the hand?

"You've bewitched me," I growled, pinching the sticky edge and stalking back upstairs.

It was the only explanation for the illogical offer.

With her freedom off the table, I pondered what she could possibly choose. I was a man of my word. Whatever she wanted, it was hers. Placing the note on her nightstand, I peeked into the bathroom.

Penelope was completely relaxed, body tipped back and eyes gently closed. The scent of jasmine and starlight filled the dimly lit space. That lush white flower would always have an association with her.

I'm obsessed with my wife. And she had no idea what kind of terrible power she had over me.

Pondering the strange turn of events, I stood there, watching her until she finally stirred. Only then did I slip into bed. Ten minutes later, she joined me.

But as always, she stayed on her side.

A silent sigh of resignation swept through me. There was still so much distance between us. So close, but so far away. I lay there contemplating the future, long after she fell asleep.

"What would it take for you to feel this way about me?" I whispered into the dark. *What can I give you that will make you want to be here?*

The crack of a fist sent me shooting straight up in bed. My lungs were bellows, gulping precious air. The blood in my veins pulsed rapidly. A ghostly pain made my jaw wince at the memory.

It was only a dream.

Scrubbing my hands through my hair, I shot a look to the side of the bed where Penelope slumbered peacefully. Good—that was good. I hadn't woken her.

Slipping out of bed, I padded from the room. Experience taught me there would be no more sleep tonight. Since it was barely four in the morning, I resisted the temptation of slugging back a whiskey to banish the tendrils of the nightmare, instead going to the kitchen for a glass of water.

Ages ago, that demon tried to break us all.

Even now, my sire's presence in my dreams succeeded in chasing away the rest I desperately needed. The bastard. Well, he hadn't won. My siblings and I had a thriving empire, and my mother had spent her final years free of his terror.

She loved him.

I shook my head. It bothered me to no end that the kindest, sweetest woman I'd known was devoted to that sonofabitch up until his last breath.

Was that what people would think about my wife? I shuddered.

Penelope was capable of that loyalty and devotion. But it would be a crime to let her think it was misplaced. No, if Penelope ever showed me that loyalty, it would be because she learned I was a good man. A man capable of violence toward our enemies, but a good man to his family.

A sigh left my lungs. When I thought Penelope was beginning to see things straight, when we took a step forward, reality sent us spiraling backward. Just like the intimate, world altering sex, and then us sleeping apart in the same damn bed.

Cool, refreshing water trickled down my throat. Given enough time, she would understand the difference. I would make her care for me. There was no other alternative.

Chapter 35 – Penelope

Spending all day with Serena at the spa, I knew exactly what I was going to use my magical yellow square of paper for. It was the perfect idea. As I wrangled myself into the soft purple gown this evening, I began to put the plan into action. Finally dressed, I tapped my freshly painted nails against the phone screen, dialing the brand-new number that wasn't being traced. This was my last phone call of the evening. After a whirlwind of text messages, group messages, and three video calls, the details were finally falling into place.

My cousin's voice was light and breathless coming over the speaker call. "Penny! Hi, how are you?"

"I'm great, actually. The girls tell me you're settling in well," I nudged.

"Yeah, I'm renting a cozy little cottage in town. Nice neighbors on both sides, and your brother Theodor's house is the next street over."

Relief swelled through me. My sacrifice wasn't all for nothing. "I'm so glad for you!"

Poppy's voice held a touch of sadness. "What's up?"

I chewed on my words. She'd taken to small town life, but to hear my sister's chatter, Poppy wasn't a big socializer. After Serena's admission about how sheltered life as a mafia princess was, I better understood Poppy's hermit-like ways.

"My sisters are planning a visit to Chicago. We haven't settled on the date, and before I booked their flights, I wanted to extend the invite to you too," I said cheerfully.

There was a long, drawn-out silence.

"Poppy?"

"You should know better than anyone why that's impossible," my cousin said quietly.

I frowned. "It's not, though. I have Alessio's card, so the tickets aren't an issue. I'm actually planning a little party for his sister—"

"Penny." Her voice shook, but without seeing her face reading whatever emotion was there was next to impossible. "I'm not leaving Carrington. I'm safe here."

Leaning on my vanity, I spun the phone around. "I don't believe Alessio holds any ill will toward you."

Quite the opposite, in fact. He'd mentioned on numerous occasions how it was me that he fantasized about. My cheeks warmed, but I couldn't resist taking a peep at my reflection. I looked damn good, like a movie star seductress. Not only was the purple shade perfect for my suntanned skin tone, but the lines of the dress were sexy without being too revealing. The hair and makeup appointment Serena made for us seemed ridiculous until the final result looked back at me now.

Yeah, I can see it. I would want a piece of that if I was a man.

"I jilted him," Poppy said, snapping me out of the lust-filled swirl of thoughts. "That's not something a man of his position is going to easily forgive."

I frowned at the phone. "Really, I think he was more than okay with the switch."

Poppy sighed. "It sounds like you two are getting along—which is great! I've lit candles for that very thing. But just because Don Mancini is pleased with his new wife doesn't mean his pride will let him forgive me."

I wanted desperately to tell her she didn't know him.

But I bit my tongue.

A voice in the far reaches of my mind begged me to consider what she said. Maybe, just maybe, there was a small truth to her fear. She did grow up in this world after all.

"Do you think you'll ever feel comfortable visiting?" I asked quietly. "Can't this be water under the bridge?"

"Made Men don't change," Poppy said reluctantly. "They aren't the heroes in these fantasy books. They are ruthless and self-serving. I find them akin to the villains."

The need to defend Alessandro was strong. It roared inside me.

I managed to wrestle it back, and instead, I asked her about the books she read. It turned out that in her new, simple life, living off the small stipend her mother set up, Poppy was content to turn into a bookish cat lady. It was shocking how many novels she consumed in a week, sometimes two a day!

We chatted for a bit longer, but a knock on my door ended the call quickly.

"Come in," I called.

The don stepped through the door. His gaze locked with mine in the mirror. It was rewarding to see the great beast go completely still. Those dark eyes heated, and I felt a rush of hunger swept through me.

My voice was a breathless rush. "I just have to put my shoes on and we're ready to go."

"Wait." That single word was rough against my skin. Alessandro prowled across the room only to stop before me and crouch. Slowly, those large hands pushed the long, full skirt over my legs.

A shiver of heat prickled across my skin.

"I'll do it," he rasped, looking up at me. Hunger showed in those black depths.

An embarrassing rush of liquid heat spread between my legs. No doubt the cotton strip in the thong was drenched.

"I'm not helpless," I protested, but the breathless quality of my voice begged to differ.

With quick, nimble motions, Alessandro snapped the delicate straps of the shoes in place. "There's a difference between being helpless and allowing yourself to be adored, vespina."

The air hitched in my lungs. Adored. Did he mean that?

Pulling a velvet box from the inside of his tux jacket, Alessandro plucked a shimmering strand of amethysts. My heart faltered as he reached to unclasp my charm bracelet. Once it was replaced by the lighter, unfamiliar cuff of gems, the desperate need to tear it off consumed me.

I struggled to swallow the reaction.

"Che cazzo, they are going to see you shine at my side and wonder how I was so fortunate to claim you," he murmured, sliding his hands up and down the smooth skin of my legs. "Do you have any idea how beautiful you are, Penelope?"

My heart stung. I lifted the bracelet, playing with it in the light.

"Do you like them?" he pressed. "I paid Blau a visit this morning and saw them. I knew they would match your dress."

I forced the hurt out of my voice. At least he'd been thinking about me. "They're nice, I suppose."

The don frowned. So I forced a smile, determined not to let him see how much the gesture, right after his brutally honest confession, hurt me. It shouldn't. I knew not to expect anything real from him.

But it did hurt, despite my best efforts. Because this was more proof that he thought he could buy me. He still didn't understand I wasn't a possession; I wasn't impressed with his opulent gifts.

Capturing my fingers, he ran his over the back of my hands. "Everyone will see you next to me. I want them to know that you are mine."

Any hope in my chest died.

Alessandro pressed his lips against my calf, continuing to stroke my leg and my hand at the same time. But the heat in my veins was gone. "Don't leave my side tonight, vespina. We are going to send a clear message that my marriage to you only strengthens my position. Those who whisper will know that I have a treasure, and that I own every fucking part of you."

Blood rang in my ears. This had quickly gone from romantic to nightmarish.

"If anyone tries to use you against me," he continued, "things will get bloody."

I pulled away and pushed to my feet. Snatching my phone and the tiny clutch that didn't hold anything more than the device and lipstick, I battled the rage stirring in my chest.

How dare he. How fucking dare he!

"Vespina?"

Rounding on him, I stabbed a finger in the air. "You can't solve your problems by shooting everyone, lupo. *'Things will get bloody'*—what the hell kind of line is that?"

His brows drew together and a dark scowl played on his face. "It's the reality of this life, Penelope."

I shook my head, Poppy's warning ringing in my ear. I hated, *hated* that my cousin's words shattered the cozy illusion. Recent events made me want to see my husband in a different light. That he was actually human.

But then he said things like that—his wife was a possession, he owned me; he would spill blood.

Villain, Poppy called him? Yes, that was exactly it.

"Let's go," I barked, storming to the door.

Alessandro took two quick steps and pushed the door closed before I could escape the suddenly suffocating bedroom.

"Penelope, what the fuck just happened?" he growled.

His presence was everywhere. The heat radiating off his body, the woodsy clean scent of his cologne and him invading my nostrils, the volatile energy that no matter how pissed I was, my traitorous body hummed desperately to have—it was too much.

"Let me go." The words sounded calmer than they felt. He began to protest, but I shoved my hands against the door. "Let me out of this room, Mancini! Your prisoner needs air."

The air around us crackled with a sudden burst of ice.

"Very well," he said coldly.

I refused to name the ache in my chest at the chasm yawning between us. He moved away just enough for me to tug the door open and slip out. In the hall, Serena emerged from her room. Her eyes widened as she read whatever was scrawled on my face.

I forced a tight smile. "Ready to party?"

Serena shot a glance behind me.

"You look lovely, sorellina," Alessandro said, voice full of ice.

"Thanks, you look great too," she responded warily. "And, Penny, wow! I'm glad the dress code was mandatory colors. Normally these stuffy functions are black tie, meaning ladies where black or other non-imaginative shades. But since it's for the children's society, we can be as vibrant as we want."

She was trying, really trying, to be a good girl friend and take my mind off whatever catastrophe she'd sensed.

"Well, you look hot in fuchsia," I smirked. In a whisper, I added. "Too bad Dante won't be there."

Serena shook her head. "I told you already, he doesn't feel that way about me."

It was true. He had someone else. But I felt bad, because Serena wasn't social enough to meet other men.

Well, that ended tonight! There would be plenty of interesting people for her to meet if she wanted. Taking long, purposeful strides away from the monster in a black tux, I joined her and looped my arm through hers. "I need a damn strong drink. Think the booze at these galas is any good?"

Serena's normal confidence wavered. "I would imagine with what we pay for a plate, donating to their cause, that we will have a decent selection of alcohol."

"Perfect." I nodded tightly, ignoring the thundercloud looming behind us. "What's your poison, dear? I'm a whiskey girl."

Serena snorted. "Of course you are, cowpoke."

Although it was forced, her haughtiness returned, gathered round herself like the protective armor I knew it to be. *I'm going to have to work on my own armor.* But first, I was going to survive the night.

Chapter 36 – Penelope

How did I think he ever cared? His illness blinded me. The symptoms that brought down the monster disguised the beast that he really, truly was. The moments of passion clouded my judgment to the point of insanity. Tonight proved that.

Well, no more.

Spun around the room, shown off and introduced to countless faces, who I didn't learn the names of, I was the prize. A pretty little trophy. Exactly what he wanted.

Alessandro's presence threatened to strangle me.

On top of that, the strappy heels were tight, pinching off the blood to my toes.

The moment I stepped into the art museum's grand event space, I was hit with a wave of opulence and never felt more out of place in my life. Crystal chandeliers dripped from the ceiling, casting a golden glow over the sea of elegantly dressed guests. The hum of conversation floated through the air, punctuated by the occasional peal of laughter or the delicate clink of champagne flutes. Waiters in crisp black and white wove through the crowd, their silver trays balanced with an effortless grace, offering glasses of sparkling wine and delicate hors d'oeuvres. The scent of expensive perfume mingled with the rich aroma of truffle-infused appetizers, creating an intoxicating blend of decadence.

The city's elite moved through the room like animals at the zoo, their designer gowns and tailored suits a dazzling display of wealth and influence. They didn't pay any attention to the artifacts and priceless treasures purposely put on display for tonight's event. Jewels caught the light, glittering at throats and wrists, while conversations played out in carefully measured tones—powerful men and women exchanging pleasantries, sealing deals with a knowing glance and a sip of vintage champagne.

I stood it as long as I could before I snapped.

"I need some air," I hissed, pulling away from the don's heavy touch.

Those cold, emotionless eyes swept over me. "We have more people to meet."

Stepping into him, I warned, "I'm not having fun."

"And I am?" He let out a harsh laugh. "Fuck, vespina, if this was about fun, I would have stayed home. With you."

The possession in his voice was twisted, convoluted. I wanted to like it. Who didn't want to be the center of someone's attention? The sole object of their focus.

But I didn't trust that Alessandro saw me that way. I was a possession, like a purse or watch. He wasn't being possessive *of me*.

Without giving him more of an explanation, I hurried away and disappeared into the bathroom. Serena left one of the stalls, took one look at me, and cursed.

"What did my brother do now?" she demanded.

I waved her away and hid in the stall she'd vacated.

But that wasn't good enough for the insistent creature. "I know he's capable of being an ass, but he's trying with you, Penny. It might not feel like it but trust me. I can see how different it is this time."

This time. "Did he love Elena very much?"

Silence pulsed in the bathroom. If anyone else was here, they were being eerily silent, probably not wanting to miss any juicy details.

"So he told you about his first wife?" Serena's words were laced with caution.

I wasn't about to tell her I pieced together the past from the nightmares and from words the maid dropped when they thought I couldn't understand their Italian conversations. But it was the old wedding photo, yellowed and torn, in the attic that confirmed everything.

"Did he love her, S?" I insisted, not lifting my dress to sit and take care of business. I stood at the stall door, leaning my head against it.

"No, but he was good to her."

I squeezed my eyes closed. While it would have hurt to hear that his first marriage was something we didn't have, this was almost worse. It proved he wasn't capable of the emotion.

"You have to understand, they were young and their marriage a business arrangement," Serena said softly. "Love was never part of the equation."

And she died because she was miserable. "I understand."

"You have nothing to be jealous about. If you can't see the way he looks at you, just know it's different."

I unlocked the door and peered at her. "How does he look at me?"

Serena wiped her hands on the thick cloth napkin. "Like you're a priceless treasure."

Incredulous laughter bubbled through me. Serena continued to smile despite my disbelief. She gave me a wink and went to the door, pausing before she opened it.

"Thanks for tonight, by the way," she added. "I'm having an *amazing* time."

At least one of us was.

As I took care of business, I thought about what she'd said. What Poppy had said. It was so convoluted. I needed air, space to think! That was the problem with the city. There was no wide-open plains where thought and feelings were able to spread their wings and soar.

Pushing into the back hall, I walked past the closed art galleries. There was a staircase somewhere in this museum. Just a few minutes, sitting and breathing. Maybe I could even take off my shoes for a spell.

I turned left, then right. The strap dug harder into my foot, making me limp.

"Shit." I spun around.

"Lost?" A voice broke through the dark.

My heart jumped into my throat. *How the hell did he find me?*

The cop stepped out of the shadows. He was dressed the same as the caterers, including the cotton gloves. "I could arrest you for trespassing."

"So do it," I dared. It might be stupid, but it was one way to prove if he was a real officer of the law.

There he stood, looming in the entryway. Looking at him, it was hard to see him as a waiter. How was anyone falling for the disguise? He clearly was up to no good.

Then again, I'd been so distracted by Alessandro that if he had been near, I wouldn't have looked twice.

"Have you thought about my offer?" he demanded.

I arched a brow. "The one where you illegally intimidated a potential witness? Yeah, screw that. I'm not interested."

Those nostrils flared, and his mouth pinched in a sour pucker. "You're going to regret siding with the mob. They're going down. You'll burn with them. You and your family."

I stepped forward. "Ooh, I'm terrified."

Part of me still didn't believe this was real and not an attempt to catch me betraying the famiglia. But I wasn't stupid. Snitches got stitches. And Alessandro's cold, unfeeling nature? Yeah, he wouldn't hesitate to hurt someone who was a threat to his organization.

A step sounded at the end of the corridor.

Whatever the cop was going to say, he stopped, looked behind him, and scowled. "This isn't over."

"Yes, it is," I snapped. "The answer is no. It will always be no."

"Then watch yourself," he said before taking off.

I resisted the urge to throw something at his retreating form. But only because the closest object was a priceless antique urn.

"Penelope."

I jumped. The don was the last person I expected to follow me.

It crossed my mind to tell the don about the Fed. But not only was I frustrated with him, there was part of me that was scared to bring it up.

Later. I'll tell him later. When I had time to cool down and properly digest the situation. Right now, there was another matter that needed my more immediate attention.

"Come to check up on your investment?" I sneered.

"Dio bono! What has gotten into you?" he hissed, turning me with a more gentle touch than I would have expected.

I glared at him. The dress was tight, the long skirts kept tangling around my legs. And there were blisters on my feet. In short, I was miserable.

Surprise widened his eyes. "You're furious," he murmured.

"Damn straight I am!" I fisted my hands at my side. "I've been trotted around, the perfect little piece of arm candy. I thought this would be a great event to learn about your world, see how the mob made business deals, and ran the world from behind the scenes. But I'm not worthy of that, am I, Alessio? I'm just your pretty little wife, who warms your bed and smiles to your friends."

His voice dripped ice. "They are not my friends."

I waved my hands. "Semantics."

"No. Facts." He tugged me to the side and pushed me against the wall. Arm braced over me, he caged me.

It should have felt claustrophobic. A sane person would scream for help. Instead, my heart began to slowly calm.

That black gaze studied me. "You want to see my world, vespina?"

I swallowed. "Yes."

"Why?" Gone was the coldness, and in its place a strange warmth. One that could almost be described as gentleness.

The answer was crystal clear. "I need to have purpose."

He nodded slowly. "And I said we can arrange that."

Why stop now? I might as well ask for the moon and see what kind of rocks he dropped at my feet. "I want to go to college. I want to make something of myself."

His jaw worked back and forth. "It's dangerous, Penelope."

"And you can figure out the logistics." I stabbed my finger against his sternum. "I want a skill set. I want to invest in me. It's my turn."

A dark smile cracked across his too handsome face. "Degrees aren't always an investment. It's the individual classes that count. The seminars, the certificates."

I shrugged. "So we'll figure out the details. But, Alessio, I will not sit around at home, shopping and being pretty, only to come to these things as your purse."

I left the *or else* out of that statement. I wasn't sure what the bad thing would be, what course of action I would be driven to, but it would be cataclysmic.

The empty threat worked better, anyhow.

Alessandro put out his hand. "Deal."

We shook, but his fingers slid up my arm. "You're mad at me. May I earn your forgiveness?"

"I'm not mad, just...frustrated." I made to step away from him, forcing my tired, sore feet to walk normally so he wouldn't see me struggle.

Alessandro pressed his palm against my sternum. "Stay."

I jerked. "No. What? Why?! This is crazy."

I moved inches before he slammed me back against the wall.

"I said stay," he growled.

"Alessio! This is madness."

The exhale that blasted from his nose was a clear dismissal.

"We're in public!" I insisted.

Pushing my skirt up and to the side, he cupped my pussy. "And the thought of being caught makes you drenched."

"I—" Words failed me.

"So wet for me," he chuckled and dropped to his knees. "Spread those legs for me, vespina."

Heaven help me, I widened my stance.

The straps of my panties snapped.

Alessandro's hot breath fanned over the sensitive flesh. "Beautiful. Everything about you is beautiful."

And then his mouth closed over my pussy.

His tongue slid against me before delving inside for a deeper taste, and I gasped, my head falling back against the wall. Alessandro's skillful mouth worked me expertly, his lips and tongue teasing and tasting. I bit my lip to stifle a moan, acutely aware of our surroundings.

This was going to be his solution to everything. We fought, we fucked. Later, when my brain wasn't sizzling with passion, I could bring myself to care.

"Let me hear you. Don't you dare be quiet," he murmured against my flesh, the vibrations sending shivers through my body.

I bit my tongue. There was no way I was making any noise. But my breathing filled the space, my pulse was a rush in my ears.

"Oh, madonna!" I cried out, using the Italian expletive.

Alessandro hummed in approval, the vibrations intensifying the sensations.

I threaded my fingers through his dark hair, torn between pulling him closer and pushing him away. The risk of discovery heightened every sensation, making me hypersensitive to his touch.

Alessandro's hands gripped my thighs, holding me in place as he devoured me. His tongue circled my clit before flicking across it rapidly, drawing a strangled cry from my throat.

"That's it," he encouraged, his voice husky with desire. "Give in to me."

My breath came in short pants as the pressure built.

Footsteps clacked across the floor. With a desperate whimper, I tried to move away.

His fingers dug harder, holding me in place. "I didn't tell you to move."

Those words were muffled against my pussy.

I tapped desperately on his shoulder. "They're going to find us!"

He continued to suck and lick as though we had all the time in the world.

"Alessio!" I hissed.

The dark chuckle was a delicious friction. "Then fucking come, vespina."

I looked desperately down the hall. Shapes moved in the shadows. Voices rose and fell in a distant hum.

Alessandro's skilled mouth worked magic, his lips and tongue exploring every sensitive spot.

Dropping my head back once more, I closed my eyes. What was the worst that would happen? They would see my husband between my legs? Letting go of the reservations, I hooked my leg over his shoulder and wrapped my shoe around his back.

The monster kneeling before me growled in approval. His strokes became faster, the contact sharp and insistent. My core tightened and pleasure built.

"More, Alessio, I need more," I pleaded in a desperate whisper.

His fingers slid inside me, curling to hit that perfect spot as his mouth continued its relentless assault on my clit. The dual sensations sent shockwaves through my body. I bit down on my lip to muffle my cries, my hips rocking against his face.

It didn't work.

My moans echoed through the dimly lit space.

The footsteps grew louder, voices more distinct. My heart pounded, a mix of fear and wild excitement coursing through my veins. Alessandro's movements became more urgent, racing against our impending discovery.

"That's it, vespina," he urged, his voice a low rumble against my flesh. "Show me what a good girl you can be and come for me. Now."

As if on command, the tension inside me snapped. Waves of pleasure crashed over me, my body shuddering as I came hard against his mouth. Alessandro held me steady, working me through my orgasm as I fought to stay quiet. Clapping my hand over my mouth, I chewed on my fleshy palm to muffle the cry of pleasure, my body shuddering as waves of bliss washed through me. He didn't let up, drawing out every last tremor until I was a quaking mess.

Just as the aftershocks began to subside, the monster shot to his feet, fluffed my dress, took my arm and guided me through the back of the hall. I stumbled blindly beside him, legs trembling and slick heat coating my thighs. It was almost powerful enough to drown the screaming in my feet.

"Hey, you're not supposed to be back here," one of the strangers called.

Plucking his silver case from his breast pocket, the don pulled out a cigar. I gaped at him.

"Mr. Dahn gave me permission," Alessandro responded without turning around.

"Oh! Mr. Mancini, it's you. Yes, no, I'm so sorry. Please, continue. Can we turn the lights on for you?" the man answered quickly.

"That would be lovely, thank you."

As we wandered away, I hissed, "You can't smoke in here!"

Alessandro pulled the lit cigar from his lips. Smoke curled from his mouth. My own watered for a taste of that darkness. "Should we find a fountain, vespina?"

I let out a rough laugh. "You're unbelievable."

Alessandro shrugged. "Life is short. We can live by the rules of others, or we can make our own."

"Like wandering a museum after hours? Everyone just jumps to your bidding?" I scoffed. "Must be so nice."

Alessandro cupped my cheek, thumb brushing under my eye. "Sometimes it's nice to be reminded I'm not a god."

The confusion was written on my face.

He laughed. "Tonight I got to pretend I was a mortal, and I fell at my knees to worship the goddess come down to torment me."

I plucked the cigar from his fingers, giving into the temptation. I took a long drag, letting the inky smoke fill my mouth. It felt sensual. Forbidden. On an exhale, the smoke plumed from my lips. Before I gave in to temptation again, I bent and extinguished it on the bottom of my shoe. One hit. That was all I needed to remind myself of the terribly sublime feeling of the vice. I gave the thick stub back to him. "Well, watch out, mortal, I'm not done yet."

"Neither am I, goddess, neither am I."

Chapter 37 – Alessandro

The caporegimes of the Mancini Famiglia sat around the long table. Several capos wanted to go downstairs and enjoy the dancers with the other patrons of the Mezza Luna. A couple wanted to be at home with their wives and family. The rest wore varying degrees of boredom on their faces. Only my enforcer standing behind me and my underboss at my right hand were alert.

They sensed the danger simmering beneath the surface.

"With your permission, don, we'll call this meeting to order." Luca tapped his stylus against the tablet screen in front of him. The assistant wasn't fazed by the group of killers surrounding him.

I straightened the sleeves of the undershirt, making sure the cuffs popped. "Gentlemen, thank you for meeting me on such short notice."

Murmurs spread through the room.

"It seems we have a problem that requires our immediate attention." I flicked my fingers, and Dante stepped forward, black garbage bag rustling in his hands.

An object sailed across the room to land on the table with a sickening thunk.

The silence that followed the enforcer's dramatic display pulsed with a heady mix of fear and disgust.

My insides churned as the stench invaded the room. The bastard hadn't bothered to freeze his prop for the meeting, but the scent of rotting flesh didn't bother the enforcer.

"Who was that?" Nuncio gagged.

"Take a close look," I commanded.

The capos winced, but several leaned forward.

"The Minstrel worked him over good," Joe grumbled. The capo was still pissy that I'd shot his men for entering my home without permission. "It's impossible to tell."

"Maybe this will help you recognize him, Adonis," I said coldly.

Dante tossed another body part on the table.

I felt the charity dinner threaten to make a reappearance as the flayed skin flopped open next to the severed head. Gruesome. Dante was downright demented.

I told him to bring the arm. Not peel off the tattoo-marked skin from the flesh.

But right now was not the time to critique my enforcer on his visual aids for this business meeting.

"That was Saint Nick!" Olando exclaimed. The capo's face going deathly pale.

The underboss cleared his throat. "Nicolo Marechetti was discovered speaking with a federal agent."

"Did you know he was using drugs, Romano?" I asked my capo.

Olando shook his head vehemently. "No, signore! I knew he was steep in credit card debt, but I didn't realize he was using."

"The fed threatened to put him away for life on drug charges," Antonio said plainly.

I nodded to my underboss. "We discovered he was passing information and took swift measures to silence him."

The unspoken subtext hung in the air. This was what happened to those who ratted out our famiglia.

"We should have been told," Joe said, pushing his fingers hard against the polished table. "There was no need for theatrics, signore."

"This *is* me telling you," I shot back.

But the capo didn't back down. "You haven't filled the position of advisor, Don Mancini. A consigliere would have told you that your captains needed to know there was a problem. He would have allowed us to take care of the issue."

I gave the capo a withering look. "To prove your loyalty by shooting the snitch yourself?"

Adonis shut his mouth quickly.

I thought so. Joe Adonis hadn't executed a single soldier in his years as a leader. He deferred punishment to his lackeys.

"Signore, have you thought more about restructuring to fill the role of consigliere?" At least Nuncio was polite about his query.

The focus of the room quickly shifted from the grotesque execution of a traitor to me. Keeping my careful mask of control in place, I slid a look from one man to the next.

"When I make such an important decision, you will be the first to know," I informed them. "In the meantime, make sure your men know what happened to Saint Nick."

Pushing to my feet, I snapped my fingers. "Dante, clean this shit up."

The bastard smirked around the piece of beef jerky he was gnawing on. I sighed inwardly. Dante and I were close, but he didn't want the position of being my counselor. And truth be told, he wouldn't be good at it. His strengths lay in information extraction and problem mitigation. No...I needed someone I could depend on implicitly. Someone who wouldn't shoot first and ask questions later.

Not a soul in this room held the potential to live up to that task.

When I sent my wife and sister home from the charity dinner, I expected they would be in bed by the time the business meeting with my commanders was concluded. Upon walking into the thick gloom of the foyer, a light down the back corridor caught my attention. I prowled forward, senses on high alert.

It was Penelope, still in her gown. My wife was curled on the sofa, reading device dangling from her sleeping fingertips. Without waking her, I pulled the eReader away, only pausing to glance at what she'd last read. Someone called a wing leader was fighting in a pit as the female soldier watched from above.

I scrolled to the next page—and the next.

The couple were in some deep argument. Some drama from their past kept them at odds, while a situation with their dragons bound them in the present. Noting the title, I resolved to read the book. I wanted to know if the female with silver-tipped hair ever forgave the brutal warrior.

I would have started reading the book tonight, but exhaustion pulled at my bones. So I covered Penelope with a throw from the hidden compartment of the footstool and went upstairs. But as I undid the fastenings of my tuxedo, my mind raced.

Too many threads tangled together.

I was the don, the leader of my organization. But I was also a husband, the protector of my family. Penelope hated the restraints I decreed were necessary for her safety. It was impossible to be cold and ruthless with her, enforcing the rules as I did with my men.

"I have to change something," I groaned, pushing my hand through my hair.

The scent of jasmine lingered in the bathroom. The moment I stepped in here, my dick twitched.

Dammit, just another thing that would keep me awake.

I glanced at the tub. My wife found soaking to be relaxing. She took a bath whenever she was wound up.

Maybe there's something to that.

And it wasn't as though my men would find out I soaked in bubbles and scented oils. It could be a secret. The decision to test the relaxation method settled over me, and I began to fill the tub with scalding water. I dumped in the salts, the bubbles, and finished with the exotic floral oil.

"This does not make me a pussy," I growled, stepping into the bath.

To make it less feminine, I plucked a cigar from my case as I removed the leather strap and pendant that only came off when I showered or slept with my wife.

As the hot water soaked away the strain in my body, I realized what I'd been missing. Sighing, I relaxed into the water, closed my eyes, and let the events of the past days, weeks, and months play through my mind on repeat. The rich tobacco soothed me, but not as much as the hot water. Not pausing to examine any one thing in particular, they danced in a chaotic revel through my mind. I let them come and go, trusting that they would sort themselves out.

I always found a way.

A teasing voice broke through the cacophony in my head. "Well don't you look comfy."

Shit. My wife caught me lounging like some pampered, lazy nutcase. I squinted up at her.

"I think you used too much oil," she mused, nose wrinkling. "It doesn't mingle well with a Cuban."

I shrugged. "I was in a hurry."

Leaning forward, my little wasp plucked the cigar. Her rosy lips pressed around it as she took a long pull. My dick stiffened at the sight.

I fucking loved that she stole my cigars to taste.

Exhaling, she set in back on the tray instead of stamping it out. The darkness inside my soul hummed in approval.

"Well, I tried to wait up to make sure you got home okay, but I must have dozed off," Penelope said with a shrug.

"You didn't have to." *But I'm glad you did.*

It was nice to know someone wanted to make sure I came back safely. I never had that before.

She yawned, but then smiled. "I'll leave you to it."

"No." Moving with lightning speed, I snatched her wrist and yanked her forward.

With a yelp, she dropped her shoes and eReader just in time before I tugged her—dress and all—into the tub. Water sloshed from the tub, the sound covered by her yelp of surprise.

"You're joining me," I growled.

The shock and mixture of emotions on her face was priceless. I cupped the back of her head, forcing her down for a swift kiss. She tasted of rich tobacco and dark sin with a hint of sweetness undercutting it that was all her—an intoxicating flavor.

"Alessio," she breathed.

"Just kiss me, woman."

She gave in to the pull. The humid air of the bathroom seemed to crackle with electricity. My fingers tangled in her hair, eliciting a moan against my mouth. The thing I'd come to realize about my little wasp was that she wasn't afraid of a little pain with her pleasure.

Time slowed as the kiss deepened. Unlike the brutal collisions of past kisses, there was something almost gentle about this one.

Penelope melted into me. I savored the feel of her in my arms.

My hands slid down her back, tracing the curve of her spine. She shivered, her fingernails digging into my shoulders. The gentleness was satiating, but I could feel the heat building between us, threatening to ignite into something wilder, to overwhelm the moment. There was something *more* here—and I was desperate to explore that apart from the fast and hard fucking we normally enjoyed.

I broke the kiss, trailing my lips along her jaw and down her neck. Penelope tilted her head, giving me better access. Her breath came in short gasps, each one sending a thrill through my body.

"Alessio," she whispered, her voice husky with desire.

The sound of my name on her lips was almost my undoing. It would be too easy to rip the dress off her body, push her down onto my hard length, and take her hard in the tub. Instead, I pressed her against me, my body flush against hers.

Our eyes met, and for a moment, time stood still. There was a vulnerability in her gaze that I'd never seen before. I didn't know how to reach it, only that I wanted to claim it for my own.

Treasure it until my dying breath.

"Tell me, lupo, what nightmares are bad enough to trouble a monster like you?" Penelope leaned down to press her lips against my throat.

My wife hates me. That wasn't what she wanted to hear. But I had to tell her something. Giving into the pull of the moment, I confided in her. "I lost a dear friend and loyal soldier late last year."

Penelope pulled back. "Gunfight?"

I snorted. "He would have rather died that way."

Her hazel eyes widened at my brutal honesty.

"He died of cancer. It was fast and aggressive, but those last weeks were filled with an unbearable pain," I said, unable to stop the story from pouring out.

"Alessio," she breathed. "I'm so sorry."

I plucked her fingers and placed a kiss on the tips. "Thank you, vespina."

My wasp had a sweet side. I wanted—no, I *craved* more of that part of her.

What price will it take to earn that, little wife?

"You miss him," she surmised, her voice impossibly soft and genuinely sweet.

"I do. But it's more than losing a friend. He was important to me. To the famiglia. Tell me, how familiar are you with the structure of a mob?" I studied her face.

That mask snapped into place. "I know what can be read online."

And you know more than that. I tested her further. "Carmelo was my consigliere. He helped when I took over the position as don. Two decades older than me, he was invaluable."

"He was your advisor." Penelope saw the truth.

Admiration filled my chest. She was clever, this little wife of mine. I leaned back further, sinking deeper into the tub, which shifted her higher on my lap. The apex of her thighs grazed against my hard length, but I didn't push her to go further.

No, I was enjoying this closeness too much to end it.

"Do you miss talking to him?" Penelope asked gently.

"I do."

There'd been no one to fill his shoes. No one trustworthy enough to unload my problems to. Not Serena, not Leo, not even Dante, who warred with me in the trenches. I was alone.

But I didn't have to be.

The hazel eyes staring back at me held a certain promise.

The outburst from the back corridor of the museum replayed in my mind. This woman had been an average student in high school. The scholarships she'd applied for had been denied. Instead of going into debt to obtain higher education, she'd taken a job where she worked hard to move as high in position as possible, and then when money was tight, had found a way to earn more to help her sister.

I wanted her to trust me enough to talk about her past. The dossier we'd compiled left too many pieces to the imagination. What lengths could we go to if we only opened up to one another?

Penelope was capable of doing far more than people—including herself—gave her credit for.

It would be a crime not to use that.

But that would require a sacrifice on my part. The empire I ruled had been won and built because of my iron control. Letting another person in was more frightening than facing an enemy in a gunfight.

"Come on, let's put you to bed," I murmured, pulling her off me.

Penelope let me lift her to stand. I helped her peel the dress off her body but then wrapped a towel around her before taking one for myself. When I helped her out of the tub, I noticed the raw spots on her feet.

My voice came out harsher than I meant it. "What happened?"

She snorted. "I played dress up for society tonight, what do you think happened?"

Despite her protests, I lifted her onto the counter. "You need shoes that don't leave blisters."

This time, her short laugh of derision was coupled with an eyeroll. I took the first aid kid from under the sink and set to work drying, cleaning, and bandaging the wounds.

"You don't have to do that, lupo," Penelope protested.

"You're right, I don't." I moved to the other foot. "But I want to."

"Did you want to with Elena?" she whispered.

Hearing my dead wife's name on her lips sent a bolt of regret through me. But I answered her honestly. "No, and I regret it every day."

Penelope nodded, taking my words into consideration. Not sure how much she knew, I was careful how much I wanted to add.

"Our fathers arranged the match, and she died before I could give her enough."

"I wonder that you were so eager to marry Poppy." There was an accusation behind her words.

"It would have been different."

"How?" she demanded.

I sighed. "Because I would have moved heaven and earth to give her everything she needed."

"And you knew what a nineteen-year-old bride needed?" Penelope countered.

"I know what my twenty-five-year-old bride needs." I gingerly touched her wounds. "I'm a better caretaker now, vespina. I understand that part of my marital duty."

Something flickered through her eyes, making the green and amber flecks sparkle. It was vulnerability laced with another emotion I couldn't quite name.

Right before I finished, my phone rang.

"I've got it," she murmured, taking the bandage from my fingers. "You'd better answer that. It's probably important."

I knew it would be. Midnight calls always were in my line of work. But as I left the bathroom, I threw a look over my shoulder. A good husband would have stayed, taken care of his wife, and then made love to her.

My finger stabbed the green button. Dante began to rattle off the latest disaster in my ear, but my only thought was that I wasn't cut out to be the good husband my wife deserved.

Chapter 38 – Alessandro

A revelation dawned on me somewhere around three in the morning. I immediately sent a message to my assistant. Luca was a soft soul, but since his family had been Made Men for generations, he'd insisted upon being brought into the business. A strong leader knew where to place valuable assets. And since I considered myself exceptionally strong, I made Luca my assistant. The role fit him perfectly.

Which was exactly what I should have done the moment I married Penelope. I saw her strengths, but I'd been too damn focused on protecting her that using her hadn't been something to ever cross my mind.

It was high time I remedied that.

Moments after I sent that nocturnal message, my assistant's response came rushing back.

Luca: On it, boss.

As usual, he didn't disappoint. It might have been the middle of the night, but the kid was always on call, always ready to do what was needed.

When Penelope joined me for our early breakfast, a designer gift bag sat on her seat. She knew the luxury brand name, and I saw her hackles raise at another expensive gift.

"Just open it," I insisted between sips of espresso.

Plucking the sheets of tissue from the top, Penelope's mask of wrath softened into a beautiful confusion. She pulled the designer model out and placed it on the table.

"A laptop bag?" She unzipped the sections and peered into the interior.

I rose and went to lean against the table beside her. "We'll find you a suitable computer."

"This is…practical." She was trying so hard to be polite.

Tugging the tip of her braid, I murmured, "How would you like to work for me?"

Something flashed in her eyes. "Do you mean that?"

I frowned. "I don't like being questioned."

Penelope yanked her braid away. "You Made Men are sneaky creatures, forgive me for questioning your intentions."

"Penelope." I gripped her waist and tugged her flush against my body. "When I say something, I mean it. Do you want to work for me?"

The pause was filled with a chaotic charge.

Breathing carefully, I forced myself to remain calm. My wife had no reason to trust me. Her statement about mobsters was likely based on the dealings she had with her uncle. I needed her to see we were not cut from the same cloth.

"What would I be doing for you?" she demanded, pulling back.

My hold on her remained tight. She wasn't running away from this.

"I don't know," I said carefully. "That is what we have to figure out—together."

Penelope nodded.

"And regardless if you like the work, we'll set you up with whatever classes and certificates you want to pursue. But I have a hunch you are a valuable asset, and it would be wrong not to see if you fit into this world." My words seemed to have the desired effect.

"That's...reasonable," she finally sighed.

"Good."

"You know, that's exactly the chance I asked my uncle for." She fidgeted with the tissue paper behind me.

I loosened my hold slightly, but she didn't move away.

"And he set you up to be married to one of his men," I surmised.

Penelope nodded.

I was going to revisit the notion of having her uncle assassinated.

"None of my men are going to touch you, Penelope." I placed a kiss on her head before returning to my seat at the table.

"Because I'm going to be guarded everywhere I go," she muttered. It was so soft, I barely heard it.

But I didn't jump to correct her. Because what she said was absolutely true. Her working for me, her taking classes, that wouldn't change the parameters of the security measures. I needed to keep her safe—while at the same time making sure that she wasn't smothered.

The herculean task was going to take every drop of cunning to accomplish. But it was a step in the right direction.

A compromise. It was all I was asking, and I had a feeling it would make her happy.

It has to.

"We'll start by taking a tour of our organization," I said.

Penelope sat down to her breakfast. "Just tell me where and when, boss."

I sighed. *It has to work.*

Chapter 39 – Alessandro

She didn't expect me to follow through. I smiled, enjoying the fascination on her face as she walked around the club. Even though the warm spring sunlight streamed through the windows, the Mezza Luna was dark, with warm mood lighting.

"Upstairs is a traditional gentleman's club," I explained. "There are billiard tables, cigar rooms, and private spaces for the elite of Chicago to conduct their business."

"With strippers." Penelope rounded on me.

"The *waitresses* aren't allowed up there, only the butler and his staff." It was hard to hide my smirk as she stewed.

"This is a lot fancier than the Sugar Daddy's on Highway 18," she muttered. "But you said you owned a strip joint."

I nodded. "Many of the waitresses are talented dancers. They perform if the mood strikes, but dancing isn't mandatory."

And if they picked up dates along the way, so be it. That wasn't my area of the business. A capo and his brother ran this place. So long as the police stayed out of their business and their contribution to the Famiglia was delivered, I let them run it as they saw fit.

Opening the door, I led Penelope down the back exit. "Well, you've seen three of our businesses. Is there anything else you'd like to know?"

Sitting back in the seat of the SUV, I watched my wife adjust herself next to me. Nico pulled away from the curb, pushing the button to close the partition and give us privacy.

"Where do *you* work?" she pressed. "And what do you do?"

"Upper management," I smirked.

Her lips pressed in a thin line at the evasion. "Fine, don't tell me."

Tell her. If she understood...if she knew the load on my shoulders.... I leaned forward. "These secrets, they don't just affect me. I'm responsible for the lives of all my men, their women, and even the children."

The way she studied me, it was impossible to tell if my words made a difference. I needed her to understand. But how could she? Women who grew up in this life didn't understand, what would make me think she would?

Gaze shifting to the window, Penelope spoke in a faraway voice. "Being the responsible one is hardest."

Was it possible that she knew something about the weight I bore? My heart pattered rapidly.

"They see the fruits of our labor but don't understand the journey to get there." A long sigh whispered through her lips. Shaking herself, she turned to me. "Thank you for showing me your empire, don."

I dipped my chin in a nod. A rare emotion, delicate and fragile, bloomed in my chest. Did I dare let hope flourish? Was this woman capable of understanding me? My role in this world?

"Show me your headquarters?" Penelope asked.

I reached for the communication button. Her interest in my work was intoxicating. Penelope was the first person close to me that wanted to see behind the curtain. And I knew in my gut she could handle it, but what she did with the knowledge remained to be seen.

After giving Nico the instructions, I sat quietly with my thoughts until the town car parked. When the driver gave the all clear, I emerged, moving to open Penelope's door, but she was already springing out. Her boots clipped across the pavement as she looked around.

"A bakery?" The confusion on her face was priceless.

Before I could speak, Tony bustled from the front door. The baker wiped his floury hand on his apron, excitement radiating from his burly figure.

"Signore, signore! You brought the signora," he beamed, words broken and barely comprehensible. He continued to ramble about the honor of us visiting him, and then he rattled off the special treats he'd just whipped up.

Penelope's smile became careful as she focused to understand what he said.

Crap.

I should have given her a heads up. Tony's garbled speech was something every member of the famiglia was used to, and we understood him well enough. But it was hard to remember how shocking it must seem to a newcomer.

"Penelope, meet one of the best men I know," I said, sweeping a gesture between them. "Tony, this is my wife."

The baker ambled over with his equally broken gait. They shook hands, and Tony excitedly pointed to the inside, lisping and spluttering about the fresh batch of pastries cooling on a wire rack.

Penelope nodded and eagerly followed. We had to accept coffees and pastries before the loyal soldier let us escape to the upper level.

"Tony is the best guard a man could ask for," I said by way of explanation.

"I can see that," Penelope said as she climbed the stairs before me.

When we reached the top, I put a hand on her shoulder. "A rival mob got their hands on him. It's been years, but the damage is irreversible."

"What did they do to him?" Penelope whispered.

"Broke bones beyond repair. Cut off part of his tongue." I left out that they'd used his body as a dartboard for weeks on end. The horror in her eyes showed her innocence. No…Penelope might have adapted well to the underworld, but I doubted she would ever be able to understand. What happened to Tony was what drug me from bed every day. That would not happen to anyone so long as I was in power. Each soul was mine to protect.

I pushed into my office.

Penelope wandered around as I took a seat behind my desk and turned on the desktop. I watched her from my peripheral as she explored each nook and cranny.

"It's like your home office," she said with a huff, sinking into a chair opposite my desk. "Anal retentive neat. No torture chambers. Not even a tech wizard command center—just a boring office."

I smirked. "Sorry to disappoint."

Plucking the coffee from my desk, Penelope stared at the liquid. It wasn't her extra-large, American swill that she consumed by the pot-full.

"Tell me," I coaxed, unable to take the silence any longer. "What thoughts are playing in your mind, beautiful?"

Penelope snorted. "How do you work above a bakery and not weigh a thousand pounds?"

It was my turn to let a harsh laugh out. "Discipline."

That word was a spark. Desire lit in her eyes.

"You're very good at discipline, aren't you." She trailed her finger over the edge of my desk. "It makes me wonder if that's the type of boss I want to work for."

Heat struck my veins as though lightning flashed from the heavens. Blood shot to my groin, and my dick hardened instantly.

"Should we find out?" I urged.

"But I haven't messed up," Penelope protested. "That's hardly fair."

I loosened my tie, drew it slowly from my neck, and ran it through my palm. The little wasp tracked every movement, gaze glued on the piece of silk.

"Are you sure?" I drawled.

Those hazel eyes snapped to mine. "Quite."

"I think you're keeping secrets." It was a broad guess, but the flash of surprise on her face confirmed there was indeed something.

There always was.

"Do you feel like making a confession?" I coaxed.

Penelope shifted. "Well, there is one thing. I wasn't sure how to bring it up, though."

I rose and moved toward her. "It's better to confess your sins on your knees, vespina."

Her chin tipped up. "This is a serious matter, Alessandro."

Darting forward, I wrapped my fingers possessively around her throat. "To you, and you alone, it's Alessio."

There wasn't much pressure on her slender neck. But her words still came out hoarse. "Just the other day you insisted it was Alessandro. Now you've changed your mind?"

I had.

While my siblings sometimes called me Sandro, Penelope was the first to use the other form of my name. She would be the only one from now until death parted us.

"Here's what's going to happen," I growled. "You're going to lock that door and take your clothes off—but not your bra or panties. Those are mine. Then I'm going to fuck you hard. Whatever else unfolds will depend on how well you listen."

Anticipation crackled between us. My thumb slid over her pulse, feeling the wild beat of her heart. Penelope wasn't scared. She wanted this as much as I did.

"Go. Lock the door," I instructed, giving her a squeeze before releasing my hold on her.

Penelope arched a brow. Defiant as ever.

"I suggest you obey, or your punishment will be far more severe." I wanted to dominate her, force her submission.

No...not force. Earn. She was the kind of creature that a man needed to earn the respect of. Make her feel comfortable enough to submit.

Penelope took two steps back. Her fingers gripped the hem of her blouse, shucking it over her head. Those full breasts greeted me, nipples hardening under my gaze. Penelope flicked the button on her jeans, and the pants shimmied to the floor.

There she stood, completely naked in the middle of my office.

"I was in a hurry because I took too long deciding what to wear for the tour," she said by way of explanation. "I didn't put anything on under this."

Desire pulsed through me like a current of electricity.

I remained silent as she lithely tripped to the door and threw the lock. Turning around, she leaned against it, an innocent smile playing on her lips.

What I wouldn't give for a roll of plastic wrap from the bakery to bind her to the furniture. And why didn't I have a hook in the wall that I could suspend her from?

Making quick mental notes to be better equipped for the future, I stalked forward. "You didn't follow instructions, vespina."

"I didn't?" she asked coyly.

I reached her, feeling the heat radiating from her skin. The tie dangled from my fingers, a silent promise. The silk whispered against my palm as I folded it in half, watching her eyes track the movement.

"Hands," I commanded.

Penelope hesitated, that delicious defiance still flickering in her eyes. "And if I refuse?"

"Then I'll have to teach you what happens to wasps who defy their leader."

"Don't wasps have queens, not kings?" Slowly, she extended her wrists, a challenge glinting in her eyes. "And here I thought you were the king in this scenario."

"Kings and queens rule together," I murmured, wrapping the silk tie around her slender wrists with practiced precision. The crimson fabric contrasted beautifully against her pale skin, each loop tightening just enough to hold without hurting. "But make no mistake, in this room, I command."

The silk slithered between her wrists as I secured the knot, testing it with a gentle tug. Her breath hitched, pupils dilating until those hazel eyes were nearly black with desire.

"Too tight?" I asked, voice rough with need.

She shook her head, brown braid cascading over bare shoulders. While she might be a vision of beauty, her words held a bite. "Not at all."

With her bound hands before her I guided her away from the door, my palm pressing between her shoulder blades. She moved with me, her naked body radiating heat against my touch.

"This will only work if you communicate with me. You don't like something, you tell me. I'll stop." I brushed my knuckles across her cheek. "Can you do that for me, vespina?"

Penelope nodded.

"Good." I pushed on her shoulders. "On. Your. Knees."

She didn't have a choice. I was taking what we both wanted.

Penelope dropped, but she wasn't done struggling.

The harder you fight, the more fun we're going to have.

I moved in front of her, fisting that long braid and wrapping it around my hand. It kept her down.

"Undo my belt," I instructed.

Penelope raised her bound hands, fingers working deftly at my belt. The metal clinked as she pulled it free, her eyes never leaving mine. There was something almost predatory in her gaze despite her position.

"Now the zipper," I commanded, my voice dropping an octave.

She leaned forward, the warmth of her breath teasing through the fabric of my trousers. Her bound hands struggled with the button at first, then slowly dragged the zipper down, the sound unnaturally loud in the quiet office.

"Good girl," I murmured, the praise causing her to pause momentarily, a shiver visibly running through her.

"I'm not your good girl," she countered, her voice husky.

I tightened my grip on her braid, pulling just enough to force her head back, exposing the elegant column of her throat. "Today you are. Tomorrow, we'll see."

Rebellion sparked in her eyes.

Mio dio, she made my structured, carefully planned life far more interesting.

"Suck," I ordered.

This was fire I played with.

My rock-hard dick sprang free after her fingers viciously tugged open the boxers. That feisty mouth opened, and her stinging tongue darted out. She was a venomous force, coiled and ready to strike as she licked from root to tip, igniting a fire that consumed me whole.

I tugged on her hair. "I said, suck."

A growl rumbled through her.

The stakes in this game raised to a dangerous level.

Penelope's bound hands trembled slightly as she leaned forward, her eyes locked onto mine with a hint of defiance. Her lips parted and her tongue darted out to lick me again, leaving a glistening trail on my hardened length.

Before I could correct her, she swallowed me.

Fucking hell.

The wet heat of her mouth engulfed me, sending shockwaves of pleasure up my spine. My fingers tightened in her hair involuntarily, the silky strands wrapping around my knuckles as I fought to maintain control. The groan deep in her throat was the only indication she noticed the unforgiving grip. Her tongue swirled around me with expert precision, mapping every vein, every ridge, every sensitive spot as if she'd studied my body for years rather than minutes.

"Fuck," I hissed through clenched teeth, watching as those perfect lips stretched around me.

My wife was perfect.

The sight alone was almost enough to undo me—Penelope on her knees, wrists bound by my tie, her naked body trembling slightly with each movement. But the sensation... Cristo santo, the sensation was beyond anything I'd experienced before. Each slow drag of her mouth sent lightning racing through my veins, pooling molten heat at the base of my spine.

Her tongue—that clever, wicked instrument—swirled around the head of my cock before she took me deeper. Those hazel eyes remained locked on mine, defiant even in submission.

I let her continue. It was a fight to maintain a hold over my body and not explode down her throat. I wanted to, and someday I would. But right now was an exercise in control and power.

If I was being honest, I wasn't the one in charge. She might be bound on her knees, choking on my thick length, but it was clear who was dominating whom.

When I was confident she was well adjusted to me, I forced her head still.

Penelope squeaked in protest.

The sound was cut off when I began to pump into her.

"Do you know how perfect you look, vespina?" I rasped.

She glared at me.

"That's it, eyes on me." I drove into her hot mouth.

She took everything I offered and more. The slick heat of her mouth engulfed me like molten silk, drawing a guttural groan from deep in my chest.

The world outside my office—deals, enemies, family obligations—all evaporated into nothing as my universe narrowed to the exquisite pressure of her lips around my cock.

Penelope hollowed her cheeks, creating a vacuum of pleasure that sent lightning crackling up my spine. Each nerve ending ignited, a symphony of sensation that made my knees nearly buckle. The wet sounds of her mouth working me echoed in the quiet office, obscene and perfect.

"Cazzo," I hissed between clenched teeth as her tongue found that sensitive spot just beneath the head.

Three more quick pumps, and then I pulled away. Her lips popped, and a strand of saliva trickled from her lips. She reached to catch it, smirking deviously.

I caught her bound wrists.

"No." I reached to wipe her mouth. That was mine. She was mine.

Tugging her to her feet, I let her go and marched to the closet. My fingers fumbled with the buttons on my shirt. I tossed my suit jacket on the chair, where it slid to the floor. Inside the closet, I opened the garment bag with my spare change of clothing.

There was another tie.

But it was the backpack on the floor that caught my attention. The go-bag held necessary items if I was called suddenly to a fight. A feral grin spread across my lips as I took out the length of rope. There wasn't any need to use my shirt to bind her.

I undressed in the closet, making sure I was completely naked—even the leather cord and metal talisman on my neck left my body for this. Only then did I walk back to Penelope.

Her eyes narrowed suspiciously, but she didn't fight me. The silk was smooth and luxurious, its deep red color a stark contrast against the suntanned skin of her face. As I wrapped it around her head, her bright hazel eyes disappeared, and she became a blindfolded figure at my mercy.

Drawing the length of rope down her torso produced a shiver of anticipation. The rough rustle of the cord echoed in the quiet room, creating a sense of tension and uncertainty. Her tight nipples tempted me to take a taste, but I snatched her hands and gave her a tug. The sound of her breathing quickened as she realized what was happening, and her small whimper made my heart race.

By the bookshelf, I tossed the rope high and managed to secure it on the top. While it wouldn't hold her weight, it would create the desired effect.

"Give me your hands," I commanded.

A little huff was the only way she fought back.

Grabbing them would have been all too easy, but when she offered them, a dark surge of triumph shot through me.

She learned quickly, my little wasp.

I secured her hands high above her head, forcing her to stand on her tiptoes. And then, the real work began. The rough pads of my fingers trailed down her torso in a long, smooth stroke. I turned her body, exposing her back to me, and repeated the gentle touch along her spine.

"Bound and at my mercy," I crowed.

An expletive muttered under her breath.

But the words were muffled by the sound of my belt sliding through the loops. I folded and snapped the leather. The belt was cool against my fingers.

The next moment it burned against her ass in a swift snap.

Penelope yelped.

"I want you to count," I breathed. "Five sins, Penelope. Five strokes for each."

"Screw you!" she hissed.

I popped the belt against her again. "Count."

"I think that's two," she spat. "But are you sure a country girl like me can handle something as important as math, lupo?"

The belt cracked across her skin—and then again with a deafening snap.

With each stroke on Penelope's gorgeous ass, it left behind a thin red line that quickly turned into a deep, angry red mark. The skin around the welt was raised and inflamed, creating a stark contrast against her paler backside.

"You sell yourself short, even as you struggle to climb higher." I paused to massage her. "I want to see you soar, regina mia."

"That was four—quit stalling and get it over with," she fumed.

I moved my fingers between her legs. This raw act of discipline turned my beautiful hellion on. She was drenched, the evidence spreading down her thighs.

"Give me a confession, and I'll stop," I tempted her.

"Never."

The belt sliced through the air with a loud 'whoosh!' before making a harsh connection with the skin. Three more strokes I placed with careful precision on her beautiful ass. Each snap echoed through the room, creating a beautiful mix of pain and fear. Each stroke was accompanied with a brush of my fingers against her clit.

On the last, I drove my fingers inside her.

"That was seven, you bastard—"

And then, a violent string of Italian exploded from her lips. She cursed me, damning me to hell, and praying that the devil fucked me hard.

I snatched her shoulders, dragging her around to face me. "Ah, there's the first secret, vespina. My wife is fluent in Italian."

Chest heaving and lips twisted in a snarl, she was the perfect picture. "Yes! Yes, I fucking speak Italian."

The sight of her bound hands above her head, the crimson silk of my tie stark across her eyes, and the angry marks on her backside, was almost my undoing.

Chapter 40 – Penelope

The blindfold was torn off my face with a vicious yank. I blinked into the daylight lit office, immediately focusing on the roguish face in front of me. Alessandro was smiling. That predatorial look was more triumph than anger.

I didn't back down.

"Don't worry, little wife, I knew your secret even back in Detroit," he mused darkly.

I stilled. I'd been so careful!

The chuckle that escaped Alessandro's lips was like a glass of aged whiskey, smooth and deep. It carried a hint of danger and playfulness, like a predator toying with its prey. It was a sound that could make one melt and shiver at the same time.

"I've wondered when you would reveal that little secret. It almost isn't fun to make you confess it now." He cupped my chin and leaned in for a kiss.

Damn him, but the gesture consumed me.

His lips tasted of power and vengeance, a heady cocktail that clouded my judgment. When he pulled away, my breath came in ragged gasps.

His voice was husky and sultry. "Anything else you wish to confess?"

It crossed my mind to tell him about the Fed. But that was a far more serious conversation.

And my pussy ached. If we stopped this power struggle because he needed to deal with the threat to his organization, I didn't think I could survive the denial.

"I confess that I want you to fuck me," I seethed. "I shouldn't. Not after you spanked me like a naughty girl, but damn you, I want it."

Alessandro's eyes glittered with amusement. "Again, that's something I already know, vespina."

"Then why don't you do it," I challenged.

With an animalistic growl, the last thread of the monster's control slipped.

Alessandro gripped me around the waist, lifting me off the ground. I hooked my legs around him as he drove into me.

I was instantly full. Stretched. But not yet sated.

"More," I demanded, clawing at his shoulders as he pinned me against the wall. The books beside us rattled dangerously.

The wolf's teeth grazed my neck, biting just hard enough to make me gasp.

"So greedy," he murmured against my skin. "After keeping secrets from me."

His thrusts were punishing, deliberate, each one driving me higher. My head fell back against the wall with a thud I barely registered.

"You—" I gasped as he hit that perfect spot inside me "—keep plenty of secrets too."

His laugh was pure darkness against my ear. "The difference, vespina mia, is that I'm allowed to."

I wanted to argue, to fight back with words since my body had already surrendered, but he shifted his angle and coherent thought fled. My nails dug crescents into his skin. The pleasure mixed with the smarting from the belt marks to create a heady sensation.

But I wasn't the only one coming undone.

His thrusts were merciless, each one driving deeper than the last.

"Look at me," he commanded, his voice a dark whisper against my ear.

I forced my eyes open, meeting his gaze. The pitch-black intensity I found there nearly undid me.

"You think your little games can outmatch mine?" He punctuated each word with a thrust that sent sparks shooting through my core. "I've been playing this game since before you knew the rules, little wife."

My body betrayed me, responding to his dominance with a shameful eagerness. Each stroke pushed me closer to the edge, and I bit my lip to keep from begging.

"Rules can change—or be broken," I rasped.

"Such strength," Alessandro murmured, his thumb brushing across my nipple before he gave it a hard tweak.

I gasped.

"It's time for you to finish," he commanded.

"Make me."

His eyes darkened to obsidian.

Alessandro's hand slid between us, finding that sensitive bundle of nerves with unerring precision. His fingers worked me with practiced skill while his hips never faltered in their punishing rhythm.

"You forget who you're dealing with," he growled against my throat, teeth scraping the tender skin. "I own every inch of you."

The dual assault was too much. My body tensed, hovering on the precipice as I fought against the inevitable. Not because I didn't want it—mother of god, how I wanted it—but because surrendering felt like losing this round in our eternal game.

"Let go," he commanded, voice like velvet-wrapped steel. "Now."

My body obeyed even as my mind rebelled. The orgasm crashed through me like a tidal wave, obliterating thought and reason.

"That's my girl." The sound of his rough voice was the only thing powerful enough to break through the haze of pleasure.

I watched as the monster came undone, beautifully violent face contorting in a mix of pain and pleasure.

I did that—I brought the beast down.

His roar echoed through the room. His body shook with powerful spasms as he gave one last thrust, his muscles tensing against mine as he emptied himself into me. I could feel the pressure and warmth of his release inside me, filling me and marking me as his conquest. The sensation was both overwhelming and intoxicating, a physical manifestation of the power he held over me. Every thrust and spasm only added to the intensity, consuming me until I was nothing but a vessel for his pleasure. And in that moment, I was completely under his control, my body his to dominate and possess.

But he was equally under my spell. That knowledge was a heady euphoria.

Everything after that collision was a blur. Alessandro untied me. He took me to his desk where he rubbed an ointment from his backpack on my bottom. Then he dressed me. Each small act was done with the utmost gentleness.

As he knelt to place the flipflops on my feet, I got the courage to ask, "How exactly did you discover my secret in Detroit?"

He chuckled softly. "Your journal had passages written in Italian. I didn't confirm your fluency until we scanned your phone and found the language learning app, but I had my suspicions."

"You snooped in my room!" I dug my fingers into his scalp, forcing him to look up at me. "What if my uncle caught you?"

A glint sharpened in those onyx depths. "It would have been dangerous, but as I've proved on numerous occasions, I don't mind the challenge, Penelope."

I sighed and leaned back against his desk.

"So, will you come work for me?" Alessandro rose, bracing a hand on either side of the desk.

I fidgeted with the bottle of Arnica ointment, realizing it came from a first aid kit. "As far as interviews go, that was the strangest one I've ever had."

The wolf smirked.

But he didn't push the decision. That was up to me.

"You made time for me today. I didn't think you would," I admitted, meeting his gaze and letting some of my feelings show. If I trusted him enough to bind me, to spank me, I could trust him with this.

"I promised myself when we married that you wouldn't feel neglected. You said you needed to see, to understand. So I showed you."

He showed me as much of the darkness as he dared.

I studied him. He remained still, letting me see what I needed. "Alessio, there's something I have to tell you."

"Tell me."

Despite my resolve, my body trembled. "I'm scared to," I whispered.

With impossible softness, he cupped my cheek. "You have nothing to fear from me, vespina. But if you need time, or something else, you have it."

That gave me a touch of courage. "I promise, I'll tell you. Let me find the words, and then I will."

He nodded. "In the meantime, would you do the honor of joining me for dinner?"

This man—from bondage to a meal invitation. "If that is the don's wish, so be it."

"Wear the green dress in the black Atilla bag. Nico will pick you up at seven," he instructed, that controlling nature still in place.

"So bossy," I teased.

Alessandro placed a kiss on my forehead. "You like it, vespina."

He was right. I did.

Chapter 41 – Alessandro

I should pick her up.

I finished my business early. Ignoring the mountain of less urgent tasks, I left my office, swung into the florist shop for a bouquet, and made it home in record time. Tonight's dinner was going to be a true romantic gesture.

A real date.

How the hell had it taken me so long to think up this idea? I lamented the fact that I wasn't a family man, that I never grew up with a good role model in that regard, that my life wasn't conducive to normal events, when really it was something as simple as clearing space to eat a meal with her.

I'm starting to figure this shit out. Pride rushed across my chest. Instead of viewing it as an unchangeable fact of life, I was conquering the seemingly impossible problem—like I did with every issue that came about in my life.

Standing in the foyer, a rush of nervous excitement shot through me. This was going to be the first of many small gestures. As I walked to the front parlor, I admitted that part of the desire to make time and work differently was the beauty herself. Penelope made me want to fulfill my husbandly duty.

"Shall I bring you a cocktail, sir?" Shepherd appeared at my heels.

"Yes, that would be—no." I fisted the flowers tighter. Tonight was going to be special. "We'll take a bottle of champagne and two glasses."

If my instructions surprised him, the wizened butler didn't say.

I sent a text to my wife and smoothed back my hair once more. Ideas and plans distracted me so I didn't hear the soft footfall until Penelope cleared her throat.

A vision stood in the doorway. My wife wore that green dress. The soft tones draped her body, pooling around her bare feet, and while it wasn't a provocative cut, the simplicity was utterly sensual. As she moved, it seemed to have a mind of its own, an otherworldly aura radiating off her that made me weak at the knees.

Beautiful.

That word didn't describe it, but there wasn't another that came to mind.

"Don Mancini," she murmured.

Lost in the vision of my wife, I didn't realize she was distraught. The tone I'd heard in her voice was etched in her face.

The urge to go to her, to comfort her, seemed natural.

But I didn't have the first idea how to do that. So I stood in the middle of the room, flowers tipping from my hand.

"I need to speak with you. Before dinner." Penelope worried the straps of her shoes, shifting in the doorway. "It can't wait."

"Talk to me, vespina."

She moved into the room, her steps slow. I wanted to yell and demand whose head needed removing. My jaw clenched tight. The molars in the far back of my mouth threatened to crack from the pressure of holding back the explosion. That was the dilemma of thinking linearly. I problem solved—but Penelope needed me to listen.

I can do that. For her.

I took a deep breath and didn't jump to fight her battles. Not until she showed me where the trouble lay. When she gave the command, then I would lay waste to her enemies.

Just as she reached the middle of the room, Shepherd appeared behind her. I cursed the old man for his timing. But the butler was only doing what he'd been told to do.

Penelope stopped short. Her gaze darted between me and the butler.

Shepherd ignored the tension. He went about his business of setting up the ice bucket, flutes, and uncorking the bubbly.

To fill the terrible pause, I stuck out my hand.

"Here," I said gruffly.

The abrupt gesture of offering the flowers didn't alleviate any of the terrible energy swirling around us. Penelope crept forward and took them gingerly—as if they would bite.

Cristo Santo! What happened since this afternoon? Did she regret what happened at the office? Dread coiled through me.

Penelope brushed the tips of her fingers reverently over a purple bloom. "They're lovely."

She meant it. That was good.

However, it wasn't the delight I hoped to create with the gesture.

Fuck.

Could I do nothing right? She didn't like anything I gave her.

"Shall I put those in water, signora?" the butler offered.

"Thank you, Shepherd. That would be awesome of you." Penelope graced him with a smile.

"I'll take them to your room. Unless you would prefer them to sit on the dining room table or the coffee table where you read?" The butler was going out of his way to be helpful to her.

I studied the faithful servant.

My wife had done the impossible. She'd won the heart of the old man. I never doubted her sunshiny disposition for a second, but I'd had my reservations about the stuffy old man coming to accept her as lady of the house.

When he finally left and closed the door, Penelope began to pace. The soft green material fluttered around her.

On the second pass, I stepped in front of her and caught her shoulders.

She was fucking trembling.

Dio! I forced my voice to be as gentle as possible. "Talk."

"Do you know about the bargain my uncle and I struck?" Her words were barely a whisper.

That was not how I expected her to begin. I bristled. "No, only that he tried to marry you off within his organization."

She nodded. "He said he would allow me a place in the organization. It was my birthright to belong, you know."

I cupped her face. "Why did you go to him, vespina?"

She shuddered.

"There was a reason. I just never discovered it," I added.

"My mother is sick."

The revelation crashed into me. There was a sweet tendril of relief that it wasn't something worse—something involving her specifically. But that was quickly squashed by seeing the pain glisten in her eyes.

"I told Uncle Tito I would work off the debt if he helped her. Hell, I was willing to clean his house, Alessio! Anything!" Her voice broke and she stopped talking, taking deep gulps of air.

And the wretched uncle tried to sell her.

I reaffirmed my desire to assassinate Caravello. Only this time, I would be the one to slit open his fat neck.

"He isn't going to pay," I guessed.

Penelope shook her head. "My sister called to say the operation was canceled. She hasn't told my parents yet, but she's going to have to. She gave me tonight to figure it out."

I pulled her close, but she struggled back.

An ache formed in my chest. I let her have her space and dropped my hold.

"It's worse," she whispered.

How the hell that was possible, I didn't know.

"Mom is going to be kicked out of the Bismarck hospital. The treatments there are the only things keeping her stable. If she goes to hospice, it's a death sentence."

"Penelope...."

Before the words formed to assure her that was never happening, my wife fell to her knees.

"I'm begging you, Don Mancini. Help her! I'll do anything. I won't fight you again. I swear it."

This was what every mob boss wanted. The perfect wife, willing to do anything.

Only that idea was long gone, replaced with a different desire. I found something better—her, regina mia. The only thing she was missing was a damn crown on her head. I touched the small metal pendant I wore around my neck. This one I was keeping, but I would buy one, properly sized for her head.

She would hate the opulent gesture. Laughter barked in my head as I pictured that scene.

I pulled Penelope to her feet and sat with her on my knee, cradling her close.

"No strings, vespina," I promised. "Your mother will have whatever care she requires. You have my word."

"I won't divorce you—"

I snorted. "*That* was never happening."

"The procedure is expensive," she continued, not seeming to have heard my determination. "Insurance won't cover a cent because it's an experimental surgery."

"Done." I brushed my fingers through her hair. Unbraided, it was long and silky. "It's done, Penelope. She'll have the surgery."

A single tear trailed down my wife's cheek. I caught it on my thumb, bringing it to my lips. This was what the other side of my wife tasted like. The side of her that lacked fire, the part that was sweet and wholesome, yet filled with that unbreakable determination.

My fingers trailed down her neck, my hand cradling the curve of her jaw as I leaned closer. Our lips met, soft and warm, sending tingling sensations through my body. As she exhaled, a gentle breath caressed my face, adding to the already intoxicating moment.

There was fire here, simmering below the surface.

But it wasn't the usual inferno. It was a warm, rich glow that seemed to burn where her heart beat rapidly.

The taste of her lips was like fresh air of open fields, bursting with sweetness and a subtle tang. As we kissed, my senses were overwhelmed by the combination of softness and flavor, leaving me wanting more.

Blood heated in my groin. For the first time in my life, I was embarrassed by my reaction. It was unavoidable. I was mad for this woman. But this wasn't the right moment to feel arousal.

Penelope needed comfort, not a rough fucking.

I shifted so she wouldn't feel it.

Too late.

She reached down and tenderly brushed her fingers over the stiff length in my slacks.

"Would you—?" She hesitated.

"Yes?" I murmured roughly.

"Would you make me feel better?"

My pulse beat harder. Pulling her to her feet and standing to join her, I spoke again to make sure she'd heard. To make sure she understood. "I am going to take care of your mom, Penelope. Not because you worked for it, or you danced for me. But because you're mine. By extension, your troubles are my troubles."

I slid the zipper down her back. The teeth clacked as they separated. The cool air hit her skin, making her shiver.

"Your family is my family—and I take care of us." I bent and kissed the smooth skin of her shoulder. "You can always come to me."

I needed her to know that, needed her to know I was the one who would move heaven and earth to fix even the smallest problems. So when something big happened, she would never go looking for another to be her champion.

My soul recognized hers as its home, and there was no undoing what had been bound.

Penelope pushed the suit jacket from my shoulders. The tie was next. The slick material slipped from my neck.

"Do you want to use this one?" she asked, a smile playing on her lips.

I closed my eyes and suppressed a moan. Dio bono! How I wanted that. But.... "Not tonight."

The tie fluttered to the floor. Her fingers plucked the buttons of my shirt, and then her lips were on me.

Each press of her mouth against my chest was like a brand, marking me as hers as surely as she was mine. Her hands, delicate yet purposeful, slid beneath my open shirt, pushing it away from my shoulders until it joined my jacket and tie on the floor.

"You're sure?" I whispered, even as my body screamed for her touch.

Penelope looked up at me, her eyes glistening with a mixture of vulnerability and desire. The shadows from the lamps caught the edges of her face, illuminating the curves I'd memorized with my fingertips. She was hauntingly beautiful. I was possessed.

"I've never been more certain of anything," she murmured.

Her gaze dropped to my chest as she leaned forward to kiss my throat. But she stopped.

"You!" she gasped.

I smiled wickedly. "Yes, me."

Penelope plucked the small metal crown in her fingers. "I thought I lost this!"

Capturing her fingers around the charm, I shook my head. "I stole it."

"Why?" Those hazel eyes shown, the green leaching into the amber to create a mesmerizing effect.

"It was only fair." I brought her fingers, still clutching the pendant, to my lips. "You stole something from me that day at the airport. I didn't know what to call it for the longest time."

Her voice came out in a breathless whisper. "And what do you call it now?"

"An enchantment." Kiss followed kiss, until each of her fingertips wore my mark. "You put a spell on me, vespina, that first time your viperous temper stung me. I haven't been able to shake it since."

"Ah, crap," she murmured. "I can't be mad at you when you say sweet things like that."

I chuckled and brought her closer. "I'm not giving it back. It's mine now."

The smile on her lips beckoned me for another taste. I pressed her to me. Her dress hung loosely from her shoulders, the zipper I'd drawn down revealing a tantalizing glimpse of her spine. I slipped my hands beneath the fabric and gently pushed it off her.

As she unfastened my pants, her mouth moved across my chest, warm and reverent, tracing a path that left fire in its wake. I threaded my fingers through her hair, cradling her head against me. The feel of her tongue against my skin nearly buckled my knees.

"Penelope," I whispered, my voice barely audible above the sound of our breathing.

She looked up at me, her eyes liquid with desire but ringed with vulnerability. That combination was my undoing. Stepping out of my shoes and letting the pants fall, I lifted her into my arms and brought her over my lap as I sat down in the chair.

Straddling me, Penelope sank onto my erection. As she lowered herself onto me, I felt myself harden and grow within her. Each movement she made, each flex of her muscles, sent jolts of pleasure shooting through my entire body.

No foreplay, no teasing, just the raw connection of us coming together.

Our exhales mingled in the space between us. Pleasure ebbed, and the primal urge flared bright. We began to move as one.

With the heat between us intensifying with each thrust, I marveled at the perfect fit of our bodies. Penelope lifted her hips slightly before sinking back down to take me deeper.

"You're perfect," I confessed.

"You're not so bad yourself."

I surged forward to capture her smirk in a fast kiss.

Her hips ground against my own, and it felt as though we were melting into one another, becoming one entity in this moment of pure pleasure. The sensation was overwhelming, almost dizzying, but all I could focus on was the way she moved against me, her hands gripping my shoulders for support and her breath hot against my neck. It was a dance of passion and desire, and with each movement, our bodies became more entwined, until we were completely lost in each other's touch.

I wrapped my arms around her, one hand splayed across her lower back while the other tangled in her hair, guiding her face to mine for another kiss. There was something almost sacred in the way our bodies moved together, a rhythm as ancient as time itself, yet uniquely ours.

"I've got you," I whispered the promise against her lips, feeling her tremble as I thrust upward to meet her movements. I would tell her as many times as it took her to believe it.

Penelope's fingers dug into my shoulders, her breathing growing more ragged with each passing second. Her skin glistened in the dim light, a fine sheen of sweat making her luminous. I traced the curve of her breast with my tongue, relishing the soft moan that escaped her lips when I took her nipple into my mouth.

"Please," she gasped, her voice thick with need. "Don't stop."

As if I could. As if there was anything in this world that would tear me from this moment.

I cupped her breasts, feeling her heartbeat vibrate against my palms. Her skin flushed pink beneath my touch, warming like embers catching flame. Penelope arched her back, pressing herself harder against me, seeking more contact, more friction. I obliged, my hips rising to meet hers.

"I needed this," she whispered, her voice breaking on the last word. The vulnerability in that confession undid something in me.

My hands found her waist, guiding her movements while I watched her face transform with pleasure. Her eyes fluttered closed, lips parted, cheeks flushed. She was transcendent in her abandon, and I was humbled to witness it.

"Look at me," I commanded softly. When her eyes opened, I saw everything I'd been searching for my entire life. "I'm right here. You're staying with me."

Her eyes locked with mine, wide and filled with trust that humbled me to my core. The intimacy of that gaze—more than our joined bodies, more than the pleasure building between us—was what threatened to undo me completely.

"I'm not going anywhere," she whispered, her voice catching as I shifted beneath her. "You're stuck with me now, lupo."

Finally! She was finally giving into this!

"Good," I growled. The fierce urge burst from my soul, eager to consume her.

I caught her mouth with mine again, swallowing her soft moans as our pace quickened. Her thighs tightened around my hips, her body tensing as she approached the edge. I could feel her trembling, could sense the moment building within her like a gathering storm.

The chair creaked beneath us, our bodies moving with increasing urgency. I could feel her tightening around me, her muscles fluttering with the approach of her release. My own control was slipping, the pressure building at the base of my spine, spreading outward like wildfire.

"Let go," I urged against her ear, my voice rough with restraint. "I'll catch you."

Penelope's head fell back, exposing the elegant line of her throat as a shudder ran through her. I pressed my lips to her pulse point, feeling it race beneath my mouth. Her breathing became shallow, punctuated by soft moans that grew louder with each thrust.

"Together," she gasped, her fingernails digging half-moons into my shoulders.

I nodded, unable to form words as the tension built between us. Her body began to tremble, small spasms that intensified with each roll of her hips. I gripped her tighter, one hand splayed across her lower back while the other tangled in her hair, anchoring her to me as though she might float away without my touch.

When her climax finally broke, it was like watching a star collapse into itself before exploding outward. Her body arched against mine, her lips parted in a silent cry before sound finally escaped—my name, broken and breathless on her tongue. The sight of her coming undone pushed me over the edge, and I followed her into that blissful oblivion, my release pulsing deep within her as I buried my face against her neck.

For several seconds we remained locked together, breath mingling, pulses a joint staccato.

Whatever just happened between us, I wanted *more*. Did she feel it too? That connection that transcended the physical? She had completely captured me, and there was no escape—not that I'd ever want one.

A rough chuckle rumbled from my chest. "I'm afraid we've missed our dinner reservations, vespina."

Penelope sighed. "We could go somewhere else, or...."

"Yes?"

She pulled back, her hazel eyes sparkling from the rush of the unexplainable intimacy. "I can make us something."

That—I wanted that. "I'll help you." I brushed my fingers up and down her spine.

Penelope cocked her head. "You cook?"

My shoulder lifted and fell. "You'll tell me what to do, and while I do it, you'll call Luca with the details about your mom. Put him in touch with your sister. By the time dinner is done, and the dishes washed—because I know you wash your own dishes every chance you get—" I plucked her fingers and kissed them "—it will all be settled. And then we'll take this to the bedroom."

The sweetest mixture of relief, joy, and happiness swept over her. Penelope closed the distance and kissed me. The taste of those emotions on her lips was like something warm and buttery, topped with a burst of sweetness. Her lips were hard and insistent against mine, radiating a sensation of pure contentment and elation.

I had to pull away, or we were going to combust yet again. "Let's get moving, vespina. The sooner you make that call, the sooner it will all be settled."

"Thank you, Alessio," she breathed. Her fingers brushed through my hair. "I can't find any more words than that."

I smiled. "You don't need them."

She didn't. Her heart told me in a language only mine understood how much this meant to her. It was a step in the right direction—a step toward something truly profound and shatteringly beautiful.

Chapter 42 – Penelope

The next few days were something out of a fairytale. Work filled the don's day, but Alessandro checked in no matter how busy he was. We ate at least one meal together, usually breakfast. And I spent two afternoons in his office, although if I was actually any help, it was hard to say. We ended both of those workdays naked, sweating, and craving more.

When I sailed into the kitchen, the maids looked up from their work and smiled. They didn't run away as I wandered to the counter where my coffee pot waited, shined and polished, ready to be used. Today, the plan was to take a crash course on spreadsheets. The new computer waited in the parlor, ready for my lessons.

Setting my journal on the counter, I reached for the filters and grounds, only to pause. Next to my coffee pot sat a small brown gift bag with my name scrawled in bold letters. I plucked the tissue from the top and gasped. A chunky, cheesy "Welcome to Chicago" mug nested inside. Frowning, I plucked the rolled note from the center.

Sorry I can't join you for breakfast, but this is so you can drink your American swill properly. Dinner is at eight. I'll pick you up.

-Alessandro

He got me a mug.

A real coffee mug. Not the dainty cappuccino cups or the teeny tiny espresso shot glasses. And the mug was...perfect. There would be no more drinking glasses for my vice. The mug was exactly the kind of junk I wouldn't hesitate to snap up at a booth when playing tourist in a new town.

I traced the name at the bottom of the note. The fact that he took the time to do this sent a strange burst of something through my chest. It was surprisingly thoughtful of him.

"Don't be too impressed, he probably sent a lackey for it," I scolded myself quietly so the maids wouldn't hear.

But he had the idea....

I shook my head. The don was a dangerous man, but something had changed between us. While I had no illusions about my husband, there was a different side of him that shone through his iron mask of control. I rubbed my chest. I needed to be careful.

I was in real danger of falling for the monster.

Letting down my guard around him would be nothing short of detrimental. Yet all my reasons for keeping my feelings in check were muddied. This monster had me seeing my life play out differently.

My fingers drummed against the countertop.

"Am I the sort of girl who can play with monsters?" I whispered.

But I didn't need to keep it quiet; the maids had disappeared to other parts of the house.

I was caught between worlds. I wasn't one of them, I always knew I held the potential to forge a different path in this world. But to venture into the dark and work for the don? Would Alessandro, with all his rules, actually give me a real chance? Or was my future destined to be in the shadow of the powerful man?

Sighing, I poured the fresh brew into the mug. I still didn't know what I wanted to do with my life. But the opportunity to learn new things had ceased to be a dream and was my reality. I took the mug and journal to the front parlor, opening my new laptop. For the foreseeable future, I didn't have to make a decision. Going to college, taking a job with a legitimate business, or working for the Mancini Famiglia were viable options.

There was time to test the waters.

There was time to learn. To grow. To *flourish*.

As I flipped to a clean page, the yellow post-it fluttered from the past pages of the journal. If worse came to worse, this little square of paper held great potential. It could be used to manipulate the don into whatever crazy idea I settled on for my future.

But I didn't want to use it.

No...I wanted Alessandro to trust me enough to ascend whatever position struck my fancy.

He says he believes in me.

My heart hoped that was true.

"Knock-knock," Serena called from the doorway.

Turning around, I smiled at her. "You're up early."

"I had an international phone call," she yawned.

"Oh?" My interest was piqued. "Who called?"

"Her name is Annaliese Hertz. We went to school together." Serena folded onto the piano bench.

The practiced sound of the scales filled the room as she warmed up her fingers. It was mesmerizing to watch those long, elegant digits float over the ivory keys.

"I thought you didn't have any friends," I teased.

The A minor scale turned into a soulful melody. Serena gazed over the top of the grand instrument, looking at something far away.

"She's more rival than friend. We got along because her father was as strict as my brothers—brother." She caught herself, but I noticed the obvious slip.

It wasn't the first time a ghostly sibling had been mentioned.

Judging my sister-in-law's mood, I knew an interrogation would only reveal one thread of information this morning—if even that. So I chose to pursue the mysterious friend and let the secret of a third Mancini lie dormant for another day.

"So how is your frenemy?" I coaxed. "In Europe?"

"She was living with her grandmother, who died. She'll be coming back to the States after the funeral tomorrow. She wants to have brunch. We lost touch over the years, so I don't know if it's a good idea." Serena's words were clipped and short, completely at odds with the haunting melody ebbing and flowing from the piano.

"It's a great idea! That will be so fun for you!" I encouraged her.

Serena shrugged. "I guess."

I let the other woman exorcise whatever emotions she wasn't able to express through the music and opened a blank spreadsheet on my laptop. Putting an earbud in one ear so I could still enjoy her music, I began my lesson on the various functions and formulas.

But something ate at me.

I might not have it all figured out, but the desire to make something of myself drove me. Serena was woefully lost, floundering like the notes of the music.

Alessandro groaned. Smoke from his expensive cigar curled around him, blending in the shadows of our secluded spot in the restaurant.

I smiled over my glass of wine, enjoying his discomfort. "I swear, you won't even know they're here."

His look could turn water to stone. "Two Greenbriar girls under the same roof, and you expect me not to notice?"

"Well, there'll be three of us," I corrected and plucked the cigar from his fingers.

His gaze darkened as he watched me suck on the same spot his lips had been. Each time I'd done this, he'd been closer and closer to pouncing. Part of me wished the wolf would come out and play, table etiquette be damned.

"No." Alessandro shook his head. "You're not a Greenbriar, vespina."

My insides warmed at the possessive note in his voice. "Oh? What am I?"

"Mine. My wife." Hunger simmered in his gaze. "A Mancini."

I planned to skip dessert and take him home as quickly as possible. But teasing the poor creature was proving to be a great deal of fun. I let the smoke curl from my lips before taking another taste. These cigars were nothing short of addicting—much like the man who smoked wherever he damn well pleased.

"We're not cut from the same cloth, you know. Most siblings aren't. Take you three Mancinis, for example."

The flash of surprise in his eyes was the smallest tell. He didn't comment on the number, however.

"You and your sister can't be any more different. The same goes for me and mine." I cradled the glass against my chest.

Alessandro sighed and took back the cigar I offered. "I will welcome them under my roof as family, Penelope. You have my word."

"Oh, did I mention I'm taking them out for a night on the town?" I took a long sip of my wine.

The don squirmed. He tried to hide it by extinguishing the cigar on the ash tray, but it was noticeable.

"Since we don't want my family knowing I'm involved with the mob, it would be really cool of you if we didn't have guards, you know, acting like guards." Another sip filled my mouth.

"And your solution to that?" Alessandro said through clenched teeth.

"Simple, they can be friends of your sister's who are coming out to party with us." I grinned.

"Not happening."

"Oh, come on! Are you going to make me use my *get out of jail free* post-it note for this?" I set the glass down a little too harshly. The slim stem cracked. "Shit," I gasped.

Alessandro snatched my fingers away, looking over them for cuts. When he was satisfied I was uninjured, he pressed a kiss to the fingertips. "I can't bear the thought of anything happening to you."

I rose and tugged his hand. "Let's go home."

He followed me to the door, where the guards joined us. As a whole, we filed out to the waiting town car.

"You do realize I didn't ask for *no* guards," I muttered as we slid into the vehicle. "But I want a reason to explain their presence."

"It's the being at a bar or club that I don't like, Penelope, not the M.O. you give my men." Alessandro pulled me onto his lap.

The kisses became hot and heavy. My pussy ached at the delayed gratification. This man was teasing me, knowing where I wanted him to touch but focusing solely on my mouth.

"Alessio," I moaned.

He cupped my face. "Nothing can happen to you."

I gazed down. He cared. It wasn't the same way a normal person cared, but the feeling was still there.

"How about this," he offered, threading his fingers through the hair I spent a painfully long time curling. "You girls take my yacht."

I blinked. "You have a yacht."

The don nodded.

"Of course you have a damn yacht," I muttered. "When's the last time you used it?"

"This would be its maiden voyage," he chuckled. "But it's a good option. Throw a little party for your sisters, have the best food and wine, see Chicago from the water, and you'll be safe."

It did sound rather perfect.

"Okay," I agreed. "I'll write it down on the post-it."

"Save that for another time. Spending time with family is sacred; I want you to do it whenever you can."

A warm rush of emotion flooded through my chest. He was really trying.

Alessandro's touch ran down my sides, skated under my dress, and up my bare thighs. My breath hitched in anticipation.

There was a knock on the partition.

Leaning forward, Alessandro opened it a fraction.

"Signore, security called. A car arrived at the mansion," Nico clipped out.

The don stilled. "Whose?"

"Signor Adonis."

That name chilled the fire in my veins.

"Call Dante," the don clipped out.

"Yes, boss." The partition closed.

Alessandro's touch continued to explore, but it was absent, almost robotic. We remained silent for the rest of the short drive back to the mansion.

"I'll make this quick," he promised, before opening the car door and helping me out.

There was no escaping to our room and avoiding the visitor. The capo stood in the middle of the foyer, a dangerous glint in his beady eyes.

I didn't mind one bit that Alessandro kept himself in front of me as we pushed into the space.

"You'd better have a damn good reason for being here, Adonis," Alessandro growled.

"Oh, I do. It's of the utmost importance, signore." Joe might be speaking to his boss, but he was staring at me.

I pulled my mental armor on and stepped beside the boss.

"Shall we go into your office?" the capo intoned.

I didn't like the freedom with which he seemed to assume the liberty of our home. Neither did the don.

"Speak and get out," Alessandro ordered.

Joe shrugged. Reaching into his breast pocket, he pulled out an envelope. When the don didn't step forward to take it, the capo glowered.

"You're going to want to see these, signore," he sneered.

"What are they?" Alessandro demanded.

Joe laughed, a slimy sound that slithered across my skin. "When we had the problem with the mole, I took it upon myself to ensure our ranks were secured."

Alessandro's voice was thunderous. "You weren't asked to."

"You can thank me later," the capo offered and placed the photos in the don's hand.

Black and white images from a security camera showed a woman speaking with a man. Me. I was the woman. And the man was that Federal agent harassing me.

My heart shot to my throat. I'd delayed telling Alessandro under the assumption it was a test. When I realized it was an actual threat, I meant to warn him, but in the chaos of our lives and the development of my mom's situation, it lost precedence.

Shit. The black look of wrath clouding the don's face told me that was a mistake. A big old fuck up.

"It seems we have a second traitor in our midst." Glee shimmered from the capo. "Care to explain yourself, donnaccia?"

Alessandro moved with lightning speed. His fingers clamped around the capo's throat. With impossible strength, he lifted the squat man off the floor.

"No one speaks that way to my wife," he raged.

I swallowed hard. Panic vibrated through my veins.

"She betrayed you!" the capo squealed, his words choking from the restricted airflow.

"I knew she'd been approached, and I've dealt with it." Alessandro shook the capo.

I frowned. He had? Or was he lying to save me? Neither option was good.

"Let me go, Mancini," the capo croaked.

"You come to my house a second time without an invitation and you insult my wife. What makes you think I'm going to let you walk out of here with your head attached to your body?" Alessandro snarled.

"Because if you don't, those photos go to the other capos," Joe menaced.

In one fluid motion, Alessandro slammed the capo into the ground. "Threatening me, Adonis?"

"No, signore. Just covering my ass in case you've been bewitched by her cunt."

"Dante!" Alessandro shouted.

From out of nowhere, the enforcer materialized. *Like a fiend from the shadows.*

"Take him. I'll join you soon." Alessandro squeezed once more for good measure, before standing back.

Adonis began to squeal.

My family didn't raise pigs. But the neighbors did. As kids, we'd helped with the butchering in exchange for a hog. The sounds coming from the capo as the enforcer pounced, secured him, and drug him through the front door were exactly the same.

"Alessio, I can explain—"

"Don't." Alessandro smoothed his hand through his hair. "Just don't."

He lied to the capo for me. A shudder racked my body. I swayed forward.

"I thought it was a test," I pleaded, not heeding the sixth sense that screamed at me to back away. I approached him, desperate to make him see reason. "I made a mistake."

The monster reared over me. Nostrils flared, teeth bared, he was every bit the wolf ready to strike.

But he never touched me.

"You should have come straight to me, Penelope."

"I meant to," I whispered. I had. But after I realized it wasn't a test of my loyalty, things moved fast and I missed too many chances to come clean.

His voice dripped with venomous ice. "Go to your room."

"Alessio, please!"

"Go. To. Your. Fucking. Room." He threw his arm out, pointing at the stairs.

Something deep inside my chest cracked. This was what I feared most.

I'd fallen for this man—this monster—knowing full well what he was. And now, after letting down my guard, he struck where I never allowed anyone. It hurt.

I fled, my heels tripping me and making me clutch blindly for the banister. Tears blurred my vision. Short, hollow breaths became sobs. Somehow, I managed to make it to the room without falling, only to collapse behind the closed door.

Chapter 43 – Alessandro

"You know the rules, Mancini. Don't touch a hair on his fucking head," Mier growled.

I shot the Fed a dark look. "I'm not an idiot."

"You're not. But that kid in there went after your wife." Mier passed me the lighter.

Flicking the wheel, I lit the cigar and inhaled. The inky smoke filled my lungs. The buzz was immediate, giving my drive the edge it needed.

"Thanks for arranging this," I muttered, not forgetting my manners.

Mier snorted. "The bastard doesn't know it was me. I'd like to keep it that way."

That was understandable. The Bureau didn't need to know Mier's source. It would risk his position in the Organized Crime Division, and it would flag me with more than the limited suspicion that was always directed at me.

Taking one last drag, I extinguished the smoke. The coffee shop was busy for this late at night, but the masses' caffeine consumption wasn't my problem. I marched inside, pulled out a chair, and glared at the Special Agent across from me.

He was young, but there was something familiar about his features.

That niggling feeling unsettled me more than I cared to admit.

"You wanted to speak to me, I'm here," I growled.

The kid crooked his foot, resting it atop his opposite knee. "I didn't want to talk to you."

"Then why did you corner my wife?" Fuck, even thinking about Penelope, how I left things last night, twisted my insides in knots.

"Just another innocent caught in the web of your treacherous world, don." The agent studied me.

"Cut the bullshit, Tribiano," I snarled.

"Why? I have every advantage here." As he spoke, he set a tape recorder on the table between us. "Just in case the fierce boss of one of Chicago's notorious mobs incriminates himself."

"We both know I'm smarter than that."

The agent hummed and shrugged. "If I was a betting man, I'd say not."

Where did I know this punk from? Those eyes, they were too damn familiar.

I both regretted taking the cigar and wished I had another. My blood buzzed in my veins.

"Here's the deal: My wife is off limits." I leaned forward, speaking into the device. "You want to take me down, fine. Bring it. But leave her out of this."

"Nothing is off limits, as you've proven before. Not family, not wives." The first hint of anger spike hot in the kid's features.

I felt the thread and gave it a tug. "Are you married?"

"No," he snapped.

"But you do have family."

He glared at me. "Not anymore, Sandro."

The puzzle piece clicked into place.

Dio mio. It all made sense.

"You grew up well, Francesco." I plucked the recorder from the table and began dismantling the device.

"That's destruction of government property and interference with an active investigation." He straightened in his chair.

"It might be, but calling this witch hunt an investigation is a poor misuse of your resources." I placed the pieces neatly in front of him. "Why don't you admit what really brought you to Chicago?"

Those dark eyes simmered with hate. "My sister didn't stand a chance with you."

"She deserved better, we can both admit that." It was my turn to take the cool, relaxed stance. Now that the cards were on the table, it was easier to navigate the waters.

Or it would have been if those waters weren't flooded with the tragedies of the past. Elena's face swam to view, haggard and sad. She was drowning, and I'd never been around to save her.

"I am coming for you, don," the agent vowed. "I'm going to burn your organization to the ground and use it as a funeral pyre for your corpse."

"What would Elena say if she heard you?" I pushed. It wasn't a smart tactic. This kid was ready to explode.

"Don't you dare speak her name," he spat.

"Why not? She was my wife, after all." Regret surged through me, a relentless tide I couldn't hold back. It was the only thing I felt when I thought of the late Signora Mancini. We had been so young, and everything seemed like a desperate struggle to survive. Even when I took charge as the boss, I realized there was nothing more I could offer her.

"I'm going to kill you," the agent responded.

He had every reason to want my end. Part of me understood, even accepted it. I was a wretched soul, unable to save an innocent I had vowed to protect in front of so many witnesses. Pain from the past clawed at me, threatening to break through my carefully maintained facade and overwhelm this moment.

"You can try. But before you do, know that I am truly sorry for how it ended. I should have seen her pain, should have eased her suffering. But I swear, I didn't kill your sister—"

"Lies! The moment she married you, she signed her death warrant."

The accusation hung between us, a testament to the conflict tearing at my insides.

I shook my head and pushed to my feet. Too many eyes were watching our exchange. "I wasn't a good husband. But you were so young, practically a baby. You probably didn't realize your sister had severe depression, even as a teen. While it's not an excuse, I didn't know any better. And I thought the sleeping pills she'd been prescribed would help her."

"She killed herself because she married a monster—"

I lunged forward, getting right in the kid's face. "She never killed herself," I said, my voice low and controlled. "Her overdose was an accident. One we could have prevented, but it was an accident."

I could feel my hands shaking, my heart racing. The memories flooded back, raw and painful. I could still see her lying there, her body convulsing as the paramedics tried to save her. And then the emptiness that followed, the crushing guilt that I couldn't shake off.

Turning on my heel, I left. I needed to get away from this place, from the memories and the pain. Mier watched from his position across the street, but didn't move to intercept me. Whether it was to keep his cover or because he sensed the torrent of emotions raging inside me, it was hard to say.

But I was a mess. I walked blindly down the street, not even stopping when the sidewalk ended. Somewhere, my men followed me, but they too kept their distance. What happened to my first wife was a deep scar that I would carry until death claimed me.

I came to a stop in front of a small neighborhood park. In a twist of fate, this looked eerily similar to the one where I had proposed to Elena. Even though it was an arranged marriage, the proposal had been real. The chemistry between us, though a faint fire, had been a flame—one that was easily squelched. I couldn't help but look at a random bench, remember how her youthful face glowed with love and happiness. And then a single tear rolled down my cheek as I remembered how I never was able to save her.

"I'm sorry," I whispered, my voice breaking. "But I swear to you, my sweet Elena, it won't happen again."

I had to do it better this time. Remembering Penelope's distraught face made me wonder if I'd destroyed yet another relationship. I was still mad at her—mad that she didn't trust me enough. If I was fair, her reluctance to tell me made perfect sense.

"I will fix this," I vowed.

I needed time to cool off. I needed space to find a way to forgive Penelope's mistake. Once the damage control in my organization was fixed, there would be time to heal what this turn of events had hurt. This time, I would fight like hell for my marriage. Unlike the infatuation of youth, what I found this time was something more. Something that wouldn't just leave a scar. This time, if I lost Penelope, I would die.

Chapter 44 – Penelope

The bubbles were almost popped, and the water stopped being hot thirty minutes ago. I scraped my fingers across the surface. A fresh burst of anger bloomed in my chest. If I thought I was a prisoner before, it was nothing compared to the restrictions placed on me now. I wasn't allowed to accompany Serena to the stores. There were four guards, strangers who wouldn't speak to me when I walked laps outside. There was no more running. I hadn't passed through the front gate since my evening out with the don.

No, the monster made it clear I was a captive.

"I need to escape," I whispered.

Mom's surgery was next week. My sisters were coming into town tomorrow. And I was stuck.

After the bath, I was going to call them, tell them the trip was canceled. They needed to stay the hell away from this house of horrors.

It wasn't like I'd been able to talk to the don. I wanted to, just to try and clear the air. The two times he'd been home, Dante shadowed his every step. Alessandro didn't talk to me. Didn't look at me.

I shivered. The lukewarm water didn't hold back the ice the monster's actions formed on my heart.

Sinking under the water, I let out a scream.

I opened myself to the man, and the monster crushed me. I should have known better. How could I have been so stupid? It would serve my heart right if I cut out the weak organ and smashed it to a million pieces! It got me into this mess. I knew better than to feel for the monster.

Hard hands gripped me and plucked me from the water.

"Penelope!"

"Let me go, you bastard," I gasped, struggling from his grip.

Alessandro shook me hard. "What were you doing?"

I clawed at him, but he pulled his face out of my reach before pinning my hands. The familiar scent of his body sent a rush of emotion through me. I held my breath, but it was too late. The spicy, woodsy smell brought a volley of memories. That, coupled with his touch, gave life to the feelings I hated. I struggled harder. The water splashed and churned, some of it sliding out of the sides of the tub. The don's grip slipped, and I bucked to the side, breaking free and moving fast out of his reach.

Plunging to the edge of the tub, I glared at him. "What do you want?"

"Why were you under the water?" The look in his black eyes was nothing short of wild.

There was a small sting of pity in my chest to see the pain. But as my fingers gripped the cold piece of metal I'd hid on the other side of the tub, I shoved that reaction away. I refused to give into the terrible longing for the man.

"Where the hell did you find that?" he growled.

"My insurance policy?" I laughed roughly and pointed the barrel at his heart. It wasn't hard to find a hidden weapon in this mausoleum. There were guns concealed everywhere in case of an attack. I'd just had to look. "I don't want you near me, Mancini."

"Fuck, Penelope." Alessandro scraped a hand down his face. "Are you really willing to shoot me?"

"Come at me again and find out."

"I was saving you!" he snapped.

"And I wasn't drowning, lupo." The term wasn't endearing, but it felt wrong to use it. "I told you before, I don't need a man saving me."

"You weren't harming yourself?" he pushed.

"No! I'm tired of screaming into pillows," I seethed. "Now that you know your prisoner is safe, go away. You're ruining my bathtime."

"This isn't a fight, vespina." He bent, gripping the edge of the tub. "We need to talk."

Now he wanted to talk? After two days of freezing me out? No. *No!* That wasn't happening. He missed his chance. My decisions were made. It was time for action.

"You're right, this is a war. And no, we don't need to talk. You've made yourself *very* clear in this matter."

"I needed time to think," he said through clenched teeth.

I shook my head. "Without all the facts? Yeah, I'm not sure I care to hear your conclusion."

"Cristo santo, woman! You act as though this was simple!" His knuckles turned white.

"It is." Emotion threatened to crack my voice. I paused to clear it.

We were married. Even if it was a sham, there was a certain level of communication and trust that went into that relationship. My mistake was not telling him about the threat harassing me. I was human; I messed up. There were reasons if he'd only cared to listen.

He hadn't.

He jumped to the conclusion that I was a threat to his organization.

He chose the famiglia over me. That was how it would always be. I was blinded by his actions, wooed by his attention, and thought he might be giving our arranged marriage a real chance.

Stupid me.

My voice came out strong, sharp, and biting. "You proved you don't trust me—so why the hell should I ever trust you again?"

With lightning speed, Alessandro snatched the gun from my hand. I shouldn't have been so close to him.

I should have pulled the damn trigger.

The don tucked the weapon in the back of his pants and rose. "We're hosting a dinner. Get dressed and be downstairs by seven to greet our guests."

"Let me guess, I have no say in this." I pushed to my feet, water sousing off me.

That dark gaze heated. The don looked down my body. I felt his desire burn against my skin, even as my nipples tingled from the chill.

"Move so I can go shower," I snapped.

There was water on the floor, but I would be damned if he saw me clean it. I would wait until he left.

"I'm fixing this, Penelope," he growled. "Please don't do anything reckless tonight."

"Wouldn't dream of it, signore." I moved past him and disappeared behind the frosted glass of the shower stall.

Alessandro stayed in the room for a few more minutes. I thought he would try to talk to me again, but he left without saying a word.

That was it?

His silence hurt.

He doesn't want to fix this.

The damn ache in my chest threatened to suffocate me. It was heavy; it squeezed tight. Rubbing my sternum, I pressed my head against the tile wall and closed my eyes. It took the idea of self-harm to make him crack. Was that really the only way to catch his attention? A sob croaked from deep inside.

Alessandro was broken, incapable of changing.

Well, he didn't need to worry. There was no reason to harm myself. This situation sucked, but that wasn't my way out.

No, when I escaped this prison, it would be to find my freedom.

And then, he might feel a sliver of regret.

Who was I kidding? That was a fool's last hope. I knew from the beginning that he was cold and unfeeling. It took my mistake to remind myself what manner of creature he was. He didn't care—not about me, only the thought of losing his possession and how that would look.

"I won't let him in again," I vowed.

Slamming the water off, I emerged to paint my face and ready myself for the part I needed to play. Before I began, I bent to clean the water from the tub.

It wasn't there.

The drain was pulled, the water swirling out of the bath. And the floor was cleaned. There wasn't a wet towel; Alessandro had taken that away with him.

Confusion flickered through me. I didn't know what to make of that.

"It doesn't matter," I growled—because it was either be mad or cry.

Fisting my hands, I vowed not to read into the gesture and marched into the bedroom to find a dress. If only it was easy to forget.

Chapter 45 – Alessandro

She hates me.

Work piled on my desk. There were projects Penelope would have been able to help me with, and I'd saved them for her. Thoughts muddled in my mind. The goals for my organization lay dormant and untouched. Problems threatened to bury us.

None of that was a priority.

It had been two days of sheer hell, working long hours to destroy the biggest threat to my family and my organization. In that time, I made a fatal misstep.

I hadn't gone to her.

I left Penelope alone.

And now I was paying for it. The little wasp was incensed.

The door to our bedroom cracked open, and my gaze snapped to the second level where her unhurried footsteps sounded. Dio mio, she was a vision. It might have been a compliment when I called her a goddess before. But there was no mistaking the divine now.

Penelope descended the stairs with a regal defiance, her chin held high as if daring the world to challenge her. Her long brown hair cascaded like a waterfall down her back. The purple scrap of fabric masquerading as a dress clung provocatively, stopping at midthigh and taunting me with the tantalizing glimpse of her powerful, sculpted legs.

The instinct to fall to my knees and beg her forgiveness for my behavior flared bright inside.

But time was against us. What was more, I was going to kill someone tonight. There was no doubt in my mind. Once my men saw this unearthly being, they wouldn't be able to help themselves.

But I wasn't going to order her to change.

No, that would be a mistake.

She was here, and we had a power move to make.

I thrust my hand toward her with determination. Her eyes flickered downward, and a single eyebrow shot up in sharp defiance. Her lip twisted into a sneer of revulsion.

"Please," I insisted. "We go in there together."

"Who's here?" she demanded.

"My capos."

Uncertainty flickered in her eyes.

"It's important we stand united." I took a step forward, reaching for her but not touching.

"Are you sure you want me present?" She tossed her head.

"Yes," I snarled. "It's time they meet you and know your place in this organization is unquestioned."

Her snort of derision hurt. "Can't have your newest employee be seen as a weakness."

"Starting tonight, they will know that you work with me, Penelope." That statement broke through her mask of rage.

"You've always said I worked for you. I was going to be a player in the background," she pushed, crossing her arms over her chest.

I shook my head. "That's changed. It's time you—and everyone else—knows that."

"Fine." She smacked her hand in mine. "Let's go save your image, signore."

Her sharp words sliced through the air, leaving a sting.

How did I expect her to see this any differently?

I was torn by regret, wishing I had followed her that night, yet doubting whether it would have made any difference. She should have been my top priority, but I couldn't shake the feeling that maybe things were meant to unfold this way. I wasn't made to be someone she deserved.

Something yellow flashed in the corner of my eye. Looking down, I noticed the post-it note. It was blank. Confusion made me waffle.

Penelope didn't offer an explanation, and we began to walk to the dining room where the leaders of the famiglia waited. As one, my men rose.

"Buona sera, signori," I intoned.

At the head of the table, I pulled the chair to my right but placed a hand on Penelope's waist to stop her.

"Mark this well," I told my men as I moved my wife into the seat. "I found Carmelo's replacement."

Surprise flickered through the group. Without Adonis there to speak out, none of the men were eager to question me.

Penelope's face was a careful mask. She had to realize what happened. But just to make the gesture clear, I placed a hand on her shoulder.

"I trust my wife completely. I expect the same from you." I pulled out my own chair. "Tonight, Penelope makes her oath and assumes the role of consigliere."

Looking down into her eyes, I begged her to accept—but not this life or the position.

Choose me.

"Do you accept the nomination I put forth?" I threw the question out to my men.

As one they spoke their agreement.

"Make your oath," I encouraged her.

Penelope plucked the steak knife, holding the handle to me as a challenge. "Aren't you forgetting an important part of initiating me into the famiglia, Don Mancini?"

The plan had been to present her, swear her in as a member, and begin the business of the evening as dinner was served. There'd been no intention of cutting her, of making her swear a blood oath.

"It's expected, is it not?" she pushed.

This woman was hell-bent on turning my existence into a nightmare. I realized that from the moment I married her. That was what made her ideal. She was destined to be one of us. Yet, I'd sooner drive a blade into my own flesh than let hers bleed by my hand. An unspoken, desperate plea hovered in the charged air between us.

Don't force my hand in this.

But her grip on the knife only tightened, a defiant promise of unyielding resolve.

A sigh pushed from my lungs. "Hold out your hand."

Her eyes glinted with challenge as she extended her palm toward me, the delicate skin of her wrist exposed beneath the dim chandelier light. The room fell silent, the collective breath of my capos held in anticipation. This wasn't how I'd planned the evening. A blood oath was a test in and of itself—something we'd never asked of a woman before.

"I don't want to hurt you," I whispered, my voice carrying only to her ears.

A dangerous smile curved her lips. "Don't tell me you're afraid now, lupo."

The knife gleamed between us, catching the light like a warning. My fingers closed around the handle, feeling the weight of tradition and consequence. The silver was cool against my palm, but my blood ran hot.

I began the ancient words, watching her face for any sign of hesitation. "Per la mia famiglia, il mio onore, il mio sangue."

The room fell into a sacred hush. My capos leaned forward, their weathered faces a mixture of shock and reverence. This was unprecedented—a woman, my wife, being initiated formally. Yet none dared speak against it.

I continued the oath. "Penelope Mancini, do you swear your blood to the famiglia? Your loyalty above all others? Your silence to the grave?"

Her eyes never left mine as I pressed the tip of the knife to her palm. A single bead of crimson welled beneath the silver point.

"I do," she said, her voice unwavering. Not a whisper of fear crossed her face.

With a swift, practiced motion, I drew the blade across her palm—gentle enough to avoid real damage, but deep enough to seal the pact. The silver edge glided across the smooth surface of her skin, leaving behind a trail of crimson that glittered like rubies in the dimly lit room. The sound of the knife slicing through flesh was almost imperceptible, drowned out by the heavy silence that hung in the air. And then, like a sacrifice to ancient gods, the blood pooled in her hand, a dark and glistening symbol of her loyalty to the famiglia.

Valentino pushed forward a crystal tumbler filled with amber whiskey. I guided her hand over the glass, watching as three drops of her blood fell into the cup.

"As we drink, you become one of us," I breathed, before taking a sip and passing it to the left.

I plucked a napkin and pressed the linen tightly into her hand.

She jerked her hand away, lowering her gaze.

Look at me!

Instinct roared within me, a primal urge demanding I seize her, whisk her away to a secluded place and mend what was shattered. Her words echoed relentlessly in my mind. She believed my actions were a desperate attempt to protect myself. How could she not understand that this was all for her? She craved more, and this was the next highest position in the mob. It was the ultimate opportunity, tailor-made for her—she had fought for it, she deserved it!

The moment dessert was cleared away, I dismissed the men. My wife rose to leave, but I caught her wrist.

"A moment, Penelope."

Exhaustion was etched into her face. After the blood ceremony, the men had each put her to the test in their own way. I allowed the ebb and flow of questions only because this was a battle that needed to be won.

And it had.

"You did well tonight." I ran my fingers along the inside of her wrist.

"Thanks." Penelope jerked away, plucked the empty square of yellow paper, and stepped toward the door.

Growling, I sprang after her and caught her body against the wall.

"Why the post-it, vespina?" I demanded, bracing a hand above and another beside her. "What do you want?" *I've given you everything.*

She gave me a challenging look. "My sisters come tomorrow. I was told we were going to spend an evening on a yacht."

Relief, sweet and pure, surged through me. "I already gave you my word on that. You don't need this."

I plucked the post-it note from her.

With a yell of outrage, she snatched it back. "Hey! I earned that."

"You don't need it." My hand curled into a fist. I was seconds away from driving it into the wall. "Whatever you want, it's yours. Hell! I've given you a seat at the table. If that doesn't prove I'll give you the world, what will?"

The smile that curled over her lips was impossibly sad. "If you think it's the world I want, you still don't get it."

"Tell me, then!"

Penelope shook her head. "Thank you for honoring your promise to host my sisters. We'll stay out of your hair."

I let her go. Every fiber screamed this was the pinnacle of the fight, and I was losing. But I didn't have the first clue how to right the wrong.

Chapter 46 – Penelope

If my sisters were confused why we went straight from the airport to the marina instead of going for drinks and dinner on the town, they didn't say. Dressed in country chic, they looked like relics of my past. The strappy heels and flirty dress covering me were uptown girl. It was a wonder they recognized me.

I didn't need to worry.

The change in circumstance didn't matter. The moment they rushed through the baggage claim area, and we squealed in a long overdue hug, the trivial things faded.

"So where is the sister-in-law?" Jillian asked as the marina attendant ushered us along the docks and docks of boats.

Karen's brows shot to her forehead. "Sister-in-law? What the hell does that mean?"

I sighed. Jillian knew more of the secrets than any of the others. I began to explain the abbreviated version of my marriage as we walked. As promised, the guards kept their distance, not joining us at the airport, tailing me in a car and only emerging to greet us in the parking lot. They sauntered ahead of us now, leading the way, not looking like they were scouting for danger. We rounded a corner, taking a horizontal stretch of dock. At the end of it were two women. It was hard to say if they were standing off or reuniting. Nico and Giulio went to stand with Serena's guard near what I assumed was the boat we were taking. It was the biggest in the marina—naturally.

"Serena's the one in red," I said, pointing.

Karen hurried forward, stuck out her hand, and ended up giving Serena a hug. The rumpled look on the mafia princess was priceless. Jillian had a little more reservation, but only because she was a nurse and her people skills were better.

It's going to be so good going back with them.

I steadied myself. Tonight, I would play my cards carefully. If all went well, we wouldn't be in Chicago to see the sunrise.

"Your sisters are as wild as you were," Serena observed, giving me a pointed look.

I shrugged. "It's all the fresh air out west."

My sister-in-law hummed politely. She had her manners and grace wrapped around her as if her life depended on it. I swept a curious look over the other woman, whose sailor stripe outfit was more costume than practical.

"Penelope, this is Annaliese." Serena gestured between us.

"I was going to take the sailboat out and ran into my old crony." Annaliese smiled broadly. "But it seems she can't do dinner, since she has other plans."

"Why don't you join us?" I offered. "We have plenty of room, and then you and Serena can catch up."

Serena stiffened. For this being her old friend, there was some kind of strange tension simmering under the surface.

Annaliese's eyes lit up at my invitation, a smile tugging at the corners of her mouth. "I'd be delighted," she said, ignoring Serena's subtle head shake.

The Mancini's yacht was even more magnificent up close—a gleaming seventy-foot beauty with three decks and chrome railings that caught the late afternoon sun like liquid silver. The name *Fortune's Kiss* was emblazoned on the stern in elegant script. As we approached, a uniformed crew member met us on the boarding ramp.

"Welcome aboard," he said with a practiced smile, his Italian accent thick but understandable. "There are cocktails on the upper deck."

"We're ready to cast off, Salvo," Nico said, but he wasn't looking at the crew member.

No, his eyes were focused on Karen.

Mother of god, I didn't think I would have to fight off the soldiers when it came to my sister. Thankfully, Jillian's ring would keep the others at bay.

Karen whistled low, her eyes wide. "When you said boat, Penny, I was thinking something with, I don't know, oars maybe?"

"The Mancini family doesn't do anything small," Annaliese said, wandering off with my sisters in search of the drinks.

"Hey, S, are you okay?" I tugged my sister-in-law aside.

Serena nodded. "Yeah, it's just…she's a reminder of everything I'm not."

"Oh. Oh, gosh, S, I had no idea." I lifted my arms, thought better of hugging her, and dropped them.

"I want to travel. I want to see the world without my brother guarding my every step. I want to meet people, Penny." The truth tumbled out, as if the dam was broken and the terrible longing could no longer be contained.

"Maybe there's a way," I began, but she cut me off.

"No, not for me. Annaliese grew up strict, but she found a way to do exactly what she wanted. In a way, she reminds me of you. Life doesn't hold you down—"

"It does," I insisted.

"Not for long, Penny."

Serena pulled herself straight, set a smile on her face, and led the way where the others had disappeared up a staircase.

I padded after her. The upper deck of the yacht was breathtaking—a wide-open space with plush seating, a bar stocked with crystal decanters, and an unobstructed view of Lake Michigan stretching to the horizon. The sun was beginning its descent, painting everything in gold.

My sisters had already made themselves comfortable, drinks in hand. Karen was chatting animatedly with Nico, who seemed genuinely amused by whatever she was saying. Jillian was examining the Chicago skyline with Giulio, her practical nature on full display.

"So, how long have you and Serena's brother been married?" Annaliese asked, materializing beside me with two glasses of something amber and expensive-looking.

I accepted the drink. "A few weeks. Still in the honeymoon phase, I suppose."

Her laugh was musical but sharp. "You don't have to sugarcoat it with me, darling. With the Mancinis, there is no such thing."

Serena's face tightened at the comment, but she busied herself with accepting a flute of something sparkling from the bartender.

"How was Germany?" I asked, trying to turn the spotlight off myself. This woman was intense. While it was possible to envision myself being friends with her, there was too much turbulence at this moment to risk a deep conversation.

"Do you know any Germans, Penelope?" Annaliese cocked her head.

"My dad is mostly German, actually. Granted, that was a few generations ago, but they married amongst themselves and I assume that's how the character traits passed down to us," I laughed.

"Well then, you'll understand when I say they're a harsh, unforgiving sort." Annaliese slammed the rest of her drink. "Come sit with me, Penny. I want to hear all about how you tamed the wicked, soulless Mancini heir."

Groaning, I grabbed Serena's elbow and forced her to come with us.

"You know I had a crush on Alessandro in middle school." Annaliese leaned against the railing, gazing into her empty cup.

"Tell me!" I leaned forward, suddenly interested. "What was he like?"

Annaliese snorted. "Late-twenties and ambitious. He didn't give us girls the time of day."

We gabbed for another quarter of an hour. Serena warmed up after the second flute of bubbles, and the excursion seemed to be off to a good start.

As we grazed on a charcuterie board, inching farther into the lake, the city becoming a miniscule portrait of blinking lights set against the red-gold sky, another boat came cruising down from the north. Since it was the only other ship out here, it drew our attention. It easily was the size of this yacht, if not bigger.

"Good Lord, Baldwin is in town!" Annaliese gasped, sitting up straight. Her eyes blazed bright.

"Anna," Serena warned, jumping to tug her friend away.

"What the hell was that about?" Karen giggled.

Nico looked like he wanted to say something, but a dark look from Giulio silenced him. I wanted desperately to know but knew better than to talk about business in front of the girls. My fingers fidgeted with the bandage on my hand. This was how it would always be, me keeping secrets from my family. If only the new family I surrounded myself with filled the void better.

One of Serena's guards carried a sleek, portable speaker onto the deck, and soon, lively music filled the air, its rhythm spreading overboard to tease the waves. My sisters, with mischievous glints in their eyes, mercilessly teased the city boys about their eclectic music choice, their laughter mingling with the tunes. A spirited battle of songs quickly ensued, each group trying to outdo the other with their selections. As we polished off another round of colorful cocktails, the mood shifted, and we were all drawn to the makeshift dance floor, our bodies swaying and moving in time with the infectious beats.

I felt weightless, like I was suspended in a dream where nothing mattered but the rhythm that pulsed through the floorboards and up into my bones.

Annaliese and Serena reappeared. This time, the tension seemed less.

We sailed closer to shore, cruising along the length of the city. The night turned dark, but I barely noticed. The music and good times had me now.

Gasping, I clutched the railing.

Jillian stepped beside me. "You're not wearing his ring."

I held up my empty finger. "What ring?"

"Your husband's."

She might be younger than me, but I felt the guilt in the face of a seasoned adult.

"Shit, Pen, you love him." Jillian turned me around.

"What? No!" I stammered. I hadn't even told her I was married until the other day, but she read me like a damn book.

"It doesn't take a genius to figure out how you found the money for mom's surgery," she said dryly and took a sip of her cocktail. "You married money. But now...you fell for him."

I snatched her drink and downed it. A hiss escaped my lips. I frowned at the cup.

That was soda water and lime.

"There's no booze—Jillian!" I squeaked.

My sister clapped her hand over my mouth. "Don't you say a word. It's too early, and with everything going on with mom, I don't want to add to their plate by worrying about a pregnant me."

I tugged away from her. "Then you'll understand when I say don't you dare tell them about my life choices."

She snorted.

Together we gazed over the water. Here, more boats sailed by. Karen and Nico waved and shouted to them.

"It's nice to see one of us is still carefree," I muttered.

"You've always managed to do the impossible." Jillian leaned on me. "Thank you, Pen."

"Don't mention it."

"What do you need?" she pressed.

Looking behind me, I dropped my voice. "Actually, we're going to cut your vacation short. Here's the plan."

Once I laid it out, my sister let out a long whistle. "I don't know who your husband is, but my guess is he's not going to like this."

"Fuck him. Are you going to help me or not?"

"I'll leave the fucking to you, but yes, of course I will." She took the empty glass. "It's a good thing one of us is sober enough to drive tonight."

I nodded.

"Look at the colorful lights!" Karen mused.

Wandering to her, my heart shot to my throat. Three patrol boats were bearing down on us, red and blue lights flashing. Sirens blared over the water. They were coming straight at us.

"Get down!" Nico shouted, suddenly all business as he moved toward us with purpose.

My stomach dropped. This wasn't some routine harbor patrol. Something was very wrong.

Giulio was already on his phone, barking orders in rapid Italian. The party atmosphere evaporated.

"What's happening?" Karen asked, her voice rising with panic as Nico gently but firmly guided her away from the railing.

"Coast Guard," I muttered, trying to keep my voice steady. "Or police. Either way, not good."

Jillian shot me a look that said everything: *This is what you married into?*

I shrugged. There would be a harsh interrogation later—if we made it to the rental car place and left the city as I planned.

Annaliese, surprisingly, seemed the least concerned of all of us. She sipped her drink with almost theatrical calm, watching the approaching boats with something like amusement. When she caught me watching, she smirked and went to my sisters. "Go below deck and wait for the law to board. They won't hurt you two."

My sisters wavered. Panic clawed inside me. What if they were hurt because of me?

"They're after you two," Annaliese said pointedly, dragging Serena and I aside. "You shouldn't be here when they board."

"How do you—"

"She knows about our family, Penny," Serena said pointedly. "Her dad has made it his life's mission to destroy the mob. That was part of our last big fight."

"Yes, yes, I know I was stupid about it," Annaliese snapped. "Ancient history. Right now, you two mafia princesses need to get off this boat. The cops can't touch us, since we don't know anything and the guards won't blab."

"One phone call to Daddy and this will all be forgotten," Serena said, rolling her eyes in disgust.

Annaliese only smiled. "So long as you two aren't here, yeah, that's what will happen."

"You'll protect my sisters?" I insisted.

The woman placed her hand over her heart. "With my life."

"Can I trust her?" I demanded, rounding on Serena.

My sister-in-law studied her old friend. "She hates her dad more than he hates the mob. So yes, she'll use him and his resources to protect your sisters."

"Glad you realize that now, Serena. Now! Time's wasting. Get off the boat," Annaliese said pleasantly.

"We're on the lake, where the hell are we going to go?" Serena spewed.

The patrol boats swiftly closed in, their sirens screaming as they flanked the yacht, which gradually decelerated until it came to a complete halt. The yacht's graceful motion ceased, and the air was filled with the metallic clatter of the anchor's chains rattling somewhere in the depths below, echoing a garish tune over the waves.

Annaliese and I shared a look.

"Oh, madonna, no!" Serena groaned.

"You're a great swimmer," her friend coaxed. "I'll have Daddy's lawyer clean this mess up, and we'll hang out another time."

Annaliese hurried us to the front of the boat. "Jump, bitches." She gave us a shove.

As I lost my balance and tumbled forward, my arms flailed wildly in a desperate attempt to regain control. The plunge into the water was a jarring shock, the icy chill striking me like a sharp slap against my skin, contrasting sharply with the lingering warmth of the humid evening air. The murky depths surrounded me, swallowing me whole and obscuring my vision in an inky blackness that pressed against me from all sides.

Strong fingers clutched me.

Serena dragged me to the surface, and I coughed out the dirty lake water.

"Can you swim?" she hissed, tugging me along.

"Kinda sorta." I began to paddle after her.

"Try to keep up," Serena called.

After just five minutes, my limbs trembled uncontrollably, the muscles quivering with exhaustion. My lungs burned, each breath a desperate gasp as I fought against the relentless pull of the waves trying to drag me down into their depths. In the distance, a black raft bobbed on the water, a beacon of hope. Serena, her strokes powerful and deliberate, altered her path, her arms slicing through the water with determination as she swam toward it.

She called out in Italian, and a male responded.

There wasn't oxygen enough to battle the confusion. I simply followed.

"Get Penny first," Serena hissed, smacking at the hands reaching for her.

Just as my lungs burned with desperation and my strokes weakened, the raft bobbed closer through the choppy waves. A large man leaned forward, his grip firm and reassuring as he hoisted me from the frigid water and into the cramped safety of the small vessel.

An impossibly familiar face, covered in shadows, stared back at me.

"Pen, I have the distinct pleasure of introducing you to the owner of the *Fortune's Favorite*." Serena gestured to the yacht anchored twenty yards away.

"The world knows him as the reclusive business mogul, Leonard Baldwin," Serena drawled, leaning back in the water, expertly treading the waves. "But that's just a front. Penny, meet Leonardo Mancini, my big brother."

Chapter 47 – Penelope

"You're fidgeting," Serena grumbled.

I wouldn't blame her if she was seconds away from smacking me.

"Sorry," I muttered.

We were close to the docks. The air is thick with the murky, stagnant scent of the lake, mingled with the faint smell of diesel fuel and the musty odor of old wooden piers. Boats of all shapes and sizes bobbed in the harbor. I scanned the area for the best place to slip away unnoticed.

The moment was coming. Jillian already knew where to meet so it was up to fate if we made it to the rental company without interference.

"What has gotten you so worked up?" Serena pushed. "It's like you're expecting a fight. Oh, Santa Maria, you're planning something!"

My sister-in-law gripped my shoulders hard. I gave her a smile, but she likely saw right through it.

"Talk." She was a force of nature, much like her brother.

"I'm not going back with you," I whispered.

"I guessed as much," Serena said, surprising me.

"How did you—"

"Please," she drawled. "Ever since my brother acted like an A-class dick, I've been hoping and praying you left. I figured when you went to the airport, you'd slip away. I thought meeting your sisters was a decoy."

She wrapped her arms around herself.

"I wasn't missing the boat party." I stepped closer, wondering if she'd let me reach out and hug her.

A raw and real emotion filled her voice. She sounded vulnerable. "I'm glad you didn't. I'm glad we had one fun memory together, even if my brother's goons watched us like hawks."

"I am too." I laughed, because I was seconds away from crying myself. "I'll be back, S."

She blinked at me. "Why?"

"Sshhh, keep your voice down." I looked back, but there was no sign of the mysterious third Mancini. There was no time—and this wasn't the place—to sate my curiosity on the subject.

"You have a chance to escape," Serena insisted.

That was the thing. I didn't want to, and it wasn't because a pair of black eyes haunted my dreams and the memory of his touch was a ghostly presence that stalked my days. "My place is here."

I held up my freshly bandaged palm. It was the only part of me that was cleaned from the lake water.

"That's fucked up."

"It is," I agreed. "I can't explain it, but for the first time in my life, I feel like I belong."

"My brother will turn this city upside down looking for you." There was a hint of dark amusement in the woman's voice.

"Give him a message from me?" I shifted back and forth. When she nodded, I still didn't have the words.

"I'll tell him you disappeared to teach him a lesson."

I smacked my forehead. "Don't do that," I moaned. "I've written a note; it was in my purse. If you can't find it, just tell him I'm safe and I'll see him in a couple weeks."

He could lock me up again, this time for good. Part of me hoped it wouldn't come to that. He made me a member of the famiglia. I hoped he'd honor that, if only to save face with his men.

But I was willing to risk his wrath. I had to be there. For my mom and siblings—for my dad. I missed him the most. That man was always able to make the worst days better.

We were going to go through her surgery as a family, just like we'd done with every crisis. Dad was the stable rock we would lean on, and I was the voice of determination that kept the others in line.

The perfect team.

"I'll go distract Leonardo while you slip off the yacht," Serena offered.

And then she surprised me again. She threw her arms around my shoulders and squeezed.

As I hugged her back, I caught the faintest scent of her perfume—sweet and spicy, the same one she always wore. It was comforting and familiar, like a warm embrace on a chilly day. Underneath the floral notes, there was a subtle hint of musk, adding a touch of sensuality and mystery. In that moment, I felt safe and loved. If I came back, it was partially for her.

She was just as much a prisoner in this life, and I wasn't leaving her behind.

The crew shouted and threw ropes to the dock attendants.

"Now's your chance," Serena whispered in my ear. "Hurry!"

Serena helped me over the railing and then disappeared to find her brother. My bare feet hit the dock with a soft thud. I slid past the crew, ducking under a rope as they secured the yacht to the pier. My heart hammered in my chest, but years of slipping out of my bedroom window after curfew had trained me well. Stay low, move quick, don't look back.

The wooden planks creaked beneath my feet as I darted between stacked crates and coiled ropes. A seagull screeched overhead, making me flinch. I forced myself not to look over my shoulder, knowing Leonardo's or the don's men might be around.

"Watch it!" a weathered dock worker growled as I nearly collided with him.

"Sorry," I mumbled, lowering my eyes and hoping he didn't get a good look at my face.

Once on the road, I took a deep breath. The first hurdle was over. But I didn't settle down until I turned the corner. The rental kiosk was just ahead—a weathered blue shack with peeling paint and a hand-painted sign. Jillian was already there, pacing nervously in front of a battered Fiat.

They'd slipped the guards.

The cops showing up had to be the best thing to happen to us. It solved the problem of sneaking away from Mancini's men.

"I thought you weren't coming," she hissed when I reached her, relief flooding her features. "The guy's getting antsy about the paperwork."

"Just had to say goodbye," I whispered, taking the keys she thrust into my palm. "How did you two sneak away?"

"The boys were arrested. But Annaliese dropped us here," Karen pouted. "I really liked that guy, Nico. You think you could get me his number?"

Over my dead body was my sister dating a Made Man. They were too much trouble—the bad kind of trouble.

The kind that left a girl wanting more.

The rental agent—a squat man with a cigarette dangling from his lips—barely looked up as we finalized the transaction. Five minutes later, we were pulling away from the marina.

Chapter 48 – Alessandro

The elevator opened to the penthouse apartment. I barreled through the businessman's front doors, not bothering with the courtesy of knocking.

Baldwin clicked on his laptop. Serena nursed a drink by the large window that offered a panoramic view of the city. And Penelope....

"Where the hell is my wife?" I shouted.

Baldwin looked up from his work, shot our sister a pointed look, and then started typing again. "This one is all her."

I marched over and slammed the computer lid closed, narrowly missing his fingers. "You said you would keep an eye on them," I snarled.

"I did. And when these two went overboard to escape the raid, I took a life raft for them myself," Baldwin shot back. "They were safe and sound right up until we docked."

"And then?" I growled.

"Sorellina," Baldwin sang out. He picked up his phone and began to tap a message.

Cristo santo, he couldn't put work away for five minutes!

I rounded on Serena. "Where is she?"

Serena threw back her drink. "Gone. And good riddance to her too."

Time blurred as I marched forward. Without thinking, I grabbed my sister's shoulders and slammed her into the window. The cocktail glass fell, shattering with a deafening finality.

In the background, Baldwin muttered. The sound of his chair scraping on the floor, of his hurried steps, sounded, but I focused on my prey.

"Where is my wife, sorella?" I growled.

"She needs time and space." Serena didn't fight me, but there was a dark satisfaction in her gaze. "She left you, Sandro. Just like they all do."

I shook her. "You tell me where she is—"

Baldwin ripped me back, leaning right into my face. "Don't lay a finger on her."

I was about to shout I would never, but I stopped. Was I the sort of monster who hurt his own flesh and blood? What was this madness consuming me?

Leaning around him, I tried a different tactic. "The Feds are looking for her—for us. She's not safe."

"Safer away than with you," Serena spat.

I lunged, but Baldwin shoved me back. His fist snaked out and clipped my jaw for good measure.

Rubbing my face, I circled my brother.

"It's what you fucking deserve," Serena hissed, heading back to the kitchen. "You are cold and unfeeling, Sandro. No wonder she didn't want to stay."

But I wasn't. Couldn't they see that?

I stopped, dropped my guard, and surrendered to my brother. He didn't move for the strike, merely watched me.

"I have to bring her back," I insisted.

"Why? So you can punish her?" Baldwin cocked his head.

"No, he'll just lock her up and not give her the time of day," Serena added unhelpfully. Two large ice cubes rattled in a new cup, and she splashed some of Baldwin's expensive whiskey over them.

I collapsed into a couch. "I fucked up."

Silence pulsed in the room.

My confession was the last thing my siblings expected.

I ran a hand through my hair, tugging at the roots. The pain centered me.

Baldwin's eyebrows shot up. "Well, that's a first."

"Save it," I muttered, raking my hands through my hair. "I need to find her before they do."

Serena sauntered back, drink in hand, studying me with newfound interest. "What exactly did you do, Sandro?"

The weight of my mistakes pressed down on my shoulders. "I kept her at arm's length. Made her feel like a prisoner in our own home." I looked up at my siblings, the truth clawing its way out of me. "I was afraid."

"The great Alessandro Mancini, afraid?" Baldwin scoffed, but his eyes held something else. Understanding, perhaps. "I thought Papà beat that out of us."

Apparently not.

"Of what?" Serena pressed, her earlier venom softening.

"Of feeling too much." The words hung in the air, raw and exposed. "Of losing her like I lost Elena." The mention of that name still cut like a blade after all these years. I closed my eyes briefly, letting the pain wash through me rather than fighting it. Perhaps that was my first mistake with Penelope—trying to bury the past instead of letting her see those wounds. "Then I saw a path to fix it. I made her my right hand."

"Let me guess, you fucked that up too," Serena drawled. She came over and offered me the drink.

I downed it. The cold fire slid down my throat, burning but not numbing the pain radiating through my chest.

My siblings were witness to my failure. There was no stopping the feelings from showing.

They'll see me as weak for loving my wife.

"Call it what you want," I said, setting the empty glass on the coffee table. "But I need her back."

Baldwin crossed his arms. "She left you a note."

Serena groaned. "I told you that in confidence."

My head snapped up. "What? Where?"

He reached into his jacket pocket and pulled out a folded piece of paper. I snatched it from his hand before he could change his mind, unfolding it with trembling fingers.

Alessio,

You made me your queen on a chessboard where I could only move in the directions you permitted. I need to remember who I am without your rules.

Don't look for me.

Penelope

The paper crumpled in my fist. "This tells me nothing."

"It tells you everything," Serena said, her voice softer now. "She's suffocating."

That made two of us. How could doing the right thing—what I thought was the right thing—create such a disaster?

"I gave her power. I brought her into the business—"

"Loving her isn't weakness. It's what dear old Papà never understood," Baldwin said quietly, surprising me. He sank into the chair across from me, his perpetually busy hands finally still. "It's the way you did it. Or didn't do it."

I looked up, meeting my brother's eyes. For once, they weren't judging me.

"Of the three of us, Papà messed you up the worst. You locked her in a gilded cage, Sandro," Serena said, sitting beside me. The hostility had drained from her voice. "Made her your right hand without giving her your heart. What did you expect?"

"I gave her everything," I argued, but the protest sounded hollow even to my own ears.

"Everything except yourself," Baldwin countered. He leaned forward, elbows on his knees. "You gave her the mansion, the clothes, the jewelry. You gave her a position in the family business. But you never let her see the man behind the don."

A hush fell over us like a heavy blanket, stifling even the faintest whisper of sound. Serena approached with the bottle of whiskey, its amber liquid catching the dim light. She poured a generous measure into my glass, the rich scent of oak and smoke filling the air, and offered another to Baldwin. Together, we raised our glasses, the clink of crystal ringing softly in the silence. As the warm, fiery liquid coursed down my throat, the gravity of the situation pressed down on me, enveloping my thoughts in a dense fog.

"Mama told me once that love is the greatest curse a soul can have," Baldwin said, breaking the silence. "She'd whispered it to me one night after our father beat her so badly she couldn't leave her bed for a week. I swore then I'd never love like that—destructively, completely. But...." My brother tipped his glass toward me. "Looks like you're cursed, brother."

I was.

By trying not to be like my father, I destroyed one marriage and was about to repeat history with a second.

I'll be damned before that happens.

"Where would she go?" I asked, my voice hoarse.

"Think," Serena deadpanned. "Where would she feel safe?"

Serena exchanged a look with Baldwin. My brother sighed. "We're not telling you unless you promise not to drag her back against her will."

"I'm trying to protect her," I growled. "That's all I'm ever trying to do with any of you."

"From what? The Feds?" Baldwin scoffed. "Or from making her own choices?"

I slammed my fist on the table. "They'll use her to get to me. They'll tear apart everything we've built."

"Oh, shut up!" Serena groaned. "She wants this life, Sandro! She was made to be your queen. So stop fucking screwing it up."

My heart stuttered. "I can—I can do that. I just need a chance to make this better."

"Then you know where to look." Serena rose and went to the cabinet, pulling out another bottle.

As I watched her, knowing that these two understood me better than I did myself, it dawned on me.

"She went home," I breathed. *She's safe.*

Serena shook her head. "The mom's surgery is in a few days. They didn't go as far as North Dakota, or wherever in bum-fuck-Egypt they come from."

"Come with me?" The offer fell from my lips before I had a chance to think it through properly. But it felt right.

"Do you mean that?" Serena pinned me with a look.

"You know he does," Baldwin snorted. "Quit punishing him and accept, sorellina, before we start another fight."

"Thanks for the offer, but I have plans with an old friend of mine." Serena tossed her hair, but I didn't miss the side look she shot Baldwin.

I didn't know what that was about, and right now, I couldn't bring myself to care. Serena didn't have friends, so I should have been grilling her about this other person. But my focus was otherwise consumed. My sister was a grown woman, and she knew the rules. I had to set my priorities straight. First thing in the morning, I was winning my wife back. I would use tonight to strategize with these two lunatics exactly how that was going to happen.

Chapter 49 – Alessandro

The Greenbriar family was staying in the penthouse suite of the Grand Inn. As I walked to the door, I felt confident with my rehearsed speech, which I'd spent the flight to Rochester, Minnesota preparing. It was perfect. It highlighted what had gone wrong and presented the case for our future together. The moment I convinced her to see me alone, I would lay my heart out to her. But first, there was likely to be resistance. With her family present, it would be tricky to force a moment alone.

How had she explained my existence to them?

If she'd even done that....

It didn't matter. I was here to talk to my wife. Not even her family could stop me.

Raising my fist, I rapped on the door. The blood in my veins pulsed rapidly. Air came in short bursts, not quite filling my lungs. A myriad of scenes played out in my mind.

I was prepared for any of them.

The door swung open, and I found myself face-to-face with a middle-aged man with salt-and-pepper hair. He could be the postcard model for a Western rancher. From the hat on his head to the dusty boots on his feet, he reminded me of when I first met Penelope. His physique was rugged and sinewy, a testament to years of toil under the relentless sun, and his eyes bore the steely resolve of a man shaped by a life of grit and endurance. A hard life made for hard men.

"Can I help you?" he asked.

Her father. It had to be. I'd never met him, never seen photos. Penelope had kept that part of her life walled off from me, a fortress I wasn't permitted to breach.

Just as I'd done with parts of mine.

That stopped today.

"I'm here to see Penelope," I said, scanning the room behind him which seemed empty.

His expression shifted, hardened. "And you are?"

The question hung between us. What was I? Lover? Captor? The man she'd fled from?

"Alessandro," I said simply. "Her husband."

The word landed like a grenade. His eyebrows shot up, and he sucked in a low breath that whistled. His body stayed tight to the door, but he made no move to slam it in my face.

"You best come in, young man. You've got a bit of explaining to do," he drawled.

"Thank you, sir." I stepped inside—

And froze.

The cold steel of a barrel pressed against my skin with a chilling threat that was impossible to ignore. I had to hand it to the old man, few were crafty enough to draw a weapon on me.

They never lived to brag over the feat.

"In the middle of the room." The door slammed closed. "Hands up where I can see them."

I obeyed. "My weapon is in my waistband."

"Hmm," her father grunted.

Once I was disarmed, he walked around to face me.

"Mr. Greenbriar, I came here to apologize to Penelope."

The rancher waved his pistol in the air. "First, you owe me an apology. If I like it, I'll think about letting you speak to Penny."

The rush of surprise was quickly replaced with respect. This was a good man...which meant he was dangerous. The best always were. His violence was held by a tight leash, but I had no illusions it would break free if I pissed him off. And clearly Penelope had said something, because I was skating on thin ice here.

"Tell me, sir, how have I wronged you?" I asked pointedly. The sooner we cut to the chase, the sooner I could find my wife.

The rancher's weathered face cracked into a humorless smile. "You married my daughter without so much as asking for my blessing. That's strike one." He circled me slowly, the gun never wavering. "Strike two is whatever you did that sent her running back to us with those haunted eyes. And strike three—" He paused, studying me with a gaze that cut like a knife. "—is showing up here unannounced like you own her."

I kept my hands visible, steady. "Fair points, sir. But there's more to the story than what Penelope has told you."

"Oh, I'm sure there is." His voice dripped with sarcasm. "There always is with men like you."

"Men like me?" Did he know?

"I've been around long enough to know your type. Expensive suit, that watch." He gestured with the barrel toward my wrist. "And the scar on your palm. A Made Man. You reek of violent sins."

"I saved your headstrong daughter from a worse fate," I started.

But he cut me off by pulling back the hammer of the pistol. "I doubt she sees you as the hero in this story."

"I told her from the beginning that I was the villain. I don't hide behind illusions, sir."

The rancher circled me slowly, his boots making soft thuds against the plush hotel carpet. The gun never wavered.

"Her mother ran from that world. I kept her safe." When he stepped back in my line of sight, a haunted look consumed his face. "Keeping my family away from those demons has been my biggest accomplishment. And yet, in a twist of fate, it's come undone. I failed, and my oldest daughter fell into the den of vipers."

"Penelope is strong. She faced those vipers and bargained without fear. I took her away when her uncle played her dirty."

The rancher spat on the carpet, showing that maybe he wasn't quite tamed. "That pig has been nothing but trouble since he came squealing out of his mother."

A genuine smile curled my lips. "And I fully intend to make him squeal once more before he journeys to meet her."

That statement didn't amuse the father. "And what makes you think I shouldn't do the same to you?"

I saw myself in his eyes. That fate was something I earned. There was no hiding from the truth. "It would be your fatherly right."

He pointed the gun point blank at my chest. "I ought to shoot you right here. It's what you deserve."

"It is," I conceded, my voice steady.

"But I won't." He inhaled deeply, the air hissing through his teeth, before gently releasing the hammer and sliding the gun back into its holster with a swift, controlled motion. "Because it would devastate my girl, and she's suffered enough."

A spark of hope ignited in my chest.

"I'm here to set things right, Mr. Greenbriar. I'll move heaven and earth to prove that to both you and Penelope."

"It's her you need to convince, boy." The rancher yanked off his hat, swiping sweat from his forehead before jamming it back on. "Let's go. She's at the hospital with her mom and brothers."

But I stepped in front of him. "I am sorry that I didn't ask you, sir."

He narrowed his eyes. "With any luck, you have plenty of time to make it up to me." He stuck out his hand. "The name's David."

I took his hand, feeling the calluses that spoke of a man who'd worked the land his entire life. His grip was firm—a warning and an acknowledgment all at once.

This was not a man to be trifled with.

"Alessandro Mancini."

His eyes flickered with recognition. "Mancini—a Chicago family. I should've known." He released my hand with a sigh that seemed to come from somewhere deep and old. "Penny never mentioned your family name."

My little consigliere. She kept my secrets from her own father. The woman was a fucking treasure, and it was time I won that back. If only the prospect wasn't filled with uncertainty and doubt.

I'll let you sting me as many times as it takes, little wasp. I would take every barb as a trophy that earned the right to rule at her side.

Chapter 50 – Penelope

The door opened, and the telltale clip of boots and jangle of spurs sounded behind the curtain. I knew without looking that it was my dad. A swell of warmth bloomed in my chest. I was ready for another hug. That noise was part of my childhood, promising the comfort to come.

Mikey shot to his feet, finger on his lips to shush Dad.

"I hope he brought food," Nicholas muttered. "The hospital stuff is crap."

"Then have something delivered," Karen hissed. "Either way, quit complaining."

"I'm not complaining!" Nicholas said in a stage whisper. "I'm just starving."

A few of us snorted quietly in agreement. Mikey gave us a warning look. Mom *just* fell asleep after a restless couple of hours.

A second pair of steps sounded, and a look showed the glint of shoes under the gap. My heart jumped to my throat. I knew that custom-made, black leather pair.

Dad moved into the room and came straight to me. The grave look on his face said it all. I rose and rushed into his outstretched arms, and he gave me a hug.

"He showed up," he rumbled into my hair.

"Sooner than I thought," I muttered into his plaid shirt.

"Want the boys to throw him out?"

I pulled back and saw the way my father's eyes danced.

Crap. He liked the don.

It wasn't hard to see why. They were fundamentally cut from the same cloth. My dad might not run a crime syndicate, but he was rough and wild. An old-fashioned cowboy who took the law into his own hands when occasion called for it.

Before I answered, the four boys stood as one. A wall of muscle and grit, facing off the monster from nightmares. It would have been comical, if the thick feeling of dread hadn't descended on the room. My sisters looked between each other and began whispering. The beeps from my mother's machines pierced the air, her only contribution to the moment.

"How dare you show your face here," Theo spat.

That brother had the blackest hair, the most olive skin—a lethal dose of Mom's Italian heritage.

And it was going to get him killed.

"Don't." I stepped forward, untangling myself from the safety of my father's arms.

As one, my brothers moved into a tighter grouping. A wall of flesh to protect me. Their instinct would have been sweet. But I didn't fear this monster—I never had, and I never would.

"I'm not going to fight you," Alessandro said pointedly. "I just want to talk to my wife."

"Well, she don't wanna talk to you," Nicholas fumed.

I walked right up behind the most blond of my brothers and clapped him upside the head. "You don't speak for me."

Nicholas yelped and ducked. "Pen! You said this piece of shit got on your last nerve."

"And if that warranted a beating, you all would be black and blue right now! Honestly, boys, you're acting like this is a bar on Friday night." I pushed them aside.

And met the wolf head on.

"Come on, lupo, there's a park outside we can talk in," I snapped, walking past Alessandro.

Joseph snorted. "Best say 'yes, ma'am' and hop to it, Mr. Fancy Pants."

Oh, mother of god, one of them is going to die.

I managed to extract my husband without the blood of my brothers spilling. His heated gaze crackled down my spine as I led the way to the elevator. Once the metal doors shut, the air evaporated, filled with a thick, turbulent energy.

"You look well," Alessandro said, his voice a low rumble in the confined space.

I refused to look at him, watching the floor numbers tick down instead. It was too much. Too intense. We'd been apart for less than three days, and his presence overpowered me. He didn't reach for me, but I knew he wanted to—because I wanted to reach for him.

"Don't," I managed to croak.

"Don't what? Comment on my wife's appearance? You look like you, Penelope. You look...refreshed."

The blue jeans, boots, and long-sleeved shirt were my sister's and didn't fit in key places. But they might as well have been strangers' clothes. I wasn't that country cousin, come to the big city with a drive spurring her forward anymore. But I didn't feel like a don's wife either.

I wasn't sure right now who I was.

The elevator doors slid open, and I marched out, feeling his presence behind me like a physical weight. The late afternoon sun cast long shadows across the hospital courtyard as we found an empty bench beneath a maple tree.

I sat, leaving as much space between us as possible. Alessandro didn't seem to notice, settling himself with that effortless grace that had caught my eye in Detroit.

"Your mother?" he asked, his voice thickening. "She's recovering well?"

"She is, thank you." I looked up at the afternoon sun. "If I have any say in what happens next, I want to stay until she goes home. Then I'll come back to Chicago—and I won't run away again."

"Vespina."

The hurt in his voice had me snapping my gaze to his. Pain shone in those black depths. The echo of it hiccupped in my chest, but I swallowed the sob. I hadn't shed a single tear the last three days. Staying awake, staying busy taking care of my family, had kept away the feelings I didn't want to wrestle with.

Alessandro slid off the bench. That custom suit scraped on the sidewalk as his knees hit the ground.

"There are so many things I have to tell you, but I can't find the words other than to say, I'm so sorry." He reached for my fingertips. "I'm sorry I didn't see what was before me the whole time."

"What was that?" I breathed.

"That every breath, every heartbeat, every thought belongs to you. I messed up, vespina." He knelt there, hands fisted at his sides. His body shook, and his gaze was filled with a wild desperation.

Emotions tightened in my chest. "You expect me to think you changed? That a mere apology can solve it?"

A breeze stirred his dark hair, and I hated how my fingers itched to smooth it back. Three days away and I was still weak for him.

"You've never apologized to anyone in your life, have you?" I asked.

His eyes—those deep, unfathomable eyes—held mine. "I'm doing it wrong, aren't I?"

"We were doomed from the beginning, Alessio. The moves were always against us. I don't think you fucked up any more than I did. And here we are." *Messed up beyond repair.*

A ghost of a smile played at his lips, but it didn't reach his eyes. The vulnerability in his face was new—raw and unfamiliar on features I'd memorized. "Where do we go from here, Penelope?"

He was asking, not telling.

That was...surprising.

I drew a deep breath, the familiar scent of his cologne reaching me even through the fresh air. It wasn't fair how he still affected me.

"I don't know," I admitted, hands gripping the edge of the bench. "This whole marriage was a business arrangement from the start. We both know that."

Alessandro's jaw tightened. "Is that what you believe? After everything?"

A bitter laugh escaped me. "What am I supposed to believe? You married me to secure a relationship with my uncle. I married you to protect my family. We made a deal."

"And then I fell in love with you," he said, his voice so quiet I almost missed it.

The words hit me like a physical blow. We'd never said that to each other, not once in all our heated nights or quiet mornings.

"No, you didn't," I whispered, pulling away from his touch. "Monsters aren't capable of that."

He dropped his hand. "I know you have no reason to believe me, but let me prove it to you."

My eyes prickled. The stupid tears I fought for so long were going to conquer me. I squeezed my eyes closed, refusing to let them fall.

"Alessandro, I can't. I just...can't."

"You can't what, Penelope?" He clasped my hands. The heat of his touch was a shock. I was cold, chilled—numb.

"I'll come back with you, but I can't do this anymore," I pleaded, opening my eyes and looking down at him through glittering lashes. The tears stayed firmly caught, safely trapped away.

"Then don't." His thumbs rubbed the back of my hands. "Stay with your family, and only come back when you're ready."

"You mean that?" I coughed.

"I do. I would rather love you from a distance and stand a chance at winning you back than force you and lose everything." One more squeeze, and then he rose. My fingers fell onto my lap. "Because, Penelope, you are everything to me."

The don moved away, a shadow swallowed by the sunlight.

His name was on the tip of my tongue. A scream in my chest formed, struggling to call him back. But my mind was in firm control of my body, and my lips pressed tight.

After a few tumultuous breaths, I rose and began walking slowly toward the medical building. The boys needed food. The surgeon would be in to do an update in the next hour. Dad hadn't finished his nap, and I needed one eventually.

A shout cut through the air behind me. With the bustle and rumble of cars on the road, the throng of people going hither and thither, there was so much noise that I didn't bother to look at the commotion.

The pop of gunshots stopped me in my tracks.

Dread crackled through my chest as I spun around. I knew, even before I saw, who was involved in the shooting. The scream that stayed silent before released now from my lungs.

"Alessio!" I ran.

The don turned, dark eyes flashing dangerously. "Stay back."

I tripped, pitched forward, and barely caught myself. Alessandro seemed fine. Air cut my throat as I gulped for the next few breaths. After scanning his body for any signs of damage, I slowly began to take in the scene. My gaze traveled past him to where Dante came running up, weapon poised at the ready. And then....

Oh, good lord, no. There was a body on the ground.

I snapped my gaze back to Alessandro. He was unarmed.

Good, that was good. He stood over the body, but it didn't seem as though he was the shooter.

"Go back inside, Penelope," the don commanded.

I stepped toward him.

His voice came out hard and filled with warning. "Go! This is going to get messy."

Dante stopped beside him and plucked at his arm. Alessandro swatted him away, but the way he held his arm—

I ran forward. *He's hurt!*

Rational thought vanished. I had to reach him. I had to—

"Penelope!" the don growled. "The police are coming. Get the fuck out of here."

Before I could disobey, strong arms wrapped around me from behind. The momentum from being tackled caused me to pitch forward, but we didn't hit the ground.

"Baby girl, we're going to listen to the mafioso." My dad's voice was firm. How long he'd been out here, it was impossible to say. "Come on, Pen. Let's go."

"But Dad!" The protest came out as a strangled cry. "He's hurt."

"It's a flesh wound. He's fine, but we need to leave him to this business," Dad said sternly.

"There are witnesses," I protested. "He's going to be in trouble."

"It was self-defense. But that's for the law to sort out. Come on, honey." Without waiting for me to move, my dad lifted me and began to haul me away.

The last thing I saw was Alessandro on his phone, his dominant arm hanging limp at his side. Those black eyes were focused on me as he spoke rapidly into the phone. The sliding doors to the building closed. Forced air blasted over my skin, and I was suddenly freezing.

"But I didn't tell him that...."

"He knows, Pen." My dad wrapped his arm around my shoulder, letting me lean my weight on him. He had me. I leaned my cheek against his chest. The steady patter of his heartbeat became the calm against the beeps and buzzes.

"He knows. And when you're ready, you'll find a way to tell him," Dad added as the elevator doors closed behind us.

Chapter 51 – Alessandro

The metal handcuffs clinked against the table. Because our lawyer wasn't present, we had to sit in a room with cameras. It was a blatant attempt to catch me talking out of turn with my "friend."

"Mier says it's a cut and dry case," Dante drawled. "They found evidence in Tribiano's apartment."

"Yeah, I saw the file. For a Fed, he left quite the paper trail showing my death was premeditated." I ran my tongue over my teeth. "You'll be out in a few days."

The law wasn't going to catch us plotting in here as a last-ditch attempt to convict Dante or me.

"How are you doing?" Dante tipped his head to the side.

"Me?" I snorted. "I'm fine."

"Bullshit."

"You're the one behind bars." I spun a finger through the air, gesturing to the setting.

"And you're the one whose wife left."

The ache in my chest pulsed. "I'm getting her back."

"Of course you are." Dante leaned forward, bracing his manacled hands against the table as far as the restraints would allow. "The question is *how*?"

If it was any other woman, I would shower her with expensive gifts, promise her whatever boon her heart desired, and make her see life with me was far better than the alternative. But not Penelope. No, I had to prove myself worthy with her.

"Um, any advice?" I watched Dante from under my brow and braced myself for his teasing.

"What do you know about her?" Dante drummed his fingers against the table.

I watched his long, thick fingers tap-tap. Tap-tap. Tap. If he wanted, he could escape. Those handcuffs were nothing to a man as cunning as him. It would be all too easy for him to kill the guards and walk out of here and disappear to a country without extradition. He was playing nice because the stakes were set in such a way as to make the case that he was a bodyguard, doing his duty to a businessman who'd been maliciously attacked. I envied him. The knowledge to free himself and disappear was a rare gift, one I would dearly love to possess. I might be the boss of a criminal empire, but I lacked the assassin-level knowledge of my friend.

"Alessandro." My name cut through the escape plan. "Quit stalling and answer the damn question."

I sighed. "I don't know her. Not well."

"Again, bullshit." Dante shook his head. "You know everything you need to win her back. You just have to talk it out. And that's what you're clearly avoiding."

I shifted in my seat. The metal chair was bolted to the floor, rigid and uncomfortable.

"What's her favorite flower?" Dante pressed.

The light on the camera above blinked red. The one-way mirror no doubt had Feds watching from behind it. What did they think of me? A man who was unable to answer even the simplest of questions.

"Find out," Dante advised. "And don't just send them to her. Make them a statement."

"Flowers that make a statement." *Check.*

"What else?"

I shrugged.

"You're not even trying." Dante's voice cracked through the room, a low and volatile whip.

"That's what you're here for," I drawled.

My right hand looked as though he would gladly slit my throat to end the conversation.

"Please." I leaned forward. "Help a dumbass out, will you?"

Dante sighed and shook his head. "You really are a dumbass."

"And I'm going to do better this time."

"I can see that. Okay, so, I bet she loves food," Dante mused, his eyes flicking to the camera with subtle defiance. "Not just any food—something specific. Everyone has a weakness. Even our sunny queen Penelope."

I leaned back, the chair creaking in protest. "Tiramisu. She devours it like it's her last meal." The corner of my mouth twitched at the memory of Penelope licking mascarpone from her fork, her eyes half-closed in pleasure. "But that's too simple."

Dante's laugh was sharp. "Nothing is too simple when you're groveling. "And make no mistake, Alessandro—you are groveling."

The truth stung, but I couldn't deny it. I, Alessandro Mancini, who had men killed for looking at me wrong, was planning to grovel for a woman. Not just any woman. My wife. The one who took life away when she left.

"Okay, I'll make sure there is tiramisu in the house at all times—"

"No!" Dante laughed again. "No, you're going to make it for her. Randomly. Or better yet, since she enjoys cooking, make it *with* her some of the time."

"I have to convince her to come back home first," I grumbled. "I don't think tiramisu will survive the mail to North Dakota."

"Baby steps, my friend." Dante's mouth curved into a knowing smile. "What does she crave? Not just physically, though I'm sure you've got that covered. What does she hunger for deep down?"

I rubbed my jaw, the stubble rough against my palm. Penelope wasn't like the other women who'd flitted through our world. She was complex, a labyrinth I'd barely begun to navigate before everything imploded.

"Independence," I finally said. "She hates feeling controlled."

"Bingo." Dante's eyes gleamed. "And what did you do, Alessandro? You caged her. Made decisions without her. Protected her so thoroughly she couldn't breathe."

The truth stung worse than any bullet I'd ever taken. "I was keeping her safe."

"You were keeping her prisoner, even if the bars were made of gold." Dante leaned back, chains rattling. "Making her a part of your company—" we both knew what he really meant "—was a good first step. Send her some work. Let her know it's not just an empty title."

"I was planning on her helping me with some jobs with the clubs," I countered. "But there's not a lot she can do."

Dante stabbed a finger at me. "That kind of thinking is what led to your fuck-up. Drop all your preconceived notions of what she can and can't do and start involving her. Together, you two will figure out her limits."

There was a buzz at the door. The surly officer of the law walked in with an authoritative swagger.

"Time's up, Mancini," he snapped.

"I wasn't done." I gave him a cold stare.

But this was his playing field. The Fed shook his head. "As entertaining as your marital problems are to the guys, we're done listening to your tale of woe."

I rose and gave my enforcer a long look. "Thank you, my friend."

"I'll see you soon." Dante smiled.

"I'm counting on it." I walked out, letting the suit escort me to the checkpoint.

There was work piled up at the office, calling my name, yet I didn't find myself driving toward the bakery. Instead, I sped home, my mind torn between obligations and desires. Grabbing a legal pad and pen, I drifted to the sitting room where Penelope often immersed herself in her books and journal, wondering if I should be there or elsewhere. But it felt right to concoct a battle plan in the space of the object of my obsession. This was where she spent her days, that journal always within reach.

The journal that she didn't take back with her to North Dakota.

My pulse quickened, and a flutter of excitement stirred in my chest.

Turning sharply on my heel, I wandered to our room and began to search. Two hours later, frustrated and defeated, I returned to the sitting room. I swore her scent lingered in the space, haunting me with her absence. Sitting on the sofa, I bent and inhaled. Yes, the faintest whiff of jasmine lingered on the seat. I started to scribble on the lined sheet of paper, looking up every so often to regroup my thoughts.

When one page was filled with ideas, I flipped to the next. But the bookshelf caught my eye.

Launching to my feet, I padded over to the furniture. Sure enough, hidden in the decorative tomes was a leather-bound book that didn't belong. I snatched it, cradling it to my chest.

This was my golden ticket, the insight into the woman who I was going to move heaven and earth to bring back.

Slowly, I opened it, hands trembling with eagerness. I traced the scrawled lines on the first page with the tip of my finger. The letters were fluid, some smooth and evenly paced, others scrunched and jagged. Without reading the words, I could tell how she'd felt when writing different passages.

I spent the rest of the night pursuing the contents and jotting down my own brain dump of ideas. This was going to work—it had to. I would settle for nothing less.

Chapter 52 – Penelope

The late afternoon sun beat down on my back. Laney's hooves clopped along the hard-packed earth as we wound around the bend in the field. Leaning back in the saddle, I tipped my head to the sunlight. Heavens, I'd missed this.

There was nothing better than being outdoors in such incredible weather with an animal I'd bottle-raised, trained, and nurtured. But....

My heart wasn't in this. Not all of it.

It was too quiet out here. Granted, the breeze whistled over the plains, and an occasional pickup rattled down the dirt road. The cows lowed in the distance while a bird cackled in the trees along the pasture's edge. Those sounds didn't add up to enough noise to create the distraction I desperately needed, though.

I was home and homesick at the same time.

"Mother of god, I miss him," I whispered.

It'd been a week since we brought Mom home. There was enough to do at the ranch, cooking, cleaning, and caretaking, to keep me busy. The nights were the worst. It wasn't that my room was too small—it wasn't right!

I angled the mare toward the mailbox. Dad asked me to check it on my way back, otherwise I'd already be up at the house prepping dinner. Stopping Laney, who immediately began to nibble at the grass, I slid from her back and went to the large metal box. There were enough letters and Amazon packages to fill the drawstring bag. I dropped them unceremoniously into it until my name caught my eye.

Frowning, I opened the bubble mailer, knowing full well I hadn't ordered anything. A colorful box of aromatherapy shower steamers stared back at me.

"I definitely didn't order these," I muttered.

A white slip of paper fluttered to the ground.

I stooped, plucked it, and gasped softly.

Vespina, I don't know if you have a tub to soak in, but I figured these would be a safe bet. Enjoy your next shower.

There was no signature, nor was there a name on the gift slip, the slot was blank.

My heart skipped a beat. It was so simple. So...perfect. I placed it in the bag with a smile and mounted Laney, kicking her into a gallop down the half-mile driveway to the house.

Mikey met me at the barn, taking the reins. "I've got her; you get supper ready."

I laughed. "Famished?"

"You know it." He grinned. "With Mom down and you gone, we'd been eating nothing but frozen dinners and beans."

I shuddered. "Living like the cowpoke you are."

He shook his head. "Karen doesn't have your inclination for cooking."

Translation: my younger sister was lazy. Not that she didn't want to help, but because I did everything when Mom wasn't doing it, there was no room for another chef in the kitchen.

"Poppy tried cooking for us once," Mikey quipped, leading Laney away. "She's eager, but damn, she needs to learn what an oven does."

At the mention of my cousin, I slid my phone from my pocket and checked the messages. She'd said she was coming for dinner tonight. There were no new messages.

As I began to prep the meal, Dad sauntered into the kitchen. He took the drawstring bag and sorted the mail. My hands were covered in flour, egg, and breading when he came up behind me.

"Say, Pen, what's your favorite flower?"

His abrupt question made me drop the chicken breast back into the bowl of eggs. My brows drew together, and I gave him a quizzical look.

"That's not a random question at all," I countered. "Where'd that come from?"

Suspicion flickered through my mind.

"I'm growing your mom a garden, in here, and I wanted to add some of your favorites, since you're back home," he explained with a breezy air that felt rehearsed.

"Uh-huh, well, Mom and I both have a thing for wildflowers. So just go down to the tractor store, get a variety pack, and you'll be set." I turned back to my chicken.

The tap-tap of his fingers against the phone screen made me sneak a glance. Dad concentrated on the screen for a moment longer before clicking his phone off and putting it in his back pocket. For a man who rarely texted, that was even stranger than the question.

"Where are you putting the flower bed?" I demanded.

"The living room. That way the light from the south windows will keep it warm through the fall, and I can hopefully keep the blooms going all winter." Dad leaned against the counter. "It's good to have you back, Pen. You know that, right?"

I sighed under my breath. This conversation was long overdue.

"Are you mad?" I laid the chicken in the cast iron skillet full of sizzling bacon grease.

"That you made a deal with your uncle, the mob boss?" Dad snorted. "Furious."

Grease popped, and I jumped back, but not before my wrist caught a healthy drop.

"Shit," I hissed, running cool water over the angry red mark.

Dad handed me a dish towel. "But I understand why you did it."

I patted my wrist dry, surprised by his admission. "You do?"

"Your mother needed that treatment. I was too proud to ask Tito for help." He leaned against the counter, his weathered face softening. "I've never liked your uncle's business, but he's still family. And so is that man of yours, I suppose. You can't escape family, baby girl."

My heart stuttered. He was my family. I couldn't cut Alessandro out of my life if I tried. The ache in my chest bloomed fresh.

"I did what I had to do," I said, turning enough to look him in the eye. "And I would do it again to save any one of you."

"I don't think you'll have to," he said quietly.

My cousin saved me from answering that loaded statement. Poppy came into the house with the dogs at her heels. She slipped into the kitchen and gave my dad a side hug.

"Wash up and come help," I offered her with a smile.

Poppy peered at the mess on the counter. "Is that...healthy?"

Dad laughed. "Bacon grease? Super! They've debunked fats being harmful."

"Although, pigs aren't the cleanest," I countered. "Beef tallow would be better, dad."

He wrinkled his nose. "Doesn't taste the same."

I laughed. It didn't.

"Alright, I'll leave you ladies to it. Oh, and here, Pen." Dad held out a letter. "Where do you want this?"

A quick glance at the tilted handwriting sent my poor heart skittering yet again. I spoke past the sudden lump in my throat. "In my back pocket, I'll read it later."

Poppy grabbed a chicken breast and held it gingerly. Sarge and Gunner watched her eagerly from where they sat at the edge of the kitchen. Sarge was drooling. They knew better than to sneak in here, but if anything dropped, their training went out the window.

The weight of the letter in my back pocket felt like a stone. It was all I could think about as I breaded chicken alongside Poppy. His handwriting, those elegant slants and curves—I'd recognize it anywhere. My fingers itched to tear it open, to devour every word. But I couldn't, not with an audience.

"You're a million miles away," Poppy observed, her voice low enough that Dad couldn't hear from the living room. "Is it him?"

I nearly dropped the spatula. "What?"

The grease crackled, and another pop sent more splashing onto my skin. I hadn't burned myself this badly in ages.

"The letter." She nodded toward my pocket. "The one you're dying to read. Is it from the don?"

My cheeks burned. "How did you—"

"Please." Poppy rolled her eyes. "I'm not blind. When you came back, you were...different. And not just because of what happened with Aunt Rosa's surgery." She paused, studying me.

"It's not the first he's sent," I confided.

"And?"

I placed the golden-brown chicken on a plate covered with paper towels. "He hasn't ordered me back."

"That's...good."

"Yeah, I suppose." I put a fresh lump of creamy bacon fat in the skillet.

"You want to go to him." It wasn't a question.

"I don't know what I want," I whispered, but the lie tasted bitter on my tongue.

Poppy gave me a knowing look, one that saw right through me. "You're a terrible liar, Pen. Always have been."

I turned away, focusing on the sizzling chicken. My cousin was right. I knew exactly what I wanted, who I wanted. The problem was reconciling that desire with the life I'd once known here—the safety of the ranch, the simplicity, the quiet rhythms that had once been enough.

"It's complicated," I finally said.

"Love usually is." Poppy bumped my hip with hers. "Especially when it involves a man who has bodies buried somewhere."

I shot her a warning glance, but my denial never made it past my lips. The truth was, I knew what kind of monster Alessandro was. What he did. And lord help me, I wanted to rush back to that world.

"I think," I began and stopped.

Poppy dropped a chicken breast into the skillet, but her lack of technique sent grease spewing up. She shrieked and jumped back.

Laughing, I shook my head. "You're going to burn yourself."

"Then I guess I'm doing it right." She gestured to the angry red marks on my skin.

I opened my mouth, but she cut me off.

"Stop making excuses, what do you think? Spit it out."

Summoning the rush of courage, I let the cards fall. "I think he's changed. But is it enough? Is it permanent? Or will I go back to the same disaster I saved you from?"

Poppy dredged another piece. Her lips pressed tight, moving as she considered her response. Her half-focus meant the piece wasn't fully coated, and then she dropped it into the pan, not having learned from the first time.

"Here's the thing: I wouldn't have thrived there. You saw that. You saved me." She moved close, attempting to give me a hug.

"Chicken! Raw meat!" I squeaked.

"Sorry." She laughed. "But I'm serious. I can never repay you what you did for me, Penny."

"You don't have to," I rushed to say.

"Thanks, but let me help you with this." She took a deep breath. "From what I've gathered, you fell for Don Mancini. You two are *good* together. You tamed him, but he brought out something in you. And you need to go back and see what life set free looks like."

She's right. It wasn't about loving the man; I adored the beast equally as much.

"I didn't tame him," I whispered, turning the chicken with more force than necessary. "I just...saw him."

The truth of it ached in my chest. I'd seen Alessandro—all of him. The ruthless don who commanded an empire with blood-soaked hands. The man who dealt with nightmares he wouldn't speak of. The lover who'd traced my body with reverent fingertips, as if touching something sacred.

"And he saw you," Poppy said, her voice soft. "That's rare, Pen. To be truly seen."

My chest tightened.

"You two were meant for each other, no matter the twisted circumstances of your coming together. If I had that, I wouldn't throw it away—I'd run back to it as fast as my feet could carry me," Poppy whispered, flipping a chicken breast with surprising dexterity.

We are, and it's time to go home.

The screen door slammed, and Mikey's boots thudded across the floor.

"Smells amazing in here," he called out, rounding the corner.

The conversation mercifully ended, and I lost myself in the routine, ignoring the letter burning a hole in my back pocket. I just had to figure out how to leave my family in a sustainable way. That would give me time to figure out how to go back—and make sure that was what I really wanted.

After spending the evening teaching my cousin the fine art of frying chicken, baking biscuits, and sauteing veggies, I didn't have time to look at my letter until the boys were washing the dishes. I should have been spending time with them, because there was no knowing how long I would be allowed to stay.

But the letter pulsed in my pocket the entire time, consuming my thoughts and distracting me enough that three chicken breasts were hopelessly burnt.

At least the dogs were happy.

Wandering out to the back porch, I curled up on a wicker chair, tucking my legs under me. I hated how my fingers trembled as I popped the seal, the edge of the envelope tearing slightly. A sheet of plain white legal paper fell into my lap.

I closed my eyes, bracing myself for whatever was written on the page.

"It doesn't matter. I'm coming back," I whispered, testing the words.

They felt...right.

Unfolding the page, I scanned the contents. Like the other three letters, this one had a block of text from a book. I laughed softly. Alessandro copied the passages from fiction, crossing out words and improving with his own thoughts to tailor the reading to our situation.

This one was from a fantasy novel, a profession from a wing leader to another dragon rider.

Vespina,

I'm sorry if you expect me to do the noble thing. I warned you. I'm not sweet or soft or kind, and ~~you fell anyway~~ you chose to be with me anyway. This is what you get, ~~Violet~~ Vespina— me. The good, the bad, the unforgivable. All of it. I am yours. You want to know something true? Something real? I love you. <u>I'm in love with you, Penelope.</u> I have been since ~~the night the snow fell in your hair and you kissed me for the first time~~ the day you pushed me into the fountain. You have bewitched me, and I'm grateful my life is tied to yours. I can't bear the thought of facing a day without you in it. But I will be brave, I'll wait for you, even if it takes years. Because it means I won't have to face a future without you in it. My heart only beats as long as yours does, and when you die, I'll meet ~~Malek~~ St. Pete at your side. My only prayer is that you love me, too, because you're stuck with me in this life and every other that could possibly follow. I'm not giving up on us. And if you have, I'll carry the weight of that for both until you change your mind.

Yes, I'm the fool who stole another's words; I can't find a better way to say this, to convey what I feel, but the confession is all the same. It comes from me, as if he's speaking what I feel. This story rang true for me. It made

me see us in a different light. If you can bring it on yourself to embrace the darkness in which you were sacrificed, then I have hope of a brighter future.

With all my heart,

Alessandro

Another tear dropped to the page.

"Ah, crap." I pressed my fingers to my lips, stifling a sob. The words swam before my eyes as tears threatened to spill over. Alessandro—my beautiful, dangerous don—had laid his heart bare in these crossed-out lines of someone else's story. There was something so vulnerable, so honest about the way he'd marked up the text, using another's words to express the truth of us. That was the beauty of fiction. The ink on the pages captured our feelings in a tangible way.

"Dammit," I whispered, clutching the letter to my chest.

The screen door creaked open behind me. I hurriedly wiped my eyes with the back of my hand, but not quickly enough.

"Penny?" My mother's voice was soft, concerned. Somewhat shaky. I hadn't heard her come down the stairs.

"Mom, you should be resting," I said, folding the letter and tucking it back into the envelope.

She eased herself into the chair beside me, her movements stiff.

"I could feel your heart bleeding from the bedroom," she murmured, brushing my hair back into the braid. "Talk to me."

I looked over the fields. "I want to go back. I...belong there."

"Then what's stopping you?" she asked gently.

"I don't know if he's changed permanently."

Mom's hand stilled in my hair, and I could feel her studying my profile in the fading light of dusk. The crickets had started their evening concert, a familiar soundtrack to our quiet conversations on this porch.

"People don't change," she said finally, her voice carrying the weight of her years. "Not completely. They just...reveal more of themselves."

I turned to look at her, surprised by the wisdom in her words. "What do you mean?"

"Your Alessandro." She said his name without judgment, which surprised me. "He was always capable of tenderness, of love. Just as he's always been capable of violence. The question isn't whether he's changed, but which parts of himself he chooses to nurture."

A breeze lifted the corner of the envelope in my lap. I smoothed it down, tracing the edge with my fingertip.

"And that's why you love the mob. It brings out a part of you that is stifled here." My mother gave my fingers a squeeze. "That's why you feel like you belong."

We sat there in silence, her words hanging between us. The path back home suddenly seemed clear. If I went back, it would be to embrace the dark, but to also bring Alessandro the light he swore he needed.

Chapter 53 – Alessandro

I had to admit the stink of horse and barn was far better than the stench of blood and death, although equally as disgusting. Leaving the windows down on the car would help a little, but I was going to have Shepherd spray the interior. Next time I visited the riding stables, I would take a motorcycle. The air whipping past me would lessen the effect.

Instead of entering the house from the garage, I left toward the backyard to check on my newest project. The last three weeks, I spent more time indulging in things that were not business related. I found…joy in alternate pursuits. In my teens, I devoured anything that would make me strong. The twenties found me tightening my hold on my reign. Doing anything else, including having a family, made me afraid.

I didn't want to acknowledge the possibility of fear, but now that my second wife was absent, it was time to call a spade a spade. I acted in fear.

Now I was rearranging everything to fit other pursuits into my life. So if—when, *when* my wife came back, there would be ample room for her here.

I plucked the watering can from the side of the house, pausing only to fill it from the rain barrel that the internet article said was the best way to collect water. Rounding the corner, I stopped short.

There, sitting beside the flower bed, was my little wasp. Her fingers were covered with a film of dirt as she plucked some small sprouts from among the blooms.

Standing still, I watched, hardly daring to believe my eyes. If I blinked, would she disappear?

Something must have caught her attention, because she started, sat up straight, and turned. I held my breath as her gaze met mine.

"Shepherd said—" Penelope gestured to the flower bed.

I could only imagine what the decrepit butler had been tattling about. "Do you like it?"

Penelope reached for a new blossom, tracing her fingers over it. "They're the same that grow in the meadows."

Exactly why I chose to grow them.

"Vespina, I—"

I never finished. Penelope launched from the stone ledge and rushed me. Jumping high, she leapt into my arms. Dropping the watering can, I caught her, wrapping her tight. There was nothing overly sensual in the act, it went far beyond that. There was an intimacy, a familiarity.

A homecoming.

Her weight settled against me, a perfect fit, and I buried my face in her neck, inhaling deeply. Even after all this time, she smelled the same—wide-open spaces and sunshine. My heart thundered against my ribs, a caged beast finally glimpsing freedom.

"You're here," I murmured, the words muffled against her skin. "You're actually here."

Her fingers dug into my shoulders, clinging as though afraid I might vanish. She clung to me with a sense of urgency, as though the very act would keep us together.

"I couldn't stay away," she whispered, her voice breaking. "I tried, Alessio. Heaven knows I tried."

I shifted her gently, reluctant to let go. My hand lingered on her waist while the other reached to cup her face. The watering can lay forgotten at our feet, water pooling around our shoes. I studied her face, searching for signs of what had kept her from me, what had driven her away in the first place.

"I'll do whatever it takes," I promised.

"Don't change too much, Mr. Don." Penelope leaned into my touch. "I've learned to love your monsters, and I want to continue, as before."

My brows furrowed. "I won't cage you."

"No, you won't. You'll take me into the dark and be my guide."

"You'll never see my demons again," I vowed. She needed to know, she needed to understand!

Her eyes flashed with a fire I'd missed, her fingers suddenly gripping my wrist. "Don't you understand? I don't want you to hide them from me. I want all of you—the darkness and the light."

I stared at her, disbelieving. In my world, women wanted security, luxury, protection—not the blood-soaked reality beneath.

"When I left," she continued, her voice softer now, "it wasn't because of what you showed me. It was because you stopped showing me anything at all. You built walls, Alessio. You kept me in a beautiful cage while you disappeared into your darkness alone."

My jaw clenched. "To protect you."

"To protect yourself," she countered, and the truth of it struck like a blade between my ribs. "You were afraid I'd see too much and leave. So you pushed me away first."

Her words warmed something deep inside me, a frozen place I hadn't realized existed until this moment. The idea that she could accept all of me—the blood, the darkness, the violence—was intoxicating.

"The last three weeks...." I began, but couldn't finish. What could I say? That I'd been drowning without her? That I'd killed men with my bare hands just to feel something other than her absence?

Penelope's eyes, those dangerous pools of ambers, greens, and browns that had haunted my dreams, softened. "I know. I felt it too."

Penelope's fingers traced the line of my jaw, her touch reverent yet possessive. I pulled her closer, my hand sliding to the nape of her neck. The familiar weight of her against me felt like absolution.

"Now, as your consigliere, we have a lot of missed ground to cover." Penelope's smile was nothing short of divine.

"Later," I promised. "It's been too long, and I'm famished."

Her grin turned mischievous. "What do you want me to cook us for dinner? Or if you'd rather go out?"

My touch slid around the back of her head. A fire surged through my veins. Her lips found mine.

The kiss was savage, hungry, a desperate claiming after too much time apart. My fingers tangled in her hair, tugging just enough to make her gasp against my mouth. I swallowed the sound, greedy for every part of her.

"You know damn well I'm not hungry for food," I growled against her lips.

Her body melted against mine, soft where I was hard, yielding where I was unyielding. But there was steel beneath that softness—the same steel that had allowed her to walk away from me, to survive in a world designed to break women like her.

"Alessio," she breathed, and my name on her lips was both prayer and curse.

I lifted her, one arm beneath her thighs, and carried her toward the house. The flowers could wait. Everything could wait. Three weeks of emptiness demanded to be filled.

"Your shirt," she murmured, fingers plucking at the buttons.

But she stopped after plucking a few.

Ah, crap. This was not how I wanted to ask her. Not on the staircase. I lowered us, holding her close.

"You weren't supposed to see that," I confessed.

"Is that for me?" A wicked slant formed on her mouth.

Suddenly, it didn't matter that this wasn't the perfect spot. She was the perfect woman, and I wouldn't rest until my ring was on her finger.

"Penelope June *Mancini,* will you do me the honor of being my wife?" I clasped her hands against my chest.

"Forever and ever." She tugged at the string. "I'm going to stay with you."

That was all I needed to hear. I pulled the cord loose, taking care not to let the silver charm fall as I took the specially made ring from the length. It slid perfectly on her finger, and I made a mental note to thank Blau for catching her size before he made it.

I captured her lips again, sealing our promise with a kiss that bordered on violent. My teeth scraped her lower lip, drawing a whimper from her that shot straight to my core. The ring glinted on her finger as she threaded her hands through my hair, pulling me closer.

"We're already married," she whispered against my mouth. "This is just making it official."

She was right. From the moment she'd stepped into my world, defiant and unafraid, we'd been bound together by something beyond paper and ceremony. But the sight of my ring on her finger awakened something primal in me.

"Mine—my wife," I growled, lifting her again and continuing our journey upstairs.

She laughed, the sound like music after months of silence. "Yours. Always."

Epilogue – Serena

The brush slid through my hair like a knife through butter. The dark gold lengths were a work of art. They hadn't seen a blade in years, not even a trim. A small investment went into making them the poster-picture of health. Other women were jealous. They complained that they didn't have the patience to grow their hair out.

But what else was a princess in the tower supposed to do?

A knock sounded on my door.

"Come in," I called, twisting a length to accentuate the curl.

"Did you see?!" Penelope beamed, sailing into my room.

"My idiot brother falling—again?"

Penelope nodded, her winning smile shining like a damn light bulb. "He can't stay on to save his life!"

At least he was trying. Ever since he behaved like an ass and upset his wife to the point where I feared for their marriage, Sandro had been going above and beyond to step out of his comfort zone. He gardened—the plants died from over-watering and needed replanting. He baked—burnt the damn cake so bad the dog he brought home from the shelter for Penelope wouldn't eat it. He bought a four-wheeler—which he tipped. And he took horseback riding lessons.

Where he fell every single time.

"Are the capos here?" I asked, smoothing a hand over my dinner dress.

Penelope shook her head. "Only Dante and Luca."

I nodded. "So the pre-business meeting has started."

"Should we go down?" Penelope fluffed her own hair in the mirror behind me.

"I'm good. But as the consigliere, maybe you should be there."

"Nah, I spent all day working with Luca. And Dante has nothing to do with me."

"Yeah, the enforcer is like a chained dog. Only useful when he has a job to do."

Penelope's eyes glittered. "Say, when are you going to shoot your shot with Dante?"

I swept my hair over my shoulder and stood. "His attentions are focused elsewhere. Shouldn't you know that?"

"Yeah, well, it's been months since his girlfriend abandoned us."

"Was abducted," I corrected.

"That remains to be proven," Penelope said with a sharper edge to her singsong voice.

But as I reached for my phone, she slid into my personal space. "You've been mopey for weeks, S. What can I do?"

The look of pity that crossed her face made me want to slap it off. I didn't need her sympathy. With a bitter sigh, I brushed past her. Nothing. There was nothing to be done.

"You know, Anneliese has a theory—"

"I don't care about her or her theories." I pulled open the door.

"You should get away from here. Find some space to discover yourself."

The door closed with a slap, my hand pressed tight against it. "Don't."

Penelope cocked her head. "Don't what?"

"Just...don't."

It was hard to hear my deepest desire so flippantly discussed. I wanted nothing more than to be free of this place. Not because they were cruel. But because their love was stifling. Made Men suffocated their families.

"Is that what you want? You get so jealous when Annaliese talks about her time in Europe."

Santa Maria! My sister-in-law was so damn annoying. But it was because she cared.

"You said once," Penelope continued, either not sensing my rising temper or not giving a damn, "that you wanted to travel. To see the world without your brother hovering over your every move."

"You know as well as I do that it's not an option for me." My heart bled, but the truth was unavoidable.

I pressed my fingertips to my temple, fighting the headache that always arrived when I thought too much about my gilded cage. "It's not jealousy. It's...." I trailed off, unsure how to explain the hollow ache in my chest whenever I heard stories of freedom.

"Then what is it?" Penelope pushed, leaning against my dresser with that knowing look in her eyes. She always could see right through me.

"Longing," I admitted quietly. "But it doesn't matter. You know Sandro would never allow it."

"The don isn't your keeper," Penelope insisted. "I don't give a shit about his rules."

Launching toward the door, she scampered away.

Sometimes she was spastic like an animal on crack.

I followed at a slower pace. At the top of the stairs, the ball of energy appeared back at my side.

"Here! Give this to the don." She thrust a small piece of yellow paper into my hand.

Confusion knit my brows as I looked at it.

Freedom for Serena Mancini to travel indefinitely without guards. Enough money to fund a long trip. No restriction as to destination.

"What the hell is this?" I snapped, unleashing the pent-up annoyance at my sister-in-law.

"Trust me." She gave me a side squeeze before hurrying us down the stairs. "You can add any stipulation to that, but the language is vague enough that he can't dispute it."

I almost crumpled the piece. Almost ripped it to shreds and yelled at her too optimistic view. Just because she had Sandro twisted around her finger....

I could be free.

I might as well try.

Following Penelope into the sitting room, a wave of fear trickled through me. What if I tried, and Sandro shot it down?

What if I tried and it worked?

I marched right up to him as Penelope said, "Alessio, it's time to honor your debt."

Keenly aware of Dante and Luca watching us, I held out the sticky note. There was no way in hell a piece of paper would subvert the don's strict rules. Alessandro ruled by a certain code. His word was law. There was no breaking free.

And yet as he plucked the piece of paper from my hand, his eyes widened, and hope flickered in my chest. That emotion was so foreign, it made me dizzy with the soft rush.

"Ah. You finally used it." Alessandro's face darkened as he read the sticky note. His jaw clenched so tight that the muscle twitched beneath his skin.

Penelope squeezed my hand, grounding me. I wished I had her confidence. She clearly didn't care about the risk. Asking the don for anything—especially freedom—was like stepping into a minefield blindfolded.

"Absolutely not." His voice cut through the room like a blade.

My heart plummeted, but Penelope stepped forward. "A debt is a debt, Alessio. I earned that, fair and square."

I glanced between them, confused. The way she stood up to her husband was admirable. But he also worshiped the ground she walked on, so that determination wasn't wholly misplaced on her part.

"This isn't what we agreed to," Sandro growled.

"You said whatever I wanted, except *my* freedom," Penelope countered sweetly. "I'm naming this."

Dante shifted in his seat, his dark eyes fixed on the scene playing out. Luca fidgeted with his tablet. This was an intimate family matter that my brother no doubt hated their witnessing. However, as the don, his honor was in question in front of his men.

"She wants to travel. I want you to let her." Penelope left my side and moved to her husband's. Her hand rested gently on his arm. "We need to let her find herself."

Alessandro ran his tongue over his teeth, a sure sign that he was incensed.

I opened my mouth, an automatic apology on the tip of my tongue.

"Fine," Alessandro ground out. "You may go."

The world tilted. Astonishment rushed through me. I stood frozen, afraid to move in case this was some awful trick.

"You owe me big time," Penelope mouthed to me with a wink.

"Conditions," Alessandro barked, his tone brooking no argument. "I want a check-in every day. A physical check-in, not just a text message. You will have a panic button on you at all times. Fake I.D. must be used at all times, and you'll tell no one who you really are. And one more thing."

My heart, which had soared briefly, began to sink again. "What is that?"

"I choose your first destination," he added, his expression softening slightly, becoming the brother I knew he could be, not the don he always was. "You'll stay in the States and see the important, historical places. Williamsburg, Virginia has a rich culture. Move south after that and stay out of the bigger Eastern Cities—we have enemies there."

This was my dream come true. My mouth opened and closed like a fish gasping for water. Words failed me. I was getting away—actually getting away from the family.

"I...I don't know what to say." My voice trembled, caught between elation and disbelief.

"Then say nothing." Alessandro's inky black eyes bore into mine. "But understand that if you break these rules, I will drag you back here myself."

"She understands," Penelope interjected, shooting me a look that screamed 'shut up and take the win.'

A small square of paper won me freedom. A regular, unimportant square of yellow. Impossible. *Priceless.*

I nodded quickly, afraid he might change his mind. "When can I leave?"

"Two days," Alessandro said, his jaw still clenched tight. "That gives me time to arrange your documentation and accounts. Enough time for you to pack. And you can stop by Baldwin's to say goodbye. He would like that."

He would. I spent more time with that older brother this summer than I had in the previous years combined. I wouldn't leave without a farewell dinner. Two days. Just forty-eight hours between me and a taste of freedom. Just thinking of the new places, the interesting people I would meet, the adventures I would have.... I could scarcely believe it.

I'm free. Never to be caught again.

To Be Continued in *Onyx Realm*

Thank you for reading *Twisted Crown*! Are you a good girl? I bet you are! Would you take a moment and leave a review for your fellow book lovers? Reviews are the best way to tell the world what you thought about this captivating love story!

Want more of the queens? *Onyx Realm* continues Serena's story and the aftermath of the yellow post-it. But there's more content about the fiery FMCs you met in this story. Good girls get rewards; flip the page to find yours!

The Consigliere

He rules the underworld with bloodstained hands and an iron will—until her.

When the Don takes a wife, it's not for love. It's for power. But what begins as a strategic move turns into obsession, and soon, he's not just protecting his empire—he's ready to burn it all down for her. She was never meant to wear the crown, but now she sits on the throne beside him, fierce, fearless, and untouchable.

In the shadows of crime and desire, she becomes the queen no one saw coming—and the only one he'll ever bow to.

Read Now: https://BookHip.com/XBTPVMB

Stalk Alexa & Become One of Her Villainous Darlings

Want to show me what a good little stalker you can be? The more places you follow me, the more updates you'll find!

Do you like exclusive content? Want more access to me? All you have to do, darling, is look!

https://linktr.ee/alexa.michaels.author

I have blog posts about the dealings in the Underworld. Want to know what the queens have been up to? Join my Patreon as a FREE subscriber to read the latest!

https://www.patreon.com/alexamichaelsauthor

About The Author

"**M**onsters deserve love too!"
Obsessed with sunshine and salty air, Alexa lives near the coast, where the waves crash wild and untamed. She writes dark romances where love is sharp-edged, loyalty is everything, and every heroine knows how to walk fearlessly through the shadows. Her heroes? They're not soft. They're sinners, kings, criminals, and Made Men — rough around the edges, scarred by their pasts, but desperate for something real. Something fierce. Someone who sees the worst in them... and stays anyway.

Alexa believes every villain deserves a love story; and she's here to write them. Coffee-fueled, ocean-hearted, and forever obsessed with stories that bite back — welcome to her world of dangerous love.

Made in United States
Orlando, FL
18 April 2025